"Woman, Your Hour is Sounding"

"Woman, Your Hour is Sounding" Continuity and Change in French Women's Great War Fiction, 1914–1919

Nancy Sloan Goldberg

St. Martin's Press
New York

ISBN 0-312-17707-0

Library of Congress Cataloging-in-Publication Data
Author Goldberg, Nancy Sloan
    Woman, your hour is sounding : continuity and change in French
women's Great War fiction, 1914–1919 / Nancy Sloan Goldberg
        p.   cm.
    Includes bibliographical references and index.
    ISBN 0-312-17707-0
    1. French fiction—20th century—History and criticism.   2. French
fiction—Women authors—History and criticism.   3. World War,
1914–1918—France—Literature and the war.   4. War in literature.
        I. Title
PQ637.W35G65   2000
843'.91209358—dc21   99–37963
                                                                                      CIP

Design by Letra Libre, Inc.

First edition: December, 1999
10 9 8 7 6 5 4 3 2 1

" . . . *Woman, your hour is sounding . . . tear off your shroud. . . .*

Be confident in yourself. . . ."

"*Femme, ton heure tinte . . .Arrache ton suaire . . .*

Sois confiante en toi. . . ."

From "Aux Mères" (To the Mothers), 1917, by Noélie Drous, pseudonym of Léonie Sourd, feminist pacifist and socialist teacher, writer, and activist, born in 1886.

For Harold
who always did have great ideas

Contents

Acknowledgments

A study encompassing the works of so many obscured writers requires the help of many individuals in both obvious and unusual ways. I would like to thank the members of the Faculty Research Grant Committee and the Non-Instructional Award Committee at Middle Tennessee State University, as well as Dr. Donald Curry, Dean of the College of Graduate Studies, for their support of my requests for released time from teaching and funds to conduct the research and writing of this book.

I appreciate the persistence and forbearance of the staff of several libraries both in France and in the United States, in particular Betty Mc-Fall and Karin Hallet at the Todd Library of Middle Tennessee State University, Derek Smith and Kevin Reynolds at duPont Library of the University of the South, Madame Durix at the Archives of the Académie Française, Geneviève Grambois at the Bibliothèque Nationale, Pierre Maubé at the Bibliothèque de Documentation Internationale Contemporaine, Fehl Cannon at the Library of Congress, and the reference librarians at both the Bibliothèque Marguerite Durand and the New York Public Library.

Most importantly, I am indebted to colleagues and friends for their wise counsel and pertinent suggestions concerning a variety of issues relating to this study. I would like to thank in particular Professors Julie Berebitsky, Harold Goldberg, Carmen McEvoy, Gayle McKeen, and Steven Trout for their insightful reading of this text in its various stages. I am also grateful to Professors Scott Bates, Jane Clement Bond, Jackie Eller, Rosemary Kew, June McCash, Anne McGovern, Mona Siegel, Tom Spaccarelli, and especially my mother, Shirley Sloan, for their individual efforts to help in the completion of this work.

Preface

Women in France faced challenges and circumstances significantly different from those confronted by other participants in the Great War. To speak of French women as a group, however, is not to suggest that they responded to the war with one voice. Moreover, to examine their specific situation is not to diminish the tremendous hardships of soldiers or of other civilians. Certainly, all French civilians, as inhabitants of a country invaded and partially occupied from the earliest days of the war, struggled with deprivation, the risk of famine, the need to do the work normally done by men who had left, and the continuing threat of direct violence from an enemy army. However, French women encountered, in addition to traditional gender-related laws and practices, distinct societal demands directed specifically at them as women, and these requirements were different from those faced by men, whether civilian or soldier. Collective and individual entities that represented traditional patriarchal structures, such as the government and the press, continually addressed women as a single and distinct group during the war, instructing them in the fulfillment of a specific set of war-related tasks, behaviors, and attitudes. In general, these stipulations stressed patriotic duty, charitable work, and above all, the stoic and even cheerful acceptance of death and personal sacrifice, while simultaneously reaffirming women's traditional maternal role, both symbolically and concretely. Such imagery and rhetoric went beyond the obvious concern of maintaining civilian morale and support for the war by its quantity and ideological specificity. Although propaganda directed at men also exhorted their duty, service, and sacrifice, it expressed itself in traditionally masculinist terms of action, bravery, and heroic defense. The call to service aimed at women reproduced equally gendered designations of passivity, resignation, and submission. French women in vast numbers responded favorably to these instructions by seeking war-related work, either paid or volunteer. Women of letters, too, registered their talents in service to the nation. During the period 1914–1919, many of France's best known contemporary female authors and scholars produced a large collection of war-centered fiction, in the form of poetry, short stories, and novels, and they also published a substantial number of histories, economic analyses, scientific reports, essays, and personal narratives that recorded the individual and collective French war experience.

It is in the novels and short stories especially that the writers illustrate their individual perceptions of the impact of war on the lives of both women and men. The following pages examine how these women writers created characters, plots, and employed other novelistic conventions to relate their understanding of the personal and social transformations taking place as they were writing. I follow the approach of Judith Lowder Newton, and explore in this fiction the intersection of ideology and gender in the context of events that changed society and the social construction of gender.[1] Chapter 1 presents the historical and cultural evolution of French maternal ideology, Republican Motherhood, and its specific war-era manifestations in the context of the public debate concerning the proper nature of women's behavior. Questions concerning the ways in which each writer viewed and articulated her comprehension of the meaning of war and of women's roles in its process formed the basis of my investigation of over 40 novels and short stories; specifically, whether constructions of the feminine and gender relationships reproduced, rejected, and/or redefined contemporary societal value systems. Expanding on Sharon Ouditt's goal in her book about British women writers of the Great War to discover "how women, at that historical moment, related their gendered identities to their possible roles in wartime," I have analyzed in chapters 2 through 6 the ways in which the writers then translated this understanding into works of fiction.[2]

The tradition of war literature privileges the testimony of direct, usually male, participants, and thereby imposes preestablished notions of authenticity, language, and content. Conversely, fiction by its nature grants appreciable freedom in form, plot, and characterization. The French women novelists and short story writers studied here participated in a literary heritage that had long had as its goals the illumination of psychological reality and the complexities of the human personality. These authors applied the traditional components of fiction, such as fully developed characters and a gradually unfolding series of incidents, to examine the interaction of the war environment and their women protagonists. Ultimately, the freedom of fiction allowed them to meditate and disclose a personal vision of truth that went beyond the experience of a single individual. Thus, I have considered only those texts by French women authors that define themselves specifically as works of imagination, and have excluded autobiographical and semiautobiographical accounts in the form of correspondence and personal narratives. For example, while Colette's novella, *Mitsou ou comment l'esprit vient aux filles* (Mitsou or How Intelligence Comes to Girls) is included, her articles published during the war in the newspaper *Le Matin* and collected under the title *Les Heures longues,* fall outside the scope of this investigation. Similarly excluded are the semiautobiographical *Dans le puits* (In the Well) by the prominent novelist, playwright, and critic of the period, Rachilde (pseudonym of Marguerite Eymery), as well as collections of vignettes about civilian life by some other well-known novelists, including Élisabeth de Gramont de Clermont-Tonnerre's *Du côté de la guerre* (Passageway of War), 1918, and *Parisiennes de Guerre 1915–1917* (Parisian Women of War 1915–1917), published in 1918 by Jacques Vincent, pseudonym of Angèle Dussand Bory d'Arnex. Since the reality of the war was experienced differently in each country, novels and fiction by French-speaking authors in Belgium and Switzerland, such as Marie Gevers and Noëlle Roger, are also outside the purview of this study. Finally, as the postwar period saw further shifts not only in cultural and political attitudes, but also in literary practice, I have restricted my study to novels and short stories published between 1914 and 1919, when official censorship ceased.

Readers today, educated through the arduous and tenacious efforts of feminist scholars to recover the works of women writers in many languages, understand the cultural values and professional mechanisms that combine to suppress women's writing. It will surprise no one that the scores of novels and other fiction these women wrote, before, during, and after the war, are absent from nearly all literary histories and bibliographies.[3] Nonetheless, that such an extensive body of writing could remain locked in the past seems perhaps unusual, especially in light of the celebrity of the majority of these writers. Winners of multiple literary prizes and civic honors, the numerous authors whose novels and stories form the basis of this study enjoyed substantial commercial and critical success for their war works, as well as for countless other works of fiction and poetry published from the 1890s through the 1940s. Fame and prosperity, however, could not insulate these books from several deeply entrenched prejudices that determine the canonization of French literary works in general and of war novels in particular. A ubiquitous gender bias against women writers, the traditional nature of the style and structure of their novels, and the notion that only combatants were qualified to write war stories, combined to categorize these books as *paralittérature,* peripheral fiction not worthy of sustained, critical analysis. Such marginalization extends beyond the period during which these women published their books to this day. French literary historians continue the conventional practice of segregating at the end of their books a short chapter discussing the works of a few disparate women authors, massed together under the rubric, *littérature féminine.* As recently as 1986, the authors of a study of the history of French publishing stated that Colette was the only woman writer publishing between 1900 and 1950 whose talent was comparable to that of the twenty-odd male authors "of exceptional value" writing in the same period. To emphasize their point, the authors specifically discounted such respected authors as Simone de Beauvoir and Marguerite Yourcenar, the first woman elected to the Académie Française.[4] Moreover, as Jennifer Milligan reported, even today's literary historians and critics whose work includes the recovery of women authors, such as Susan Rubin Suleiman, tend to support the traditional view that Colette is the only outstanding woman writer of the early twentieth century.[5]

While several of the war writers received praise from contemporary critics for their stylistic innovations, in general their works duplicated time-honored conventions of the French novel. Rooted firmly in the tradition of Madame de La Fayette and Honoré de Balzac, these novels recount the efforts of well developed characters to confront and overcome obstacles to their happiness; but above all, their aim is to tell a good story. Such stylistic fidelity to the past is rarely rewarded in the canonization process in French literature. The literary limbo inhabited by the novelists studied here is also home to male writers whose works replicated, rather than challenged, nineteenth-century forms. In addition to sustaining a perspective that favors innovation in language and style, French critics and literary historians continue to support a traditional bias against works that evoke the topical. In spite of the universal acclaim for the political works of authors like Voltaire and Hugo, scholars maintain a belief that creative projects that center on historical or public events are not literature and therefore do not merit critical inquiry.

In addition to the biases against women's writing in general and derivative and ideological writing in particular, another device has effectively obscured much of French women's war fiction. Critics have long designated realism in combat as the major criterion for evaluating the worth of a war text, a determination that minimizes the importance of literary qualities and erodes the distinction between fiction and autobiography. It also eliminates the writing of many, if not most, women, who did not share in the battlefield experience that traditionally defines authenticity in war. Indeed, most bibliographies of war literature, including the seemingly inclusive five volume annotated list of French works, *La Littérature de guerre* (War Literature) by Jean Vic and the often cited listing of soldiers' memoirs, *Témoins* (Witnesses) by J. Norton Cru, validate the prevailing importance of realism.[6] Present-day scholars, like Margaret R. Higonnet, rightly indicate the subjectivity of such a restrictive definition of any war literature that excludes the experiences of women and other civilians. Higonnet in particular argues that this interpretation avoids examination of the social and economic implications of war. Noting the distinction between combat and war, she enlarged the definition to reinscribe in the narrative of war realities other than those endured in the course of actual armed conflict.[7]

It is this comprehensive account of life during the Great War that the French women writers related in their novels, and in general, their stories focused on the experiences of women.[8] This nearly exclusive emphasis on the impact of the war on women is significant. Not only did the authors record the voices of women in the narration of the war, but they did so while successfully avoiding the snare of certain social prohibitions concerning women's knowledge. Unlike the fiction by women writers in other combatant nations, French novels generally did not depict actual battle scenes. They presented the frontline experience far more often through indirect means, and the women characters learned about the war in much the same way as noncombatant readers then and now, through the testimony of soldiers. By concentrating on women's experiences, the French novelists avoided the charges of pretense and impropriety that plagued other women war writers, and they did not challenge the notion of combat as a definitively male activity. As Higonnet has observed, women who write about war are judged to be trespassers, both on the literal field of battle and on the figurative terrain of worldly knowledge deemed the exclusive right of men.[9] The majority of French fiction writers strengthened the authority of their voices among their contemporary readers by faithfully reproducing the experiences of women, rather than seeking to represent those of men. The authors insisted on the far-reaching significance and moral value of what the women endured, even while asserting that the war their characters witnessed was different from that seen by the men. Nonetheless, the writers insured the worth of the women's experience by demonstrating that both realities shared many characteristics. The war required women, as well as men, to develop and exhibit courage, to make choices in the interest of others rather than themselves, and to face physical injury and loss of life.

Despite a marked variety in the construction of the plots and development of the characters, several common threads unite the novels. Support for the war as necessary to the defense of France remains virtually unchallenged in the texts. Even those novels published after 1917, the year that saw publicly-expressed dissatisfaction with the (lack of) progress of the war, confine their critique of war to an evocation of the problems of social reintegration of soldiers and their families. Secondly, the novels have strong female protagonists, all forced by the circumstances of war to take decisive action in a way that is new or different for them as individuals. Finally, a clear valorization of an historically-sanctioned version of maternal ideology, Republican Motherhood, informs the novels' and stories' themes and the actions of their characters. This approbation of the mother role is not merely the reproduction of a conventional and biologically-determined definition of the feminine. Prestige and moral authority had been associated with maternity in France since the early nineteenth century through the conviction that female citizenship was manifested through procreation and education. The following pages will demonstrate how acceptance of the responsibilities of the *mère-éducatrice* (mother-teacher) became a vehicle in French women's Great War fiction to explore new realities for women in a changing social context.

That the authors supported the war unequivocally through such traditional imagery should not imply that they accepted without question contemporary definitions of the feminine. These fiction writers appreciated the growth in women's moral and social stature afforded by the doctrine of Republican Motherhood. Their appropriation of its tenets is another illustration of the fluidity and constancy of an ideology that has a long record of empowering as well as manipulating the political thinking of women. As Jean Bethke Elshtain and Sara Ruddick, among others, have shown, maternal images have served concurrently and alternately throughout history (and to this day) to promote war as well as peace.[10] Nonetheless, although depictions of women as givers of life grant them in patriarchal society a certain moral authority, the state, especially a nation at war, often succeeds in appropriating this force for its own objectives. Contemporary critics on women and war have long observed that political leaders, from those in ancient Greece, to those in the United States in both world wars, and in the recent revolutionary movements in Latin America, have understood the vital importance of women's participation to the success of their various endeavors. Lorraine Bayard de Volo especially noted how nations rally support for war by adopting maternal symbols to forestall the opposition of mothers to the deaths of their children, while simultaneously reworking the social definition of the "good mother" to conform to the reality of war.[11] The application of maternal ideology has succeeded even when confronted with contradictory doctrines, as well as distinct time periods and historical circumstances. Joyce Berkman and Leila Rupp have demonstrated how an expanded national version of the protective role of mothers promoted acceptance of both world wars. Such representations privilege the welfare of the larger family of the nation over that of any individual. Rupp also recognized a continuation of the concept of a "mother class" imagined by Jane Adams in 1907 as the agent of community improvement in both Charlotte Perkins Gilman's notion of "world mothers" in 1923 and in the Nazi ideology of "spiritual maternity."[12] As Nancy Scheper-Hughes affirmed, " . . . maternal identity has no essential position; instead it may be used ambiguously to structure very different, even antagonistic positions—from promoting peace to advancing war to mobilizing political resistance."[13]

That maternal ideology, regardless of its representation, has succeeded in strengthening the position of disparate and incompatible viewpoints throughout history is no doubt rooted in the inclination to accept such notions as intrinsic and universal. Maternal ideology is difficult to refute or debate, even by advocates of women's rights, because it carries the weight of history, tradition, and acceptance by both women and men who fail to recognize its contingent and politicized context. Even those activists who understand how such a traditional definition of the feminine is constructed may choose to appropriate it in order to subvert its application. For French feminists in 1914, maternity had long granted to women a unique responsibility that secured for them an active role in both the home and the community. Many women considered their biological specificity as the root of moral authority, and thus the indisputable justification for suffrage and additional improvements in women's material condition. Other women regarded maternal sacrifice and renunciation as primary expressions both of their love of France and of their duty to the nation. That these political and transcendent interpretations of the mother's role could exist concurrently and compatibly mirrors the inconsistency of social forces set in motion by war. Joan W. Scott has written that "[w]ar is the ultimate disorder, the disruption of all previously established relationships or the outcome of earlier instability," while Jennifer Turpin asserted that "war magnifies already existing gender inequality and women's subordination."[14] The validity of such contradictory statements underscores the paradoxical nature of war, which, in the case of the two world wars, saw both improvement and decline in women's political and material condition. In acknowledging the phenomenon of such discontinuities, Margaret R. Higonnet and Patrice L.-R. Higonnet reiterated Steven Hause's assertion of the importance of nationalism and the perception in France of its inconsistency with feminist goals.[15] While the French women fiction writers whose works are studied in the following pages upheld the priority of patriotism and dedication to their country, they nevertheless confirmed the existence of an independent and intelligent woman, whose accomplishments benefitted herself, her household, and the larger family of the nation. It is an intermediate position that both accepted the discourse of the past and expanded its meaning to encompass the future. The modern French woman who emerges from the experience of the Great War in these novels and stories fulfilled her duty to a family beyond the limits of biological reality. For these authors whose celebrity assured them a large and continuing readership, service to the nation in the public sphere was a right that belonged to women, and the war provided the opportunity and the obligation to manifest that responsibility.

Chapter One

Republican Mothers All 🌑

Marcelle Tinayre, prolific author of the turn-of-the-century, published one of the first novels that featured French women in the Great War. Her 1915 work, *La Veillée des armes: Le Départ: août, 1914* (The Call to Arms: the Departure: August, 1914; translated in 1918 as *To Arms!*), retains even today a level of recognition enjoyed by no other woman writer of the period 1914–1919, with the exception of Colette. Repeatedly cited as either the sole or one of a very few examples of French women's fictional response to World War I, Tinayre's narrative nonetheless resembles more the static and symbol-laden imagery of the war poster than a novel.[1] Its shallow, tableau-like plot, and its one-dimensional characters, mere emblems of traditional gender stereotypes, seem to justify the charges of superficiality and jingoism that traditionally eliminate didactic and circumstantial literature from scholarly consideration.

Despite its notoriety, Tinayre's work is, in fact, atypical. While it shares several general themes with the dozens of other war novels and stories written by French women during the period 1914–1919, such as homage to the unity of the French nation, the sorrowful resignation of women, and the heroic courage of the soldiers, it differs from all others in a fundamentally important way. While many other books, like *La Veillée des armes*, educate and comfort civilians during a time of extraordinary upheaval or reiterate the aims and goals of the war, these works go beyond a simple evocation of patriotic discourse. Unlike Tinayre's comic book character Simone, who plays the nearly silent and subservient supporter of her conventionally valiant husband, these novels and short stories feature complex and intelligent female leads who ultimately act in accordance with decisions they make by and for themselves. From Marie Reynès-Monlaur's Claude Harteveld in the ruins of Reims Cathedral to Isabelle Sandy's Chantal Daunoy, isolated in southwest France, the main characters struggle to understand and resolve a variety of adverse situations encountered specifically by women in war. Despite diversity in the theme and characterization in these works of fiction, the women protagonists, nearly all members of the middle and upper classes, find themselves in exceptional and abnormal situations, suddenly bereft of the certainties that formed the core of their lives. Compelled to face alone and unprepared circumstances unimaginable before the war, these characters begin a process of analysis that combines reasoned judgment, empathy, and a sense of personal worth to determine independently a course of action.

The outcomes of the choices of the individual women are as varied as the story lines in the narratives, yet they share several important attributes. Whether the character is safe at home or besieged in occupied territory, whether she faces economic hardship or is financially secure, and whether she possesses a modern higher education or the more traditional training in domestic responsibilities, she will freely choose to serve the cause of France. Moreover, this act of patriotism will increase her degree of independence and will lead to future opportunities for self-determination. This emphasis on female agency and individual responsibility, while certainly provocative to contemporary readers, nonetheless avoided any direct assault on patriarchal social structures. The vision of women in these works was liberal rather than radical, for nearly all of the characters rely on or develop traditionally constructed feminine qualities, such as dedication to the family and devotion to service, in the process of determining their choices. Faced with the freedom of movement and the opportunity to exercise responsibilities outside the home, the majority of the characters in these narratives evolve successfully into modern, postwar women precisely because of their confirmation of those values traditionally defined as female. The authors thus depicted the social transformation created by war in the lives of women as an asset and not a threat to the French nation. For them, autonomy and self-determination were inseparable in particular from the maternal compassion and dedication to civic duty their characters acquired and demonstrated.

Such overlapping of the historically separate private and public "spheres" and the association in France of maternity with civic duty did not, of course, originate with women's Great War fiction. Rooted in long-established maternal ideology, the image of the Republican Mother had already defined French women for nearly a century. In the backlash against women's political influence in the *Ancien Régime* and in the rejection of the demand for women's civil rights following the French Revolution, a new image of women had begun to take hold in nineteenth century France. Anchored firmly in the Rousseauean tradition of *Émile,* in the statutes of the Civil Code, which defined women's civic function as procreative and educational, and in Michelet's widely-read *La Femme* (The Woman/Wife), the *mère-éducatrice* or mother-teacher role became the ideal for middle- and upper-class women. From the 1830s on, a wave of domestic and school manuals stressed the moral and psychological power that mothers possessed, an influence considered far more potent and enduring than any activity in the public sphere.[2] Roddy Reid noted that books such as Comtesse de Flesselles's *La Jeune Mère institutrice* (The Young Mother-Governess), published in 1830, and Louis Aimé-Martin's *De l'éducation des mères de famille ou de la civilisation du genre humain par les femmes* (Of the Education of Mothers of Families or of the Civilization of Humankind by Women), 1834, in fact clearly advocated an exchange of domestic authority for participation in the public arena (43–45). Linda Clark confirmed the impact of nineteenth-century primary school texts, such as Alice Durand Gréville's *L'Instruction morale et civique des jeunes filles* (Moral and Civic Education for Girls), approved by 1889 for use in over 90 percent of French departments. For Gréville and other educators, women's service encompassed the household as well as the larger family of society, and through their school texts, they taught French girls that sending their husbands and sons to war was an important patriotic duty (414–15).

The widespread dissemination of these manuals, magazines, and books for children inculcated a specific set of values for women that fused motherhood and obligation to the community in the form of the nation (Pope 225–32; Reid 45–52). The emphasis on *utility* and *service, sacrifice* and *piety, seriousness* and *duty,* as well as *honor* and *virtue* through fulfillment of the maternal function, became key words that articulated and established an ideal code of behavior for women. Constructed on the attributes of dedication, self-sacrifice, and service that were deemed inherent in women's nature, the Republican Mother image continued to gain strength throughout the nineteenth century. As a durable compromise between the public and the private, it created a rapprochement that made it possible for middle- and upper-class women in many countries, including France, to work in projects outside the home, especially efforts at social reform, including the eradication of alcoholism and of prostitution. Anne Martin-Fugier reported that the advances women made in certain professions, especially teaching and nursing, were expedited by the perception of these occupations as extensions of the mother role.[3]

The ongoing debate over women's responsibility for France's declining population that intensified in the second half of the nineteenth century demonstrates the solidity of the connection between maternity and duty to the nation. Hundreds of essays, articles, and books expressed anxiety over the ability of France to withstand in particular the military and industrial threat posed by Germany's increased population and economic advances. Despite the variety of possible remedies proposed to solve the depopulation problem, the rhetoric of these ideas confirms the degree to which the Republican Mother ideology was firmly entrenched in contemporary consciousness. Further, doctors, politicians, and sociologists charged that selfishness, greed, indolence, careerism, and the aspiration for social and material advancement had caused the population crisis.[4] Significantly, these negative attributes privilege the desires of the individual woman over the needs of the state, and as such, epitomize the antithesis of the Republican Mother image. While both men and women were deemed responsible in varying ways for the problem, the insistence on women's culpability begun at this time would increase with the beginning of the war. Whether considered a "luxury doll" who spent her time at parties and had no time for children, or the emancipated "new Eve," who refused marriage in favor of education or a profession, women would bear the blame for a depopulated France, whose assumed weakness fueled the aggressive aims of Germany. While these two female stereotypes are certainly opposite, they both illustrate the belief that damage to the family, and by extension, the family of the nation, would necessarily follow women's autonomous actions, regardless of their intent. Both Michelle Perrot and Annelise Maugue noted the turn of the century public anxiety throughout Europe concerning the future of the family. A modern female ascendancy, epitomized by the so-named new Eve or new woman, fueled the perception of a decline in male identity and authority.[5] For Maugue, the virilized image of the new Eve in fin-de-siècle French fiction denoted women's increasing exercise of power, incompatible with the traditionally required attributes of femininity, including "devotion, abnegation, [and] self-effacement" (529). The time-honored association of autonomy with maleness implied an absence of femininity, for them, the maternal, in women who demanded or achieved independent action. Thus feminists, even those with families, were believed to be "unsexed" and abnormal, and therefore posed a threat to the future of society by their assumed rejection of maternity. As we will see, the novelist Jeanne Broussan-Gaubert's novel, *Reviendra-t-il ?* (Will He Return?) attempts to unravel and neutralize this convoluted condemnation associated with the demand for women's rights.

The dualistic concept of women's role that formed the basis of the Republican Mother ideology became the foundation of a major strand of French feminism.[6] The double foundation, "feminist, yes, but feminine," expressed succinctly reformist feminism's insistence on the primacy of motherhood in a woman's life and the power of that role to affect lasting change.[7] Anne-Marie Käppeli noted the paradox inherent in this position that sought equality for women while valorizing their difference from men (483), yet, as

Karen Offen pointed out, it was the insistence on the uniqueness of women, summarized in the phrase "equality in difference" that led to an increase of male support for women's rights late in the century (664–65). Historian Christine Bard described the majority of French feminists as reformist, who, although represented by several organizations of different tendencies, nonetheless had the common goals of seeking the gradual improvement of women's condition through judicial reform, including suffrage. Public support for women's right to vote had reached a high point in the spring and summer of 1914, and many suffrage activists felt that victory was imminent.[8] It is significant that the importance of the moral and social duty of women permeated the projects launched by the most powerful of the revisionist feminist groups, the *Union française pour le suffrage des femmes* (French Union for Women's Suffrage) (Bard 22–23; 32–33). The Republican Mother ideology informed not only mainstream organizations such as the U.F.S.F., but also the philosophy of militants, including the radical feminist-pacifist Madeleine Vernet. Vernet, a well-respected pioneer in educational reform, based her opposition to war on an approbation of the maternal in opposition to masculine destructiveness, ideas she expressed consistently in the periodical she founded in 1917, *La Mère éducatrice* (The Mother-Teacher) (Bard 139–41). Vernet continued until her death in 1949 to urge women to recognize the power of their love for their husbands and children to end all war.[9]

As the discourse that had constructed and maintained the Republican Mother ideology for nearly a century, the exceptional importance of mothers to family and nation, founded on the "natural" maternal virtues of self-sacrifice, piety, and seriousness, pervaded and informed French women's Great War novels. Nonetheless, the numerous authors whose works form the basis of this study accomplished more than a simple confirmation of this omnipresent image. In fact, they achieved nothing less than the proof of French women's qualifications and competence to engage in public activities, including exercising the vote, the restoration of their moral reputation, assaulted and maligned both before and during the conflict, and, finally, the permanent inscription of the voice of women in the history of the Great War. By applying a contemporary version of the long-accepted tenets of the Republican Mother ideology to the present situation of French women, the novelists established a middle course that supported feminist goals without challenging the construction of patriarchal society. In fact, their portrayal of dynamic, unique, and self-directed women, whose maternal qualities enabled them to meet and overcome the various challenges of a modern society at war, vigorously defended the national importance of mothering to claim for women an extension of political rights and social roles. The image in many of the novels is that of an autonomous woman who, as an intelligent individual, chooses to be a traditionally defined, responsible citizen. While some authors occasionally camouflaged the degree of self-reliance of their characters, the fictional women nonetheless achieve sufficient agency to realize their personal objectives within the larger context of the family and the nation. This new generation of Republican Mothers thus reclaimed and enacted the prestige and political power long associated with the ideology of patriotic motherhood. It is an achievement the French war novelists accomplished from within established French society, without assaulting the foundation of patriarchal structures.

It is significant that this conciliatory stance of the fictional works in fact reproduced the liberal social and political agenda of reformist feminists, who pressed for increased political rights while maintaining the importance of women's biological uniqueness. This successful fusion of a traditional notion of the feminine with independent decision making and action exemplified a mode of being for modern women acceptable to a wide spectrum of both women and men; it assumed a more extensive public role, yet mitigated concomitant male anxiety over gender relations. Moreover, this depiction of women's dedication, courage, and perseverance through volunteerism during the war replicated the effort of French feminists to prove their defense of national over gender interests and their hope that such accomplishments would hasten the advent of suffrage.[10] By extending a traditional image of women that could not be contested even by the most ardent of antifeminists, and by demonstrating the value of the contribution of these modern Republican Mothers to a nation at war, the Great War novelists proved that emancipated women would enrich and elevate, rather than endanger, French society.

It is also important that through the portrayal of their protagonists as modern Republican Mothers, the authors contested vigorously the widespread public accusations of vanity, parasitism, and licentiousness that plagued real-life French women during the war. The fictional characters who employ their newfound freedom of movement and opportunity for independence of thought in favor of France thus establish a progressive, yet middle, ground between a variety of extreme and damaging female stereotypes. While suspicion concerning women's morals, behavior, and motives was certainly firmly anchored to traditional gender stereotyping and anxiety concerning female sexuality, it had expanded during the war with the increased visibility and presence of women in the workplace and civilian projects. When government officials and journalists alike urged women to assume various new activities in support of the war effort, they responded enthusiastically to this call to duty. The 1919 report by Marguerite Borel (war novelist Camille Marbo), *La Mobilisation féminine en France (1914–1919)*, (The Female Mobilization in France [1914–1919]), written for the Société l'Effort féminin français (French Women's Effort Society), provided a precise and statistical documentation of women's activities in many different sectors. Drawing a parallel between women's service and that of frontline soldiers, perhaps in response to the argument that suffrage should not be extended to those who did not serve in the armed forces, Borel employed military vocabulary to detail the contribution of this "French women's army."[11]

The participation of women of all social classes was extensive. In agriculture, commerce, and later in munitions factories, as well as in hospitals and charitable organizations, women assumed jobs and responsibilities necessary and vital for the continuation of the war. The home front thus became, in historian Françoise Thébaud's words, "a theater where women apparently played the lead roles," a transformation in women's social condition that incited numerous judgments and analyses of their conduct and morals.[12] Although Borel and other writers like Hortense Cloquié and Marie de La Hire believed that the monumental contribution of French women would be rewarded by the right to vote, the majority sought to serve their nation in whatever capacity possible without any hope of personal or political gain.[13] Nonetheless, cynicism and distrust, especially concerning middle- and upper-class women, arose regarding the reasons for their activities in support of the war effort. Such imputation of women's patriotism, exacerbated by the implication that prewar female individualism had induced German aggression, magnified the suffering that French women already endured due to the loss of family members in battle. Responding favorably to the demand to support the war through the stoic acceptance of death as well as active service in hospitals, factories, and charities, while at the same time being suspected of the unwitting contribution to Germany's cause or of personal aggrandizement, was an untenable situation whose injustice was obvious to contemporary women of letters. In addition to the novels and short stories that French women authors published during the war era, extensive commentaries and histories by writers such as Berthe Bontoux (Berthem-Bontoux) and Yvonne Pitrois, were among dozens of nonfiction books and articles that attempted at that time to exonerate and acclaim the conduct of French women.[14]

It is important to analyze here the particular ideas and arguments contained in this wartime debate on French women's comportment and motivation that raged in much of the French press, for they correspond to similar themes and judgments in many of the novels in this study.[15] Although the issues of the controversy were specific to the war, its underlying assumptions replicated the historically sanctioned belief in the universality of (potential) motherhood. Thus the degree to which a woman exhibited well-understood maternal qualities, such as caring and sacrifice for others, determined the propriety of her particular activity.

Although no wartime accomplishment was immune to imputations of immorality or self-interest, activities that could be viewed as extensions of the mother role, such as nursing and charity work, received more praise than factory and office work that replaced men and were considered by many to be a usurpation of male privilege. Thus, regardless of the nature of her activity or the gender of the commentator, approbation or reproach depended on how well, that is, how maternally, the woman in question executed her pursuit, irrespective of the presence of any real or symbolic children. Moreover, nationalist sentiments were clothed in maternal metaphors, so that any attitude that denied priority to total sacrifice for France rejected simultaneously motherhood and the only acceptable role for women. Consequently, women who repudiated the importance of motherhood, whether real or symbolic, were immediately assumed to be immoral or unnatural. A succinct example of this wartime link between patriotism and the Madonna/whore polarity is located in the criticism of women factory workers who participated in strikes for fairer wages in 1917. Mathilde Dubesset, Françoise Thébaud, and Catherine Vincent reported that the women were showered with recriminations for their action. It is significant that the reproaches concerned the women's morals and behavior, rather than any injury to the national defense. Newspapers denounced the women's language and attitudes as "hardly feminine."[16]

The long tradition of such a paradigm of cultural definition and judgment of women insulated it somewhat from challenge, even by defenders of women, who seldom questioned the motives of antifemale accusations.[17] The essays and articles that deliberated the issue of the war activities of French women often disclosed extravagant assertions and insulting innuendo that both condemned and glorified their participants. A few examples illustrate the wide range of contradictory and convoluted opinions. The internationalist humanitarian Romain Rolland blamed women for not using their maternal influence on their childish husbands to prevent the outbreak of war.[18] Tony D'Ulmès (pseudonym of sister novelists Renée and Berthe Rey) praised upper echelon or "society" women for recovering their instinct for devotion through volunteer nursing by asserting that their previously selfish lives had accustomed them to abandoning home and children without regret.[19] The fiction writer and essayist Berthe Bontoux, while recounting examples of women's heroism, nonetheless reinforced the accusation of women's vanity and luxury as the basis of Germany's view of France as too mired in pleasure-seeking to defend itself.[20]

These statements expose the aura of suspicion and speculation that surrounded women's activities during the war, mistrust voiced by advocates and adversaries alike. Equivocal praise of those considered the least productive members of society satisfied the requirement that writers elevate civilian morale while simultaneously shielding them from evaluating the significance of women's achievements. Such ambiguity and disingenuousness allowed well-known male journalists like Claude Laforêt and Robert de Flers to comply outwardly with the government's demand that intellectuals and writers become "moulders of public opinion"[21] without appearing to condone the implications of women's increased visibility and mobility. Laforêt, in an article that appeared in the *Mercure de France*, seemed to acclaim women's willingness to substitute for men in various functions without succumbing to despair. Nonetheless, immediately following this compliment, he commented on the accusations of moral impropriety. He finally concluded that although such laxity was deplorable, it was understandable as the result of French women's natural sensuality, for which men were grateful. "The French woman is courageous, intelligent and cultivated, she is also voluptuous. It is a reproach that we would not be able to level against her without [showing our] ingratitude."[22] Robert de Flers wrote in a similar equivocal style in his article "La Vraie Charité" (The True Charity), published just after the mobilization in the large-circulation Parisian daily *Le Figaro*. De Flers's oblique allusion to women's alleged snobbery overshadows his praise for their eagerness to staff the volunteer hospitals. While such petty criticism seems improbable especially in the first few days of the war, de Flers, while appearing to minimize the reproach, nevertheless indulges his own wit at the expense of the nurses. A sarcastic flourish enhances his suggestion of impropriety by using the homonym "panser," to bandage, in the place of "penser," its more famous counterpart in the allusion to the quotation by Descartes.

> Without doubt, alongside these prolific initiatives, we have sometimes noticed in this zeal for volunteer nursing a few excesses and perhaps even a suggestion of snobbery. One caustic wit had gone so far as to remark that certain society women had taken as their motto: "I bandage, therefore I am." That shaft is unjust.[23]

The practice of undermining the speed and dedication with which French women responded to the call for action with insinuation and imputation of their morals and patriotism often occurred, as in the examples above, alongside sincere praise. It was especially prominent in the discussion surrounding two wartime occupations that attracted the greatest number of middle- and upper-class women: volunteer nurse and *marraine de guerre,* the "war godmother" who sent letters and packages to soldiers. That concern over these particular activities should elicit an extensive controversy is located in the fact that they enacted the greatest amount of social change for their participants. Although adult single and separated women had gained full legal status in 1893, married women, who had only recently in 1907 won the right to dispose of their own salaries, were still minors under the law.[24] The war set into motion events that altered not only the material reality of women's existence but the social patterns as well. For middle- and upper-class women especially, who had led lives of semisequestration and had rarely, if ever, ventured anywhere alone, the war suddenly created an environment that provided more freedom of movement and a wide breadth of knowledge in many different areas of social and political life. Circumstances forced women of all classes to develop their decision-making skills and the habit of directing their own day-to-day lives. For working women, the war presented the additional problem of the loss of income and job security, as many workers, especially in the luxury industries, lost their jobs. The modest war allocation from the government and services from volunteer organizations helped until other jobs were found, although in general women did not enter the work force in large numbers in France until the end of 1915. Many of the charities set up by bourgeois and well-to-do women endeavored to help working women and mothers experiencing economic hardship, but in many cases unintentionally aggravated the deterioration of their financial condition. With space and materials donated or bought at cost, the women created goods that were in turn purchased at prices lower than prewar production expenditures, and consequently, the women earned less money. Wholesalers were eager customers for the clothes the women made, realizing a substantial profit while outwardly supporting the war effort. Writing in 1915, Louise Compain noted the exploitation of working women, who had no choice but to continue to labor for wages that became progressively lower.[25] Social patterns changed the least for agricultural women and those whose families owned small shops, for they continued to work as they had traditionally, even while assuming increased and different responsibilities.[26]

Expression of the disruption of established gender relationships that Joan W. Scott, Margaret Allen, and Margaret Darrow have characterized as distinctive of war occurred in a variety of accusations leveled at women of all social classes.[27] The anxiety over male identity and authority, as well as the fear of the virilization of women employed at jobs traditionally held by men that had surfaced at the end of the century, expanded as war work and responsibilities increased women's economic independence and social visibility. The absence of the men, coupled with the small war allocation women with children at home received, exacerbated the customary misogynist discourse to allege avarice, indifference, merrymaking, and infidelity, especially against those women whose activities brought them into proximity with civilian men.[28] The degree of suspicion voiced against nurses and godmothers was particularly prominent. This was due, as previously stated, to the proportional change these activities produced in the lives of women of "society," but also to the fact that the journalists and academicians who published their disapprobation were more concerned about women of their own social rank. Nonetheless, these accusations duplicated in essence the fear of loss of male authority expressed by men in other segments of society.

Perhaps no activity stimulated as much controversy as nursing. Fraught with contradictory imagery, the volunteer nurse embodied the major shift in middle- and upper-class women's social experience. Traversing the streets alone and unescorted to the hospital, she entered a world without privacy, where bodies and bodily functions were openly visible. Whether young or old, single or married, the nurse came in direct contact with sights, sounds, and smells that had been previously unknown to her. Moreover, she encountered, perhaps for the first time, people of different social strata, races, and nationalities, acquiring knowledge and developing ideas that would have otherwise remained outside her purview. Replicating the contradictory image of women enshrined in the Madonna/whore polarity, the understanding of the nurse's task of caregiving and comforting as an extension of her motherly duties competed with the opposite view that the maternal qualities of purity of heart and selflessness had been lost through this worldly experience.[29] The veil that framed the nurse's face caused her to resemble not only actual nursing sisters of religious orders, but also, as some commentators noted, to embody the spirit and example of the Virgin Mary, the ultimate mother figure. Yet, that same veil, along with the uniform's white blouse, blue cape, and modern length skirt, figured prominently in accusations of coquetry and vanity.[30] Sexual curiosity, flirting, and husband-hunting were considered motives disguised by the mask of saintliness and dedication. Even well-known feminists such as Marguerite Durand and journalist Marcelle Capy criticized the women who "paraded themselves" in the white blouse, high heels, and fancy hairdos.[31] Still Capy's views on nurses were typical of many, in that while she admonished women who "flutter about" and refuse to perform unpleasant assignments, she also praised the "serious" Red Cross volunteers whose "devotion inspires unanimous respect" (79–81; 85). Academician Frédéric Masson, whose patriotic articles appeared regularly in *L'Écho de Paris,* stated that the vehement and numerous attacks against bourgeois and upper-class women were part of enemy propaganda aimed at weakening the war effort of the French people. While he conceded that the place of young women under 30 was not at the bedside of a wounded soldier, he defended this "shocking" practice by asserting that none of the women and girls actually looked at the men whose wounds they tended. His comments on the nurse's veil were equally ambiguous and contradictory. Identifying the religious symbolism of the nun's veil with that of the nurse, while simultaneously asserting the flirtatiousness of the women, Masson praised the volunteers for "taking the veil" that they folded and draped "so coquettishly."[32] In their nonfiction portrait of nurses, "Ces Dames de la Croix-Rouge" (These Ladies of the Red Cross), Berthe and Renée Rey (Tony D'Ulmès) remarked in 1915 that the volunteers, with their detractors and defenders, were the subject of nearly everyone's conversation. Their article voiced the common view that the war had taught sacrifice and service to affluent women previously steeped in egotism and frivolity.[33]

Writing in 1916, historian Yvonne Pitrois also noted the beneficial social leveling that resulted from the work of the volunteers, women "whose white hands had never accomplished any vulgar chore" (87). Similar to most laudatory accounts of women's support activities, *Les Femmes de la Grande Guerre* (The Women of the Great War) described the heroism and personal sacrifice exhibited by women in the dangerous conditions of the hospital, validating its praise in terms inscribed by the Republican Mother ideology. The following passage was typical of many of these narratives in its insistence on the universality of the maternal impulse and the ability to enact motherly behavior regardless of any real-life experience. Moreover, Pitrois, like other contemporary observers, skillfully acknowledged the charge of coquetry only to neutralize it more effectively, while simultaneously reasserting the mother-child relationship that existed between nurse and soldier.

> The ladies of the Red Cross, all clothed and coifed in white, with their flowing veils and armbands adorned with the symbol of redemption, surrounded the heartbreaking new arrivals with attention; from this time on, they [the soldiers] were their property, their treasure; they were "their children," as they all said, and nothing is more beautiful than to see such a young girl of twenty, with fresh and rosy cheeks, hold up a seasoned foot soldier, already old, a courageous papa with a gray moustache, and get him to climb the stairs, while repeating, encouraging: "Go on, my child!" (86).[34]

Like Pitrois, Berthem-Bontoux reiterated the maternal character of the nursing task in her extensive history of women in the war, *Les Françaises et la Grande Guerre* (The French Women and the Great War), published in 1917. Dismissing the familiar accusations of coquetry and "misplaced curiosity" of the volunteers as infrequent, Berthem-Bontoux cited instead the dangerous conditions of the hospitals where nurses died from disease and enemy bombs. She also presented many statistics from the Ministry of War that demonstrated the effectiveness of the nurses in caring for the sol-

diers and returning them to the front (148–64.) Feminist writer Marie de
La Hire likewise reproduced the Republican Mother ideology throughout
her historical account of 1917, *La Femme Française, son activité pendant la
guerre* (The French Woman, Her Activity During the War). She also reported many pages of statistics on the thousands of professional and volunteer women who cared for the wounded and the indigent, as well as the
numerous nurses who received the Croix de Guerre and other commen-
dations for bravery. De La Hire carefully distinguished the importance of
gender in her assessment, stating that men did not possess inborn devotion,
as did women, for whom it was natural to care for the wounded. Her praise
of the nurses who died from typhus or enemy shells, as demonstrating a
"[p]atriotism of courage, but above all, of love and pity for the defenders
of the homeland," encapsulated the essential duality of Republican Motherhood by privileging maternal qualities over those traits deemed masculine, and even recasting accepted male characteristics in female terms. The
women's patriotism she honored was "one of the heart" (80–81).

Maternal imagery similarly pervaded interpretations of the future impact of the nurses' activities. According to many of the commentators, the
social leveling effected through volunteer nursing and other charitable activities would benefit the country in several ways. They concurred with
Tony D'Ulmès's opinion that the war, "rich in surprises, will have had unexpected results" ("La Mobilization des femmes," 79). In providing an opportunity for service to women who had led the lives of idleness and
triviality dictated by their social standing, the conflict had taught them the
true values of abnegation and sacrifice. Not only had these women revived
the innate, though dormant, qualities of devotion and pity they had always
possessed as women, but by putting these virtues into practice, they had re-
futed the world's opinion of French women as "luxury dolls," an image ex-
ploited by the Germans.[35] Further, as D'Ulmès, essayist Comtesse de
Courson, and critic Maurice Donnay theorized explicitly in their respective treatises, the spirit of entente that had developed as a result of the
mother-child relationship of nurse and soldier had minimized and even
collapsed class distinctions between the bourgeois and upper-class women
and the soldiers, most of whom were from rural agricultural areas. These
writers considered the mixing of social classes begun in the hospital as a
democratization that would continue after the war, and that, by creating
understanding among the different social strata, it would end the threat of
class conflict. Such fear of class war, voiced in France since the labor un-
rest of the 1880s and the anarchist attacks of the 1890s, had expanded with
complaints during the war that the casualties were borne unequally by the
laboring and agricultural classes. Rumors of a postwar revolution surfaced
as early as December 1914 (J. Becker, 96). Thus for these editorialists, the

upper-class women, forced by the war to enter public service, had not only learned lessons about themselves, but had, through the enactment of their conciliatory maternal role, brought about the pacification of, like so many unruly children, the common soldier. The notion of political harmony imagined by these writers replicated the solid maternal values of home, pity, and love. Stronger than political doctrine, the family relationships established between nurse and soldier would override class differences and create civic stability, despite the fact that each group had resumed its former social position.[36] Courson denied, however, the right of suffrage that many other writers thought would recompense women for their service in the war, and visualized the profound political influence women would have in the future, not by voting themselves, but through the reeducation of the soldiers.

> In a completely domestic atmosphere, the wounded have the time to reflect and compare; more than one, seeing close at hand these "aristocrats" and these "bourgeois," whom they heard vilified in public meetings of the past by their friends, will wonder, with his simple and correct good sense, if these same friends had ever studied closely those whom they denounced so vigorously. His suspicions aroused against revolutionary doctrines in this way, the wounded of yesterday, having become the voters of tomorrow, will have, after the war, a healthier and more clear-sighted attitude; the Red Cross, healer of bodies, will have contributed to creating a new soul for [future] French generations (42).[37]

Two personal memoirs that recounted the actual nursing experiences of their novelist-authors illustrate well the polarities of the nurse controversy. These accounts, J. Delorme Jules-Simon's *Visions d'Héroïsme* (Images of Heroism), serialized in 1915 in *L'Écho de Paris* and published the same year in book form, and Geneviève Duhamelet's *Ces Dames de l'hôpital 336* (Those Ladies of Hospital 336), 1917, both vigorously defended the nurses' skill and maternal devotion and depicted the mother-child relationship that existed between the attendants and the wounded. Nonetheless, the tone is strikingly different in each book.

The reverent, almost eulogistic language in Delorme Jules-Simon's account expressed the view that hospital service was the sole occupation possible for women. Not only was it the only way for women to be truly useful, it was also the means to increase their own self-esteem and assuage their guilt for the loss of husbands and sons who died protecting the women and children of France. For devout Catholics, such as Delorme Jules-Simon, usefulness was a value that earned merit for loved ones and would save their souls, if not their lives.[38] Her presentation directly countered the charge of pleasure-seeking and parasitism, while at the same time supporting the belief that the war benefited women by bringing out their best qualities. In this passage, she reiterated these themes by insisting that although women might act as individuals, it was in accordance with the guidance of the men in their lives.

> To serve! To be able to say that we are not useless. To serve, to try to elevate ourselves in our own eyes and before the eyes of those whom our soul follows, by forcing us to make that soul a little like theirs. To serve with that hope that we will thus redeem the lives of those who are dear to us.[39]

The opportunity for many women to serve their country would continue in her view even after the end of the war. Delorme Jules-Simon evoked with reverence and a sincere note of envy the women whose lives would be spent attending their permanently disabled husbands. Her attitude in *Visions d'Héroïsme* resembled that in her novels and in those of other writers, that such a situation was the ultimate expression of a woman's natural role of renunciation and self-sacrifice. Her assertion, "What a dream of abnegation! To serve. . . . To serve. . . . For the woman, what a mission, what a reason to be living!" (23), reinforced the appropriateness of such a permanent mother-child relationship. Moreover, she disagreed with the impassioned public praise of young women for not breaking off their engagements with their crippled fiancés because for her, such denial of the self was simply an expression of the patriotic and protective obligation of all women.

For Delorme Jules-Simon, the dual role of the Republican Mother was evident not only in a woman's personal relationships, but in the primary duties of the nurse as well. In addition to acting in defense of the nation by caring for the soldiers and enabling them to return to the front, the nurses used their natural maternal abilities of resignation and forbearance to comfort and pacify the soldier. Delorme Jules-Simon underscored the spiritual side of the mother role, as she recounted scene after scene in *Visions d'Héroïsme* in which the nurse, through soft words and little stories, was able to convince the soldier to accept with dignity and bravery the loss of a limb or even his life. Such a representation of the nurse as mother corresponded in part to that of the ubiquitous *mère douloureuse* (sorrowful mother) image, symbolized by the Virgin Mary of the Pietà. Many writers, in both fiction and nonfiction, expressed the anguish that mothers felt because they were not present to comfort their dying sons or to close their eyes after death. In this sense, the nurse in *Visions d'Héroïsme* became both a substitute for the absent mother and an instrument for the soldier's spiritual salvation. Disagreeing with a journalist who compared a young and pretty nurse's ability to calm the soldier on the operating table to an anesthetic, Delorme Jules-Simon responded that the man saw only one thing when he was in pain, "the image of his mother" (25).

In contrast to the solemnity and piety with which Delorme Jules-Simon evoked the patriotic and maternal task of volunteer and professional nurses, a relaxed, warm, and even humorous depiction of these same values characterized Geneviève Duhamelet's memoir, *Ces Dames de l'hôpital 336.* Yet the difference in tone does not undermine her portrayal of these virtues, but rather adds a note of realism. Even the least serious of all the volunteer nurses in Duhamelet's narrative exhibited the single-minded devotion to the soldiers, and the nursing sisters, the seasoned professionals, were more like saints than nuns. Duhamelet further countered the charge of frivolity and vanity among the volunteers, accusations denounced in the book's preface as the work of uninformed writers like François Le Grix, by portraying the superficiality and pettiness of male volunteers. Her vignettes of hospital life are balanced, revealing the fear of invasion that caused some of the volunteers to leave their posts, but also demonstrating the maternal caring that enabled the women to command the soldiers without intimidation. It was the desire for renunciation that made the women "the humble servants of the pitiful soldiers" (87).

Duhamelet often linked words that evoked maternal qualities, like abnegation, pity, and humility, with piety and spiritual sacrifice. Moreover, words or gestures of the people in the anecdotes she related allude simultaneously to Mary and to the soldiers' mothers, thus uniting divine and earthly motherhood in the person of the nurse. Nonetheless, Duhamelet showed the human side of the women by portraying their foibles alongside their saintliness. Nurses, whom she chided for having too much pride in their uniform, also sought the most humiliating tasks in the hope of earning merit for the souls of their wounded (120–22). Although these bourgeois and upper echelon women might never have scrubbed a floor before, they did so now to diminish the suffering of the soldiers by their own sacrifice (39). Several times Duhamelet pointedly drew a parallel between the agonizing situation of the soldiers and the Crucifixion of Jesus, equating the ministrations of the volunteer nurses with those of Mary and other Holy Women (122; 184).

The charges journalists leveled against the *marraines,* or godmothers, resembled the accusations against nurses, but centered more explicitly on women's sexuality. *La Famille du Soldat* (The Soldier's Family), founded in January 1915, was the first organization to coordinate the custom of writing letters and sending packages to soldiers separated from their families in occupied territories. Soon expanded by the efforts of many other organizations, such as *Mon Soldat* (My Soldier), and by the encouragement of public figures like the well-known nationalist novelist Maurice Barrès, the practice quickly became a vogue, linking countless soldiers of all regions and women throughout France. Borel reported that French women sent over one million packages to soldiers by January 1917 (66). Generally, the correspondents did not know each other, but answered ads in newspapers, or were "introduced" by other soldiers or civilians. The civilians were most often women of various ages, although some men, *parrains* (godfathers), also participated. Since the sending of packages involved a certain expense, while letters sent to and from soldiers were free, the godmother was generally a society woman who also took part in other charitable activities.[40]

The concept of *marrainage,* or godmothering, illustrates well the application of women's traditional private and maternal role to the public sphere. The godmother would be a substitute mother for her *filleul,* her godson, the soldier whose parents were unable to communicate to him the necessary guidance, courage, and morale building required at the front. While the underlying premise of the godmother certainly supported the combined patriotic and maternal values required of the Republican Mother, the social implications of the *marraine's* self-determined and above all, unsupervised contact with the soldiers quickly led to accusations of impropriety against the women. As in the case of the volunteer nurses, denunciation or defense of the godmothers reproduced in a contemporary patriotic version traditional anxieties concerning the possibility of an increase in female autonomy. It is significant that while the nurse's activities involved far more freedom of movement, independent decision making, and direct contact with men than that of the *marraine,* the reaction to godmothering was analogous to that of volunteer nursing. Encapsulated in the Madonna/whore polarity, the defense of the *marraines* invoked the same image of maternally-derived emotional, material, and spiritual comfort provided to the soldiers, while the reproach repeated the assumptions of vanity, sexual misconduct, and husband-hunting. Neither the mostly male critics of the godmothers nor, surprisingly, their female defenders disputed the complaints or questioned their origin. Instead of challenging the motives that prompted the accusations, the woman essayists asserted that abuses were rare and more likely to involve dishonesty on the part of the soldier.

Henriette de Vismes devoted a long book to a defense of the godmothers, and this best-selling work of 1917, *Histoire authentique et touchante des marraines et des filleuls de guerre* (Authentic and Moving History of War Godmothers and Godsons), received the Fabien Prize from the Académie Française. De Vismes concentrated on the civic stability enacted by the maternal care of the women, reiterating the benefit of the social leveling also attributed to nurses. As most of the godmothers were of a "superior station," they were able to alleviate the soldier's physical and emotional poverty, impressing them with "their hearts and their hands." The privileged or "society" women overcame the traditional mistrust of the working class through their efforts, teaching their godsons wisdom, reason, moderation, as well as unity by erasing the divisions among soldiers. The soldier treated the godmother like his mother, listened to her advice, and became easygoing and gentle. De Vismes's assertion in 1917 that the godmothers succeeded far more than most other civilians to pacify and thus maintain the morale of the soldiers and the political truce known as the *union sacrée* (sacred union) is important. It reaffirmed the steadfastness of women's loyalty and the vital and continued importance of their maternal conciliatory and educational role to the nation during a period that witnessed strikes, mutinies, and general civilian fatigue with the war (253–55).[41]

Like de Vismes, other critics emphasized the combined maternal and patriotic function of the godmother, a role dependent on good will, rather than age or experience. In citing the letters of one young woman and her middle-aged godson, Berthem-Bontoux demonstrated the impact of the godmother on satisfying the spiritual needs of the soldier. The girl's motherly question, "Are you well behaved, my godson?" elicited an appreciation of her efforts to provide religious guidance, something the war prevented his own mother from doing. Despite his mature age, he wrote, he had found the path back to God through her words, and his mother would be thankful that the godmother had completed the task she herself had started (190). Essayist Comtesse de Courson also stressed the maternal influence of the godmother, whose presence provided compassion and physical comfort similar to the sustenance and moral instruction given in the past by the soldiers' own mothers. True to the Republican Mother ideology of selfless service to the nation through maternal caring and charity, Courson's godmother remains anonymous, expecting no recognition for nurturing her adopted son.

> . . . their pity extends to strangers, to war "godsons," whom their benefactresses have never seen, whom they will never see, but whom they adopt in order to clothe them, to nourish them, and to comfort them (46).[42]

The commentators acknowledged some problems with the godmother program, but dismissed the accusations directed at the women as exaggerations of innocent "flirtations" or too infrequent to be of consequence. It is significant that while criticism of soldiers on any subject is exceedingly rare, Courson, de Vismes and Berthem-Bontoux all deflected censure of the women by placing responsibility for abuse with the men. They cited the women's enthusiasm for charity as the source of their occasional and naive inattention to the offensive motives of their godsons. Courson regretted that putting on a uniform never conferred virtue and delicacy to the soldier but conceded that most men distinguished themselves by their gratitude and reserve (46). Berthem-Bontoux also exposed the dishonesty of some of the soldiers who took advantage of women's self-sacrifice and compassion (187), and de Vismes related the story of one godson who had 53 godmothers. The soldier received so many packages that he set up his own illegal business, trafficking in the items the women had sent him (3–4). Still the writers confirmed the benefits of the relationship to both godmother and godson, and de Vismes characterized the bond as an expression of the French national spirit, rooted in tradition and history. Her allusion to the ransom of the fourteenth-century knight and popular hero, Bertrand Duguesclin, by the women of Brittany pointedly underscored the venerable and pivotal role of French women in determining their nation's fate.

> . . . the adoption of soldiers of the front, isolated and unfortunate, by the people of the rear, the friendship of Godmothers and Godsons, is worthy to be mentioned among the most beautiful features of a history of France's fleeting moments. Wouldn't it be proper, for example, to designate as sisters of the women of Brittany spinning flax for the ransom of Duguesclin, these women of our time, the godmothers, knitting wool to clothe the defenders of our homeland, orphans, or separated from their families? (7)[43]

The difficult first few months of the war found journalists deliberating the level of France's state of readiness, and women were among the targets of their speculations concerning the reasons for the beginning of the war. As in other subjects of debate involving women, the defenders invoked maternal and patriotic imagery, while detractors alleged selfishness or impugned the moral conduct of the women. Many of these writers blamed an extended period of peace and prosperity for creating a generation of selfish women, unduly naive in their faith in internationalism or too mired in the pursuit of individual pleasures to fulfill their duties to the nation. In addition to challenging the sincerity and loyalty of French peace activists, who played a visible role in the European pacifist movement during the two decades before the war, such castigation charged women with leading men into a lifestyle that rendered them ill-prepared to defend the country.[44] According to this reasoning, an alert and rapacious Germany would not have begun the war without perceiving this weakness in its ancestral enemy. Significantly, defenders as well as critics of women ascribed validity to these accusations of "delilahism," an extension of the prewar negative judgments against expressions of female individualism.

The allies of women, however, considered the war as a benefit that had taught women the values of service and devotion, rehabilitating them from lives of useless frivolity. Critic Maurice Donnay identified Parisian women's independence and individualism as the cause of their having become in his view the slaves of fashion and the easy prey of German dress designers, but he credited the war with ending their freedom, as well as the vogue for bizarre inventions and overpriced antiques. "Disorder, independence, egotism, blindness, all of that becomes order, discipline, altruism, and clear-mindedness" (26).[45] Writing in 1915, the ubiquitous woman of letters and feminist *salonnière* Aurel (Aurélie Mortier) proclaimed a new era of gender relationships based on esteem acquired through the adversity of war. Despite her reputation as an advocate of equality in marriage, Aurel's image of the future granted primacy in the couple to the man. Like Donnay, she applauded the decrease in women's independence.[46]

As for the women, haven't they been led by the war to renounce their fluttering idleness, their young peacock's self-conceit, their enslavement to ruinously expensive embellishments? Look at their faces. They have been, it seems, *stirred by respect.* Each one carries in her heart a companion, a friend, who suffers for victory. And the agitated Eve of times past who drew everything to herself, has become a reliable and strong woman, she who, again, respects, admires man.

He lived in times past for his creature comforts. How could she have respected him, she who bows down only to suffering? In the eyes of the woman, the war has made the man again the great sex, great by the fatigue overcome, great by the war well borne.

I do not think at this moment that there is a woman alive who looks down on man. In returning women's respect to men, the war has opened a whole future of magnificent moral standards.[47]

Despite public misgivings concerning their tenacity and determination, French women did support the war effort, largely because of the immediate threat to the territorial integrity of France. While many European and American feminists were ontological pacifists, considering their goal of world peace as a natural outgrowth of their special status as mothers, mainstream French feminists had concentrated more on the ideal of justice between women and men.[48] Their immediate and positive response to the call of *la patrie en danger,* the endangered homeland, stemmed from their concept of republican feminism and belief in the rule of law. These reformist feminists supported, like most French people, the idea of a just war of legitimate defense that should not end until German militarism, unleashed on France twice in 44 years, was destroyed. Moreover, prudent foresight led mainstream feminists to avoid even the appearance of inconstancy to the cause of France. While individuals may have agreed in principle with the small number of feminist pacifists such as Hélène Brion, Gabrielle Duchêne, Louise Saumoneau, and Madeleine Vernet, reformist leaders saw women's advocacy of the war as solid proof of their loyalty to French national interests above those of international feminism.[49] Support for suffrage had never been greater than it was during the spring and summer of 1914, and many activists had predicted at that time that their first votes would be cast in 1915. In adhering to the political truce, termed the *union sacrée,* the majority of French feminists, along with socialists, trade unionists and others, agreed to postpone their demand for social and legal reform until after the war. Many suffrage activists felt certain that the extensive contribution of women to the well-being of the nation at war would result in attaining the vote.[50] As Marie de La Hire proclaimed in 1917, no one would ever again mention the supposed weakness of women, who would be granted the right to vote as just compensation for defending their country (57; 299).

During the war, writers openly exulted that neither the women nor the soldiers had proved to be as selfish or as ill-prepared as generally assumed. Essayists like Louis Madelin glorified the image of an awakened France, roused from its stupor of pleasure and its habitual contentiousness to defend not only land and people, but also Christianity and civilization against godless barbarians.

The third of August one thousand nine hundred fourteen! Frivolous pleasures, dazzling luxury, political quarrels, religious discussions, social struggles, all appeared forgotten in an hour. The country on its feet, facing the enemy, facing danger, facing death, revealed itself more beautiful than it had ever been. All idealism melted into one élan, the spirit of the crusades and the spirit of '89 because along with the Homeland they were going to defend the Law against Barbarism and the God of our fathers against Odin, the destroyer.[51]

In contrast to the aura of suspicion and doubt that surrounded women and their activities during the war, there was one female identity that received only reverence and adulation, the passive and silent *mère douloureuse,* or sorrowful mother, modeled on the image of the Virgin of the Pietà. Unlike other women, accused of enjoying in various ways the economic and social changes set into motion by the war, the grieving mother was exempt from any form of mistrust or cynicism.[52] The representation of the sorrowful mother varied little in the press, with journalists of both genders acclaiming her resignation, her willing offering of her sons, but above all, her silence. Such serene and stoic self-abnegation in service to *la patrie,* the homeland, reflected the precise expectations for French women during the war. It was the supreme duty of the Republican Mother, called upon to put the moral instruction of her sons to the test and to sacrifice her personal happiness to the needs of the nation. Often called "cornélienne" in French after that seventeenth-century playwright's tragic heroines who fulfilled their public obligations to their own detriment, the sorrowful mother appeared in fiction and nonfiction alike as both a woman to be revered and to be emulated. Prolific propagandists, such as René Bazin and Frédéric Masson, continually praised the resignation, piety, and composure of French women, who had taught their sons the meaning of civic duty and whose bravery stemmed from these lessons of faith and sacrifice. Similarly, Berthem-Bontoux noted the formidable resolution of French mothers, whose refusal to revolt against the war in order to save their remaining children disproved German assumptions of weakness (251). Significantly, these characterizations of women's obligation to the state invoked maternal imagery on both a personal and national level, for France was a greater mother, a higher mother than any individual. Nonetheless, the commentators also emphasized the courageous struggle of French women to overcome their natural maternal instinct of protection in order to support their nation through the sacrifice of their children. This momentary conflict between the individual and the nation was significant because it demonstrated that while French women were patriotic, they did not take pleasure from death and killing, as the popular image of German mothers purported. A particular anecdote that appeared countless times in the press illustrated the symbolic identification of the maternal with France. While the woman uttering the patriotic phrase was different in each retelling, the speech was always the same. At the news of her husband's death, she proudly proclaimed, "He gave his life for France, he did well. France was his mother, I am only his wife."[53]

Editorialists commonly associated an imperiled France with the Catholic Church and Latin culture, thus merging the political with the religious and the historical. Regardless of whether the men in their family were sons, husbands, or other family members, writers expressed the obligation of French women in maternal terms, enlarging the familial metaphor to embrace spirituality and nationhood. In several articles, Eugène Martin compared the fate of French women to that of the Virgin Mary, who, in the willing sacrifice of her son became herself a coredeemer of humanity. Similarly, French women were helping to realize the preservation of their homeland, as well as the civilization created by the deeds of the heroes of France, figures who in their own actions fused Catholicism and national history. Like Martin, many journalists referred to Joan of Arc, the revered warrior-heroine who had roused her king to the defense of France and whose beatification, a prelude to her later canonization in 1920, had occurred only recently in 1909. Similar to allusions to Saint Genevieve, whose prayers deflected an invasion of ancient Paris by Attila, another invader from central Europe, the image of Joan had, since the mid-nineteenth century, signaled the convergence of national and religious identities, as well as the sanctification of political interests through her defense of France from the enemies of Catholicism and Latin culture. Moreover, Joan's patriotism and faith were considered ideals to be emulated by French women.[54] Martin, among others, reiterated the long-standing notion that France was "the eldest daughter of the Church," and thus, the war was necessary to preserve the future of a civilization "created by nineteen centuries of Christianity."

> French wives and mothers, the Lord, through the voice of the endangered homeland, asked you for your husbands and sons. . . . In giving your husbands and sons, o French women, you have thus contributed to the redemption, to the salvation of our France! . . . by means of your dear and greatly mourned casualities, you have protected the homeland from the most fearsome peril that ever threatened it . . . and, with the homeland, the civilization that numerous generations of Christian women have made to blossom, beneficent, in the land of [saints] Clotilde, of Saint Louis, of Joan of Arc, of Vincent de Paul, of Peter Fourier.[55]

Such rationalization of war, whether appropriating maternal or religious imagery, served to annul the incompatibility of motherhood with warfare and to assuage the guilt of mothers for allowing their sons and husbands to leave. Most essayists and historians ignored the paradox inherent in a cycle of birth and death determined by the needs of the nation. They, along with most feminists, supported the heightened emphasis on increasing birthrates as a means to offset the casualties for the future economic and military defense of France. Few agreed with the political analysis of maternity voiced earlier in the century by neo-Malthusians like Nelly Roussel and reiterated during the war by a few anarchists and radical feminists. Recognizing the power of women to realize civil justice on both the personal and the public levels through the control of the number of pregnancies, their call for a "grève de ventres" or "womb strike," remained unheeded. The majority of French feminists maintained their traditional support for a feminine identity defined by a connection between biological specificity and civic responsibility. Moreover, many reformist feminists considered the fall in population as a grave danger to France, and during the war they joined antifeminists in their pronatalist pronouncements, despite a rhetoric that repudiated some of their long-standing objectives (Bard, 27; 47–49; 65). Among those deemed most culpable were modern women, especially professionals, intellectuals, and those who considered themselves emancipated

(Thébaud, *Femme,* 276).[56] Notwithstanding the seeming incompatibility of pronatalism with feminism, in 1916, Cécile Brunschvig, the general secretary of the largest and most influential of the prewar feminist groups, the *Union française pour le suffrage des femmes* (French Union for Women's Suffrage), announced that the first duty of every woman after the war would be to have numerous children.[57] Christine Bard explained this incongruity by suggesting that feminists regarded the dangers and discomforts of pregnancy as the counterpart to the risks of injury and death encountered by men in the military, and that through maternity women paid a "blood tax."[58] While suffrage activists were especially sensitive to the argument that only those who served in the army should have the right to vote, it was also likely that women experienced guilt during the war, since defense of the family was one of its most publicized objectives (51). Nonetheless, Marcelle Capy, the pacifist socialist who published articles in many feminist newspapers, pointed out the irony of pressuring women to have more babies, children who would be born while their fathers were dying. "Forward! The crusade for cradles . . . sing of the white baby clothes after the mourning crepe of the widows."[59]

Journalists of various political and religious orientations responded favorably to the crusade for repopulation in terms that reiterated the principles of Republican Motherhood. Most agreed that Germany had viewed France's diminished population as evidence of its weakness and the inability to defend its borders or infrastructure. Although some critics, like Dr. Jacques Bertillon, a longtime activist for repopulation, cited the irresponsibility of French men, others blamed women directly for choosing to drain France's vitality. The editors of the Catholic daily *La Croix* faulted the attraction of modern pleasures and independence for luring young girls from the ideal of a Christian and moral marriage.[60] Similarly, Berthem-Bontoux decried the higher education before the war that diverted women from training as wives and mothers, adding that France needed fewer university graduates and more highly skilled homemakers if it were to regain its former worth (48–50). Frédéric Masson intimated that population control advocates were anarchists in the service of Germany.[61]

Despite the diversity of the criticism, there was nonetheless consensus concerning the solution and the responsibility of women in its implementation. Most commentators agreed that the war had brought about an unforeseen benefit in causing French women to refocus their attention on the priority of the family. Typically, they characterized this attention to maternity as a reaffirmation of compassion and duty to the nation, values inherent in the ideal of Republican Motherhood. "They will have pity on the French race," wrote the editors of *La Croix,* "already so weakened and so impoverished before the war, so decimated and so battered by the war;

and they will allow themselves to rebuild and revive it."[62] The feminist historian Henry Spont concurred in his well-known study of the economic condition of women. In spite of his advocacy of work outside the home as a personal and social benefit for women, he insisted nonetheless that "[t]he essential function of the woman, her reason for being, is procreation and the conservation of the species."[63] Even writers who disagreed with each other on most issues, concurred that motherhood was the fundamental duty of all women. The internationalist Romain Rolland, vilified in the press for his call to European intellectuals to withdraw their support of the war, urged women to resist war in natalist terms, asserting, "It's not in making war on war that you will suppress it, [but] it is in preserving first of all your heart against war, in saving from the conflagration *the future, which is in you*."[64] Marthe Borély, who attacked feminism as pro-German and anti-Catholic, asserted that "Maternity is the patriotism of women" (16), a statement shared by suffrage advocate Hortense Cloquié, who declared succinctly, "We have to repopulate France" (24).[65] These assertions support Thébaud's contention that from 1917 a general consensus established that the main role of women after the war was, in the words of two physicians, "to give birth, to give birth again, to give birth continually." Significantly, these doctors considered the exercise of women's rights dependent on maternity. They declared that a refusal to have children negated claims to any rights whatsoever and lowered women to the level of prostitutes (*Femme*, 282). Such an analysis of the primacy of women's biological function, while expressed here sensationally, reiterated the time-honored principles of Republican Motherhood: "before their arms, the wounded country wants their wombs."[66] The anxiety concerning the birthrate also brought about some reforms in working conditions and child-care facilities during the war, as writers debated the effects of factory work on fertility and the health of young mothers and their children (47–52; 76–77).[67] After the war, new legislation, including a 1920 law that sought to enforce existing antiabortion statutes and repress all information on contraception, underscored the heightened emphasis placed on maternity as a means to rebuild France (Bard, 127). In insisting on women's reproductive obligations, this pronatalist discourse effectively undermined the potential resistance to the return of French women to full-time domestic duties.

The compulsion to increase the birthrate was so pervasive that it promoted adoption and other forms of surrogate motherhood. In 1915, critic René Bazin renounced his former opposition to education for women because of new programs designed to develop the moral character of girls and to train them to be good mothers and homemakers. His praise of teachers as "miraculous mothers" not only reiterated the Republican Mother vocation of "mother-teacher," but enlisted women who were often celibate in the campaign for repopulation.[68] As educators, the women fulfilled their required maternal role through their training of future mothers, teaching young women to resist the temptation of individualism and selfishness.[69] The power of the natalist rhetoric was such that it even overrode the irony of conscripting for its crusade the very women, celibate teachers, who exemplified the choice of lifestyle antithetical to its purpose and ideology.

Adoption was considered a remedy to several cruel realities of war as well as a means to bolster the sagging population. As casualties rose, so did the anxiety of populationists and young women who had lived their entire lives in anticipation of marriage and nothing else. Historian Henry Spont criticized the narrow upbringing of these middle-class girls who lacked the education or training to earn a living and consequently became the financial burden of their parents, while contributing, by their celibacy, to the ruin of France (viii-ix; 32). Other essayists praised the willingness of these so-called surplus women, or *veuves d'espérance* (literally, expectation widows), to assist other women with their children or to adopt war orphans themselves. Such approval, beyond the humanitarian concern for children's welfare, promoted motherhood as well as civic responsibility by demonstrating that even unmarried women could participate in the regeneration of France. One of the anecdotes that circulated widely in these articles was the remark made by a member of the "Noëlistes," a group of young girls who took their name from the word for Christmas, and who made baby clothes for the newborn children of soldiers at the front. When asked what would be the fate of the "excess" women who would result from the deaths of so many men in the war, the girl replied, "We will not be too many mothers for the orphans." One of the many writers who repeated this semiparable was Louise Zeys, a journalist whose feminist views did not conflict with, but rather supported, pronatalist assumptions on marriage and the family.[70]

The promotion of marriage also figured in the repopulation campaign, and emotional accounts of bedside and hospital weddings between young women and severely disabled soldiers appeared regularly in newspapers like the ultrapatriotic *L'Écho de Paris.*[71] Berthem-Bontoux, like others, praised a group of girls in Nantes who had promised to marry only men who had seen action in the war, publicly rejecting any man suspected of being an *embusqué,* or war slacker (203). In 1915, novelist Marie Laparcerie published the pamphlet *Comment trouver un mari après la guerre* (How to Find a Husband After the War) that advised young women to reject both feminism and "coquetry" to provide the nurturing and healing atmosphere required by the returning soldier. Similar to other commentators, she also praised the patriotism of women who married disabled soldiers, as an expression of national pride and civic duty. Writing in 1916 on repopulation, Frédéric Masson commented on the essential role that morality and religion played in the formation of a family. While he decried the injurious effects of alcohol on marriage, he reserved his most dramatic attack on voluntary childlessness and celibacy. In this extended portrait of young girls who chose not to marry, Masson evoked the culturally-charged terms essential to Republican Motherhood, such as devotion and compassion, patriotism and victory, obedience and personal sacrifice, anti-individualism, and duty to the nation.

> The first victory to prepare is to propagate moral law and re-establish a religious law, to induce to marry by piety, by patriotism, [and] by pity, young girls who adopt celibacy, at first as a mode of waiting, and later permanently through the spirit of independence, through fear of family obligations, through lack of having met *Prince Charming,* [and] through not understanding that the first duty is the formation of a family.[72]

Adoption also became the answer to a more serious problem that beset especially the women of the invaded territories of France.[73] The fate of children of rape victims was a question particularly difficult to resolve because the issue contained in microcosm many of the long-standing and contradictory views of women and their role in society. Judith Wishnia reported that a protracted debate began in early 1915, during which feminists, intellectuals, doctors, and others argued the viability of several solutions, including relaxing the ban on abortion for a temporary period and providing varying degrees of state assistance to the mothers and their children.[74] While fears of racial contamination by German blood were a factor in the debate, the implication for the future if women exercised the right to determine whether they would bear and/or rear unwanted children, posed a far greater threat to the acknowledged need of the state to increase its population. Access to abortion implied the liberty to control one's own body, a freedom of sexual action that conflicted sharply with the tenets of Republican Motherhood. It is significant that the reality of war and the invasion of enemy troops in areas without adequate protection did not outweigh the stigma of dishonor or neutralize the questioning of women's morals usually associated with rape. Suspicion of wantonness and adultery, fueled by the soldiers' increasing anxiety about their wives' loyalty, conflated with fears of women's sexual agency. The long-standing determination of patriarchal society to maintain its control over women's bodies, along with the immediate concern for repopulating a nation at war, impelled the French government to agree to accept the children in state-run orphanages and to guarantee the anonymity of the mothers.

Many of those who entered the debate, including novelist Lucie Delarue-Mardrus and feminist leader Jane Misme, were sympathetic to the plight of the unfortunate women, but rejected abortion as a violation of the sanctity of motherhood. Significantly, the solution many critics envisioned reiterated the maternal and patriotic qualities of Republican Motherhood. While the letters sent to various periodicals, such as *La France* and the feminist *La Française* expressed worry about the native brutality present in the blood of the children of partial German ancestry, they also assumed that the loving heart of a "true" French woman and the long history of French cultural traditions would civilize the child and nullify the presence of the "barbarian." In growing up French, the children would avenge the unfortunate circumstances of their birth and the sacrifice of French soldiers in the war by becoming soldiers in the army of the future (Wishnia, 34–36). There was general agreement that the child's family and education, with its classic French and Christian values, would purify the youngster. Its deep-seated and powerful civic virtues would expunge any trace of what novelist Odette Dulac would call in a 1917 article the "barbarian stain." In a short story published that same year, pacifist Madeleine Vernet considered the opportunity to exercise maternal love as the proper way to avenge the hateful act of rape. "With the fruit of evil," she wrote, "[the mother] will create goodness." While for these mothers, the infants may have been *petits indésirés* (little unwanteds), *petits vipéreaux* (little vipers), or *petits intrus* (little intruders), populationists and pronatalists viewed the children as an unexpected benefit for France. Their comments emphasized the women's patriotic duty to offset the number of casualties in the war and urged them to give birth to the children, instead of choosing abortion.[75] Like many others, Berthem-Bontoux claimed the right of such children to sit at the family table of France and cited the "divine generosity" of women who would make the children "doubly French" (78).

The support of reformist feminists for the repopulation campaign was indicative of a larger view many French women had of the role they would play in society after the war. It was a position that did not refute either long-accepted gender divisions or traditional assumptions rooted firmly in the biological determination of women's nature. Rather, it appropriated the tenets of Republican Motherhood, especially the subordination of the needs of the individual woman to those of the nation, to expand the socially acceptable domains of women's agency. Since the ideology of Republican Motherhood originated in the principles of the French Revolution, it was not necessary for women seeking increased civil rights to subvert its emphasis on liberty, equality, and fraternity. It was instead a matter of extending these ideals to all citizens, a position of irrefutable logic. Thus, to oppose the emancipation of women, as Marie de La Hire asserted in 1917, was to call into question the principles of the Republic

(32). Activists like de La Hire understood that the call for justice for women that had dominated feminist rhetoric before the war had a different meaning in the new context of women's outstanding contribution to the national war effort. Although before 1914 the claim for civil rights under the principles of the Revolution remained open to a charge of opportunism and selfish convenience, the record of women's massive achievements and the value of their work in defense of the nation proved women worthy of all rights of citizenship. Politically astute writers like de La Hire and Marguerite Borel documented in painstaking statistical detail the extent of women's activities, from those who replaced the men in fields, shops, and factories, to the thousands of volunteer nurses and charity workers. They and other essayists like Louise-Amélie Gayraud and Hortense Cloquié recounted hundreds of anecdotes, along with lists of groups formed to respond to every possible need of a nation at war. While sometimes these writers were not declared feminists, their portrayal of French women nonetheless enhanced the feminist call for emancipation by providing corroborative evidence. Their histories of women's activities during the war showed the impact of the increased freedom of movement, the necessity to reflect and act in unusual situations, and the urgency of wartime responsibilities. The effect of those activities, however, was not what traditionalists and antifeminists had feared. Rather than nullify or destroy the essential feminine characteristics so ingrained in the image of Republican Motherhood, the writers demonstrated that the experience of French women in the world outside the home in fact intensified their devotion to family and nation. Using a line of reasoning that both affirmed and defeated accusations of frivolous conduct before the war, these historians and essayists applauded the fact that the war had finally given women the opportunity to activate their innate but underused qualities of devotion and sacrifice for the good of the nation.

Encoded in this approbation of the positive change in women's mental attitudes and physical state was the affirmation of a new and modern rendering of the Republican Mother image. In describing activities that subverted an established social order restrictive for women with the very terms and symbols of the values of that society, the writers effectively redefined the cherished image of patriotic maternity. Appropriating the rhetoric of those who had opposed expansion of women's active sphere to valorize those same activities hindered criticism and normalized behaviors previously considered shocking. The new Republican Mother became in nonfiction and, as will become apparent in the following pages, also in fiction, a self-directed and intelligent adult who could competently discharge her private, familial responsibilities and, additionally, execute diverse public roles. Rather than claim such freedom of action as a right, the women essayists and fiction writers alike insisted that it was a patriotic and moral obligation.

It is significant that very early in the war suffrage proponents began to assess the impact of women's war activities on their role in the future. As early as 1915, when it was already apparent that the war would continue far longer than people had thought, books and articles appeared that carefully explained the expanded responsibilities women would fulfill in society when the hostilities were over. While the anecdotes and examples in these writings promoted in different ways women's independent action, they also linked this conduct through traditional female imagery to service to the community of the state. Moreover, commentators often cautiously distanced themselves from the politically charged term *féministe,* while unmistakably advocating a clear feminist position and definite feminist goals. Such pragmatism had the effect of substituting evasion for confrontation. For example, essayist Hortense Cloquié imagined a new life for all of France after the war, with the most important roles going to women. She described the war as a tragic benefit, but one which would convert people from lives of indolence and comfort to seriousness and purpose. Women would have to assume the financial responsibility for themselves or the family because of the dearth of able-bodied men. For Cloquié, meaningful labor educated women both morally and physically. Nonetheless, while she advocated activity outside the home ("work is the beginning of wisdom"), she also disparaged higher education for women and reminded her readers of the importance of family life (15; 17; 32–33). Similarly, while she cautioned her readers to resume as quickly as possible the role of wife and mother when returning from work each evening, so "that the husband may recoup his wife and not a legislator," Cloquié was candid and direct about suffrage and the changes those very legislators would enact. "We will claim the right to vote to make laws to protect the women who work, single mothers, and abandoned wives" (15–16; 21).[76] Cloquié also warned her readers to remember always that their husbands were superior by virtue of their service in the war, yet ended her volume with a call for an army of women to protect the frontiers of France (15; 35). As contradictory as such assertions may seem, in fact they reiterated succinctly the traditional duality of the Republican Mother, with one very important difference. Whereas patriotic motherhood had always subordinated the private to the public by emphasizing civic duty through maternal virtue and practice, the war had expanded the definition of a woman's maternal "sphere" to include the greater family of France. By insisting that all women always acted as mothers regardless of the situation, both nonfiction and fiction authors drew on women's successes in the war to create an unlimited and certainly public domain for the new Republican Mother. Such two-sided statements as Cloquié's in fact reassured anyone fearful of women's emancipation that new freedoms would continue to benefit the larger community of France. Pauline Valmy was another writer whose proposals for new legislation confirmed the necessity of freedom for women to insure the long-term well being of France. In 1915, she advocated the termination of parental rights concerning an adult woman's right to marry. While her argument appropriated military vocabulary and rested on the themes of the repopulation debate ("The salvation of a nation requires battalions of cherubs") it nonetheless asserted the right of women to determine their own future in an area where that power did not then exist.[77] Such a position, although confined to the traditional domestic arena of women's lives, implied a more comprehensive notion of the legal ability of women to dispose of themselves as they wished.

Some proponents of the new Republican Mother rejected women's right to vote as dangerous to the future of the nation, while nonetheless supporting increased autonomy for women in the public sphere. Essayists like Louise-Amélie Gayraud and Pauline Valmy celebrated the advent of a new partnership between men and women, born of the exigencies of war and forged in a newfound maturity and seriousness of purpose. However, they considered the demand for suffrage a serious impediment to the creation of the cooperative spirit needed to rebuild a weakened nation. They were, moreover, indignant at the suggestion by many feminists that the right to vote should be granted to women as compensation for their war work, arguing that patriotic service was required of every citizen. Both Gayraud and Valmy heralded the death of prewar feminism that "treated men like enemies" and, much like Aurel, proclaimed the era of the couple, under the guidance of the husband. Gayraud encouraged women to discard the separatism of the past to unite with men in the performance of the nation's work, characterizing such a coalition as mature and reasonable, in contrast with feminist demands for legal autonomy, which she deemed selfish and childlike ("L'Œuvre féminine," 538–40). Similar to Valmy and other observers, she alerted women to the inevitable changes the war experience would engender in their husbands' personalities and the impact of these differences on their own lives, creating, in a sense, two conflicting realities. Her advocacy, like theirs, of a new relationship between women and men located all responsibility for its success with women and thus ordained that they reject previous social roles, from the subservience of the past to the self-assertion of the future. Neither the *femme esclave,* the slavish woman, nor the "egotistical" and "coquettish" feminist would be an appropriate partner for the postwar man ("Féminisme et la Guerre," 610–27; "L'Œuvre féminine," 539–40). These authors, fearing a continuation of the pre-1914 "war of the sexes," imagined with alarm the consequences for a postwar France if the divergence between women's and men's sensibilities were not resolved quickly. Valmy, like Gayraud, considered the hardship of war a benefit, since it forced women to alter their prewar life goals, whether traditional or modern, and created in them the basis for a new partnership with men.

> The war has united, in the same spirit of patriotic faith, fellow citizens separated by their other convictions, it has also given birth to a second miracle: men have discovered in the enriched and reformed soul of women the foundation on which to establish the couple of tomorrow, no longer in accordance with a blueprint of demands, but [one] of love and of intelligence (310).[78]

The comments of Valmy and other journalists signaled the emergence of a new role for French women, one that recognized the legitimacy of certain educational and legal advances of modern society without rejecting completely the customs of the past. It combined both action and stability and provided an image of women who would accomplish their responsibilities as full citizens of France and of the world, while maintaining their cherished position as mother and wife. Although the conciliatory stance of this New Republican Mother was far from revolutionary, its emphasis on the process of growth and change occasioned by the war repudiated traditionally-conceived gender roles for both men and women.

Despite the solidity of the image of the New Republican Mother in the essays, histories, and other nonfiction texts of the war period, it was in the era's novels and short stories that this representation developed considerable depth and power. Compelled by circumstances beyond their control, the women protagonists of these novels and short stories, like their real-life counterparts, engaged in activities rarely imagined or desired, which required them to exercise independent judgment and action. In performing their civic duty, they overcame the anxiety caused by inexperience and the unknown and acquired increased self-esteem and a renewed sense of dedication to the nation of France. In 1916, commentator Louise-Amélie Gayraud predicted this transformation in the lives of the real-life women who served as volunteer or paid workers, "They will have become aware of their value, of their personal strength, they will have tested themselves."[79]

Rather than the stereotyped and one-dimensional characterization of women found in Tinayre's famous novel, *La Veillée des armes,* the complex reality of women's psychological and social condition during the war informed the representation of women in dozens of French works of fiction published between 1914–1919. While in general these stories demonstrated how the war experience challenged and caused the characters to develop the positive qualities required of citizens during a war, the authors did not present a homogeneous portrait of women. The female novelists explored and analyzed the effects of war on women's lives and their evaluation disclosed a variety of views on the content and purpose of war, the nature of interpersonal relationships, and the impact of the war on women, men, and the society of the future. Nonetheless, the novels and stories shared several comprehensive assumptions about French women and World War I. Foremost, they established the vital importance of women's contribution to all sectors of the war effort, demonstrating through characterization and plot that such participation was indispensable and as fundamental to eventual victory as that of combat soldiers. Significantly, the fiction demonstrated that the experience of war, far from corrupting women with its increased freedom of movement and opportunities for decision making, in fact gave women the opportunity to develop and improve as individuals, to the benefit of their families and the greater family of France. The war emerged in these novels and stories as a great teacher of civic duty and of other valuable lessons, often restoring to the social mainstream women whose pursuit of independent goals was portrayed as excessive and dangerous to the hegemony of the doctrine of Republican Motherhood. Egotism and self-concern, whether the result of traditional practices or modern freedoms, submitted in the fiction to a renewed sense of the importance of the community in its various forms. The protagonists were, or became, serious-minded individuals who loved their country and were willing and physically capable of sacrificing their own lives, their security, and comfort to defend their homeland. Although nearly all of the characters are wives or fiancées, the themes and plots of the stories portray them as sexless mother figures whose desires are limited to the preservation of the family of France. With rare exception, these women protagonists are thoroughly chaste, and their fidelity to husbands and fiancés is unequivocal. This narrative stance duplicates the virtue and devotion of Saints Joan and Genevieve, role models for the women of France. It also refutes soundly the widespread accusations of sexual promiscuity assumed by the press and expressed by soldiers in their correspondence and by male writers in their fiction, such as Paul Géraldy's best-seller of 1916, *La Guerre, Madame* (The War, Madam), reissued regularly for the following 20 years.

It is important that the actions of these characters attested that the desire and ability to serve the nation stemmed from the exercise of what the authors established as "innate" womanly qualities and not from any usurpation of male privilege or assault on male social roles. The underlying assumption of these novels and stories was that women's active participation in the society of modern France did not endanger, but rather, enhanced and sustained the performance of maternal and wifely duties. Thus, for these authors, being active in the world did not corrupt the womanly virtues of devotion, love, and caring, but instead reinforced in French women these ideal qualities traditionally required of the *mère-éducatrice,* the mother-teacher so integral to the Republican Mother ideology. Whether volunteer nurse, fiancée, *marraine,* or biological mother, all women in these novels (eventually) exemplified the profound and enduring significance of maternal care, thus refuting definitively the accusations of immorality and selfishness leveled at women during the war. Further, the novelists carefully documented the beneficial service that middle- and upper-class women, freed by the war from the idleness and inutility of their socially-imposed semisequestration, eagerly accomplished. Their conclusion, that the activities of women outside the home supported, rather than threatened, traditional societal values and structures complemented and reiterated the dual philosophy of reformist feminists of the period. It combined a biologically-determined view of women and their role in society with a modern insistence on the value of women's independence, self-direction, and the social worth of women's work outside the family. Like their journalistic and political counterparts, the fiction writers advocated an image of self-reliant and autonomous women choosing to promote the traditional interests of France, cooperating and working with men for the greater good of their nation.

In addition to establishing the record of women's achievement while rehabilitating the image of female volunteers and paid workers, the novelists registered permanently the voice of French women in the history of the Great War. Their acceptance of the contemporary model that synthesized the traditional definition of the nurturing mother with the modern desire for legal and social emancipation verified, rather than denied as recently suggested, the importance of women in the national memory. The novelists duplicated the philosophy of reformist feminists, a compromise that imagined active and autonomous women, empowered by maternal qualities of caring sacrifice and loyal devotion. Such a rapprochement between the public and the private in these novels and stories collapsed the distance noted by Joan W. Scott between official pronouncements on the meaning of war in the twentieth century and women's experiences. For Scott, this divergence facilitates understanding of the ways in which and by whom a national memory is constructed (28). In recounting these tales of those whom Berthem-Bontoux called "true French women with manly hearts" (46), the women fiction writers used the prestige of their established literary careers to claim for their compatriots an important and enduring voice in the retelling of their nation's history. Yet, these novels and stories are more than documents that record permanently the experiences of French women during the Great War. In interpreting the various effects of war on their characters, the authors ascribe meaning to the events and, in Scott's words, "articulate their understanding of war and its consequences . . ." (29).

By retaining their works of fiction within the realm of women's separate "sphere," the authors recounted the distinct story of that particular war without challenging the definition of battle as the quintessential male experience. In effect, their narrative position did not question the enduring assumption, noted by several present-day critics, that only combatants had the moral authority to express knowledge of war.[80] With few exceptions, the subject of the fiction French women writers published during the period 1914–1919 was an existence that not only differed from that experienced by men, it was also the disclosure of a reality of which men were largely unaware. Rather than dispute the masculinist definition of war, as Claire Tylee found among British women writers, French women authors evoked a parallel reality that existed simultaneously with the battlefield experience of men. It was a didactic project that informed women of their responsibilities as well as demonstrated to men the determinant role women would have in securing an eventual victory. Complementary, rather than competing, definitions of the truth formed the basis of these novelists' point of view. Instead of expressing openly or subversively a bipolar rivalry such as the one that both Gilbert and Goldman perceived in British women's war fiction, the French writers affirmed their part of a shared and communal experience.[81] Support, and not opposition to what Suzanne Raitt and Trudi Tate have termed the "discourses of femininity," exempted these predominantly mainstream and established authors from the expectation of silence, inherent in the traditional view of women's role in war.[82] By reasserting and simultaneously expanding women's separate "sphere," the fiction writers calmed social anxiety over the blurring of gender lines occasioned by women's activities in the war. Most importantly, they also normalized those new behaviors by incorporating them into a long-accepted definition of the responsibilities of French citizens to their nation.

Chapter Two

The Anguish of a Fearful Freedom ✿

S everal novels focus on the exceptional situations that many middle-
class French women faced because of the war. These stories detail
the protagonists' efforts to confront the challenge to their previously tranquil and assured lives and also illustrate their eventual triumph
over these difficulties. The women in the novels by Mathilde Démians
d'Archimbaud, J. Delorme Jules-Simon, Geneviève Duhamelet, and
Marcelle Tinayre have little experience outside the narrow circle imposed by traditional obligations to their families, and thus they lack the
knowledge necessary to guide them through the complexities of their
particular circumstances. Nonetheless, their devotion to both God and
France serve them as sure and steady signposts in their successful attempts to navigate the unfamiliar landscape of intense emotions where
the reality of sudden death invites every excess.

As dedicated wives and mothers, the protagonists in these novels exemplify "model" French womanhood, and ironically, it is their scrupulous
sense of obligation to this ideal that places them in the most morally trou-
blesome situations. Nursing the wounded and caring for refugees and orphans fulfills their traditional duties of service and charity. However, these
activities by necessity replace the protected environment of the home
with the possibilities of freedom and choice inherent in the outside
world. Such liberty of movement and thought is a revelation to them, but
it is not a happy discovery, although it is for Gérard d'Houville's character, Cécile, in *Il faut toujours compter sur l'imprévu* (Always Count on the
Unexpected), published in 1916.[1] As a didactic *proverbe dramatique*, it
demonstrates how the lapse of strict social decorum so common during
the war allows a man and woman to speak openly and honestly with one

another. Their relationship thus begins in friendship and integrity rather than with the normally required conventions of coquetry and courtship. Unlike d'Houville's couple who appreciate the value of this "unexpected" break with custom, the characters in the novels discussed below regard the prospect of freedom with anguish and fear, for they have experienced only the dangers of such autonomy. Having glimpsed the consequences of liberty, they will assert that independence to choose to resume their traditional and socially accepted roles. Thus the war tests, but eventually strengthens, their long-held qualities of self-denial and sacrifice.

A travers le tourment: une vie intime (Through the Torment: A Private Life) was Mathilde Démians d'Archimbaud's second book on the Great War. Born in 1883, she had also published *Notes d'une infirmière* (A Nurse's Notes) in 1914, but it was her 1917 novel that brought her notoriety with the award of the Jules Davaine Prize from the Académie Française.[2] *Une vie intime* is the story of a young married woman with two small children who discovers love and passion through a relationship with a soldier. The novel chronicles the awakening of her passionate nature, her struggle to resist the temptation of her love for Jean, and finally, her resolution to rededicate herself to the duty imposed by family and country.

The successive losses of her parents and grandfather had made Madeleine Delaitre an austere and obedient young woman. Having learned to suffer for others, she avoided knowledge of romance and frivolity and accepted with indifference marriage to a man twice her age. A model wife, Madeleine wins the respect and admiration of her husband and all of Lyons society, yet she seems somewhat detached. Her older friend, who serves in the novel as a mother figure, notices this aloofness and accurately predicts that motherhood will provide an outlet for Madeleine's suppressed emotions. When war is declared, Madeleine's husband is assigned to the Supply Corps, leaving Madeleine alone with her two young children. She serves as a nurse at a local hospital, establishing a noteworthy reputation as the embodiment of her principles of honor, duty, and Catholic faith. Incarnating the very image of maternal care, Madeleine cheers the wounded and consoles the dying in a remarkable display of patriotic fervor and the redemptive power of suffering. Perhaps because of her austere and nun-like demeanor, she is especially effective in counseling off-duty and recuperating soldiers who feel tempted by the reported opportunities for sexual license at the home front. Moreover, she convinces several amputees of their patriotic duty to marry and have families, despite their fear of being objects of pity. Their role, she assures them, will be to remind people in the future of heroism and glory (115–16). Démians d'Archimbaud's emphasis from the beginning of the novel on Madeleine's purity and maternal qualities is significant because it ensures

that the reader will judge her later activities in the context of the atmosphere of permissiveness that resulted directly from the war. Moreover, in
examining so closely the character's struggle to resolve the conflict between self-interest and the needs of her family, the author creates a parallel to the soldier's acceptance of self-sacrifice for the good of France. The
insistence on piety and love of country here also imparts poignancy to
Madeleine's subsequent brush with temptation, while at the same time establishes the means for her final triumph.

At the hospital, Madeleine renews her acquaintance with the handsome officer Jean de Vermelles, a childhood friend, and quickly falls in
love with him. Astonished by the intensity of her emotions, she tries to
suppress them through meditation and prayer. The many innocent hours
she spends with Jean end when he returns to the front. When he is severely wounded in a major offensive, Madeleine flaunts social convention
by traveling unescorted to his bedside. There she inadvertently reads a letter Jean wrote in the event of his death, and learns that he shares her love.
Resisting the powerful urge to renounce home and family to live openly
with Jean, she obeys a "secret inner law" and returns home. There
Madeleine endures the tacit reproaches of her husband and older friend,
while silently mourning the loss of her happiness. She proves her resolve
to end the relationship with Jean by convincing him to marry the daughter of a friend. Her decision, however, is less personal than it is patriotic.
Madeleine finds the strength to return to her children and passionless
marriage in the realization that her "rival" can give Jean the home and
family every French soldier deserves and that the country requires. Thus
in taking on the traditional married woman's role as matrimonial agent,
she guarantees the stability of two families, her own and Jean's. Confronted with "the anguish of a fearful freedom" (293), Madeleine chooses
the interests of France, represented by the preservation of the family unit,
over her own and Jean's individual happiness. The last scene of the novel
confirms the virtue of her choice. Her young son reads a letter he wrote
to his father, telling him that they love him and that everything at home
is unchanged. As in many other novels studied here, a child symbolizes the
truth and enacts a mother's redemption.

Démians d'Archimbaud presents the process of Madeleine's struggle
and victory over self-interest in the context of other women's efforts to
continue their lives under the extraordinary conditions of war. The shoe-
maker, Madame de Bizolon, has a son at the front, and although she is very
poor, she spends all of her resources on supplies and gifts for the soldiers
who stop at the Lyons train station. When her son is killed, she redoubles
her efforts for the other soldiers (46–47; 183–84). The grief of Madame de
Saint-Julien, Madeleine's older friend, for her son, is so profound that she

cannot speak of it (306–07). Strangers Madeleine meets on the train on her way to Jean's hospital also recount stories of suffering, resignation, and sacrifice (220–28). It is significant that Madeleine encounters these people and learns of their anguish at critical points in her own story. Each time she faces a difficult decision and seems about to yield to the passion she feels for Jean, Madeleine comes in contact with a mother whose dignified bereavement forces her to accept the idea of her own happiness as selfish and almost indecent. These mothers function as teachers whose collective example stimulates Madeleine to compare her life with theirs. The examination of her conscience leads her to respect the stoic acquiescence with which these women endure their losses, and to accept the relative unimportance of her own sacrifice.

Madeleine's decision to return to her home is more than a reaffirmation of the primacy of the family and the acknowledgment of the need to rebuild France's population, certainly popular themes in French women's war fiction.[3] Rather, Démians d'Archimbaud privileges the resumption of those qualities of self-denial and care for others that Madeleine exhibited before the war as the means to guide the young mother through her experience with war. Like other authors, she underscores the attitudes of resignation and abnegation as the proper responses of women to war. The various characters in her novel reinforce the view that it is a woman's duty to live and suffer for others, especially for her children. Romantic love is a fleeting distraction from a woman's true vocation of service and duty to her husband and children. It is significant that it is Madeleine's son who voices the affirmation of the family that also indicates the proper conduct to his mother. Madeleine's older friend, Madame de Saint-Julien, reinforces this view by admiring submission as the greatest of maternal attributes. In fact, she considers the war part of a divine plan to rescue men from self-indulgence, remind women of the redemptive role of suffering, and, in general, to reaffirm human spirituality (52–53; 307). While other war novelists like Duhamelet and Reynès-Monlaur emphasize the war's curative effect on the shortcomings of an individualistic French society, Démians d'Archimbaud here underscores the sexual nature of those transgressions. Madame de Saint-Julien clarifies her viewpoint to Madeleine:

> We have avoided suffering too much. Providence reminds us of its redemptive role. You see, men who were slaves of pleasure are called as if to a direct atonement through the martyrdom of their flesh. . . . And women share their expiation, it's the law (53).[4]

Personal happiness, then, comes from the generosity of self that typifies for Démians d'Archimbaud the joys of motherhood. It is an altruism, symbolized by children, that preserves the larger community of the French nation and parallels the soldiers' sacrifice of their lives for the future of France. Like many war novelists and activists for women's civil rights, Démians d'Archimbaud considers childbirth and maternal practice as a civic duty that in its specificity for women parallels combat as the unique domain of men.

While Démians d'Archimbaud elevates the involvement of women in the war to a spiritual level nearly commensurate with that of men, she nonetheless retains a properly respectful tone toward the soldiers. Servicemen are not simply combatants; they are "volunteers for the supreme immolation" (38) and "our heroic defenders" (63) who offer their lives freely and joyfully (130; 187–93). The portrayal of the lingering demise of a teenage soldier in Madeleine's charge evokes this attitude of willing sacrifice (149–51). The pallor of his face contrasts sharply with its expression of peace, a calmness that could only come with the approach of death. Despite his desperate condition, the boy insists on being carried into the chapel to witness his sister's wedding. Her happiness is a sincere joy to him, and since he has already begun to detach himself from the world of the living, he is not jealous of the love and life he will never have (150). The level of patriotic martyrdom and jubilant self-sacrifice confirmed in *Une vie intime* is strikingly different from the confusion and discouragement indicated in three other novels published in 1917. As discussed below in chapter 6, the books by Isabelle Sandy, Jehanne d'Orliac, and Andrée Mars, reproduce the doubt and dissatisfaction with the progress of the war expressed by civilians and soldiers alike at that time.

It is important that Madeleine chooses on her own to reject an extramarital relationship with Jean. Alone with Jean, she has no friend to talk to or to counsel her; nonetheless she feels the strength of an "inner law" that emanates from her own mother's love, her thoughts of home, and her religious principles (268–75). Although the temptation to stay with him is great, and she does hesitate for a few minutes, she sadly obeys a collective force that overcomes her desire for individual happiness.

> With sadness, but without resistance, the young woman obeyed the impulse that ordered her to hurry away without delay. Yet, the chaos of circumstances isolated her in a total freedom. Around her, no advice, no support. But inside her all the power of a secret law that emanated from deep-seated and invincible influences: from her love for her children, from the thought of her husband and their home, from her jumbled misgivings, her religious sentiments, from all the harmony of her life (268–69).[5]

That Démians d'Archimbaud characterizes Madeleine's decision as an impelling force is significant because it emphasizes the subconscious and intrinsic characteristics of her moral stance, qualities that preserve it from interpretation and possible transgression. Thus it is not until she is at a safe distance from Jean that she begins to contemplate her decision rationally. She concludes that the marginalized life she and Jean would have been forced to live would eventually make them despise one another (284–86). The importance of her inner voice is substantial because it indicates that freedom and independence for women will not threaten the established social order. Madeleine is a woman who had the liberty to leave her husband, yet exercised that agency to preserve her family. Démians d'Archimbaud's novel shows that similar to the men who willingly sacrifice their self-interest to the idea of the Nation, so will women choose to serve the larger community of France. Her assurance of Madeleine's fidelity and loyalty counters fears concerning women's sexual behavior during the war and the subsequent possibility of their political emancipation. It reasserts women's commitment to the established and traditional values of maternity and national interest, while resisting any suggestion of separateness or insurgency.

Marital fidelity and sexual freedom are also important issues in J. Delorme Jules-Simon's *Âmes de guerre, âmes d'amour* (Souls of War, Souls of Love), published in 1917. Delorme Jules-Simon, the granddaughter of the celebrated political figure and academician, had achieved fame in her own right before the war. Her *Soldat* (Soldier), 1910, had received the Académie Française's Prix Jules Davaine; and *Plutôt Souffrir* (Suffer Instead), 1912, and *A l'ombre du drapeau* (In the Shadow of the Flag), 1914, a novel about a soldier's search for heroism in the French colonies between 1912–1914, had secured favorable reviews. In addition to *Âmes de guerre, âmes d'amour*, awarded the prestigious Prix Montyon by the Académie Française in 1917, she published *L'Impérieux Amour* (The Essential Love)[6] and *Visions d'Héroïsme* (Images of Heroism) during the war period.

As noted previously, Delorme Jules-Simon served as a nurse during the war and the long essay, *Visions d'Héroïsme*, records her impressions of the military hospital. Serialized in *L'Écho de Paris* from August to September 1915, and adorned in its published edition by a laudatory preface by the most visible and famous patriot-writer, Maurice Barrès, *Visions d'Héroïsme* reveals a theme of central importance in all of Delorme Jules-Simon's war works, the defense of volunteer nurses. Bedside scenes described in minute detail recount the wounded soldiers' efforts to comprehend the gravity of their conditions. It is in this profoundly maternal role of consoler that Delorme Jules-Simon's nurse accomplishes her greatest task, for it is she who helps the soldier accept his permanent disability or imminent death. In insisting on the motherly or sisterly relationship between the nurse and the soldier, Delorme Jules-Simon refutes the public criticism of nurses. The motive of the vast majority of nurses in Delorme Jules-Simon's account, as in *Ces Dames de l'hôpital 336* (Those Ladies of Hospital 336) by Geneviève Duhamelet, is neither praise nor ambition, but simply service to France in the only way open to women. The fulfillment of this obligation is also important because it removes the stigma of women's inactivity and moreover, it seeks Christian redemption for the lives of their own husbands and brothers. It is this dual objective of women's service that also informs Delorme Jules-Simon's two novels of the war, *L'Impérieux Amour* and *Âmes de guerre, âmes d'amour.*

Âmes de guerre is an epistolary novel that recounts the lives of four people during the first year of the war: Madeleine, her husband Jacques, her friend Janine, and Henri, a friend of both Madeleine and Jacques who falls in love with Janine. The novel's substantial length and confessional structure allow Delorme Jules-Simon to treat a variety of complex themes, especially the psychological effects of the war on both men and women. Passages depicting in minute detail the reality of life in the trenches, on the battlefield, and in military hospitals in France and Greece transmit an unusually precise degree of realism (11–16; 35–38; 44–48; 100–03; 121–77; 220–23; 240–49; 260–73; 330–349). While the few descriptions of trench and battle scenes in the works of other writers are generally short and serve as encapsulated episodes separated from the main plot of the novel, authenticity in Delorme Jules-Simon's story is the foundation for her characters' meditations on distinct moral issues. It is not a question of whether or how to serve their country best that concerns these four people, but how to uphold their personal moral principles in extraordinary and unfamiliar situations.

Contemplative reflection rather than action fills the novel. Madeleine, married for over 20 years to a career soldier, balances her responsibilities as the mother of three young adult children with her duties as volunteer nurse and director of a center for refugees. Janine, a widow without children, is a full-time nurse at a military hospital for severely wounded and contagiously ill soldiers. One of her patients there is Henri, the married father of three children. In Janine's letters, Madeleine discerns the slowly developing love between Janine and an unidentified officer, and confides her fears and dismay to her husband. Many of the letters between Jacques and Madeleine concern the general issues of sexual morality and marital fidelity in a climate of intense emotional and physical need (67–69; 95; 104–06; 192). Jacques, promoted to general, also comments on the Allied armies' strengths and weaknesses, Germany's economic reasons for beginning the war, and the organization of soldiers' daily lives in the trenches. The letters between the two men, similar to the restrained and virtuous correspondence between Henri and Janine, concentrate on the politics of war and daily life at the front (87–88; 103; 112–116; 220–23).

Janine resolves to volunteer for a dangerous hospital assignment in Greece, in the vague hope that her death would resolve her hopeless situation with Henri.[7] She returns unharmed, but Henri has suffered severe wounds in the battle of the Marne and will be blind. Despite the fact that his wife has died of an embolism, Henri refuses to marry Janine. His permanently dependent condition eliminated his natural roles of protector and guide to his family, and thus, he feels that any relationship with Janine would be unnatural. The last letter of the novel speaks to this issue of the future of the French family and presages the eventual union of Henri and Janine. With dramatic and poignant images, Jacques praises the generosity and sacrifice of French women who marry the wounded (350).

Although the epistolary structure of the novel is sometimes cumbersome, it provides an authentic means for the depiction of the characters' often intense introspection. As in real life, the individuals here reveal to one another their misgivings and frailties, and Delorme Jules-Simon skillfully evokes her characters' bewildered attempts to understand and perhaps resolve their painful personal situations. As the letters continue, the writers sometimes return with new insights to concerns voiced in earlier communications, evidence of the process of their own private reflection or a subsequent incident that influenced their reasoning. Such evolution of thought characterizes the correspondence between Madeleine and Janine.

The issues that concern Madeleine and Janine reflect in several ways the differences in their individual situations and the manner in which they live their lives. Madeleine, the army wife, has had for many years the sole daily responsibility for her children and home. Her letters show that while she is used to contemplating an issue, formulating an opinion, and then carrying it out, she also never takes any action without the prior approval of her husband. It is clear that the couple is used to long separations, and that Madeleine is conscious of public scrutiny of her behavior when Jacques is away. She is completely certain of her duties, even during wartime (3–6; 24). She executes her responsibilities with a steadfastness and conviction that amaze the people around her. Several letters praise her strength and refer to her public reputation for reliability and efficiency (37; 41; 182; 206). Although her life has focused on the private and inner-directed world of her family, she overcomes her reticence and becomes a nurse. She was able to conquer her horror of the men's wounds by thinking of her husband, for she felt that her successful completion of the most gruesome tasks would redeem and protect Jacques's life in battle (15; 24).

Janine's life is quite different from that of her friend. Married and widowed at a young age, she enjoys the freedom of her life, while sincerely regretting the absence of a child or the experience of romantic love (7; 41). While Madeleine's interests center around home and family, Janine's attention gravitates toward issues that reflect the worldly and public sphere in which she operates. Her status as widow insulates her to some extent from the accusations of impropriety that would normally beset a young single woman, and it allows her more freedom to circulate unescorted. The military hospital dormitory in which Janine lives provides a socially acceptable home with little surveillance of her activities (19–22). While the hospital environment protects her, it also exposes her to a variety of different people, unconventional ideas, and unique experiences that she would never have encountered under normal conditions. Many of her letters chronicle the questioning and reappraisal of her own ideas that such connections engendered (31; 54–57; 71–73; 202–10; 251–2).

Janine's work at the hospital involves long hours and constant danger from contagious soldiers. At one point in the story, she nearly dies from tetanus contracted from a soldier's wounds, but is cured by an injection that she had almost declined out of fear (66). Confiding to Madeleine that she thought she would succumb to the effects of either the illness or the inoculation, Janine nonetheless feels gratified by the idea of dying for France like any other soldier, "inasmuch as the hospital is our very own battlefield!" (66).[8] Her letters often contain such patriotic statements, tinged with regret at the limitations imposed upon her as a woman. She had volunteered for a hospital close to Alsace in order to share as much as possible in the men's suffering and planned to demand the most hazardous assignment to compensate her for being "just a weak woman" (20). It is not easy for her to accept the indirect nature of her contribution to the war as a nurse, and she imagines herself with a rifle, killing Germans (20–21). Moreover, the shame she feels at not being able to offer herself bodily to the war cause deepens because she has neither child nor husband to sacrifice to France (57). This solitary status also degrades her in the eyes of the other nurses, whose frontline family members grant them a status proportionate with their numbers and degree of potential danger (208). As in many novels studied here, especially Maryan's *Un mariage en 1915* (A Marriage in 1915) and Delorme Jules-Simon's second war novel, *L'Impérieux Amour,* a woman's actions during wartime contribute less to her own and others' judgment of her individual worth than those of the men in her life. Regardless of Janine's indefatigable dedication and her several near-death experiences in the line of duty, the other nurses refuse to listen to her ideas about the war and often ridicule her. For them, Janine has no authority on any matter relating to the war, since she has no one at the front. Janine's own attitude does not dispute that of the other women, and she tells Madeleine that she considers the young soldier to whom she gave her blood to be her child, and so that even she was able to offer her son to France (208).

Janine is outspoken in her letters to both Madeleine and Henri concerning women's activities during the war, and her comments reinforce a traditional image of abnegation and service. She praises those who accomplish anonymously the humblest jobs, such as the women who take care of the soldiers' bloody clothes in the basement of the hospital, as well as the women who married at the beginning of the war, despite the possibility of raising a child without a father (209–10).

There are several letters in which Janine disagrees with the commonplace view that mothers sacrifice their sons to France with joy, and she insists that such a depiction lessens the value of their loss (54–57). She counters this emblematic vision of mothers with that of stoic women willing to die in their children's place. In suggesting a future army of mothers, her argument evokes the traditional notion of women's inborn pacifism, since such a military force naturally would avoid conflict. Analyzing the various attitudes, she concludes that women in war are the same as they are in peace: there are the lovely parrots, the gossips, and those who seek public martyrdom. She has particularly harsh criticism for women who do no war work at all, and whose perpetual tears and lamentations attract attention but accomplish nothing for France. Moreover, she exposes the special form of arrogance of "grief snobs" who consciously seek out people to console so as to feel the intense enjoyment of an emotional outpouring (205–06).

> . . . besides, there are some [women] for whom this habit of thinking of disaster has become a veritable snobbery of suffering. A curious category is the excessively compassionate woman, this one seeks out the grief of others, she always has a friend to go to console; I truly think that she obtains some voluptuous pleasure from that (206).[9]

Still, neither Janine nor Madeleine is immune to this sensation of enjoyment that results from the expression of strong feelings. Similar to characters in other novels, they report experiencing sensual delight (*volupté*) and exhilaration (*ivresse*) when thinking of the sacrifice and bravery of the soldiers at the front (231–32). While the two women seem not to recognize the sexual component of their emotions, Madeleine's husband Jacques speaks frankly in his letters of the link he believes exists between love and war (67–69). His assessment of the ways in which war arouses all of the senses, including the erotic, seems decidedly emancipated, for he finds it normal that both men and women are equally affected by the heightened emotions of the war situation. He tries to allay Madeleine's fears concerning Janine's possible affair with a married man by explaining that such behavior is the understandable reaction to a climate of anxiety, pity, sexual abstinence, and the intimacy of the hospital atmosphere. Jacques's similar explanation of soldiers' love affairs and his own attraction for other women prompts a protracted discussion between him and Madeleine on the subject of marital infidelity (95; 104–06; 192). He ultimately convinces her to accept his opinion that women should be tolerant of their husbands' "little indiscretions" during wartime, since for them the act is merely physical and has little meaning. Moreover, she also adopts Jacques's view that husbands need not have the same attitude of forbearance for their wives because the consequence of sex for women, presumably pregnancy, is far more important, and also because, for them, affection always plays a part. Madeleine not only acquiesces to her husband's liaisons, but also counsels her friends to forgive their own husbands' infidelities. When her friends accuse Madeleine of immorality, she answers that it is women's role to pardon and absolve (106). Thus Delorme Jules-Simon, while seeming to advocate parity in viewing men's and women's sexual conduct, in fact underscores the traditional view of the fundamental differences in their sexual needs. Further, by neutralizing the ridicule that her friends direct toward Madeleine's Christian view of forgiveness, the author reinforces a well established and gender-determined standard for extramarital sexual behavior. It is equally significant that Janine's chaste relationship with the married Henri is based on a mutual love of duty and patriotic ideas, and that Janine notes that women and men can work together in the hospital without initiating gossip (20; 231).

Foregrounding the permissive attitudes of valiant soldiers allows Delorme Jules-Simon to acknowledge the atmosphere of sexual license reportedly prevalent during the war while simultaneously exonerating the behavior of dedicated nurses like Janine and Madeleine. Her defense encompasses the real-life Janines and Madeleines whose war work attracted both widespread public praise and also much suspicion concerning possible personal motives for performing such tasks. Delorme Jules-Simon does not dismiss or ignore the insinuation of vanity, promiscuity, and husband-hunting that beset the reputation of women war volunteers. Rather, she creates characters who confront the dilemmas and temptations of situations that are both disturbing and unexpected. She shows how the attributes of dedication and forgiveness, traits considered innately feminine, empower Janine and Madeleine to conquer the unknown and retain their traditional modesty and virtue.

Further, Delorme Jules-Simon demonstrates that the work experience the two women had during the war will not lure them to abandon in the future their conventional roles of wife and mother. Madeleine decides to find husbands as quickly as possible for her 19-year-old twin daughters, since she feels their chances for marriage will be considerably lower after the war. She reasons that women's innate creativity can be fulfilled only by motherhood, and that her daughters would have better lives as widows with small children than they would if they remained unmarried (258–59). The novel's conclusion, which strongly suggests the eventual union of Henri and Janine, presents even more explicitly the primacy of maternity for all women, for Janine, the childless widow, will become the mother of another woman's orphans. Janine imagines women's influence in the future in the recovery of the values of the past, for the complex role of the postwar woman will not be in the public sphere, but in the home (251–52).

> The war will have put woman back in her true place, it will have provided her with the means to give intensely her devotion, her pity, her admiration, her cheerfulness. I see the extent of women's influence in the future, so that I wish to be all women at the same time, to be a mother, a wife . . . (252).[10]

While Janine and Madeleine represent two different lifestyles and personalities, they are equally dedicated to the cause of France and share an assessment of women's attitudes and activities that is firmly based in the traditional values of maternity, service, and self-sacrifice. In *Âmes de guerre, âmes d'amour,* Delorme Jules-Simon eases her readers' anxieties by affirming that women did not seek the autonomy they acquired in service to France. Moreover, she demonstrates how this freedom in fact fortified women's "natural" qualities of devotion and compassion and would help to rebuild, rather than endanger, the traditional social order.

Like J. Delorme Jules-Simon, Geneviève Duhamelet (1890–1980) understood personally the problems and dilemmas faced by women volunteers. Her experiences as a nurse during the war, recounted in *Ces Dames de l'Hôpital 336* (Those Ladies of Hospital 336), earned for her a commendation from the French government, the Médaille d'argent des Épidémies. An accomplished poet and respected novelist and playwright, Duhamelet won numerous literary prizes throughout her long career, including the Prix Montyon from the Académie Française for *Les Inépousées* (The Unmarried Women), 1918, the Prix Jacques-Normand in 1923, the Prix Spiritualiste in 1926 for *La Vie et la Mort d'Eugénie de Guérin* (The Life and Death of Eugénie de Guérin), and the Prix de l'Académie de l'Humour Français for *Rue du chien qui pêche* (Dog-Fisherman Street), her best-selling story about the difficulties of working-class life in a Parisian suburb. A consummate woman of letters as well as an indefatigable teacher for more than 27 years, Duhamelet also regularly contributed short stories, literary criticism, book reviews, and essays to more than a dozen periodicals.[11]

Les Inépousées is the story of the profound impact the war has on the lives of three women in their early twenties. The novel begins during the summer of 1914, as the three friends contemplate their respective futures with both fear and excitement. Monique Hautier is pious and devoted to her brother, Thérèse Orcines spends her time writing fanciful letters to her great "Unknown Love," and Marthe Jacquin is engaged in the serious pursuit of advanced studies. Monique's brother Bernard is a poet, beginning to gain a reputation especially in the elite social and literary circles where he reads his work. No one suspects that the real reason Marthe intends to continue her studies at the Sorbonne is because she is in love with Bernard and hopes to prove herself worthy of him. Much of the action in the first third of the book focuses on whether Marthe will succeed in attracting the attention of Bernard. A few days before the mobilization, Bernard declares to his sister Monique that he loves Jacqueline, the rich society daughter who introduced him to the Parisian literary circles. When war is declared, Marthe asks Monique to advise her about whether a woman should reveal her true feelings to a man who is unaware that he is loved. Monique feels that such a disclosure would weaken the man's courage, and that it is the duty of French women to wait patiently for the end of the war. Marthe, to her later regret, acquiesces in silence (5–21).

The second part begins in 1917 and concentrates on the physical and emotional hardships endured by the three friends and by other women in their lives. Bernard's death in the third week of the war devastates his sister Monique. A devout Catholic, she devotes her life to meritorious acts and charitable works among the poor, both as an effort to console herself and to assure the redemption of her brother's soul. Thérèse's older sister, left a pregnant widow, operates her husband's factory with the help of an old man who lost all of his sons in the war. Marthe, having renounced her studies to volunteer at a hospital, has become a nurse well respected for her intelligence and skill. Many passages detail the lack of coal and the scarcity of food, and recount how the war has aged people, especially the women.

In contrast to the three friends who show quite visibly the effects of three years of privation, Thérèse's much younger sister Colette is full of life and joy. A convalescing soldier decides to marry her because of her youth. His explanation for his choice makes Thérèse realize that she and her friends will never marry because the returning soldiers will associate them permanently with the war (168–71). Her own generation of women now over 25 will carry forever the tangible signs of their suffering and sadness. The ex-soldiers, needing above all to forget, will reject them in favor of women whose youth protected them from the physical and mental ravages of war. For both Thérèse and Marthe, the fearful excitement with which they imagined their future lives in 1914 has yielded to the certainty of remaining celibate and living alone. Yet this is not an opportunity they accept as an alternative to marriage with values and prospects of its own;

rather it signals the loss of their individual sense of self-worth and of their importance to their community. When they burn their old diaries for fuel, they separate themselves definitively from a time when they were ready to assume their predetermined role in French society. Moreover, they accept without question the idea that their lives will be empty without husbands and children, and they embrace their fate as *vieilles filles* (old maids). The charitable service and war work to which Marthe and Monique dedicate themselves is an attempt to find new meaning in the lives they are forced to lead. Thérèse, perplexed and bewildered concerning her own role, is the only character who does not contribute to the war effort. The last part of the novel addresses her struggle to understand and discover a direction for her life.

An important subplot concerns Fanny, the dressmaker, whose life of service to others will become a strong example for Thérèse. When Fanny's brother was taken prisoner, she moved in with her sister-in-law and parents, so that she could care for them while working. However, tragedy soon forced Fanny to expand her caregiver's role. Her brother's wife began to work at a munitions factory in order to earn the extra money needed to send him packages. After a month, she suffered a burning sensation in her lungs, began to spit blood, and died eight days later. Fanny's earnings are the only remaining source of income for the family, and she takes on the additional job of tramway conductor (129–34). When Thérèse sees Fanny on the tram, happy and vibrant despite her fatigue and the danger of her job, she feels ashamed of her own inactivity for the first time (175).

Just after Fanny dies in a tramway accident, Thérèse's family arranges for a foster mother for Fanny's infant nephew, setting into motion circumstances that will result in Thérèse's eventual redemption. In contemplating Fanny's life of service to others, Monique's decision to enter a convent, and Marthe's plans to become a doctor, Thérèse comes to realize that her own life is sterile and useless. The word *utile* (useful) appears frequently in Thérèse's meditations, especially concerning her older sister Claire's life. Despite the loss of her husband and the rigors of single parenthood, she still managed to save her husband's factory and all of the workers' jobs. Thérèse's chance to rectify her inactivity emerges when the guardian of Fanny's nephew leaves the region, and she assumes his care. Suddenly the restive consternation and self-examination that characterized Thérèse's life evaporates, and she becomes happy and calm (211–21). This change in mental attitude expresses itself in her outward behavior as well, and it echoes the view common throughout women's war writing that children are the agents of a woman's salvation. Thérèse is at first perplexed by the transformation, but after several months, she recognizes that the peacefulness she feels is the result of caring for and having a child in her life. In asking her mother for permission to keep the child, she explains at the end of the novel that what she and all of her generation seek is someone to whom they can dedicate their lives.

> I will never marry, mama. Almost all of the boys my age are dead. The sacrificed generation, someone said in speaking of them. Well, we girls, we are the generation of sacrifice. The one who would have loved me fell on the field of honor. We will thus be a legion of widows who were never betrothed. However, our sacrifice for the Homeland counts; and the love that we did not bestow cannot be lost. Monique gives it to God, Marthe to her wounded of today and her patients of tomorrow. Me, I want this baby (252–53).[12]

Duhamelet here evokes the poignant reality of the women who, because of the war, could not fulfill the social demands of marriage and maternity for which they had spent their whole lives in training. Since the men Thérèse and her friends might have married are all dead, it is as if the women are widows. However these women are not like other widows with children or happy memories to comfort them. In naming them the "generation of sacrifice," Thérèse claims for herself and her peers a title equal in honor to that of the martyred soldiers. Such a classification, however, goes beyond mere sympathy for the loss of a traditional married relationship. Duhamelet provides her characters with alternatives that guarantee them a place of value in a social structure that equates women's worth with service to family. She shows women's love to be an inviolable and innate maternal force that circumstances cannot diminish and that exists in even the most self-absorbed of women. Although the three friends will never have husbands or children of their own, they will still be able to bestow their motherly care: Monique to God, Marthe to the sick and wounded, and Thérèse to a homeless orphan.

Although the presence of the baby culminates the process of Thérèse's reeducation, the examples of the other women in the novel contribute an important part. Their activities encompass a wide range of possibilities from traditional to modern. Marie, the homemaker, went to work in a factory to earn the money needed to send better packages to her prisoner husband. Her coworkers there were uneducated and coarse, but these women often chose the most dangerous and difficult jobs in an extra effort to help the soldiers. Fanny, the unmarried dressmaker, left her own home to take on the responsibility of keeping her brother's family intact. Marthe, the most modern and independent character before the war, decided to become a doctor, while Monique, contemplative and spiritual, embarked on one of the most traditional paths for women, that of nun. Even Thérèse's sisters, certainly minor characters, demonstrate the importance of service to others that lies at the heart of Duhamelet's novel. Claire, a young widow with a small baby, was able to save her husband's factory, and the frivolous Colette spent her time learning to be a better wife. The mourning clothes of the silent strangers on the tram seem to denounce Thérèse's lack of devotion. Every woman, except Thérèse, sacrifices her own comfort and personal happiness to serve the family, whether it be her own, or the extended family of the nation. Nonetheless, the lesson Duhamelet imparts here is more complex than simply promoting women's war work, for, as in other novels, it is the war itself that is the character's greatest educator. Thérèse, egocentric, easily bored, and longing for an Unknown Love, simply takes longer to understand what the other women had already learned from the war, that duty is always a woman's first priority. All of the women's activities, whether traditional or modern, bourgeois or working class, illustrate Duhamelet's conviction that a woman's primary obligation is to her family, and through her household, to the nation. The deaths of potential husbands in battle merely eliminated the most conventional means to meet that responsibility. Rather than exempt women from their "natural" and "innate" duty to serve others, her novel shows that the war in fact provided many more ways to fulfill that requirement. Whether doctor or nun, foster mother or factory worker, Duhamelet's characters are wholly dedicated to serving others and have no other personal goals. As in so many other novels here, it is through interaction with a child, the ultimate symbol of traditional innocence and womanhood, that the character finally achieves the moment of psychological breakthrough.

It is significant that just at the instant when Thérèse understands that caring for the infant will give meaning to her life, she also resolves to acquiesce if her mother refuses permission. Her obedience to her own family parallels that of Marthe, whose plans to become a doctor depend on her parents' consent, in spite of intense encouragement from her department head, a male doctor. Marthe's compliance with parental will, however, is the opposite of the attitude she exhibited before the war. Unaware of Marthe's infatuation with Bernard, her parents had resisted strenuously Marthe's intention to study at the Sorbonne. Her father was proud of her intelligence but was not satisfied with her dedication to studies, and her mother thought of Marthe's eventual career as menial work. She wanted her daughter to live the easy, tranquil life a husband could provide, and she urged Marthe to take courses on household management and cooking instead of science and philosophy. Yet Marthe, Duhamelet's narrator explains, was the cherished only child of parents who had married very late in life and had thus enjoyed an independence rare for a young woman in 1914. When she had announced during that summer her intention to measure herself against the knowledgeable and educated of her society, that is, to create and define herself, her parents had relented (23–24). Duhamelet shows that the subsequent turnabout in her attitude, from defiant self-determination to obedient respect, results directly from her war experience. It is important to note that Marthe's desire to become a doctor is not because of personal ambition or confidence in her own abilities. Her humility and submissiveness effectively negate any criticism of her career plans, because being a doctor for her simply fulfills her obligation to serve a family, in this case, the greater family of France. Rather than threaten the established social order that depends on women's assumption of maternal and other home-centered tasks, Marthe's actions confirm the value of those responsibilities. Doctors, in Duhamelet's postwar world, would be mothers and homemakers, if only they could.

The war is also the great teacher of humility and self-abnegation in Marcelle Tinayre's novel of 1915, *La Veillée des armes. Le Départ: août, 1914.* Translated into English in 1918 as *To Arms!,* the book enjoyed success on both sides of the Atlantic, and remains even today the most cited example of French women's war fiction. Such an achievement was not unusual for Tinayre (1877–1948), whose various novels had assured her an appreciative audience for nearly two decades and would eventually bring her the Académie Française's Barthou Prize in 1938. Critical opinion for *La Veillée des armes,* however, differed from that of the public, and reviewers like the widely read Jean Ernest-Charles accused Tinayre of superficiality and prolixity. "Precisely when war was threatening France and the world," he scoffed in *La Grande Revue* in 1915, "Mme Marcelle Tinayre said to herself, 'Hey, here's a subject for a novel!' She wrote that novel without delay. . . . Mme Tinayre, to celebrate French heroism during the call to arms, has written her most insipid book."[13] While these remarks were certainly severe, Tinayre was not immune to such a charge of opportunism. A comparison of *La Veillée des armes* with her prewar works reveals a distinct departure from her exploration of women's struggle for independence and love to embrace an emblematic and shallow patriotism. Instead of the richly drawn characters that made novels like *La Maison du péché* (The House of Sin), 1902, and *La Rebelle* (The Rebel), 1905, memorable to many readers, Tinayre offers one-dimensional symbols in static scenes reminiscent of contemporary war posters. In her earlier novels, Tinayre's characters were strong women who made decisions involving moral and ethical problems and in so doing established firmly their identity for themselves and for the men in their lives.[14] In *La Veillée des armes,* however, Tinayre replaces that robust independence and autonomy with the voluntary suppression of individual interest.

Although Tinayre's vapid and dependent depiction of her female characters differs sharply from that of other novelists, her story nonetheless replicates the predominant denunciation in French women's war fiction of individualism and the insistence on total dedication to the single collectivity that is France. Tinayre's indictment reflects the prevalent viewpoint that French individualism had weakened the country and made it vulnerable to German ambition and expansionism. It is a perspective that would find an expression in many later novels and stories studied here, including those by Isabelle Sandy and Odette Dulac. The characters in those books, nonetheless, are more complex than are those of Tinayre. Instead of demonstrating how her characters gain positive qualities in response to the unexpected and distressing situations brought by the war, Tinayre simply validates the necessity of a unilateral and unquestioning support of the conflict.

La Veillée des armes chronicles the attitudes toward war of a group of Parisians during the final few days before the declaration of war and the general mobilization. While the story focuses in particular on the emotions of two married couples, it also portrays the patriotic reaction to the threat of war of their friends, neighbors, and coworkers. Rather than action, there is the depiction of the anguish of waiting, and the slow acceptance of a terrible reality. The main characters are Simone and François, whom Tinayre idealizes as perfect examples of what it means to be French, both as a couple and as a woman and man.[15] Their devotion to each other mirrors their love for their imperiled country. Tinayre contrasts the harmony and simplicity of their lives with the egotism and friction between Simone's cousin, Nicolette, and her husband Jean. Moreover, their self-centeredness has extended to their children, to whom they are somewhat distant and even indifferent (75–82). For all of Nicolette's selfish ostentation, she still cares for Jean and worries that he might be in danger (245–46). For his part, Jean feels that he has failed as both a husband and father, and cheerfully anticipates the war as an adventure and an escape from his unhappy life (262). In the portrait of these couples, as in that of all other characters, Tinayre shows how the threat and finally the reality of war instantly purifies and elevates the thoughts and actions of even the most imperfect of French people. Significantly, Tinayre indicates that such grandeur of soul arises as an immediate response to war, requiring little or no reflection.

Several minor characters represent wives and mothers of different ages and social classes, and Tinayre depicts nearly every one as instantly and stoically devoted to the cause of France. Their willingness for sacrifice is equal only to the ferocity of their patriotic courage, illustrated at one point by an old and thick-bodied woman who proclaims her desire to defend France personally (136–38). She cites Joan of Arc as a precedent for women soldiers and announces to startled subway passengers that women will fight when there are no men left. It is important that Tinayre eliminates even the suggestion of deviation from her monolithic patriotism: the one mother whose support for the war is in doubt, dies suddenly when hearing news of the mobilization (285).

This main idea of unequivocal support for the war extends beyond individual characters. Similar to many authors studied here, Tinayre refers numerous times in the novel to the unity demonstrated by all social classes, especially the workers (63; 91; 123; 155–57; 198–99; 210–11; 232–37; 255–57). François is surprised, yet proud, that the socialist workers in the factory he directs replaced their usual silent hostility with respect for him as an officer (198). The repeated emphasis on the support of French socialists, who represented for Tinayre's readers perhaps the least likely group to favor the war, is significant because the author is thus able to prove the single-minded resolve of the French people. References to actual persons such as Jean Jaurès and Gustave Hervé underscore the reality of the socialists' renunciation of their traditional antiwar position to support the *union sacrée.*[16] Tinayre's characters are certain that despite Jaurès's well-known pacifist ideas, the slain leader of the French Socialist Party had accepted before he died the need to defend France (174–76; 179). Similarly, minor characters remark with amused pride that even the noted syndicalist journalist Hervé wants to enlist (210–11; 282). Scenes with ordinary laborers draw attention to the patriotism of the working class. For Tinayre, like Broussan-Gaubert and others, it is important to indicate that support for the war effort will triumph over even long-standing class divisions.

It is also equally crucial to demonstrate the loyalty of French mothers. As stated above in chapter 1, French women's war fiction invariably acknowledges what is considered the innate opposition of mothers to armed conflict; however, it always resolves that inherent contradiction in order to prove mothers' loyalty and to demonstrate their continued support. Tinayre, no less than the other authors, gives voice to the anguish of mothers who must accept the uncertain future of the children they have loved and served their whole lives (145), and, like them, Tinayre also disarms this potentially seditious antiwar argument. Thus, when an old concierge, who symbolizes for Simone the Mater Dolorosa of the Pietà, suggests that the heart of a German mother could not be different from her own (146), Tinayre's narrator quickly reasserts the dominance of duty to country as a natural law higher than that of maternity (147). She further subjugates motherhood to the importance of the state through the portrayal of women of the world as simple-minded and captive to their instincts.

> And the women of Russian huts, primitive souls who knew nothing of the universe, and the prolific German women who lived in subjection to men, and the French women passionately devoted to their sons, all, submitting to

the law, faithful to their duty but equally tortured, uttered the same cry, the unavailing cry of the mothers which, from the time of Hecuba and Rachel, resounds eternally from age to age (146–47).

The implication contained here and in the paragraphs that follow supports a traditionally misogynist argument that mothers' desire to protect their children is natural, but that maternal instinct prohibits reason, judgment, and intelligence. Thus while Tinayre notes "the cry of distracted maternity, of naked and savage instinct" that reverberates through Simone (146), her immediate reaffirmation of the supremacy of duty, the "law," in effect incapacitates and revokes any power mothers might exert to save their sons or to stop war in general. Tinayre further emphasizes the biological significance of each woman's individual sacrifice for the nation when she notes that the France of the future would be born from the farewells the night before the mobilization (278).

One slight exception to Tinayre's tableau of total unity is the character of Simone. Throughout the story Simone struggles to control her emotions and her fear of what may happen to her officer husband. While the resolution of her inner turmoil is the only real conflict in the novel, its outcome is never in doubt. Outwardly, Simone is acquiescent. She barely reacts when hearing that her husband declined a safe assignment in Paris, and she listens approvingly when told that the principal duty of all women in war, including suffragists, is to be silent (202–04). Nonetheless, Simone suffers from a sense of separation from her husband that she feels results from the different views that men and women naturally have concerning patriotism and war. Thinking to herself, she concludes that women see war primarily as destructive because as mothers they understand better the great price of life. Men, however, experience the idea and the glory of dying for a just cause that is uniquely their own and therefore excludes women (205–06). The emphasis here on the causal link between maternity and emotionality reiterates Tinayre's adherence to the traditional notion that women are simply less rational than men. Further, despite the fact that Tinayre carefully points out that Simone's submission is the result of her will, it is nonetheless the spontaneous demonstrations in the streets of Paris following the declaration of war that conquers her last bit of resistance (233–35). Feeling the crowd's excitement, she understands that each separate person is at that moment becoming part of a single, great entity—the Nation. All concerns for individuals, even her husband, evaporate as Simone becomes "a tiny particle of France" and a desire for victory conquers her last vestige of vacillation (234). After this emotional and involuntary response, she returns to Jean and Nicolette's house, where she is hailed as "the wisest of women" and promoted as an example for her selfish cousin

(237). The story ends much as it began, with an evocation of the French public's seamless unity in the face of national danger (291–92).

In *La Veillée des armes,* not only do individuals relinquish their interests, but women, workers, and other population groups renounce their previous demands for political and social rights. Both women and men in Tinayre's book act according to the instincts of their gender, an extreme biological determinism absent from her prewar novels. The protagonists in these earlier books were for the most part autonomous women whose decisions both questioned and expanded the parameters of socially acceptable behavior, and the men in their lives often defended their actions. The obedient and unobtrusive Simone and her vigorously stalwart husband, however, presented as the ideal woman and man in *La Veillée des armes,* communicate a truly French value system. Their deep love for each other provides a positive example for others, yet their devotion to France has precedence. The defense of France here concerns not so much the actual territory as the preservation of established social constructs. Moreover, it is an act of conservation that permits no dissension or even slight disagreement. Marcelle Tinayre, like Jehanne d'Orliac, Colette Yver, and others studied here, considers France the standard bearer of the civilized world, and the war for them is a modern crusade against barbarism. For Tinayre, national culture resides, not only in cathedrals or in fertile valleys, but in the maintenance of the tightly structured traditional family unit. Unlike the characters in Démians d'Archimbaud's *Une vie intime,* in J. Delorme Jules-Simon's *Âmes de guerre, âmes d'amour,* and in Geneviève Duhamelet's *Les Inépousées,* Tinayre's idealized Simone does not experience the anguish of making choices because she does not possess the freedom necessary for evolution or change. The war confronted Madeleine, Janine, and Thérèse with situations for which they were unprepared, and in facing those challenges they developed their inner strength and acquired self-esteem and the respect of those around them.

Chapter Three

Sheroes 🏵

Many authors affirm the immense value of women's contribution to the war effort through conventional images of tireless and steadfast mother figures, whose maternal wisdom and patience brings healing both at home and in the hospital. Other writers expand the role of women in war beyond such a reactive position of healer to claim for them the proactive station of warrior. However, these authors do not accomplish this departure from customary gender-determined tasks by asserting the right of women to fight alongside men. Rather, they enlarge the definition of the battlefield to include places where readers would normally expect to find women, especially the home. Although many characters frankly regret that their gender prevents them from enlisting in the army or even dream of hand-to-hand fighting with the enemy, such as Janine in J. Delorme Jules-Simon's *Âmes de guerre, âmes d'amour,* the authors certainly do not openly challenge the authority and sovereignty of men in all matters of armed conflict. Instead, writers including Jehanne d'Orliac, Lya Berger, and Camille Mayran avoid such a revolutionary and provocative assertion of gender standardization to posit instead a revisionist parity that resides in biological difference. Their narratives contain story lines where traditionally feminine home and family-centered locations become spaces in which women who had previously led private lives are forced by the circumstance of war to metamorphose into heroes. In these narratives, main and secondary female characters act exactly according to the expectations for any soldier. The women engage the enemy, fight him bravely, and are eventually victorious, yet it is significant that they carry out these quintessential male roles without the loss of conventional "feminine" qualities, such as forbearance, propriety, and self-effacement.

Moreover, the authors do not neglect the importance of the mother-teacher basis of the Republican Mother ideology, for the war experience serves in each story as the means to achieve not only the character's heroic transcendence, but that of others for whom she serves as a model. These narratives thus create a space for a new catagory of active, independent heroine who accomplishes historically male tasks, like killing the enemy, but does so in a way that neither shocks nor questions contemporary definitions of "the feminine." Unlike the paradigmatic heroines of Western literature who, as secondary characters, help the male hero by providing information or acting as a foil, these women heroes, or "sheroes," formulate their own plans to triumph over the enemy, and they accomplish these goals alone, sacrificing their lives in patriotic martyrdom. Their stories, told in high language and dramatic plot twists, establish a fresh mythology that foregrounds a hitherto-hidden feminine force ready for action when needed. Further, the powerful and heroic women in narratives by Madame Yves Pascal, Lucie Delarue-Mardrus, and Colette Yver also expand the meaning of heroism. Although preserved from direct contact with the enemy, their characters nonetheless demonstrate soldierly courage and bravery in simple and less dramatic ways open to anyone, even children.

War, history, and legend combine to create a fable of female heroism in the novella *La Captive de Gand* (The Captive Woman of Ghent) by Jehanne d'Orliac. D'Orliac was a prolific author who published novels, plays, and poetry, in addition to some 15 historical novels. These works centered on the lives of royal women from the medieval and Renaissance period, and also featured detailed treatments of the lives of François I, poet François Villon, and the mathematician-philosopher Blaise Pascal. The celebrity d'Orliac enjoyed for such historical works as *Madeleine de Glapion,* 1919, and *Diane de Poitiers,* 1930, as well as for the fictional *Deuxième Mari de Lady Chatterley* (Lady Chatterley's Second Husband), 1934, resulted in the distinction of being named an Officier in the Légion d'Honneur.[1]

In a review of d'Orliac's 1937 work, *La Légion d'Honneur* (The Legion of Honor), critic J.-E. Weelen wrote that her book was a long monologue by a virile voice that nonetheless sang soothingly and entertained the reader.[2] Weelen's comments were typical of male critics who commonly characterized the writing of famous women authors as fundamentally masculine, embellished by a few feminine accessories. Such statements generally attributed the weighty thematic aspects of a work to the male quality of rationality, while designating any artistic or decorative aspects to female sensitivity. These assertions reinforced the opinion that women were not serious writers, while avoiding the evidence of writers like d'Orliac, whose work proved the contrary.

Published in 1917, *La Captive de Gand* is a frame story told by a French woman who receives a tattered and bloodstained manuscript recently smuggled out of Belgium by a refugee. It is the diary of her friend and former schoolmate, Marguerite Van Huyghe, who had returned to her home in Ghent before the war began. The format of a personal journal together with the frame convention allow d'Orliac to create an atmosphere of authenticity for the story, substantiating her authority to recount events in occupied territory. By using public facts well-known to her readers to advance the plot of her narrative, d'Orliac not only depicts a patriotic tale of wartime valor, she applies the prestige associated with truth to enshrine the private actions of an unexpected hero. Moreover, the central importance and universal renown of the other major "character" in the story, the fifteenth century Altarpiece of the Cathedral at Saint-Bavon, reinforce the element of genuineness, while elevating the story of Marguerite to mythic proportions. Although she is recovering from wounds and is held prisoner by a cruel and cynical German prince, Marguerite, similar to other sheroes in French women's war fiction, will defeat the enemy while preserving her public reputation and private self-esteem.

The outside story situates the narrator's relationship to Marguerite and includes a flashback of the French woman's visit to her friend and her father in 1913. While the two women had been close friends in their convent school in France, it is not until she sees Marguerite in her native Flanders that the narrator truly understands her friend's contemplative nature and her total devotion to her father, an art historian. Through the character of the father, a world-renowned expert on Van Eyck's Altarpiece, d'Orliac evokes the beauty, history, and mysticism associated with the work, as well as its multilayered symbolism. Long, detailed passages explain the factual genesis of the work, as well as its scenes that depict the Last Judgment (199–208). The episode portrayed in the central panel, that of the Mystic Lamb who breaks the first seal of God's book, becomes an extended metaphor for Belgium, her people, their Catholic faith, and eventual triumph over the evil of "barbarian"—that is German—violence.

The Lamb is a consummate symbol here, representing simultaneously Christ and Belgium, both models of redemption through the sacrifice of blood. D'Orliac insures such a straightforward identification by quoting (204–06) several long excerpts from the Book of Revelation. She skillfully compounds the link by creating in the fictional character of Marguerite a manifestation of both the spiritual and secular history of Belgium. As in other war novels studied here, the figure of the Virgin Mary combines both the transcendent and the temporal through the image of motherhood. Moreover, Marguerite's amazing resemblance to the portrait of the Virgin Mary in the panels, and thus, to the original model, Marguerite Van Eyck, imbues her with a sense of personal responsibility for the religious and cultural masterpiece. Her single-minded dedication to her father and his study of the Altarpiece parallels that of the relationship of

Marguerite Van Eyck to her famous artist brothers and connects the contemporary Marguerite with the European artistic tradition (201–08). Here d'Orliac anticipates Virginia Woolf's speculations about Judith Shakespeare in creating a gifted sister whose own work remains unknown. In d'Orliac's version, however, Marguerite Van Eyck willingly renounces her own art and the possibility of marriage, much like the modern Marguerite for her father's career, to devote her life to serve her brothers' painting. Marguerite's father describes the relationship of the three siblings in terms of the Trinity, while also underscoring the agency of the brothers and the passivity traditionally expected of women:

> Thus the three settled in [to the house] at Kautre, all three joined together to accomplish the artwork. All three not only banded together but united in an indissoluble love, creating, for me, [the image of] a perfect trinity of the spiritual world. Hubert, the father, the creator; Jean, the son, the agent; Marguerite, the spirit by way of the gentleness that she radiates, the tenderness that she puts forth (202).[3]

Nonetheless, the events of the diary, or inside story, establish the modern Marguerite as more than a passive symbol of Belgium, Christianity, and Western art and civilization. Instead, the story line constructs a legend in which she becomes their valiant defender. Marguerite's journal recounts the German invasion and the capture of her father. Injured in the attack, she awakens from a two-month coma to find that a severely wounded German prince, Otto, is also recuperating in her house, surrounded by a large staff of doctors and servants. Cruel and imperious, Otto attempts to intimidate and manipulate Marguerite by withholding information about her father. Although at first she remains stalwart and proud, eventually she acquiesces to Otto's demand that she play the piano as the price of a letter to her father. The feeling of violation that Marguerite feels at seeing the prince in her house, seated at her father's desk, is compounded by the revelation that Otto chose to invade the city of Ghent precisely because of the Altarpiece and her father's reputation. More than just occupying her father's country and his house, Otto has also desecrated his faith and his love for the Altarpiece, represented in the face of his daughter, whose life is now in Otto's hands. He is, of course, struck by the resemblance of Marguerite to the Virgin Mary, a fact that safeguards her, but also contributes to Marguerite's feeling of guilt. She feels disloyal to her fellow citizens because of the special privileges she enjoys, especially writing to her father (243–44). It is this sense of public accountability that verifies her patriotism and motivates her to commit the subsequent act of bravery as an expression of her national duty. However, her heroism also expiates a betrayal of a more intimate nature, for without realizing it, she had become attracted to Prince Otto. One day while playing, at his request, the death scene from Wagner's *Tristan and Isolde,* the still-wounded Otto faints. Convinced that he is dying, Marguerite is filled with pity for the young man and cradles his head (245–46). Looking up at her, Otto recalls wistfully that in the ancient story, a sword separates the doomed lovers. The allusion to the impossibility of their own situation, as well as the realization that her feelings are obvious to Otto, thoroughly shock Marguerite. Bewildered and dismayed by her conduct, she flees the room, wondering how her behavior could be so different from her volition.

> Are there then deeds that are independent from our wills? Wills that escape from consciences? Consciences that no longer control . . . (246).[4]

Nonetheless, d'Orliac insists on the culpability of Marguerite by carefully establishing Otto as pointedly predatory and cynical immediately before and after the fainting scene. Moreover, the political philosophy discussed by both Otto and Marguerite echoes several themes found in other war fiction by French women, and d'Orliac, like them, condemns a German predilection for violence and avarice as the cause of the war. Similar to J. Delorme Jules-Simon, Marcelle Tinayre, Gyp, and Marie Reynès-Monlaur, d'Orliac specifically denounces the German espousal of a Nietzschean-based philosophy that respects only boldness and disdains French culture as decadent (239–42; 256–58). Otto's theory of war, life, and superiority reproduces the Nietzschean emphasis on the feverish sensation of subjugation and the joy at realizing the power to create out of destruction. When Marguerite courageously chastises Otto for the brutality of the war, he explains in social Darwinist terms that violence is the means to create a better society, with justice belonging to the most powerful.

> What theorists, afflicted by shortsightedness, thought that combat amounted to forbearance; being civilized involves expanding the means to destroy in order to favor the mechanisms of choice. There is only one justice, the one that gives permission to live to he who has the power to conquer, this [is so] in peace as in war, in the past as in the present. Outside of this obvious statement, there is only darkness (256).[5]

D'Orliac here concurs with the common view that the war begun in 1914 was a defense of Western civilization against the chaos and barbarism of German expansionism. Moreover, in juxtaposing the cold determination and obstinacy of Otto's remarks to Marguerite's momentary expression of compassion for the wounded man, d'Orliac, like other authors, tacitly criticizes prewar French admiration for German philosophy and society and the failure to recognize the threat of German economic and cultural ascendance. Otto's desire to take the panels of the Altarpiece to Berlin both acknowledges the superiority of the Latin and Christian artistic tradition and also locates in actuality the French indictment of German *Kultur* as rapacious and mercenary. Readers of d'Orliac's story of 1917 knew in fact that the Altarpiece was in German hands and would learn in 1919 that the return of the Van Eyck masterpiece was a specific stipulation of the Treaty of Versailles (Article 247).

Thus, in both truth and fiction, the captured and threatened artwork becomes a symbol of a besieged Western civilization, as well as of an occupied and violated Belgium. Accordingly, Marguerite's decision to save the irreplaceable Altarpiece at any cost elevates her to the highest heroic level, equal to that of any other soldier in the war against barbarity. Still her resolve is not totally altruistic, nor is her decision without conflict. Her gentleness toward Otto implicates her honor as both a Belgian and a woman, and she understands why the prince's presence in her house has compromised her reputation in the city. A visit with the sacristan of the Cathedral alerts her to the rumors that deem her culpable of improper behavior, yet also assume that she will somehow fulfill her obvious duty to save the artwork. While she acknowledges that she has a patriotic duty to perform, she hesitates because she fears that Otto may harm her father (249–50). It is significant that d'Orliac combines as a single entity the sacred and secular communities in the moral dilemma that Marguerite faces, and that ultimately the young woman gives priority to the nation over her family. Still, it is the realization that her honor would be lost as well as the panels of the Altarpiece that resolves her uncertainty and propels her to sacrifice both herself and her father. In a dramatic moment she stabs Otto and hides the artwork. Her last diary entry before her execution proclaims her satisfaction at her choice of public good over her individual happiness: "I saved the *Lamb* and I also saved my honor, and I appeased my heart" (264).[6] Her desire to restore her honor is not only a catalyst for action, more importantly, it defines her violent deed, not as a usurpation of masculine combat, but as a socially acceptable act of womanly self-preservation. D'Orliac, however, interprets Marguerite's courage beyond a narrow and melodramatic redemption of her personal virtue to an act that recovers not only the soul of Belgium, but through the symbolism of the Van Eyck Altarpiece, also upholds Christianity and Western civilization itself.

The creation of living symbols is also very important in the short stories of Lya Berger. Born in 1877, Berger was an esteemed writer of considerable standing before the war. Her long career featured numerous honors, including several literary prizes each from the Académie Française, the Société des Gens de Lettres, and other prestigious institutions. Berger had the noteworthy distinction of being named an Officier in the Académie Française and also decorated by the French government for her contribution to the development of the arts. Known particularly for her poetry, such as *Réalités et Rêves* (Realities and Dreams) 1901, and novels, including *L'Aiguilleuse* (The Woman Pointsman) 1911, Berger also wrote plays, criticism, and essays that appeared in nearly all of the important daily newspapers and literary reviews. Beginning in 1910, she edited several well received anthologies featuring the poems of German, Dutch, and Belgian women. Moreover, the leadership roles Berger occupied throughout her career in the Société des Gens de Lettres, the Société des Poètes Français, and various other learned societies attest to the enormous respect the Parisian literary establishment had for her competence. In 1919 Berger published *Les Revanches, contes de guerre* (Revenge, War Stories), a collection of the patriotic short stories that had appeared during the war in *L'Écho de Paris*. This was the same conservative newspaper whose pages disseminated the editorial comments of some of the war's most ardent supporters, such as Frédéric Masson and René Bazin. Three years later the Société des Gens de Lettres established the Berger Prize in tribute to both the venerable author and her stories that attested to the loyalty of the people of the occupied territories of Alsace and Lorraine, as well as the unabashed evil of the Germans.[7]

In "Flirt de guerre" (A Wartime Flirtation), Berger recounts the story of a young woman of Lorraine. Alone in occupied territory since the enlistment of her father and brother in the French army, Édith Valorre has no choice but to receive alone and unchaperoned the visit of the German officer who controls the area. Despite her proper reserve and cold politeness, he addresses her in a familiar tone, and his arrogant bearing and insolent language insinuate his immodest intentions towards her. Gradually, and obviously enjoying the pain his revelation causes the young woman, the officer discloses his true identity as that of the young man she had met on vacation before the war began. He had disguised his origin by using a French name and had explained his foreign accent by claiming that he was Alsatian. Although their relationship had been conventional and proper, the young woman feels a mixture of shame and indignation at the revelation that Monsieur Voninger was in fact Herr Von Hinger (8–9). Her absolute conviction that he had been a spy for Germany accurately reflects the traditional suspicion commonly directed against Alsatians both before and during the war and explains her sense of the loss of her honor. However it is not any doubt concerning her own purity that distresses her, but rather the realization that she may have inadvertently helped France's enemies. Her dismay at the possibility that she may have compromised her loyalty is stronger than any fear of the German officer or of the personal disgrace that could result from his visit.

As the story progresses, it becomes apparent that the officer intends to rape her, thus requiring any subsequent actions on her part to enact simultaneously the personal as well as the patriotic notions of honor. The denouement, intricate and visually dramatic, satisfies the political and public-spirited obligations of an established writer such as Berger during wartime, without shocking or questioning traditional social sensibilities. Her character devises a heroic plan that succeeds on both the individual and national levels. It redeems her pride in herself, safeguards the purity of both her person and her reputation, and creates a situation of strategic importance to the French war effort. When the officer demands that she show him the isolated countryside and its beautiful river, he welcomes her suggestion that she blindfold him so that a particular vista might be more spectacular when he viewed it. Considering this proposition as proof of feminine weakness and submission to his (sexual) power, the officer cannot imagine any possible threat from the young woman and therefore does not suspect the true purpose of the blindfold. Intent on pursuing his advantage, he decides to delay a planned execution of some French soldiers, as well as an attack against a nearby regiment until his return. As she rows their boat toward a treacherous waterfall and certain death for both of them, she rejoices knowing that her act will save the lives of French soldiers. However her heroism accomplishes more than even she imagined, for at the end of the story the narrator reveals that since the drowned officer did not transmit the order to attack, French soldiers were able to surprise and capture a large German unit (12–13). Similar to Marguerite in d'Orliac's novella, Berger's character demonstrates her dedication to the cause of France through action, much like any uniformed soldier at the front. Yet while these sheroes kill the enemy, they do not take on any other male activities and their actions in fact subscribe to the most traditional notions of proper female behavior.[8]

Berger creates a more emblematic character in "Myrtille" (Blueberry). It is the brief story of a young woman, many years an orphan, who is known for her pleasant nature and for dressing in blue and white, the colors of her native Lorraine. Although a German regiment is quartered nearby, Myrtille conquers her fear and volunteers to smuggle a small band of young village men through the area so that they might serve in the French army (41). The enemy, known only in Berger's stories by the disparaging term *boche* ("Hun" or "kraut"), captures her, and they try in vain to force her to reveal the whereabouts of the would-be soldiers, hiding in the forest. Berger elevates the scene of the woman's subsequent execution by firing squad to an epic dimension with poignant visual effectiveness. With head held high and her gaze toward heaven in thanks for the opportunity to sacrifice herself for France, Myrtille falls ever so slowly to the ground. As she dies, her red blood mingles with her blue and white clothes to evolve from the flag of Lorraine to the Tricolor of France. It is this eternal flag, Berger's narrator informs us, that a few more soldiers will now be able to serve and defend, thanks to the martyrdom of this young woman (44).

Berger's narration of the story insists on Myrtille's stance as an emblem, for the little we learn about her as an individual serves only to reinforce her value as a symbol. She is an orphan, and similar to other solitary female characters in French women's war fiction, this fact explains in an acceptable manner her somewhat independent nature and faith in her own capacity to make decisions. This lack of personal family ties also serves to eliminate any bond with the temporal and the mundane, which might have prevented or impinged on her patriotic determination. As a single person, she is free to sacrifice her life without deserting her maternal duties to children or others. Berger can thus identify the young woman completely with a transcendent notion of the greater family of Lorraine and France, without questioning the traditional notion of women's proper social roles. Moreover, Myrtille's symbolic choice in clothes completes Berger's image of her as representation, reminiscent of the wartime posters that urged revenge for the lost provinces. Nearly devoid of any personality, her static nature is different from the vast majority of main characters in French women's war fiction, who engage in analysis, rational thought, and decision making. Myrtille is valiant without conscious reflection, much like the idealized image of soldiers in the trenches. The change in the final image of this young woman, from symbol of Lorraine to that of France, emphasizes the French identity and steadfast loyalty of the region's inhabitants, under German domination since the Franco-Prussian War. Berger uses this final scene to demonstrate and confirm the allegiance of the people of Lorraine, often contested during the war, as was that of the inhabitants of Alsace, also ceded to Germany in 1871 and occupied until 1918.

While the deaths of the protagonists in *La Captive de Gand* and "Un flirt de guerre" may seem at first to replicate the traditional novelistic punishment for a fallen woman, in fact neither character violated the standard of expected behavior. The difficulty for them, as would have been obvious to any contemporary reader, is that none of their moral education had prepared them for the extraordinary circumstances and inconceivable choices these women had to make. In fact, their training, with its emphasis on politeness and passivity, had in many ways left them vulnerable to danger. At one point, Marguerite in *La Captive de Gand* is so overwhelmed by the horror of her personal situation that she feels certain she must have fallen asleep on a beach, and that the hot sun is causing her to have hallucinations (249). However, Marguerite, like the other sheroes, makes a decision that sustains both the public good and her own standing within the larger community. Moreover, the obvious care on the part of d'Orliac and Berger to safeguard the sexual purity of their characters speaks to the suspicions concerning women's conduct, as discussed above in chapter 1. The denouements of these stories, however, accomplish more than the alleviation of male anxiety about possible female promiscuity. By enveloping their actions in the protective rhetoric of concern for personal honor, the authors suggest that women will continue to observe the code of acceptable female behavior, even when forced to commit acts that are decidedly "unfeminine."

Further, the deaths of the three protagonists in d'Orliac's and Berger's narratives are evidence of women's willingness and ability to sacrifice their lives in the Great War, as would any uniformed soldier in the trenches. Their loss in active service to their country adds another dimension to the conventional view that the position of women in war was passive or supportive. Rather than question the nature of this traditional view, however, the heroism of the characters circumvents such a challenge by amplifying the role of women and augmenting the value of their support. None of these characters sought personal advancement through education or employment; nor did any of them advocate suffrage or increased political rights for women. All three would have been happy to continue their private and quiet lives at home, caring for their extended families and serving the interests of the men in their lives. The war's intrusion destroyed that possibility, and instead, created a reality for which they were not prepared, but whose challenge they were able to answer. D'Orliac's and Berger's narratives assert that the opportunity to sacrifice oneself for one's homeland is a glorious prospect for women as well as men. Chances for heroism exist anywhere and everywhere, from the backyard garden to the trenches of eastern France.

While the sexual purity of d'Orliac's and Berger's warrior heroines is relatively unimportant, the openly adulterous relationship of the protagonist in Camille Mayran's *L'Histoire de Gotton Connixloo* (The Story of Gotton Connixloo) determines both the plot and development of the character. Published in 1918, this first novel brought the young author instant fame and the year's top literary honor, the Académie Française's Grand Prix du Roman. This accolade was the first of many in Mayran's long career. Her extensive repertoire of poetry, novels, and translations twice garnered the prestigious Prix Alice Barthou, once in 1945, and incredibly, again in 1952.[9] As early as 1926 a critic hailed Mayran as the best of the avant-garde writers. His praise however duplicated the bipolar classification typical of commentary on women's writing, by asserting that the keen modernism so expertly displayed in her work was the result of the fusion of her woman's natural suppleness and receptivity with a forceful and scholarly knowledge.[10]

The distinction of the Académie Française's Grand Prix for Mayran's first novel was not without controversy. The conflict centered on charges of favoritism, since Mayran was the grandniece of the revered philosopher Hippolyte Taine, and it also alleged impropriety in the book's content. The latter accusation was especially damaging since it implicated Mayran's personal life. Male critics had long postulated that women writers had inferior powers of imagination and were thus obligated to call upon their personal experiences to create plot lines. In this case, however, one reviewer assured his readers, Mayran's ability to analyze Gotton's actions with reserve and tact proved the writer's natural purity. Yet his praise actually replicated the common bias against women's writing by attributing her work to instinct rather than to her competence as a writer. "It's a bit miraculous that so much probity can describe such brazenness. One senses there an innate innocence that surpasses skill and that even the wisest and most knowledgeable male writer would be incapable of achieving" (418).[11]

Mayran's novel tells the story of a Belgian peasant girl whose cruel and abusive father blames her for her mother's death in childbirth. Like other motherless main characters, Gotton is headstrong and independent; moreover, her father is both attracted to and repelled by Gotton's sensuality and passionate nature (21–26). He soon learns that she is having an affair with a married blacksmith from another village, an older man with five children. After a savage beating from her father, Gotton runs away to live freely and happily with Luc. There she patiently hopes for the birth of a child who will revenge, so she feels, the cruel ostracism both of them suffer from the villagers, and from family and friends. Castigated by name from the pulpit, Gotton can no longer attend Church, and she finds this limitation almost unbearable. When the much-anticipated birth does not occur after three years, Gotton begins to blame herself for Luc's abandonment of his family and especially for the violation of his marriage vows. She interprets her continued childlessness as a sign of God's punishment for her transgression, for she believes that children protect their parents from damnation (80–87).

Overwhelmed with guilt for her life of sin with Luc, Gotton is certain that the German invasion of Belgium is the beginning of the Last Judgment. Ghastly details of the massacre of hundreds of peasants, the mutilation of children, and the incineration of the city of Louvain reinforce Gotton's fear that she will die outside the Church. She refuses to leave the village with Luc because she fears economic hardship if they abandon his blacksmith's shop. Moreover, she feels ashamed to seek safety for herself and Luc alone, when everyone has children to protect. "What do we have to save?" she asks herself (110), referring to the empty cradle in her house. In fact, the subsequent events in the story will provide Gotton with the opportunity to save her integrity and restore her public standing in both the community and the Church she so loves.

> The tragic upheaval that jarred everyone's spirit had resonated for her [Gotton] like the trumpet of the Last Judgment. It seemed to her like the end of the world was drawing near, and she saw herself with horror bound to a culpable love outside of Christendom (119).[12]

Like the descriptions found in the works by Marie Reynès-Monlaur and Lya Berger, the recounting of civilian deaths in Mayran's story is both visually horrifying and unsparing in its evocation of German barbarity. Luc arrives at his former home to find his wife and father-in-law eviscerated, his five children alive, but covered with blood and terrorized by the scene they have witnessed. Luc barely manages to escape before the Germans set fire to the village (130–34). Gotton immediately assumes care of the children, expertly bathing and comforting them. Sensing that her dream of a house filled with children would finally materialize, she anticipates the joys of motherhood, but soon realizes that they will never accept her. Understanding that her own mother's death and her father's abuse obscured for her the primacy of parental over spousal love, Gotton is now convinced that Luc will ultimately reject her.

> Her desire to be a mother had made her understand what the love of parents for their little ones could be. It seemed to her inevitable that this love would eventually be the stronger and would overpower the love of a woman in the father's heart (137).[13]

Rather than face this inevitable loss and humiliation, Gotton sees death as the means to escape her intolerable situation. When Luc reports that he had seen the barely hidden body of a murdered German soldier, he resolves that they should leave to avoid the inevitable collective punishment that would reduce the village to ashes.[14] As Luc speaks, Gotton feels a great wave of pity and forgiveness come over her, for she recognizes the opportunity she desires to escape her unbearable predicament and expiate her sin by taking responsibility for a German soldier's death (141–43). With the mayor, obviously uncomfortable at being in Gotton's presence, acting as translator, she confesses to the murder a few hours later. Several of the German officers believe that she is protecting her husband or some other man, and they press their superior to execute everyone in the village as they have been ordered to do in such cases. As they debate the fate of the town, Gotton prays fervently that they believe her, bringing the death that will atone for her sin (154). The German lieutenant, whose conscience is disturbed at so many village massacres, accepts Gotton's story and her sacrifice. The novel ends as the remaining characters, all male, gather at her burial in consecrated ground to forgive her sins and praise her generosity of heart (165).

Gotton's heroism is different from that depicted in the stories by d'Orliac and Berger in that it is more self-serving than patriotic and provides an escape from an untenable position. While these other characters also find themselves trapped in dangerous situations, they seek and embrace solutions expressly for the benefit of others. Gotton is a victim, both of the lack of maternal care and of her father's abusive anger and barely disguised lust for her. She grows up alone tending her flocks and leaves with the first person who is kind to her. While Gotton transgresses social and religious laws that regulate sexual behavior, her desire for children and her reverence for the maternal predict the rehabilitation she so desires. In addition to supporting the widespread emphasis on the primacy of children in a woman's life, Mayran's story shows that even a woman so hopelessly fallen and publicly degraded as Gotton is capable of heroism and redemption. Her death, however, is not the passive suicide she could have solicited by leaving the relative safety of her house. It is, rather, atonement for her sins, which requires active reparation of some kind. Gotton had thought that she could make amends through caring for Luc's children, and her intent to live for them is evident in the future she imagines (136–37). She comes to realize, however, that her situation is impossible because she understands firsthand the irremediable consequences of a mother's death. She also knows that because of the nature of her relationship with the father and the pain she had caused the children, they will never accept her as a substitute mother. In a final letter she advises her lover to marry quickly for the sake of the children and even suggests a candidate (144–45).

> I would love them, they would perhaps despise me: they would have every reason. I would die of shame and sorrow. You, now, you must live for them; you must marry: they must have a mother and she must not be an unworthy woman like me (144).[15]

Yet this aspect of her heroic sacrifice is private and as such, is incomplete. The common knowledge of Gotton's adultery requires public expiation, and her expulsion from the Catholic Church demands an act of penance so complete that it will remove the stain of her guilt. When she goes to the German officer and falsely claims to have stabbed a soldier, she does so to spare the inhabitants of the village the inevitable destruction by fire. It is important, however, that while Gotton did not commit the murder, someone in the village did, knowing that the Germans generally reacted harshly and swiftly to such acts of civilian resistance. Thus in admitting the stabbing, Gotton is doing more than saving the village. She is taking on the sin of another in fulfillment of the fundamental Christian acts of love and sacrifice that both annul her own sin and recover her soul. In death, Gotton's blissful otherworldly smile attests to the peace she has found, and her burial in the church cemetery of her native village affirms her reintegration into the community (163–65).

This dual aspect of Gotton's death as both punishment and expiation is important because it demonstrates Mayran's simultaneous support and subversion of the social controls concerning contemporary women's attitudes on marriage and the family. The sympathetic portrait of the free-spirited and natural Gotton, motherless and victimized, mitigates her behavior. Her death, however, is not a punishment for her emancipated sexual conduct as much as it is for transgressing the social and religious laws of marriage. As discussed above in chapter 1, long-standing fears about the changing attitudes of women toward marriage had been a subject of public discussion that intensified with the advent of the war. Politicians, scientists, and intellectuals, both male and female, had linked the steady decline in France's population with the increase in women's educational levels and their growing demand for a voice in public affairs. Since such a decrease was commonly cited as one of the factors in German perception of French vulnerability, this line of reasoning at least partially blamed feminist and educated women for the war. Thus Gotton suffers the ultimate punishment, sterility and death, for violating the social mandate of regulated marriage and legitimated childbirth required by the modern state to continue and survive attack by bellicose neighbors. By denying her protagonist a child and then killing her off, Mayran signals her support of the traditional view of women's role in marriage; nonetheless, she mediates this position by granting Gotton heroic status and posthumous rehabilitation in both the secular and religious communities.

Gotton's social position, that of a peasant woman, is distinctive among the novels and short stories discussed in this study, for most protagonists are members of the middle and upper-middle class. These characters enjoy the benefits of financial security as well as certain privileges afforded by their social standing. Moreover, with the exception of a few teachers and other professionals, these main characters are young women waiting for marriage or they are homemakers with children. As Gotton is one of only two major representations of rural women, the protagonists in Madame Yves Pascal's *Noune et la Guerre* (Noune and the War), 1918, and Colette's *Mitsou, ou com-*

ment l'esprit vient aux jeunes filles (Mitsou or How Intelligence Comes to Girls), 1919, are the only examples of working-class women. Pascal's narrative in particular expands the definition of heroism by portraying the financial problems that the war unleashes and the courageous efforts of women in the labor force to overcome their hardships.

Both Pascal's Noune and Colette's Mitsou are music hall performers who have relationships with upper-class men.[16] Both women are in their early twenties and consider the stage as a happy alternative to factory work or worse. Nearly nude, the two women play roles in different *tableau vivant,* that staple of the French music hall whose wartime patriotic veneer did not alter its essentially erotic and voyeuristic intent. The descriptions of the shows in both narratives disclose the distance between what theater directors presented for civilian consumption and the reality the soldiers lived in the trenches. Declining to see Mitsou in her role in "Ivy on the Battlefield," one of her lovers, the Lieutenant Bleu, expresses his amusement that there are people who actually think that plants can grow in such a hostile environment.[17]

While in the other narratives discussed here, the war occupies an important role as a plot mover or teacher, in Colette's dialogue-short story, it is simply a convenient background. Still, the exceptional place of Colette in the history of French letters warrants the inclusion of her brief story in a study of women's war fiction. Mitsou seems completely unaffected by the war, so much so that other characters feel compelled to remind her of its existence (657; 660; 672). Her colleague and friend, Petite-Chose, is a sexually expressive woman, who rejects more conventional civilian activities, such as knitting for the soldiers, to enjoy the increased opportunity of the war to meet attractive young men (672). One night, she hides two officers in Mitsou's closet, and later, one of them, the Lieutenant Bleu, so-named for his blue uniform, sends Mitsou a gift. Despite the jealousy of her older, "respectable" civilian lover, Mitsou begins a correspondence with the officer. Their letters juxtapose Mitsou's uncultivated candor with Robert's educated worldliness. However, the process of writing develops Mitsou's powers of expression, and she marvels at the fresh ideas that a few months of correspondence have formed in her mind (685). While at first the Lieutenant is charmed by the contrast between them, he loses interest in Mitsou after their first night together, for he cannot imagine a future with her (709). A long letter from Mitsou ends this brief account of their fleeting relationship, and explains the significance of the short story's enigmatic title. She thanks him for his interest in her, attention that she feels cultivated her intelligence, but she also notes that meeting him in person frightened her and concealed her new self from him. Moreover, she hopes that her continued growth, stimulated by her love for him, will cause her to become the woman he truly wants

(716). Thus Mitsou's newfound understanding does not lead her to develop her individual self; rather, it reinforces her practice of adopting another person's definition of her, symbolized by her name, an acronym for her older lover's two companies. Her desire to conform more completely to Robert's expectations is a continuation of the internment of the self that characterized her relationship with her previous lover. For Mitsou, the writing process, as in Jeanne Landre's . . . *puis il mourut* (discussed below in chapter 5), furnishes the opportunity to assume an identity created by another person.

Although the war plays a minor role in Colette's story, the idea that a woman's intelligence comes from the experience of loving another person differs little from the approbation of abnegation and sacrifice in other narratives studied here. While it is the war in those other stories that causes the women protagonists to realize the importance of service and dedication to the men in their lives, in *Mitsou,* it is a woman's emotions that bring her to perceive that knowledge. Such a representation of women's intelligence supports the conventional male view of the sentimental basis of female reason.

In Pascal's *Noune et la Guerre,* the self-knowledge acquired by the main character is a direct result of the war experience. Selfish and cold, Noune cared little before the mobilization for Jacques, the rich young man who adored her in spite of her cruel indifference. Noune liked to tease him about his pretty white hands that she judged too delicate for work, and she contrasted them to her own dark and callused fingers. While certainly resentful of the ease of his life, Noune also understood the power of his money. It had not only allowed her to leave the music hall and live comfortably, his wealth had also enabled her to escape the poverty and drunkenness of life in the Parisian working-class district of Belleville. Rather than rejoice in her good fortune, Noune's family rejects her new lifestyle as improper, socially ambitious, and opportunistic. Her mother, tired from worry and the care of six children, and her father, violent and alcoholic, consider Noune dishonored by her affair with Jacques (2–10; 47–57).

Soon after Jacques's departure for the front, his absence and the intense emotions of the war environment cause Noune to realize that she really does love him. Her transformation into "a new being," begun with the mobilization, intensifies into an open display of heroism a few weeks later during the threatened siege of Paris. As she observes the decision of those around her to leave Paris or accept meekly the inevitable German invasion of the city, a fierce pride surfaces in the young woman, and armed with a gun and a knife, Noune prepares to protect herself and her country.

And then, pride burst forth from this young woman waiting for the Huns, to feel thoroughly ready and so courageous. Forlorn, she thought of the other women who must sleep or cry uselessly.

    . . . Oh! For certain, Noune could not accomplish much, could she? But after all, she will defend herself! And besides, if they go down her street, she'll fire on them, it's understood! (79)[18]

Inspired by her historic link with the *pétroleuses,* the fierce revolutionary women of the Paris Commune of 1871, Noune embraces the opportunity to accomplish acts of equal courage, and even martyrdom. The banality of her past life fades in the image of the glory she expects, a sacrifice in keeping with the tradition of Joan of Arc and of the Parisian working class. A mental picture of the "visionary Virgin who saved France" motivates and fortifies Noune's bravery throughout the night of her vigil. When the German advance stops outside of Paris, Noune is somewhat disappointed to have missed her one chance to be magnificently heroic (79–87). Nonetheless, her identification with the legendary warrior-saint elevates her transformation to the highest level. No longer merely a pretty but selfish doll spurned by her family, Noune has become a totally different woman through her experience of war. Not only is she now devoted to Jacques and willing to fight and die for her country, but her association with the virgin warrior of Orleans symbolically restores her "lost" honor.

Noune's rebirth as a warrior-heroine, although untested, will later guide her to seek and accept the more socially prescribed manner for women to exhibit their courage, becoming a mother. "Could it be that she, Noune, useless little woman, certain of her emptiness, was put into the world only to give birth in her turn?" (212).[19] However idealistic her image of mothers, Noune's view of marriage emphasizes her awareness of its social and financial advantages. Nonetheless, despite her aspirations for the respectability of middle-class life through marriage with Jacques, it is hard for Noune to abandon attitudes considered normal in her social milieu. While imagining their future life of sumptuous dinners served by domestics, Noune expresses the hope that Jacques will someday beat her in a jealous rage (249).

Class consciousness also informs Noune's view of the war. Although she makes a few disparaging comments about Germans and seems throughout the novel to be entirely supportive of the war, in fact she is one of the rare characters in French war fiction to voice opposition to the war. Noune's plan to terminate the war is doubly significant, not only because it proposes an end the fighting, but also because its analysis of international armed conflict duplicates that of a notorious antiwar group, the Left Zimmerwaldists, long associated with Lenin and other revolutionaries.[20]

Noune's peace project does not specifically refer to their program that drew virulent criticism beginning in 1915, a fact that may explain how this passage evaded notice by official censors who remained active in France until October, 1919. Nonetheless, its affinity with the Zimmerwald call to soldiers to put their class interests before national rivalries is apparent.

> . . . I'd say to them [the Germans]: "Listen, guys, you have wives, moms, kids? Us, too. So why are we fighting? To please some bastards who aren't in any danger, and to make your wives, your moms, and your kids cry? . . . Stop fighting, come with me, become friends with all of the common people, and let's unite to knock the block off the tyrants, the emperors, the kings and ministers! . . . All are brothers, that's what we must be" (252–53).[21]

Noune's financial security departs with Jacques, and soon she finds herself in circumstances similar to many of her friends and former colleagues. Pascal evokes the heroic efforts of these women to manage the consequences of reduced income and increased responsibilities. Facing indigence, they borrow from friends and pool their resources; others supplement their inadequate government allowances with work provided by the Red Cross and other charities, such as sewing army uniforms in their homes.[22] Pascal correctly disregards the increased employment opportunities for women in factories, which did not become widespread until 1916, more than a year after *Noune* takes place. Nonetheless, she does allude to another, ironic, type of relief brought by the war. For women accustomed to their husbands' brutality or the extreme poverty resulting from the dissipation of family resources through alcoholism, the war afforded a respite from a personal reality of anxiety and violence. Nonetheless, these women hope earnestly for their husbands' safe return, despite past misdeeds or future disabilities (102–117; 122–26). As in the novels by Colette Yver, Andrée Mars, and others, Pascal affirms the unconditional willingness of French women to accept their husbands regardless of any war injuries. However, her analysis of this attitude in terms of social hierarchies underscores the heroism of working-class women who remain steadfast in the face of the inequities of class privilege and the realization that at the end of the war, the men will still have all of the rights (184). Noune analyzes the women's sentiments:

> Yes, certainly, that's the way it is among the common people: you have "a man," and then, it's forever. You're his, and he's yours; so you keep him, always, in spite of everything. You keep him, without arms or legs, even if life, thinking itself generous, consents to give him back to you one day with the same gesture of a rich kid who gives a poor one the toy he just broke. And you're delighted, and you clasp your hands and you say thank

you. They're giving him back to you, that's just too bad if he's damaged.
He's "your man" (126).[23]

Pascal spends considerable time depicting the environments of the
music hall and the cinema and the impact of the war on the performers.
While sometimes shallow and often vain, the players nonetheless dedicate
themselves to their country's cause and attempt to employ their talents to
elevate the audience. It is through her women characters especially that
Pascal illustrates the minor status of stage performers, the brevity of their
careers, and above all, their precarious financial condition. The war simply
adds more instability to their situation by increasing the competition for
jobs that demand more physical beauty than talent. Attracted by the marginally elevated salaries and fully aware of the number of women available
for the few positions open, the cast ignore the humiliation and familiarity
of auditioning half-naked. Once hired, they become obedient and model
performers, afraid that a stray remark might cost them their jobs. Neither
mourning clothes nor bereavement leave are allowed, so widows must in-
ternalize their grief and forego the support of the community. Salaries are
not high enough for anyone to become a *marraine* or to pay for packages
to soldiers. One player, frustrated that she cannot afford the expense of
adopting a *filleul,* decides to have sex with the soldiers she meets at train
stations, since that is all she can afford to give them. Moreover, the added
responsibilities of married women double the amount of time they spend
working (128–73). Pascal evokes with sympathy the quiet courage of these
women, simple entertainers for whom the theater is, above all, a job.

> Everyone knows that the theater is not an occupation for the lazy, for
> women especially. They, in addition to the roles to be learned and practiced,
> they must also maintain a house, care for the children—of whom the most
> infantile is often the husband,—accomplish each day the back-breaking
> tasks of a good housewife, and in addition, perform their roles in the evening
> (131–32).[24]

When Jacques dies of complications following severe wounds to his
hands, Noune faces class barriers she thought had been effaced by her relationship with him. Overcome by grief and especially guilt concerning
her frequent criticism of Jacques's hands, Noune rushes to his mother, sure
of finding a sympathetic companion for her misery. However, instead of
solace, Noune encounters cruel disdain and a lesson on the impossibility
of social mobility. While a spontaneous emotional outburst briefly unites
the two women, it quickly becomes clear that the mother will never acknowledge the importance of Noune in her son's life. She refuses to give

Noune even a small memento or picture of him, and advises the young woman to accept in silence the tragedy of his death. Pascal here attributes the differences in the women's reactions to social class, for Noune, a daughter of the working class, is instinctively revolted by the sacrifice of a life (276). She counters the mother's resignation with the assertion that women's cries of grief could wipe out the sounds of war and thus put an end to conflict. Instead of repudiating this traditional view of women's instinctive pacifism, as in the novels by Marcelle Tinayre and Mathilde Démians d'Archimbaud, Pascal reinforces Noune's rejection of the primacy of nationalism. "My country, my homeland, it was him, my Jacques, my guy, so handsome, my man" (284).[25] Moved by Noune's uncontrollable sobbing, the mother finally offers her one of Jacques's rings, but Noune declines, perceiving for the first time the irrevocable distance of class and privilege that separates them more completely than death (285–86).

Noune later encounters one of her fellow performers, who insists she return to the music hall for the evening show. However, this is not due to any theatrical tradition of continuing a presentation under any circumstances, but rather is in recognition of the financial loss that Noune would incur if she failed to perform. Like many others in the theater company, Noune will have to hide her grief or risk paying a fine or even losing her job (300). Thus, Noune fulfills, against her intentions, the admonition of Jacques's mother who urged submission and passivity, and despite her fleeting pacifism, she acquiesces to the reality of war. The novel ends as Noune, barely paying attention, makes her entrance in the tableau on the instruments of war, representing barbed wire. The cruel irony of such a role emphasizes the courage of women such as Noune, for whom the dignified and secluded grief of Jacques's mother is a luxury they cannot afford. Pascal's novel demonstrates that the "heroic martyrdom" Noune recognized in the older woman's demeanor, belongs to Noune and her stalwart coworkers as well.

The war also provides an unexpected opportunity for a child to demonstrate heroism in Lucie Delarue-Mardrus's second war-related novel, *Toutoune et Son Amour* (Toutoune and Her Love).[26] By the time of the book's publication in 1919, Delarue-Mardrus (1880–1945) had already embarked on a distinguished and enormously prolific literary career. From the beginning of Delarue-Mardrus's professional life, critics acclaimed the original quality of her sensuous and romantic verse and fiction. Known primarily as a poet of her native Normandy, she also published novels, plays, short stories, essays, and articles that appeared in many of the Parisian dailies.[27]

Delarue-Mardrus's literary production during the war alone is impressive. Despite serving as an ambulance driver and nurse, she managed to publish several novels, a volume of poetry, personal narratives, anecdotes, essays, and many short stories printed in various newspapers. Her articles during this period often emphasized the redemptive power of mothers, especially in the case of wounded soldiers and the children of rape victims. Delarue-Mardrus agreed with other women in the public debate on these so-called "petits indésirés" (little unwanteds) by insisting on their social acceptance. Mothers would love them just like other "handicapped" children, she wrote in an article of 1915, "L'Enfant du Barbare" (Child of the Barbarian), and the innocent child, in turn, would renew the great miracle of motherhood. Furthermore, many women who commented on the fate of these children, like Delarue-Mardrus and Odette Dulac, understood that these infants would help to rebuild a population devastated by war. In becoming French, the children would eventually take their place in the army of the future, thus redeeming the crime of their German fathers and avenging the sacrifice of the raped women and the French soldiers.[28]

Toutoune is a child who recounts her life from her earliest memories to the present, her eleventh year, coinciding with the war. From the very first pages, Delarue-Mardrus creates a sad-sack character whose complete neglect by her socialite parents quickly establishes her status as victim. Abandoned to the care of servants and disparaged by her mother and father for the double resemblance to a sheepdog (hence her nickname, a variant of the childish "doggie") and to a cantankerous and difficult distant relative, Toutoune nonetheless loves her parents (6–146). With the war, the mother is left alone and turns to Toutoune as a source of attention for herself (160–78). Toutoune, who worships her mother as a distant fairy princess, assumes many adult responsibilities in her efforts to please her and win her affection. Her successful adventures, from obtaining rare news of the war to managing the household by herself when the housekeeper dies, greatly impress her mother, who openly praises Toutoune, and this in turn increases the child's self-esteem. As the mother's confidence in her daughter grows, she reveals that she is separated from the father, who has squandered all of the family money on other women. When he suddenly returns, wearing a uniform and begging for forgiveness, the mother, bolstered by the presence of Toutoune, sends him away forever (243–52). The story ends with Toutoune remaining happily with her "love" of the title, her mother.

Toutoune does not face a German soldier, conserve priceless art treasures, or save French soldiers' lives, but her actions are nevertheless heroic. Toutoune accomplishes nothing less than the patriotic and spiritual redemption of her own mother, reclaiming her from a life of ostentation and excessive self-indulgence. When the father leaves for the front, the mother returns to the family manor in Normandy, where Toutoune lives with the servants. Bored by the quiet country life, she spends her days in bed, waiting for letters from her husband and endlessly searching the newspapers for details about the war. In these scenes, Delarue-Mardrus communicates effectively the anxiety felt by so many civilians, as well as their sense of isolation and frustration at the scarcity of news. One day, when the newspapers fail to arrive, Toutoune is so distraught at her mother's unhappiness that she decides to set off by herself on her bicycle to obtain them. This act, Delarue-Mardrus's narrator carefully explains, is such a major breach of etiquette that it threatened the family with scandal, for the girl was unaccompanied for two hours (166–77). The concern for Toutoune's public reputation signals her passage from child to adult and prepares her mother's acceptance of her as an individual.

Later the mother rejoins her husband in Paris, but returns to the country when she learns that his infidelities have continued and that he has dissipated her personal fortune in these affairs. When ten-year-old Toutoune receives her telegram that her mother is arriving on the train, she despairs that there are no carriages or cars available to meet her at the station. She sets off alone on her bicycle to find her mother, an act whose independence and daring both shock the other characters and amaze her parent (217–20). Her mother's praise makes Toutoune radiantly happy, propelling her into assuming the strong personality of her Aunt Dorothée. Whereas previously the comparison with this disagreeable relative had been a source of dismay and confusion to the young child, now Toutoune concentrates on the woman's adult qualities of resolve and determination.

> "Decidedly, Toutoune, you resemble your Aunt Dorothée completely."
> At bedtime, when the little girl came to kiss her mother, the latter began to examine her daughter as if she had never seen her. She lifted up her braids, probably to judge the effect of a hairstyle, leaned her head to one side, and then said in a kind tone:
> "You have pretty eyes, Toutoune . . ."
> The child gave a start, struck to the core. She understood in that minute that never in her life would she hear anything similar. A lump in her throat, she felt the desire to express a small part of the immense pleasure she felt, a little of her delighted surprise (194).[29]

Toutoune declares herself grown up and reorganizes the household neglected by her spoiled and inept mother to such a level of efficiency that even the servants are amazed (224–27). She assumes her adult role so completely that she becomes her mother's confidante and, finally, in a spectacular role reversal at the end of the story, her mother's mother, defender, and champion (230–39; 246–52).

This change in Toutoune's perception of herself and her relationship with her mother supports another common theme in French war fiction: that the war, although certainly tragic, had many positive effects on society. Toutoune's mother, accustomed to the advantages of wealth and social status, is unprepared for the war's disruption of her life of privilege and self-absorption. Delarue-Mardrus presents the mother as unnatural, countering her disregard and even cruelty toward her child with the depiction of a sad and lonely little girl who despairs of her ugliness and dreams only of pleasing her parents. Yet her parents' very neglect allows Toutoune a kind of freedom of action and thought that she might not otherwise have had. Similarly, the war provides Toutoune with new challenges and the opportunity to develop a positive view of herself and her capabilities. Thus the model of responsible adult behavior she comes to represent proceeds directly from the war and replaces the selfish and childlike behavior characteristic of her parents' lifestyle of endless parties and social engagements. The breakup of the mother's marriage is symbolic of the disappearance of a way of life whose lack of concern for duty or responsibility is no longer possible or desirable in a France besieged by war. Moreover, the mother learns the meaning of commitment and dependability from her daughter, as her passivity and inactivity yield to the lesson of Toutoune's little acts of heroism and her efficient running of the household. This reversal of the roles of parent and child is not only emblematic of the general upheaval of values engendered by war, but it also resolves that discontinuity by proposing a new but certainly not revolutionary kind of woman as its champion. For while Toutoune becomes a confident and self-assured person who insists on making her own decisions, her behavior nonetheless supports socially acceptable views of female activities, since she teaches her mother to become a responsible parent and homemaker. The Toutounes of tomorrow may shock a few sensibilities by riding a bicycle alone and in public, Delarue-Mardrus affirms, but their qualities of earnestness, self-assurance, and dedication to duty are the essence of the France of the future. Her acts of bravery, although scaled-down to a level appropriate for a child, demonstrate the kind of heroism needed to rebuild France after the war.

Colette Yver examines the very concept of heroism and whether it exists in the modern age in her novel, *Mirabelle de Pampelune* (Mirabelle of Pamplona), published in 1917. Yver lived from 1874 to 1953 and began writing children's stories at an early age. Her long and prolific career began with the fame that resulted from several novels written in the decade before the war, including *Les Cervelines* (The Brainy Women), 1903, and *Les Dames du Palais* (Ladies of the Palace), 1909. Many of these and subsequent novels, especially *Les Princesses de Science,* (translated in 1909 as The Doctor Wife) for which she won the prestigious Prix Fémina in 1907, detail the traditional outcome of her women characters' struggle to resolve the conflict of love and independence (Waelti-Walters, 188). Like other prewar antifeminist novels, such as Jeanne Broussan-Gaubert's *Josette Chardin ou l'Égoïste* (Josette Chardin or the Egoist) published in 1912, Yver's *Princesses* attempts to prove that women's increased education and demand for autonomy inevitably lead to tragedy for the family, for in both cases a child dies of neglect while the mother pursues her own interests. Yver's many postwar works include historical fiction, novels, and essays. Her *Dans le jardin du feminisme* (In the Garden of Feminism), 1920 and *Le Vote des femmes* (Women's Suffrage), 1932, continue her long-standing critique of the assertions of "new women" and of feminism in general.

In *Mirabelle,* Yver investigates the meaning of heroism in modern times through the simultaneous narration of two separate stories. The first recounts the daring adventures of the eponymous heroine and her warrior-knight during the time of the Crusades, and the other concerns the changing relationships between two women cousins, Édith and Louise, and the young salesclerks, Robert and Henri, who wish to marry them. The story begins just before the declaration of hostilities and quickly establishes the central obstacle to the marriages. The women find the men too ordinary and lacking in gallantry to appeal to them and they both agree that heroism is definitely missing in contemporary men. While Robert does not displease Édith, she hesitates nonetheless, and both cousins mock the self-absorption and commonplace concerns that pass for valor in French men:

> "I find him very nice. But it's so mediocre to marry a salesclerk! I would have liked a young man who had done something grand, a husband of whom I would be proud: an aviator, for example."
>
> "That's like me," says Louise. "But what do you want? In the sad era in which we live, there is no longer any heroism. Men hang on to their old junk. Their ideal is to bring back on Sunday a fish bigger than what the neighbor caught or to go play cards before dinner" (22).[30]

Yver expands Édith's conclusion that "France is fallen" to castigate contemporary attitudes illustrated not only by Robert and Henri, but also by her father and brother, Georges. Yver insists on this comprehensive reproach by juxtaposing the young women's harsh judgment with the brother's unhappiness at having to comply with the three-year compulsory military service law. Worried that such a stint would intrude on his future plans, Georges expresses sorrow for his useless sacrifice, and both men agree that no danger threatens France, despite rumors of a possible war (24–25). This scene, placed at the beginning of the novel, establishes a major theme of the book, but it also implicitly responds to doubts about France's readiness for the war. Yver suggests that perhaps her country's citizens were too satisfied with their lives, and that this complacency may have fueled German expansionism, as some critics charged. However, she also indicates that the capacity for gallantry requires motivation and that such encouragement is the task of French women. Writing in 1917, the time of increasing public dissatisfaction at the lack of visible progress in the war, Yver shows the transformation of ordinary citizens, both men and women, into valiant defenders of France and its Christian and Latin civilization.

In the medieval legend of Mirabelle of Pamplona, Édith and Louise discover two individuals who personify the ancient and noble definition of heroism for which they yearn. It is the story of a courageous couple whose love for each other is as strong as their devotion to their country and faith. Yver quickly establishes the legend of Mirabelle as a moral tale for the inhabitants of a nation at war, and she locates parallels between the historic crusade against the Saracens and the present hostilities with a Germany characterized as "barbarian." Mirabelle and the Count consider honor and service to France and to God not only as inseparable but as necessary to their love and respect for each other. In taking leave of Mirabelle to fight the enemies of Christianity, the Count affirms that love without esteem is impossible and that death with integrity is preferable to life without principle (29). After many months with no word of his fate, Mirabelle has a dream in which she sees the Count wounded by a Saracen arrow. By dint of her intense prayers to the Virgin Mary, Mirabelle miraculously changes places with him and finds herself in a Turkish prison (108–09). Her bravery and fidelity earn her the respect of her captors and safeguard her honor. The Count, although now blind, nonetheless raises an army and returns to rescue Mirabelle, but only after defeating the Turks. Yver portrays the Saracens as thoroughly wicked, an uncivilized people whose sole purpose is to subdue Latin France and thus destroy Christianity. After Mirabelle's return, she is heralded universally as a hero whose exploits are equal to that of her knight (134–37). It is worthwhile to note, however, that although Mirabelle acts to rescue the Count, her accomplishment remains within the definition of traditionally acceptable female behavior of self-abnegation. In praying to take the Count's place, she offers her life as a sacrifice for his, and she waits chastely and patiently for her turn to be freed. Moreover, her acceptance of the Count as her husband despite his blindness establishes another important aspect to the portrayal of heroism that Yver ordains in *Mirabelle de Pampelune*. For her, women work together with men in war by taking their places metaphorically and, if disabled, in reality. Still, Yver does not present such a substitution as an assumption of male roles, but as the means to aid the men to accomplish more efficiently their duty.

Interspersed in the narration of Mirabelle's story, Yver depicts with realistic detail and authentic *poilu* (soldier) slang the battle scenes that trace the heroic metamorphosis of the three "modern" men, Georges, Henri, and Robert (64–77; 82–85). Although nothing in their prewar lives had prepared them for the rigors of combat or trench life, their innate qualities quickly established them as model soldiers and leaders to their comrades. Moreover, Yver suggests that only an actual threat can generate real courage and that all else is superficial imagination. Before the war, Louise had asked Henri if he would jump off the Eiffel Tower to prove his love for her (36–7). It is important that although Henri had rejected this demand as romantic silliness, he nonetheless agreed that he would do it to save her life. Even Louise's father, a modest bookstore owner, assumes the position of heroic defender of French civilization. While many of his neighbors flee the advancing German army, he decides to remain in his shop, not to protect his investment, but to guard, like a soldier, the books and art reproductions that represent France's soul (41; 44–45).

When letters and other accounts reveal the valor and fortitude of Henri and Robert, Louise and Édith admit with shame and regret that they had misjudged the two men. They understand that people are just as valiant and noble now as they were during the time of Mirabelle, but that the modern age furnished few opportunities to show that courage. Identifying with the character of Mirabelle and her example, the young women realize that their own heroism will be to wait for and support the soldiers and to be grateful for their return, regardless of their condition. Foreshadowing the story's dramatic conclusion, Louise acknowledges women's patriotic duty to accept their men regardless of their injuries and to rebuild and continue France with them. Louise, imagining herself in Mirabelle's situation, declares triumphantly,

> For myself, I have thought several times that Henri could return disabled. Do not fear at all that I might then have to force myself to keep from running away like a fool. No, no, only too happy if he returns, even missing an arm, an eye, or a leg! (162–63)[31]

Colette Yver asserts through the lesson of the medieval legend that the performance of traditional womanly virtues results in courageous deeds. Like Mirabelle, who took the Count's place in prison so that he could fight alongside his king, so too should each woman do what she is able to empower the modern soldier to accomplish his duty. Even the most modest action may result in the heroic. When Robert is wounded, Édith is determined to go to the hospital to see him, despite the danger and impropriety of such a visit. She counters her parents' objections by declaring that she is not just his fiancée, but also his sister and friend, if not his entire family, whose solemn duty is to comfort and care for him. Her father relents by evoking the heroic nature of Édith's mission of consolation, for her death would make her "another heroine for France" (103).

Mirabelle's example also teaches that a woman must wait patiently for her soldier's return, accepting him as her husband and the future father of her children, regardless of any disfiguring wounds or amputated limbs. Yver here supports the pronatalist discourse, common both before and throughout the war period, which equated female heroism with creating the French army of the future. Moreover, by celebrating the life of abnegation and service required of the wives of severely wounded veterans, Yver echoes another lesson for women contained in much of French women's war fiction. Like Isabelle Sandy and J. Delorme Jules-Simon, Yver envisions the post war marriage as the union of patriotic mother and permanent child. Instead of his own eyes, Yver's character Henri will "utilize" those of Louise, and she will become his eyes, just as other women in real-life and in fiction will become the eyes, arms, and legs of their husbands.[32] As Louise explains, "Besides, we will love each other better this way, because I will be the one to serve as his enlightenment . . ." (186).[33] The double meaning of light in French (*lumière*) in the physical sense as well as one of knowledge underscores the ambiguity of a statement that extols simultaneously a woman's independent authority but also service to another. It accurately reflects the mediatory stance found throughout the war fiction that appears to authenticate but at the same time undermine the possibility of women's autonomous thought and action. For, as Henri's eyes, only Louise determines the nature of the reality she reports and what Henri accepts as authentic. Most importantly, only she will know what uses she would make of this knowledge and power.

The evolution of Yver's characters illustrates another common view in these novels that war is an unforeseen benefit for its participants. The transformation of the two cousins' attitude from frivolous disdain for their soldiers to total devotion, and the metamorphosis of their fiancés from mild-mannered salesclerks to wounded soldiers decorated for their bravery, supports Yver's contention that war, although tragic, helps everyone become what they need to be. The war gave the men the chance they never would have had as salesclerks to prove their courage to their country, to themselves, and to their future wives. Further, it provided Louise and Édith with the ability to recognize heroism in its modern form and to understand that even the most ordinary women and men are capable of valiant deeds. Yver concludes her novel's exploration of the different guises that heroism assumes in the present era with an acclamation that pointedly defends soldiers whose willingness to continue fighting in 1917 was questioned in that year of mutinies and disobedience. Raising his glass in salute to the two young couples, the family friend who had recounted the adventures of Mirabelle, praises their "eternal" French virtues.

Today, as yesterday, I recognize in women the same nobility, the same bravery, the same idea of honor. In the men, the indomitable courage and abnegation for the glory of country. What harmony between the centuries! In spite of the tribulations, the developments, the transformations, France is one and forever itself. As she was seven hundred years ago, under the white cloak of chivalry, so I find her today, the countenance more solemn, somewhat clouded by the contemplation of science, surrounded by the smoke of industry, of railroads, and steamboats, but arrayed with the same flame, the same youth, and the same appeal that captivates the world and disorders even her barbaric enemies (193–94).[34]

Chapter Four

Out of Sin ✤

The growth and personal change that result from the experience of war also distinguishes the characters in another group of novels. In these stories, however, events of the war induce the female protagonists to accept as transgressions previous ideas or acts embraced in the name of self-determination and personal freedom. Despite differences in plot and in the backgrounds of the characters, these novels demonstrate the judgment that disagreeable consequences inevitably arise from the realization of such independence. Yet the authors of these novels condemn women's autonomy not because they are necessarily antimodern or against increased civil rights for women, but because such values do not serve society as a whole during a time of national crisis. Their novels affirm that for a woman to assert her independence while her countrymen are fighting is both egotistical and unpatriotic, for such personal freedom is antithetical to the unity and cooperation indispensable for an eventual victory. In these stories, the tragedy of war provides an unexpected benefit for the main characters. It is through the suffering and catastrophe of war that each protagonist learns her "true" obligation to family, country, or God. Rather than contribute to the moral and spiritual degradation of women as critics had charged, the experience of war delivers them from what the authors clearly depict as a state of sin.

The war trilogy by the prolific and popular Catholic writer Marie Reynès-Monlaur, *Pages de deuil et d'héroïsme* (Pages of Mourning and Heroism) illustrates well the far-reaching effects of a woman's insistence on her right to intellectual freedom. Born in 1870, Reynès-Monlaur had achieved before the war enormous success with her spiritualist novels, such as *Jérusalem* and *Angélique Arnauld,* awarded the Prix Jules Favre and the Prix Sobrier-Arnould, respectively, by the Académie Française. Pious and strictly Catholic in orientation, her numerous works always earned the approval of diocesan authorities, and several of her novels contained the written endorsement of a cardinal or bishop. Her immense popularity ran unabated for decades, and nearly 40 years after its publication, *Jérusalem* was still obtaining excellent reviews in the international Catholic press.[1] In an interview in 1980, famed author Marguerite Yourcenar singled out Reynès-Monlaur as one of the world's most notable twentieth century women authors (Milligan, 61). Many of Reynès-Monlaur's works, including the first volume of *Pages de deuil et d'héroïsme*, appeared in English and other languages.

Reynès-Monlaur's trilogy is the story of the separate spiritual journeys of two sharply dissimilar women: the simple and devout nun Sœur Claire and the atheist intellectual Claude Harteveld. *Les Paroles secrètes* (Secret Words), published in 1915 and translated into English in 1917 as *Sister Clare*, concerns the invasion of Belgium and the nun's perilous flight into France. The bombing of Reims Cathedral in the last part of *Les Paroles secrètes* brings together the Catholic sister and the independent thinker. It is Claude's spiritual crisis and eventual conversion to Catholicism that are the focus of the remaining two volumes, *Les Autels morts* (Dead Altars), 1917, and *La Fin de Claude* (The End of Claude), 1918.

The preface to *Les Paroles secrètes* contains the author's assurance that the story to follow is completely genuine, and that she invented nothing (i). Such assertions of authenticity are frequent throughout French women's war fiction because they help justify the legitimacy of the author's claim to be able to recount events to which women would not normally have had access. Reynès-Monlaur's insistence that neither the facts of the book nor its ideas are hers, however, reverently diverts any approbation to saints and medieval mystics. Her emphasis here on the nature of women's duty during the war includes the expected call to serve and mourn the soldiers of France, but it also displays Reynès-Monlaur's larger spiritual goal. Her message is that the dead represent "flowers in the fields of invisible crops" and that it is her obligation, as it is for all women, to "harvest" their souls for God (iii). Reynès-Monlaur thus establishes from the very beginning of the trilogy her interpretation of the link between the war and the fundamental teachings of the Catholic Church. For her, the war is a divinely created trial of faith as well as a punishment for past sins. Nonetheless, the present conflict is an ultimate benefit because it revives people's spirituality, thus bringing them closer to Jesus and to eternal life.[2]

Sœur Claire is a Belgian nun whose simplicity and lack of general aptitude is second only to her loving and maternal manner. When captured by the invading Germans, she and the other members of her convent barely escape the torture and murder they witness around them. After six harrowing days alone with neither food nor rest, Sœur Claire finally reaches a village in France. Her faith shaken by the horror of what she had observed, she prays for deliverance from her doubt. That night she has a vision of Jesus and the "secret words" she hears reveal to her the reasons for war and the sacred mission that she is to fulfill.

This message and its divine means of presentation establish firmly the book's themes of sin, redemption, and martyrdom. For Reynès-Monlaur, war and other evils result from humanity's sinful misuse of free will, but war is also a test and a means for the faithful to show their submission to God. Nonetheless, she also asserts that the barbarism of the enemy purifies those who die and elevates them to a state of martyrdom. Thus sanctified, the dead exalt the souls of the living who witness their sacrifice, while also attaining for themselves eternal life and glory (130–38). Through the vision Sœur Claire comes to understand that her mission will be to serve the people by easing their suffering and preparing them for heavenly redemption. Reynès-Monlaur introduces here a major theme in the trilogy: that war is part of God's plan to force people to evolve spiritually, and that it furnishes an important opportunity to do God's work and thereby earn merit.[3] The fact that Sœur Claire, unassuming and somewhat simple-minded, experiences such a miraculous vision demonstrates clearly the transformative power of the torments and misery she has observed. To underscore the glorified status of the dead, Reynès-Monlaur locates parallels between their suffering, sacrifice, and salvation and the death and divinity of Jesus.

While many authors studied here allude to German atrocities, few present those acts as often or in as much detail as Reynès-Monlaur. Massacres, firebombings of hospitals, and the tortured murder of children and priests appear from the very beginning of *Paroles secrètes,* and these scenes are notable for their extended length and graphic description (3–5; 23; 34–38; 42; 52–54; 86–88; 95; 122; 157). The scope of the atrocities serves to efface any doubt of the truth of the allegations reported by the allied press, especially at the beginning of the war but disputed by the Germans. Perhaps more importantly, it also rescues the public reputation of members of the Catholic religious community who were the target of widespread rumors in the French press, suspected of evading service in the army and actively supporting the German cause.[4] Even Père Jean, Sœur Claire's brother, enthusiastically recounts his adventures with "his" wounded soldiers, commenting on the difference the war has made in the way he is treated. The people who considered the priests pariahs and fanatics before the war now look to them with confidence and respect (190–91).

Reynès-Monlaur also elevates the position of soldiers by presenting them, along with priests, as holy martyrs who willingly offer up their lives to a higher cause (86–88; 135–38). However, contemporary readers would

have known that soldiers who died in defense of their country were inel-
igible for the status of martyr, since that station belonged only to those
who underwent a death imposed out of hatred for Christian life. Reynès-
Monlaur, by ascribing an aura of holy war to the conflict through references to Germany's Lutheranism and to the Kaiser's expressed desire to
destroy the Catholic Church, thus transforms its orientation from political
to religious (61–63). Moreover, by insisting on the spiritual side of France,
Reynès-Monlaur brings renewed attention to the somewhat faded importance of France's Catholic identity. As discussed above in chapter 1, the defense of France, for Reynès-Monlaur and other writers, is thus inseparable
from the preservation and predominance of its Church.

Reynès-Monlaur establishes the Cathedral of Notre Dame at Reims as
the preeminent symbol of the indivisibility of Catholicism and France, for
its history unites the sacred and the secular. As the coronation site of its
kings, it recalls the country's ancient and vivid past, but it also invokes the
memory of Joan of Arc, the warrior-saint and defender of France.[5] Moreover, as a celebrated example of Gothic architecture, the Cathedral is a
nonreligious representative of the achievement of Latin civilization. At the
end of *Les Paroles secrètes,* it becomes additionally a place of reconciliation
and redemption, for love and respect for the Cathedral is the one interest
shared by Sœur Claire and Claude Harteveld. Reynès-Monlaur identifies
its partial destruction by German bombs in September, 1915, not only as
an attack on France, the Catholic Church, and all of Western civilization,
but also with the beginning of Claude's spiritual renewal.

Claude is the exact opposite of the nun. Raised in a Protestant but freethinking family, she believes in nothing except what her studies of the German philosophers have taught her, that is, to follow her own will. Like other
intellectuals before the war, Claude admires German letters and culture.

> . . . I cannot regard [Germans] in that way, as bandits or torturers. I reject
> them as a French woman as much as I admire them from the point of view
> of the mind. You know the saying of one of our professors: "Germany, the
> second homeland for all beings who study and think" (207).[6]

Despite the testimony of Sœur Claire and others, Claude refuses to accept as true the allegation of atrocities committed by the German army.
The bombing of the Cathedral dumbfounds her, since she cannot understand how the champions of culture and reason would attempt, even during wartime, to destroy such a monumental treasure of art. She feels lost
and depressed, and soon leaves her nursing duties to return to her family
home in south central France. Her spiritual crisis and the resolution she
will discover, the focus of the remaining volumes of the trilogy, result not

so much from the loss of her admiration for Germany, but rather from the large void left by its demise. For Reynès-Monlaur such an emptiness is not tragic, but in fact a fortuitous opportunity for the soul distraught by the disorder in the world of which war is a manifestation. In speaking of George, Claude's brother, whose conversion to Catholicism certainly prefigures Claude's own, a priest remarks that the evils of war have brought much that is good (212). Throughout Reynès-Monlaur's works, the human desire to understand the unexplainable will lead to God and the Catholic Church.

Les Autels morts (Dead Altars) describes Claude's battle with depression and a steadily increasing desire to end her spiritual torment through suicide. In her efforts to understand and resolve her crushing feeling of emptiness, she will come to realize the failure of her philosophy of individually derived morality and intellectual self-direction. Her war experiences will change Claude from a marginally Protestant skeptic and self-sufficient woman with ultimate trust in her own judgment to an ardent and obedient Roman Catholic who denounces free will as a categorical evil. Throughout this second novel, Reynès-Monlaur juxtaposes the fundamental Protestant concept of a person's right to self-examination of conscience with the unquestioning and unwavering faith of Catholicism. She represents Claude's belief system as more than a simple denial of the existence of God; it is, rather, a firm confidence in herself and in her own sense of what is right. Even after renouncing her admiration of German thought, Claude can still proclaim:

> But my first master is myself. . . . Christ intervenes only to the extent that I consider it good. It is the only benefit—or the only evil spell—which I keep from Germany. Moreover, I cannot speak differently from what I think (94).[7]

Through the evolution of Claude's thoughts and her discussions with family members, Reynès-Monlaur endeavors to confirm the ultimate failure of all non-Catholic belief systems to relieve a person's spiritual anguish. She specifically condemns Protestant doctrine by linking its justification of individualism with the German rationalization of violence as an acceptable expression of its national will. Moreover, her Protestant characters, in addition to being attracted to German intellectuals, exhibit coldness, pedantry, and sterile egotism, while the Catholic characters, although humble and poor, are completely French and are the models of compassion and consolation. The war with its constant threat of death provides the means to prove what Reynès-Monlaur considers as the superior substance of her Catholic faith and to censure beliefs she feels are spiritually and morally empty. Claude's fiancé, Abrham, writes from the front lines that he sees the war as a conflict between gods, contrasting Germany's pagan love of violence and hatred of the weak with France's charity and compassion. It is significant that he validates France's Christian roots and identity, notwithstanding the 1905 law that had disestablished the Catholic Church, by integrating them with her past.

> It is such a clear feeling that this war is a war of gods! In spite of our athe-
> ist government, France is here with its great Christian instincts, generosity,
> kindness, pity! Faced with a brutal adversary, she retains the chivalrous na-
> ture that fourteen centuries of fellowship with Christ gave her. We feel that
> in the hand-to-hand fighting, just as we sense life (143).[8]

Claude Harteveld withdraws to her family's vacation home in a former convent, both to care for her ailing father and to seek refuge from the "anxiety that gripped her" (43). The location both consoles and disturbs Claude, for it represents the paradox in the personal history that now entraps the young woman in a theological dilemma. Claude feels the strong Catholic faith of the nuns who lived in the convent until the French Revolution, as well as that of her own Catholic mother who died when she was seven. Madame Gautrande, the devoutly Catholic peasant woman who helped raised Claude, welcomes her home (14–20). There is also a strong Protestant presence in Claude's life: her father, a freethinking Protestant intellectual, her Aunt Coralie, whose extreme hatred of everything "Roman" is often comical, and her fiancé, Abrham Bonnier, who plans to become a minister (48; 115–20).

Before the war, her brother Georges and Abrham studied at German universities, and Claude read and discussed with them all of the works of the modern moral philosophers, especially Kant, whom she greatly admired. The war brings an abrupt end to their intellectual triumvirate, and the suffering the men experience and witness causes a deepening of their spiritual commitments. Observing firsthand the generosity and compassion of nuns like Sœur Claire so moves Georges that he embraces Catholicism; Abrham overcomes his last doubt about the divine, as opposed to the historical, reality of Jesus (52–54; 138–9). The changes the men undergo are positive in that they result in their growth or development. For Claude, however, the war brings a spiritual loss. Having based her beliefs on human-centered systems, she feels a profound sense of emptiness when she realizes that the moral strength she encountered in German philosophy could also result in acts of barbarism and savagery. "We sought our mentors among our worst enemies and I am ashamed of it," she confides to her father. His response reinforces the double condemnation of Germany as both anti-Catholic and uncivilized, "They are the enemies of our Latin souls, as well as those of our borders" (90–91).[9]

The collapse of Claude's humanistic metaphysics leaves her without the courage to endure the reality of death represented by war. Whereas Georges and Abrham consider death a passageway to a greater truth, Claude sees only an endless void. Tempted continually by thoughts of suicide, yet fearing the vacuity of death, she writes to Sœur Claire who recognizes in her anguish the first painful steps toward an affirmation of faith. When both Georges and Abrham are reported missing and presumed dead, Claude is drawn to a church, where the sight of a crudely painted representation of the Virgin Mary overpowers her remaining resistance (286).

It is understandable that Mary, symbolizing simultaneously maternity and faith, provides the means for Claude to accept Catholicism, the religion of her deceased mother. At the time of her mother's death, the seven-year-old Claude had internalized her grief and as an adult retained this emotional aloofness. Claude's stoic self-composure parallels the people and ideas associated with Protestantism and rationalism, from her father and aunt to her own respect for Kant and the categorical imperative. Yet, the freethinking father who encourages Claude's intellectualism is also unable to speak to her about her mother. Although Claude clearly needs his comfort to fill the emotional void caused by the mother's death, his own pain is too great to help her. Moreover, her Aunt Coralie, the only Protestant female presence, is a stereotypical illustration of the sterile coldness that accompanies antagonism and hatred. Conversely, all of the women associated with Catholicism are completely maternal and nurturing, with a divinely inspired gentle benevolence. With the exception of the Virgin Mary, they all represent a direct link with the essence of France: the nuns who lived in the seventeenth-century convent, the loving servant who raised Claude, Sœur Claire, and of course, Claude's mother. Finally, the bombing of the Cathedral at Reims and other German misdeeds cause Claude to reject the idea that morality can come from reason. In embracing the Catholic faith, Claude is not only reclaiming the maternal presence that has been absent from her life, she is also admitting the failure of human-based moral systems. Her struggle to understand and accept the true extent of the submission and obedience integral to her new religion will be the focus of the trilogy's last volume, fittingly named *La Fin de Claude* (The End of Claude).

A year after her conversion, Claude finds out that Abrham is alive but is nearly blind and apparently dying from third-stage tuberculosis. He had spent many months in a German field hospital, unable to communicate his whereabouts or the extent of his condition. Unsure of how Claude will react to his precarious state, he contrives with Sœur Claire and Claude's friend Geneviève, a canoness, to ascertain her feelings for him. Abrham, unaware of Claude's conversion and the resolution of her spiritual crisis, imagines that she will not want to renew their relationship because of a quarrel at their last meeting. Claude had asked Abrham to renounce all ideas, especially theological, not directly related to her, and he had refused. For her part, Claude remembers this incident with shame, mostly because she worries that he has died with that scene being his last memory of her. She longs to see him again, if only to tell him of her new faith and her certainty that his eventual death will not be a solitary journey (58–59). While many of the themes of Reynès-Monlaur's first two volumes reappear here, it is Abrham's possible conversion to Catholicism and Claude's total submission to the will of God that are the central foci of the book. In evoking the themes of the other novels, Claude's pride in her own judgment, Abrham's hesitant faith, and the link between Protestant theology and German philosophy with the brutality of its army (13; 19–20; 36; 57; 119–21; 128; 248–49; 259–60), Reynès-Monlaur again reaffirms the bond among France, Latin civilization, and the Catholic Church (23; 115–16; 152; 258–59; 272–74).

Reynès-Monlaur emphasizes another important point from those novels, that the war is part of a divine plan to bring people closer to God and to instill in them the belief in eternal life, an essential tenet of Catholicism. The joy with which several characters, including Claude, regard the proximity of death clearly affirms their anticipation of heaven. Thus, with the deterioration in Abrham's condition, the "winning of his soul" and his acceptance of Catholicism become more urgent for Sœur Claire and Claude. His conversion corresponds exactly to the nun's view that it is often women of faith who lead their husbands to God (215). Claude's unconditional love of Abrham and her quiet serenity gradually dispel his religious doubts and his prejudices against Catholicism. Moreover, the promise of an afterlife brings the dying man solace that he cannot find in his Protestant beliefs. Rather than directly criticize Protestant doctrine, Reynès-Monlaur endeavors instead to demonstrate the transcendent richness of her faith and its ability to fill the spiritual needs of believers and atheists alike (213–14; 248–49). The conversion of Abrham, a Christian headed for the ministry, would have greater lessons for Reynès-Monlaur's readers than that of Claude, who had had no faith at all. Thus, it is Claude's example, rather than any discussion, that finally brings Abrham to Catholicism, a point that reinforces its experiential quality, rather than the more rational Protestant examination of conscience.

Abrham's situation is a test for Claude. Under Sœur Claire's tutelage, she gradually comes to understand that praying for Abrham's life is presumptuous because it places her own desires before those of God. As his condition weakens, she replaces dreams of their future life on earth with images of their union in heaven and prays that they never be separated. When

Claude asks Sœur Claire to pray that God spare her from surviving Abrham, the nun refuses and instead counsels Claude's complete submission to the will of God (242). The novel reaches a dramatic ending on Maundy Thursday and Good Friday, 1918. After a prayer vigil centering on the hope for Abrham's conversion and for the couple's eternal union, Claude visits the Church of Notre-Dame de Saint-Gervais with Abrham to attend Good Friday services. As they kneel and pray together, Abrham reveals that he has embraced Catholicism, and just as Claude rejoices at the immediate favorable response to her supplication of the night before, German zeppelins bomb the church. Mortally wounded, the couple dies in each other's arms.[10]

This scene not only ends the trilogy but also reunites its most important themes. In his last few seconds, Abrham imagines that he has returned to the battlefield, and that he is again defending France. While he has been inactive for most of the book, Reynès-Monlaur depicts his death as that of a heroic soldier (272). Moreover, his impression that the red blood, the white pillars of the church, and the blue of the now visible sky have blended to become the flag of France restates the link between France and the Catholic Church so important to the three books. The novel's climax also serves to underscore another theme, that of the premeditated godlessness of the Germans. As in the bombing of Reims Cathedral in *Les Paroles secrètes,* Reynès-Monlaur skillfully depicts their almost unimaginable sacrilege as a consequence of their belief in the superiority of their national will, as well as that of their faith in modern technology and of German *Kultur.*

> From the ground rose a blinding dust, so dense that one thought at first that it was poison gas. Human fragments were thrown together indiscriminately. Even those who were spared, near the choir, were shrieking in madness . . . The Germans had chosen this day and this hour—Good Friday at 3 o'clock—to surprise the world with one of the traits of their culture. They thus made unforgettable one of the significant crimes of their race. The shell had broken a pillar, bringing down the dome (273).[11]

Reiterating the connection among modernity, technology, German philosophy, and Protestantism also repeats on a larger scale the particular condemnation of Claude's earlier belief in her own ethical authority and reason. It is significant that after her conversion, the bookish and self-absorbed Claude joins the peasants, "feeling the joy and health of this work in the fields" (7). Her presence there symbolizes Claude's rejection of the modern world of independence and individualism that had led to spiritual torment and the temptation of suicide. Cultivating the earth with farmers already identified with historic and Catholic France illustrates her recognition of their salubrious and restorative traditional values.

Claude's dying thoughts unite the religious and the patriotic, with sacrifice and redemption reiterating Reynès-Monlaur's earlier portrayal of World War I as a holy war. Claude exults that her blood will serve the singular and simultaneous purpose of the deliverance of France and of Abrham's soul. Contemporary readers would not have failed to note that Claude's death replicates the required characteristics of that of an authentic Christian martyr, with her blood replacing the water of baptism and her death in witness of antipathy for Christian life.

> God had heard her, answered her prayers, exceeding her hopes and fulfilling the wishes of her heart. Her offering was accepted. Her blood would be used to redeem this France that she had loved more than herself, for the baptism of the cherished soul that she placed in the hands of God through this heroic aspersion (272).[12]

Reynès-Monlaur continues in this scene to blend the political and the religious. The fallen mother lying in the rubble between her two dead children who cries out "For France!" with her dying gasp symbolizes another kind of Trinity, that of the tripartite unity of the maternal, the Catholic Church, and France (274). It reiterates the consistent identification of motherhood with Catholicism and France evident throughout the trilogy. This bond includes not only mother figures and substitutes like Sœur Claire and Madame Gautrande, but also Geneviève, the devout lay nun who dedicates her life to Christian charity and service in imitation and love of her mother and other forebears (49–50). Further, that the saintly Geneviève confides to Claude that her one sorrow is not having had children illustrates Reynès-Monlaur's view of the primacy of motherhood for Catholic women. Geneviève expresses this thought in the context of a visit to a new mother, during which she also regrets that the young woman did not fully understand the spiritual importance of her baby's baptism (204). Nonetheless, Reynès-Monlaur does not limit the prominent role of women in the perpetuation of the Catholic religion to mothers, for it is Claude who, as Sœur Claire predicted, brought not only her soul, but that of Abrham to God. The significance of the rather abrupt title of this last volume, *La Fin de Claude,* becomes clear, for in addition to end or death, *fin* can also mean aim and purpose.

Redemption of another person's soul is also a theme in Mary Floran's *On demande une marraine* (Seeking a Godmother), 1919, the second of her two war-era novels. Floran, the pseudonym of Marie Leclercq, was a prolific author who published more than 40 novels between 1889 and 1930.

She received two prizes in the prewar period from the Académie Française for *Un an d'épreuve* (A Year of Hardship), 1892, and *Orgueil vaincu* (Pride Overcome), 1897, as well as recognition from the Ministry of Public Education for *Mademoiselle Millions* (Miss Millions) in 1902. In addition to her novels, the indefatigable Leclercq wrote articles for a wide variety of periodicals, including *La Libre Parole, La Mode Illustrée,* and *La Revue des Revues,* and issued an impressive number of plays under the pseudonym, Monsieur Tril.[13]

Floran's book is one of several novels and stories, including those by Colette and Lucie Delarue-Mardrus, that explore the impact of the *marraines de guerre* program and the relationships that developed between the correspondents. As stated above in chapter 1, early in the war women received encouragement to write letters to servicemen at the front, especially those soldiers whose families were in occupied territory and could neither write nor send packages. However, criticism and suspicion soon dominated much of the commentary on *marraines* (godmothers) and their *filleuls* (godsons). Many authors studied here make passing references to their characters writing letters or sending needed personal items to combatants, and while they do not openly address the controversy, their insistence on the maternal motives and behavior of the *marraines* communicates a tacit defense of the women. This respectful tone is certainly not the case in Jeanne Landre's three sardonic novels, discussed below in chapter 5; however, in Floran's story, the correspondence accomplishes nothing less than the miraculous redemption of a discredited mother and her reconciliation with an estranged and embittered son.

The story consists of a series of letters from March 1916 to March 1917 between a soldier and the *marraine* he solicited through advertising in a newspaper. Neither correspondent is aware that the other is using a pseudonym. Madame Jean's first few letters seem strangely hesitant and so diffident that Jacques Louez (whose name is an exhortation to praise) fears that he is causing her some pain; nonetheless, he desires to continue writing to her. She finally consents to the correspondence, provided he does not attempt to meet her. Her tone is direct and unflinching, as she warns him not to expect too much from her. She feels that her advanced age, her inadequacies, and her disappointments in life prevent her from providing the motherly guidance expected from a *marraine*. Jacques speaks of his feelings of detachment and separation and, alluding to others' less than honorable motives for establishing such a relationship, simply asks for encouragement. His innocent motives and sincerity finally convince Madame Jean, who enthusiastically acknowledges that what she can do best is communicate to him the unity of civilians with the men at the front. She reveals that she had a son his age, a fact that would explain her initial refusal of a maternal role, despite her decidedly parental tone. The soldier, an orphan, is glad to accept his *marraine* on her terms (2–14). Thus from the very beginning of the story, Floran establishes their association in essential terms of mother and child. Additionally, the purity and patriotism of their ideas replicates all of the understood qualities of the ideal *marraine-filleul* relationship, thereby contradicting for the reader of 1919 negative views acquired during the war.

In his letters Jacques unleashes his anger and frustration at the French complacency that he feels played a role in the beginning of the war. The many years of prosperity his fellow citizens had enjoyed since the end of the war with Germany in 1871 had created an ideal existence. However, it had also engendered the conviction that these conditions would continue as an inevitable part of the modern age. Those who "languished in well-being and pleasure" could not recognize the danger from an expansionist Germany that was all too conscious of any weakness in its neighbor (24). Floran here echoes the view of many other novelists, including Odette Dulac and M. Maryan, discussed below, who focus on the negative aspects of the changes and choices inherent in modern life. They cite the self-indulgence and excessive self-satisfaction of the French population that they consider as the cause of weakened defenses, thus attracting the aggression of Germany. Later in Floran's story, Jacques will proclaim that the purpose of the war is to purify the earth of excess (148).

Notwithstanding his criticism and disappointment in the French people before the war, the soldier's attitude changes abruptly when considering his fellow combatants. He draws strength from their example and finds inspiration in their unity of purpose despite social, educational, and class differences among them (24–25). As in the novels by Isabelle Sandy and Delorme Jules-Simon, the experience of being at the front has an almost instantaneous ennobling effect on Floran's soldiers, who shed individual cares and any petty concerns to emerge as a unified whole.

Gradually Jacques recounts the sadness of his life before the war and the disappointments in love that embittered him against all women his age. He is particularly antagonistic because his fiancée had deserted him for his own father. Despite his father's trickery, the soldier's harshest judgment is directed at the young woman. This inequity elicits a long response from the *marraine,* who, unaware that Jacques is in fact her long-lost son, asks him not to condemn all women. She relates the story of Kate, a woman she knew who lost her reputation, family, and considerable fortune through the machinations of a philandering husband. He had falsely accused her of infidelity so that he could obtain a divorce and steal her money. By drugging the woman, the husband had arranged a situation so compromising that even her own family discounted her protestations of innocence. Appearing to be drunk and found in bed with a male acquaintance, the young wife was quickly cast out of her home, separated from her young son, and disowned by her own mother. The husband easily obtained the divorce, control of his wife's assets, and custody of the child from a judge who never questioned the veracity of the story. Deprived of her income and rejected by friends and family, she would have starved had it not been for a sympathetic aunt who granted the woman refuge. The saddest part, the *marraine* explains, is that the woman never saw her son again, since the father told the boy his mother was dead (117–44). This story reinforces the *filleul's* conviction that French society before the war was decadent but affirms his belief that the sacrifice of the soldiers will prevent the possibility of such incidents in the future. Floran here replicates the view of Reynès-Monlaur and Maryan in depicting the war equally as a punishment for, and expurgation of, society's past sins.

It [the war] came to purify the earth, perhaps of such monsters, or to punish it for having borne them. Believe me about this, Godmother, after the baptism of blood that has washed humanity, we will no longer experience such villainous deeds, we will no longer encounter such predilections (148).[14]

Although Jacques does not guess the identity of the woman in the story, the narrator reveals that Madame Jean's story of the young woman was about herself. At this point, neither of the correspondents is aware that they are in fact mother and son. The *marraine/filleul* relationship provides shelter and anonymity, and in the letters that follow, the two isolated and hurt individuals become more comfortable and attached to one another. The subjects they discuss are personal and do not focus on the war or trench life. Madame Jean assumes an increasingly maternal tone, and thinking about a prospective marriage for him, she advises Jacques on future relationships with women. After some months in the trenches, he and his squad depart for a château in order to wait for their next orders. There Jacques makes the acquaintance of a baron, his family, and some of their friends, including young marriageable women. The soldier relates his impressions of life at the château to his *marraine*, especially concerning the young women he has met. For her part, Madame Jean quickly detects the possibility of a favorable and socially advantageous match for the young man and imparts much advice on becoming himself and overcoming his mistrust of women. Emboldened and more confident, Jacques pursues Hélène, who agrees to marry him (150–250).

The last part of the book details the predictable revelation of the identity of Jacques as the *marraine's* long-lost son, Renaud Leuroy de Brestange. Hélène's mother is in fact an old friend of Claude de Chailly (Madame

Jean) and writes to her when he is wounded. Hélène, unaware of who Madame Jean actually is, arranges for her to visit Renaud in the hospital. Looking into his *marraine's* eyes, the soldier feels an emotion so intense that he understands that this woman is his mother (281). A happy reunion, his recovery, and marriage to Hélène quickly follow. The story ends with a letter from Renaud to his mother asking that she become a *marraine* again, but this time for a baby (273–88).

The central issues in Floran's novel are the importance and permanence of maternal love. Her book demonstrates that this is not a bond confined to a woman's biological children. Even mother-substitutes, such as the *marraine,* can provide young people with the essential maternal attributes of affection, guidance, and enhanced self-esteem. Similarly, the orphaned soldier's urgent insistence on continuing the correspondence, despite the older woman's decidedly forbidding tone, demonstrates his search to form the mother-child relationship lacking in his life. The woman's reluctance is a kind of test of the sincerity of his motives, and his persistence finally convinces the *marraine* of his integrity. It is significant that Floran establishes from the very beginning that the connection between these two people is that of parent and child, for it defends women and soldiers alike against charges of husband-hunting and licentious behavior. Moreover, the soldier solicits and receives much needed counsel on a variety of subjects, and because of the *marraine's* parental guidance, he grows and matures into a man who will accept family responsibilities. Under the motherly supervision of the *marraine,* the soldier changes from an embittered young man who despised all women and vowed never to marry, to the founder of a stable French family. As in so many novels studied here, Floran's book supports the traditional view that women's primary role is the preservation of the family, whether it is her own, someone else's, or the greater family of France.

Floran also confirms the extensive and profound value of the entire *marraines de guerre* program, for this wartime activity enabled an embittered young man and a victimized woman to reclaim her rightful mother's role to rear her son and prepare him for adulthood. Although Claude suspects that the soldier may be her son, she nonetheless decides to use the *marraine-filleul* relationship to keep her identity secret. Unaware of how much he actually knows about his mother, she fears he will reject her. Despite the pain of withholding her true feelings from him, she knows that her son can better accept the warmth and instruction he needs from a stranger than from the woman sent away from him in shame. Thus, she sacrifices the opportunity to tell him the truth and thereby reestablish her reputation so that she can be the best mother possible. Her selfless dedication receives the ultimate reward, that of her son's instant recognition of the bond they share, a connection not effaced by time or injustice. Significantly, Floran does not address the unfair treatment of Claude or implicate the legal system that prevented her from defending herself and allowed her husband to destroy her life and steal her personal fortune. Rather, the extensive degree of persecution and dishonor that Claude suffered is important because it demonstrates the durability, constancy, and inviolability of mother love. In Floran's book, maternal affection cannot be destroyed by time or circumstance; moreover, it always triumphs, no matter how great the misdeed, and is always unmistakable, no matter how carefully hidden. Additionally, the son's unquestioning acceptance of his mother reintegrates her into the family and into society, thus rehabilitating her reputation. Although she was innocent, everyone else, including her own mother, believed her to be unconditionally corrupt. As in other novels, including Andrée Mars's *Tu aimeras en douleur* and Delarue-Mardrus's *Toutoune et Son Amour,* it is the war that provides the means for a child to rescue miraculously the parent from what seems to be an irremediable situation. In Floran's book, a son's love redeems a woman and restores her to her traditionally appropriate role, that of mother and grandmother.

The power of a child's love enacts the spiritual deliverance of a selfish woman in Camille Mayran's novella, *L'Oubliée* (The Forgotten Woman). Published with *L'Histoire de Gotton Connixloo* in 1918, it relates in flashback the story of Denise, a young woman previously living in occupied France with her elderly and sick mother. Arriving in Paris in December 1916, to search for her fiancé, Denise encounters her old friend Adrienne, a young mother and dedicated volunteer nurse. The two friends spend the evening together, and Denise recounts her adventures since her village had been occupied by the Germans two and a half years before.

Denise had been engaged to Philippe, but had not heard from him since his capture and subsequent escape from a German prison camp soon after the war began. The details of her life in occupied France disclose predictable stories of German brutality, especially concerning the forced labor of local citizens and of the Russian and Belgian prisoners of war (202–06). Nonetheless, the metaphor of a machine allows Mayran to mitigate slightly her condemnation of the Germans, while at the same time reinforcing a negative view of the effects of modern technology.

> Everything is a machine to them. They themselves function like parts of one enormous machine. The most surprising thing is that, taken individually, the soldiers are not often malicious. But they are part of the machine, and the machine makes everything possible (204).[15]

Moreover, when Denise's mother develops terminal breast cancer, it is a German doctor who cares for her with respect and goodwill (215–18).

With unexpected patience, the Germans tolerated the many charitable acts the mother performed before her illness. Denise admires her mother's courage during the long year before her death, but fails to emulate her, much to her subsequent regret. She is later ashamed that, despite the death of her brother in the war and her mother's steady decline, her concern for her fiancé was totally absorbing. Even at the moment of her mother's death, she could think only of her own personal joy in the future with Philippe (230).

Released from her filial obligations, she decides to try to find Philippe and receives permission from the Germans to leave her town on a refugee train. The journey is torturous and long, since the train travels through Germany and Switzerland and includes a required eight days of quarantine to eliminate the possible transfer of any information valuable to the French war effort. As the train is about to depart, a German officer shoves a six-year-old boy into Denise's compartment. The child, wearing a tag with only his name and the classification "orphan," stays with Denise and, significantly, his presence transmits a certain composure and confidence to her. Directing her thoughts to him, she notes his bewildered and resigned demeanor and suspects that the silent boy may have witnessed his mother's death (237). However, she soon forgets him in the excitement of her arrival in Paris.

There Denise learns that her fiancé has married the nurse who cared for him while in the hospital. Gravely wounded, his arm and shoulder amputated, he had wished to die, but the serenity in the nurse's face and the singular grace of her movements had healed his depression and cured his soul. His explanation that extreme suffering changes people makes Denise begin to realize that she could have done more to protect him from despair, just as his love had been a refuge for her (247–48). Days later on Christmas Eve, she sees the couple together in prayer and sensing the sanctity and depth of their happiness, she feels almost as if she had never existed for Philippe.

Seated in another church, she reflects on her life and suffering, and her self-pity gives way to shame. She suddenly realizes that she failed to grant to her own dying mother the compassion she herself now so desperately needs. Consumed by worry and love for Philippe, she had been oblivious to her mother's silent agony, for which her present sorrow is just compensation. "I understood that my inordinately grasping heart had deserved its disaster" (269).[16] The environment of the church and the atmosphere of the Christmas holiday have a significant impact on Denise. She not only accepts responsibility for her suffering but also recognizes its potential lesson in teaching her to understand and console other people. Realizing that the time has come for her to stop thinking of herself and to act, she suddenly remembers the little orphan boy and resolves to adopt him and others like him (270–72). Thus the multilayered symbolism of Christmas, epiphany, renewal, and spiritual redemption, fuse in the manifestation of a new, wartime Madonna and Child, that of a forsaken fiancée and an orphan. Denise employs distinctly Christian images and terms to describe how the fellowship of their anguish revealed love to their battered hearts:

> When we are alone together, and the thought of our common misery and weakness overwhelms me, I take his little head in my hands, and I feel then that this poor little crumb of love that serves as our nourishment suffices to sustain our lives, he and I who have lost everything, merged in the immense communion of those who love each other. For a heart that believed itself cut off from the midst of the living, it is a resurrection (273).[17]

For Mayran, as for many authors, the war sets into motion events that provide life lessons impossible to achieve under normal circumstances. The self-absorbed Denise is insensitive to the charity and sacrifice of her mother and at first barely moved by the silent sadness of the orphaned boy. Moreover, Mayran contradicts criticism of nurses' motives and behavior in her sympathetic portrayal of Adrienne and Philippe's wife (171–76; 263–66). They both exhibit the devotion and steadfastness that Denise has yet to learn. Her long journey to generosity and mercy begins appropriately in a church on Christmas Eve, where she observes her disabled former fiancé and his pious and radiant wife at prayer. She no longer blames Philippe for not keeping his promise to her, for she perceives in his new relationship the results of compassion and self-sacrifice. In comparing herself with Philippe's wife, she finally begins to recognize her own shortcomings, especially concerning her mother. Nonetheless, it is not until she responds to the needs of a child and expresses maternal love for her adopted son that Denise is able to isolate sufficiently her own disappointment in order to emulate the Christian values these other women represent. As in many other stories studied here, *L'Oubliée* demonstrates the power of a child's love to actualize a woman's spiritual redemption. Significantly, that atonement depends on the willing acceptance of an active maternal role that dominates all other concerns. For Mayran, Floran, and other authors discussed below, maternal love is boundless, eternal, and eventually triumphs over circumstance, corruption, and sin.

Two of Lya Berger's short stories from *Les Revanches, contes de guerre* (Revenge, War Stories) also feature the capacity of children to divert their mothers from self-centered and harmful behavior. In "La Leçon des Petits" (The Lesson of the Children), Odette Debormeau, a young mother, learns solemnity and reverence for sacrifice from her six-year-old son (14–19).

Berger portrays her as frivolous and selfish from the beginning of the story. She refrains from participating in any war work, claiming fragile health, and devotes herself to her son, Tony, who is a source of amusement for her. When a shell attack kills her soldier husband, she dutifully wears mourning for a year. At the end of that time, she throws a Christmas party, although her young son is still very depressed. When the boy sees that his mother has discarded her black crepe veil for a party dress and jewels, he thinks that his father is somehow no longer dead. The mother, exhilarated by the dazzling lights and merriment, ignores the child's questions and fails to discern the gravity of his incomprehension. The turning point of the story occurs as she brings in a cake with mini firecrackers in the shape of mortar shells. The noise of the firecrackers completely frightens the child, and screaming, he declares to the astonished crowd that he will not play with the weapons that killed his father (18). The narrator concludes the story with the comment that thanks to this child's lesson, the mother finally understood.

The one-dimensional, near-allegorical depiction of the mother is typical of Berger's war stories. As in "Myrtille" (Blueberry) and "La Fée aux Roses" (The Rose Fairy), the women characters represent qualities for Berger's readers to emulate or repudiate. In "La Leçon des Petits," the mother is totally self-absorbed and thinks that her sacrifice of a year of fun during the required mourning period is certainly sufficient. Berger presents her decision to resume her normal life as a dereliction of her dual roles of wife and mother. Not only does the woman desecrate her husband's memory, but she also neglects her child and fails to provide the comfort and guidance he requires. While the story indicates that women need to respect and preserve the memory of the men who sacrificed their lives for France, it also submits that women's families should always be their primary concern. As in Berger's "Flirt de guerre" (A Wartime Flirtation), a woman's personal interests and even her life, whether selfish or devoted, always come last.

"L'Anniversaire" (The Birthday), another of Berger's stories from *Les Revanches* replicates this conviction that women who focus on their own emotional needs instead of those of their families are trivial and selfish. In this story, a grieving mother must suppress her suffering for the good of the greater family of France (77–81). The elderly woman is inconsolable over the death of her son in the war, and absorbed by her loss, she refuses to participate in any charities. Moreover, she even declines such a minimal commitment as sending packages to a soldier by alleging that her dead son would be jealous. The first anniversary of the son's death is also his birthday, and that day the parents encounter a young soldier the same age as their son. Since he is from Alsace, the soldier has no news of his family and expresses his concern for his elderly parents. After hearing his story, the mother decides to invite him to share what would have been their son's favorite birthday lunch. Furthermore, she intends to adopt him as her *filleul* and to send him letters and packages. As the story ends, she explains her change in behavior by her conviction that the soldier is somehow a messenger from her son. The lesson Berger presents here is that while a mother should be completely devoted to her children, that dedication requires a living recipient. Maternal love without a child is simply self-indulgence and impropriety. In both "La Leçon des Petits" and "L'Anniversaire," children have the power and authority to correct their mothers' individualism, thereby restoring the women's strict adherence to a conventional definition of acceptable female behavior.

Similar to "L'Anniversaire," the preeminent capacity of children to remedy maternal shortcomings is not limited by death in André Corthis's short story, "Une mère" (A Mother), published in her collection of 1917, *Petites Vies dans la Tourmente* (Minor Life Stories of the Turmoil). André Corthis was the pseudonym of prolific poet and novelist Andrée Husson Lécuyer (1885–1952). She won the Prix Vie heureuse in 1906 for *Gemmes et Moires* (Gems and Moiré), a volume of poems that evoked in an impressionistic manner her reflections on a broad group of topics including nature, acquaintances, and places she had visited. Celebrated also for her many novels, which were published by several prominent publishing houses, Corthis was awarded the prestigious Grand Prix du Roman by the Académie Française in 1920 for *Pour Moi Seule* (For Me Alone) (C. Cooper, 107).

As in many other works studied here, the responsibility of women to preserve the memory of fallen soldiers is a major theme in "Une mère" (75–113). Yet for Corthis, as for Berger, this role of remembrance cannot be self-centered, for such individualism is static and antithetical to the action necessary to benefit and continue the nation. The mother in the story is Nanon, a peasant woman obsessed with the memory of her dead son. Embittered by grief, she devotes her life to mourning for him and expects her son's fiancée to remain unmarried in order to respect and honor his memory. When the young woman renews a friendship with a soldier, a childhood friend on leave, the mother rages against her, considering her immoral and unfaithful to her son. She attempts to destroy the girl's marriage prospects forever by spreading lies about her family. Baptistin, Nanon's other son, agrees at first with his mother's judgment; however, when he sees the young couple working silently in the fields, he perceives their dedication to the land as a manifestation of his brother's sacrifice. Baptistin finally convinces his mother that the only way to keep his brother's memory alive is by enabling other people to live and to preserve the French nation. "He gave his life so that life might continue," he explains as the mother sadly acquiesces (110).

While Nanon remains angry with the young woman, her failure to block the marriage is important. Corthis portrays Nanon as selfish and vindictive, just as she presents the fiancée as obedient and industrious. Nanon's dedication to her dead son is laudable for a mother, but such devotion in a young woman is misplaced and dangerous, as it would obstruct the formation of a French family. Like many authors studied here, Corthis considers the war as a fight for the preservation of the French nation and regards its continuation as a primary responsibility of French women. The final image of "Une mère" juxtaposes the fecundity of the future with the remove barrenness of the past: the young couple work side by side to harvest the field as the aging Nanon and the lame Baptistin stand immobile.

The importance of children to a nation and the impact of population issues on women's lives are themes in Odette Dulac's complex novel of 1916, *La Houille rouge: les enfants de la violence* (Blood Power: The Children of Violence). Dulac was the pseudonym of Odette Roche, and her death in 1939 did not in fact end her long and celebrated career begun at the turn of the century. Dulac's books for children, many carrying her imaginative illustrations, continued to attract a wide audience throughout the decade of the 1940s. The novels, short stories, and articles published during her lifetime earned Dulac respect and admiration from her peers as well as honors from the French government. Elected Secretary of the Société des Gens de Lettres, Dulac was also named an Officier de l'Instruction Publique and a member of the Ordres Coloniaux. Her novels were considered feminist, especially *Leçons d'amour à l'usage des jeunes filles de France* (Love Lessons for French Girls), in which Dulac counsels women to rely primarily on themselves to earn a living.[18]

Dulac reiterates her particular notion of women's independence and demonstrates her opinions on its implementation in *La Houille rouge*. Her book blends natalism with nationalism to propose that women exercise their autonomy by choosing to rescue the nation from the errors of men (303). Women's restorative occupation, however, is purely biological and requires neither education nor civil rights. For Dulac, whether women accept their childbearing role or refuse it through abortion and celibacy, is fundamental to the future survival of France. Moreover, she links this choice with German expansionism and the origins of the present war. As discussed above in chapter 1, the impact of the declining birthrate in France had long been a source of anxiety among politicians, economists, and industrialists. The beginning of the war and its early setbacks intensified this discussion of the importance of "le nombre," the number of available or potential soldiers. Dulac engages in this debate in her book by locating the source of the change in demographics in French women's increasing demands for education and autonomy. Although cloaked in the farcical depiction of the ruinous designs of a group of German secret agents, her book in fact charges that women's desire to determine the size of their families contributed strongly to the moral and physical depletion of France.

Yet Dulac does not simply assign blame in her novel, for, ironically, she finds a solution to the population problem in the wartime violence directed specifically against women. The question of the future of the children of rape victims, the so-called "Little Unwanteds," was also the source of much discussion, especially in 1915, the year before Dulac's novel appeared.[19] Dulac was certainly not alone in perceiving a single convenient resolution to the double issues of unwanted children and depopulation. In her lectures and articles, Dulac joined other novelists studied here like Broussan-Gaubert and Delarue-Mardrus, in affirming the children's right to live and urging women to keep them instead of choosing abortion or adoption. In *La Houille rouge,* however, Dulac exploits the controversy over these unwanted children to attack women's demand for civil rights and feminism in general. The denouement of her novel returns to its underlying argument, that women must embrace the maternal role as their highest interest and sole occupation, and that nothing, not even the pain and humiliation of rape, should deter women from this supreme achievement.

The complicated plot begins in 1895 with the abortions of three women who choose to end their pregnancies for very different reasons. One woman has had an affair and wants to avoid a scandal, while another already has a large family and cannot afford an additional child. The third woman is a medical student, and while she hesitates to have the abortion, eventually she proceeds. In describing their situations, Dulac also presents the different reasons that accounted for these unwanted pregnancies. It is significant that neither the problem of adultery nor of poverty solicits much attention here. Rather, Dulac concentrates on the medical student, who chooses abortion because of professional ambition. Her reason, that since competition is so fierce between men and women, a child would cause her to fall behind irrevocably, establishes from the very beginning of the novel Dulac's view that professional life and motherhood are inherently incompatible. As the novel progresses, maternity will emerge as the only potential activity for women.

Dulac's Madame Rhœa, the midwife abortionist, is greedy, unskilled, and an apathetic traitor. She is indifferent to the political implications of her involvement with a covert network of pan-germanists, even when they reveal their ongoing project to destroy France from within. For years, the group had successfully infiltrated various sectors of French society, such as the legal system, industry, and the arts. The ludicrous plans of the spy network add sarcasm to Dulac's implication that French weakness and desire for peace had invited German aggression. In her scenario, every sector of the French infrastructure is complicit with German territorial ambition, including intellectuals and women. Reducing the French population and thus, its potential army, was the special assignment of the section devoted to French women, appropriately named "La Houille rouge" (Blood Power). Its attempt to damage and control women's bodies through fashion had succeeded better with Parisians than among the more emancipated and health-conscious women outside the capital. The Germans fear these provincial women whose robust strength and intelligence endangered the German sabotage of the French birthrate through control of style and of women's silhouettes. In infiltrating the fashion industry, they had caused the promotion of corsets to create a thinner shape, thereby forcing the womb to fold in on itself and disappear (75–90; 151; 210). By distinguishing sharply between Parisians and other French women, Dulac reiterates the analysis voiced by novelists such as Maryan and Pascal and essayists Berthem-Bontoux and Marcelle Capy. These women authors regret the universal perception of Parisian women as self-absorbed and frivolous, because, whether justified or not, they feel it contributed largely to the German opinion of France as an easy target.[20]

The foundation of the Germans' anti-Christian and anti-French objectives is a Nietzschean philosophy of racial superiority, forged through violence and blood. Insistence on the causative link between Nietzsche's theory of human evolution and German aggression conveys various other associations frequent in French women's war fiction. In *La Houille rouge,* the Germans' sadistic enjoyment of bloodletting, torture, and rape, their mockery of anything overtly Christian, and their veneration for modernity and progress (93; 151; 289) restate the condemnation found in works by Delorme Jules-Simon, Marie Reynès-Monlaur, Jehanne d'Orliac, and others. Moreover, it is significant that the general disapprobation of modernity in these novels implicates advances made by women in education and the demand for civil rights. Defining modernity as fundamentally German in effect nullifies the attraction any of its tenets may have had for contemporary readers.[21] The veneration of progress by Dulac's German spies has a sacrilegious tone, as progress has replaced the Bible:

> We have sworn on universal Progress and it alone is the goal of our undertaking; we are the pioneers of the Sublime Race (93).[22]

Many years later, during the mobilization, the three women from the beginning of the story and Madame Rhœa meet by chance as they report for nursing duty. The midwife abortionist, having successfully infiltrated the Red Cross, has acquired a position of responsibility. The bravery of the soldiers at her hospital, even as they cry out in pain for their mothers, softens her customary indifference. Moreover, during a spy mission she becomes lost near the front line and hears so many dying soldiers weep for their mothers that she regrets all of the abortions she carried out. When one of them asks her to give him his mother's picture from his pocket, so that he can kiss it before he dies, she recognizes the woman as a former client. Madame Rhœa's statement of remorse and guilt is significant because it implies that women might or should be natural pacifists because of the fundamental contradiction between childbirth and waging war. However, Dulac ends the scene with a patriotic evocation that completely invalidates this stereotypical representation of women's attitudes. She thus reiterates the importance of mothers to the nation as well as the support of women for a France at war, thereby alleviating any worrisome questions about their loyalty.

> "Oh!" Blasphemed the backstreet abortionist, "why bring children into the world, since this is what they do to them?" But the nobility of this dying cadet from Saint-Cyr retorted triumphantly: "To save France!" (129).[23]

Maternal love and sacrifice unite the stories of the remaining three women, as Dulac's narrative shifts from hospitals, to occupied territories, and finally to a prisoner of war camp. The women replicate their maternal roles by discharging their nurses' duties with endless kindness and steadfast devotion, but without neglecting their own families. They care for German prisoners when required, despite the cruel and crude behavior of these soldiers. When tragedy strikes their personal lives, they rejoice that their husbands and sons died gloriously and immediately resume their responsibilities. Dulac's defense of volunteer nurses, however, goes beyond that of other novelists like Delorme Jules-Simon and Genevieve Duhamelet, in that she criticizes directly the male-dominated hierarchy of the hospital corps. When some nurses try to improve the rudimentary conditions of their unit, the military threatens them with dismissal. Dulac reiterates the unquestionable loyalty of French women in reporting that while the nurses became submissive out of necessity, at least there were no slackers among them (219–52).

Dulac rejoins her earlier theme of abortion and national population growth in relating in detail the stories of two of the characters. Madame Breton regrets her abortion for financial reasons, assuming that the child would have been a boy and that he would have been able to help his country in desperate need of soldiers. Dulac reinforces the importance of a single life to a nation at war by revealing that the woman's only other child was the dying soldier found by Madame Rhœa (141). Thus, in fact, two lives were lost, one on the front lines, and one through abortion.

Dulac continues Madame Breton's reeducation when a German unit occupies her home. The commander attempts to intimidate Madame Breton by lecturing her on the superior results of his country's population program that corresponded with the success of the German emperor's plan to incapacitate the French birthrate through fashion. After a somewhat absurd conversation between them relating the size of French and German women's breasts and hips to the number and quality of their children, the commander orders his men to rape Madame Breton while he watches (151–56). This scene not only reinforces the image of Germans as violent and sadistic, it also restates Dulac's theme of the importance of population to a nation. It demonstrates that the increase in German population growth that made German occupation of French territory possible, intensified the negative political impact of France's declining birthrate.

The Germans also rape the daughter of the gardener, and soon after both women realize that they are pregnant. The different reactions of the girl's parents illustrate the complex social position of such women, in addition to Dulac's sympathy for their plight. Accusing his daughter of complicity in her attack, the gardener threatens to kill the girl and the baby. The mother counters his stupefaction that the daughter did not commit suicide or die of shame by charging him with failing to protect the girl adequately. As Christmas approaches, both women give birth, and resisting the Germans' attempts to buy their babies, the young girl and the middle-aged matron comprehend and celebrate the many joys of motherhood (158–78). The symbolism of Christmas not only underscores the sanctity of maternity, it also reinforces the view of Germans as uncivilized and barbaric. Along with mocking the Christmas story, they also demonstrate their particular concept of the family unit in service to the nation by claiming the babies. The violence committed against women in France and Belgium and the subsequent attempt to send the children to Germany are in fact part of an organized effort to increase the German population at the expense of those other countries. In openly loving and caring for their children, the women illustrate Dulac's personal view of the primacy of French motherhood and its capacity to overcome the "stain" of German rape.[24]

The story of the medical student from the beginning of the novel confirms Dulac's view that the importance of motherhood supercedes all other possible occupations for women. Now a 39-year-old doctor, she narrowly escapes burning to death when the Germans attack her hospital. As she flees, a large and brutish German soldier rapes her. She awakens in a German prison camp with other hostages, and soon realizes that she is pregnant. At first the brutality and unnaturalness of the child's conception so revolt her that she nearly rejects him. However, when she sees how normal and perfect the child is, she realizes that as a mother she is part of a greater mission as a guardian of life, and that whether the child is conceived in love or savagery is irrelevant. Repeating the depiction of Germans as calculating and barbaric, the nurses attempt to gain control of the infant, for they consider him German or alternatively, a future threat to Germany if left with his mother. Moreover, the Protestant prison guard tortures the doctor and an old man when they, both Catholics, baptize the child (260–89), reinforcing the assumption that Germany's desire to destroy France is inseparable from its prejudice against Catholicism.

Eventually the doctor returns to Paris with her child. A famous feminist theorist before the war, she organizes a large conference so that she may address women whom Dulac deprecates as "superstars of feminism and arrogance" (297). Instead of elaborating her usual "mannish and revolutionary ideas," the doctor shocks her audience by turning to the question of "les petits indésirés," the unwanted children of rape. Her emotional speech to those mothers, the "pitiful debris of glory," urges them to keep and love their children. Moreover, she nullifies possible objections from their husbands by locating the source of the women's predicament in the men's failure to protect them adequately (303).

The doctor's long speech is an appropriate way for Dulac to end *La Houille rouge,* for it restates and summarizes all of its significant themes, notably, the importance of the quantity of people, or "the number," to the future of a nation, the malevolent designs of an industrialized Germany, and the restorative role that is every French woman's responsibility. Dulac reiterates her view that the decline in birthrate diminished the number of defenders for France and invited aggression from calculating and depraved barbarians. In this regard, the rapes become just punishment for women who aborted their future protectors. Moreover, she asserts that maternity is the sacred duty of French women and appeals to them to save their country through unlimited procreation. For her, repopulating France is an act of heroism and sacrifice, equal not only to that of the soldiers, but perhaps even rivaling that of Joan of Arc. Dulac underscores the nationalistic and Christian aspects of women's reproductive responsibility by associating it with the Maid of Orleans and with the punishment for original sin.

For too long, backstreet abortionists, abundant love, the stupidity of fashion, and now of war, have enfeebled our Race. . . . The Number alone can save our future. . . . I saw there [in Germany] the hostile Number swarming, I saw it marching past, arrogant and pompous, I saw the innumerable factory chimneys that vouch for the industry of that mob, and I implore you to save France. If a maid was necessary to rescue a King, it takes mothers to save a Republic. The men gave their blood, let us give our own. From now on, let the laughably virginal aunts and the mystically reserved sisters be condemned. No more hands folded over flat chests, no more arrogant, pudgy, and greedy moral values. Let all women bring forth children in pain, the way our heroes died in the trenches (303–04).[25]

The militaristic vocabulary of the speech reinforces the specific idea that women must produce the army of tomorrow. "[L]et us create the battalions of future epics!" (304)[26] It is significant that the horrible experiences that Dulac's characters undergo do not propel them toward a desire for peace, for that would perpetuate attitudes that contributed in the author's view to the initial outbreak of war. Rather, her characters seem exhilarated in their anticipation of future armed conflict, exemplified by the doctor's proposal of a new motto for French women, "gunpowder and milk." Dulac uses violence against women to punish them for the egotism of their previous inclinations, and additionally, to teach them the value and importance of the maternal role they had rejected. Moreover, rape is not merely a penalty for selfishness, but the children that result are also the means of the women's redemption. Religious and nationalistic allusions combine in *La Houille rouge* to present the view that women have a distinct, purely biological, and God-given purpose in their society. Dulac's novel discards firmly the prospect of individual choice and opportunity that the modern age had begun to reveal to women.

The war also corrects the sin of pride and the error of modern individualism in M. Maryan's *Un mariage en 1915* (A Marriage in 1915), published in 1916. Maryan was the pseudonym of Marie Cadiou Deschard (1847–1927), known especially for her novels written for girls, including *La Maison hantée* (The Haunted House), for which she won the Académie Française's Prix Montyon in 1912. A prolific writer, Maryan had published an incredible 52 novels before 1919, of which 32 were part of the series "Bibliothèque de ma fille; choix de romans pour jeunes filles," (My Daughter's Library; a selection of novels for girls). Many of these stories, serialized in various magazines, were in effect *Bildungsroman,* for they focused on the psychological development of the young woman and her efforts to remove obstacles to a successful future through marriage. What unites these novels, however, is the strength of character that propels the protagonists to make life decisions in serious circumstances, actions that determine, for good or ill, the rest of their lives (Chartier and Martin, 276). Of the five novels Maryan published between 1915 and 1919, only *Un mariage en 1915* takes place during the war.

The first few pages of Maryan's novel establish one of its major themes: the clash between traditional expectations for female conduct and the young women's desire to exercise the possibilities afforded by modern independence. Similar to Geneviève Duhamelet's *Les Inépousées* (The Unmarried Women), the novel begins during the summer of 1914 as two girls contemplate their future marriages, and Maryan's story, like Duhamelet's, discloses the impact of the war on these women who were reaching adulthood as the war began. Moreover, in Maryan's novel, like in those by Dulac, Delarue-Mardrus, and Reynès-Monlaur, it is the war that demonstrates to the protagonists the emptiness of twentieth-century values, and confirms instead the worth of traditional moral principles such as service, duty, patriotism, and Christianity. To avoid losing their liberty, the girls in Maryan's novel imagine remaining single or marrying a man rich enough to have servants care for their children. Both conclude that it will be necessary to teach their husbands to respect their freedom, noting that as girls of the twentieth century, they are very independent (2–11).

Anet Raubert is the main character, the only child of a scholar-inventor and a pious mother who died young. Entrusted to her rich, society aunt, Anet has grown to be spoiled, idle, and bored, exemplifying perfectly the Parisian "luxury doll" denounced in contemporary commentary and fiction. For Anet, the world consists of two categories, one containing the men who are marriageable, and one for those who are not. She spends her days in social calls, parties, sessions with her dressmaker, and taking drawing lessons. Although she rarely sees her father, who lives alone and is totally absorbed by his scientific work, Anet exhibits a real affection for him and tries to improve their relationship. During a visit, Anet defends her frivolous and self-absorbed existence, even as she realizes how her mother devoted herself to charity and religion. As in other novels studied here, the absence of the birth-mother both causes and explains a daughter's independent nature, whether that freedom leads to virtuous deeds, as in Lya Berger's "Myrtille," or disreputable conduct, as in Mayran's *Gotton Connixloo*. In *Un mariage en 1915,* the memory of her mother is a powerful influence on Anet, causing her to begin to examine more closely her own activities. While Anet neither reads nor attends church because of lack of time and refuses to visit the sick or the poor for fear of germs, she does acknowledge that her life is shallow and would have been substantially different had her mother lived (16–18). Anet's initial reeducation has begun.

During a visit, Anet's father comments that her mother was "truly a French woman," alluding to another aspect of his daughter's attitude that will change in the course of the novel. Their conversation reiterates many of the anti-German ideas common to French women's war fiction, including denunciation of Protestantism, of Nietzschean philosophy, and the merging of science and industry. It also confirms the view that French pacifists and internationalists were naive and misinformed. Anet admires the intelligence of Germans and does not understand how French people could still wish for revenge so many years after the Franco-Prussian War.

The father, who had fled Alsace as a young boy, considers aggression as the cause of Germany's transformation to a nation ruled by pride and disobedience and denatured by the criminal notion of force imposing itself on law. He regrets that Anet is following the current fad among young people who appreciate German accomplishments and fail to recognize in these deeds an unhealthy appetite and a depraved ambition. Moreover, he fears the German predilection for blending modern scientific discoveries with corrupt business practices, citing the theft of one of his own inventions by a German pretending to be Alsatian. Anet counters with the belief that the destructive capacity of modern weapons is a deterrent, rather than an enticement for war (11–14).

When Anet meets Fabien, a young officer from Lorraine, he tells her about his ancestral home, his family's long history, and the famous hidden sword he tried to find before his parents sold the property to a man named Raubert (28). The coincidence of her father as the owner allows Anet to visit the estate, whose serenity and beauty advance slightly the progress of her self-awareness. While enchanted by the young officer and his fanciful story of lost treasure, she is also attentive to his family's impoverished financial state, and seems to prefer another man, whose rich mother is German. She realizes sadly that there are in fact two girls inside her. One is romantic and susceptible to the cozy informality of the countryside, while another is completely modern and hates silence, a restricted life, and the limits imposed by lack of money (104). Although Anet adapts well to country life, even learning piety, economy, and charity from a young nun, she also knows that she is not willing to relinquish the luxury of her Parisian lifestyle (116). Her honesty in refusing his marriage proposal astonishes Fabien, who is incredulous that a woman not yet 20 years old could be so harsh and calculating. He realizes that her obvious affection for him will yield to the other man's wealth. In a parting speech, he declares that her attitude has destroyed his ideal of French womanhood, and that he hopes to die in the war that appears imminent. The idea that soldiers need the support of women in order to defend France is an important issue to which Maryan will return. Fabien's statement dumbfounds Anet and prods her self-reflection. She finally admits to her father that she does not know herself well, but that she is aware that she does not resemble her mother or any other courageous or devoted woman (133–36).

The beginning of the war brings unfamiliar surges of national loyalty and religious faith that complete Anet's transformation. "[T]he France for which she had had so little regard, that she did not know how to love . . . suddenly took possession of her soul with a painful violence" (159).[27] Repulsed by her future mother-in-law's Germanic features and behavior, as well as her fiancé's unwillingness to enlist in the French army, she breaks her engagement. Her father rejoices that underneath "the little light-headed Parisian" was a true daughter of Alsace after all, with a real French woman's heart (159–62; 177). Maryan synthesizes patriotism, Christianity, revenge, and allusions to France's past as Anet's fears for her fellow citizens propel her to repair the estate's chapel. Inspired by a visit to Domrémy, the birthplace of Joan of Arc, Anet installs a statue of Mary bearing the Cross of Lorraine. Thus Anet's metamorphosis transcends the personal sphere of her individual life to encompass the larger environment of her country's Catholic identity, its victory over an ancient oppressor, and the hope to reclaim the provinces lost in 1870. Moreover, the delineation of Mary as the ultimate maternal figure provides a role model as well as a surrogate for the motherless Anet. Finally, in characterizing the young woman's awakening as representative of a major movement taking place throughout the country, Maryan demonstrates the unity of the French people and refutes suggestions of any irresolution.

> The church bells sounding the alarm, sounding the call to duty, have caused the real France to arise, a warlike France, a devout France which, recognizing itself tomorrow in the presence of its rediscovered beauty, will be overcome with pride and joy . . . (177).[28]

Nonetheless, awareness of one's obligations is insufficient by itself, and the tocsin in French women's war fiction always leads to action for women as well as men. In portraying the responses of Anet and her father, Maryan, like other authors, demonstrates the ennobling and transcendent power of the war in images that fuse religion and patriotism. For Maryan, as for Reynès-Monlaur, the present conflict is a holy war, because to be French is also to be Catholic and therefore, to perish in defense of France is a death sanctified by God (239). Before leaving to fight for his beloved Alsace, the now-rejuvenated father gives permission to Anet to turn the estate into a hospital. The two pray together, and the narrator notes that at the moment Anet gave herself over to her sacred duty, a selfless prayer came from her heart (181–84). Everyone, including Anet, recognizes the admirable effect of the "lightning bolt" of war on the young woman, winning for her a long-sought but previously elusive approval (183). The laudatory comments of Sœur Marguerite, the young nun, attest to the extent of Anet's transformation and also make clear the correct responsibility of all such women.

> You are no longer the young, bored, and trivial Parisian woman whom I saw arrive so little time ago, not looking for anything in life but its pleasure. The

great blow that is going to strike us all has made arise a woman eager for devotion . . . (199).[29]

The effect of the war is so comprehensive, that even Anet's socialite aunt renounces her frivolous activities and volunteers for kitchen duty at Anet's hospital. She had not only disapproved of Anet's project, but even more selfishly had opposed her own husband's enlistment in the army. At the time, she could not understand why he had abandoned the safety of his diplomatic post, and she had misunderstood his departure as a sign of a loss of affection for her. His request that she donate her time to Anet's infirmary so as to be worthy of him as a soldier, places the pampered patrician in a work environment for the first time in her life. There her observation of the dedication of the attendants and of the importance of their accomplishments gradually reveals to her the magnitude of her country's need. She feels remorse for having opposed her husband's decision, and worries that her lack of patriotism will affect his love for her (214–16; 249). Maryan here reiterates her emphasis on the soldiers' need for women's moral support, and moreover, concurs with such historians of the mobilization of women as Hortense Cloquié and Marguerite Borel (Camille Marbo) on the positive consequences of work in women's lives.[30]

The denouement of the novel affirms Anet's total transformation through an act of heroism that also serves to prove her worthy of Fabien. The Germans bomb the hospital in defiance of its Red Cross, and Anet receives facial wounds while trying to save a soldier. Although she wonders if Fabien would still love her and worries that she might prove a burden to him, news that Fabien has lost a foot does not elicit the same uneasiness for her own future life. Like the women protagonists in the books by Isabelle Sandy, Colette Yver, and Andrée Mars, Maryan's Anet willingly and proudly accepts the permanently disabled soldier as her prospective husband. Moreover, in all of these novels, the soldier resists the idea of being dependent on his wife and nearly rejects his fiancée, but in Maryan's book, Anet's wounds make her Fabien's equal. While Fabien has vowed to keep his love for Anet hidden, her injury changes his mind. Anet, learning his secret, and explaining that the world is now upside down, employs this "lapse" of tradition to rush to his bedside to ask him, submissively, if she may become his wife. Both receive the *croix de guerre* and plan to marry the following spring, that is, in 1915. The last line formalizes Anet's separation from her previous "completely modern" side and eliminates her desire to exercise her independence. Anet's miraculous transformation from "luxury doll" to an exemplar of conventional French womanhood signals her recognition of the superiority of the time-honored and community-directed values of abnegation, patriotism, and spirituality. Her smile communicates not just the joy of sacrifice, but a total submission of the self. "For apparent there is not only the affection of a woman in love, it is the faith of a Christian and the strength of a French woman" (304).[31]

Mary Floran's first war novel, *L'Ennemi* (The Enemy), published in 1916, also portrays the war's reeducation of a modern and independent young woman. It begins during the summer of 1914, when Odile, the youngest daughter of an upper-class family, seriously flouts social convention by agreeing to marry a German diplomat against her widowed mother's wishes (33–35). She rejects nationalism and ideas of revenge against Germany as antiquated and irrelevant. By the time the war begins, however, Odile has begun to worry about Otto's domineering and stereotypically Nietzschean-inflected German disposition that surpasses the limits of propriety, including suggestions of potential violence (73–76; 90–91). Nationalistic to the point of absurdity, Otto welcomes the prospect of war with France as appropriate to Germany's ascendancy as a world power and France's concomitant decline (98–110). He is outraged by Odile's proposition that they avoid the war that will separate them by eloping to a neutral country. Abruptly, Odile realizes that Otto will become an enemy not only of France, but also of her family and friends (114–55). Now acutely aware of the importance of duty and sacrifice to every French person, Odile breaks off her engagement with Otto and, considering herself the widow of a lost love, retires to the country to expiate her grief through acts of charity (183–94).

Odile and her mother flee an advancing German battalion and narrowly miss being murdered by the former fiancé, who destroys their château and the surrounding village in an extravagant display of gratuitous violence and murder, including real and symbolic rape (205–34). Safe in Normandy, Odile becomes an excellent volunteer nurse and one day encounters the wounded Otto, who tries to convince her that he will renounce his family and nationality for her. Odile refuses but recognizes that she still loves him. It is not until she overhears him bragging about the violence and murder he committed in her own village that she totally rejects him. Despite Odile's vow to remain celibate and dedicate her life to nursing, her mother happily anticipates a future marriage with a Frenchman worthy of her daughter (249–322).

In creating the story of Odile and Otto, Floran unites the personal and the public to convey specific social and political themes. Similar to the novels by Dulac, Reynès-Monlaur, and Maryan, *L'Ennemi* demonstrates the negative consequences that result from a departure from traditional values. Odile is a passionate and intensely independent young woman who defies the conventions of her upper-class society by refusing all possible suitors as boring and even hinting that she may choose to remain single. Floran contextualizes

Odile's insistence on her right to determine her own destiny, culminating in her betrothal without her mother's consent, as part of the "winds of independence, blowing from America" that have changed courtship practices forever (20–21). By showing Odile's behavior to be naive to the point of recklessness, Floran underscores the worth of the prudent and sensible guidance of her mother, who tries to accommodate her daughter's desire for autonomy while preserving her own sense of the proper role of women in family and society. Reminding both Odile and Otto that a woman's intellectual satisfaction is realized as the true companion and aide to her husband, Madame d'Averjean repudiates both the American notion of women's autonomy and the German insistence on female subservience. For her, the time-honored French relationship between spouses is an ideal partnership that enriches women's lives and increases the possibilities for the development of their characters and intelligence (72–74). Her rejection of Otto as a potential husband for Odile, with his insistence on *Kirche, Kinder, Küche,* is based not only on the past and the defeat of France in 1870, but also on anxiety concerning her daughter's future life. Thus Floran's critique of the modern effort for women's self-determination does not discard its underlying values, but demonstrates instead that traditional family alliances afford the best way to achieve those goals.

Floran carefully relates Otto's increasingly aggressive behavior to a stereotypically German predilection for dominance and brutality. She gives prominence to his belief that the coming war would be the inevitable expression of his nation's determination to realize its power (90–142). Odile seems unaware of this side of Otto, and she ends their relationship only because he decides to return to his regiment in Germany, rather than elope with her to a neutral country. In choosing duty to his country over his love for her, Otto validates his public over his private self. It is a patriotic sacrifice that Odile emulates, and yielding to the same love of country, she defines her decision to break their engagement as an act of heroism equal to that of a soldier on the battlefield.

> She would remain a widow of that dead love all of her life, being forced to hide even her grief for its loss, and the pain that she felt was so great and so profound that she compared herself to a martyr for the Homeland!
>
> This thought sustained her spirit somewhat by elevating her resolution to [the level of] heroism. To choose between her love and France, France, seemed to her a brilliant act like that which, soon perhaps, would distinguish our soldiers on the field of battle, and she consented to it with exhilaration (156).[32]

Yet any woman in France could have voiced these patriotic sentiments, and Odile's sacrifice, other than being denied the solace afforded by public recognition, is no different for her than if Otto had been French. While she yields to what she calls her "national duty," Odile's decision to remain true to her love for him stems from her perception of their mutual obligation to a superior value. It preserves her respect for him as an individual, allowing her to reject the judgment of her family that the war had provided a benefit in separating her from Otto. Odile does not identify Otto with his country's political aims, despite his extreme nationalism and his contempt of France as weak and irresolute. Similar to Reynès-Monlaur and Maryan in their novels, Floran, both here and in *On demande une marraine,* criticizes the young generation in France for their prewar admiration of Germany and German intellectualism. Further, she implicates this attitude as a contributing factor in the German decision to wage war against France. Consequently, the events of the second half of the book serve to destroy both Odile's love for Otto and her esteem for Germany by showing him actively engaged in acts of brutality and sadistic barbarism. Floran presents his deeds as the natural outgrowth of "the brutality of his race," solidified by an absolute obedience that denied the existence of free will.

> Protected against all personal disgust by this training, barbarous in its concept and realization, Otto consented to the most degrading tasks without misgivings. They saw him give orders for executions that were virtual assassinations. Conflagrations were ignited by his command, and he tolerated, before his indulgent eyes, orgies that the pen refuses to describe (209).[33]

Nonetheless, these acts of violence, while egregious, are committed under Otto's command and not by him directly, and thus it might still be possible for Odile to rationalize his participation as an officer and maintain her love for him. It is not until Odile hears Otto's boasts about personally setting fire to her family's château and its village, as well as his cold-blooded murder of her household employees, that she finally renounces her love for him. His drunken profanation of her bedroom, in addition to less symbolic rapes of young village women, portray him, not as an officer doing his duty during a war, but as a thoroughly degenerate brute. Floran leaves no doubt that such acts of gratuitous violence might be individual aberrations, and she emphasizes their connection with German ancestry and education. Moreover, she underscores this condemnation of the German nation by contrasting their acts of barbarism with French compassion and mercy, attributes derived from a dual Gallic-Christian heritage (224–42).

It is this uniquely French tradition of patriotic duty and Christian devotion that transforms Odile from "selfish independence" to "the most dedicated of all nurses" (33; 252). Floran's careful description of Odile, as a beautiful woman with a nun's soul who loves her patients as her own children, insulates her against any accusations of impropriety (253–55). Further, it establishes the legitimacy of Odile's decision to dedicate the rest of her life to the care of the sick, associating it with the principles of Catholic spirituality and Republican Motherhood. While Odile reiterates her independence by choosing to remain celibate, she will nonetheless discharge her maternal duties to her nation by easing the suffering of her "children" and bringing their souls to God. Thus, the experience of war did not extinguish the principle of autonomy and self-direction so vital to Odile at the beginning of the story. Rather, the war afforded knowledge that caused Odile to redirect these ideals from self-centered aims to altruistic objectives that would benefit the community as a whole.

While Floran leaves the notion of women's right to self-determination intact, such is not the case in a three-part story published by Lucie Delarue-Mardrus. Serialized in the *New York Tribune* from 1916–1918 and later published in the anthology, *Tales of Wartime France,* the narrative "The Godmother" recounts the life of Géo, a 28-year-old artist. She had married at a young age to escape her family, but quickly divorced her husband to pursue a career as a painter. Dropping both her family and married names, she asserted her independence by symbolically recreating herself as "Géo." Although she felt that she was a painter of genius, she nonetheless had had no success in the five years before the war began (97–100). With the debut of hostilities, she suddenly realizes that "she has no talent and had been living in a world of self-deception" (100). Too delicate for hospital work, Géo directs her energies instead to providing soldiers with *marraines,* and she also writes and send packages to several soldiers herself. Her efforts to find Charles, her ex-husband stationed at the front, prove futile. One day she opens a letter from a soldier requesting a godmother and, in amazement, realizes that the correspondent is Charles. They begin to exchange letters regularly, but Géo disguises her identity so as not to jeopardize the consolation and relief such a relationship would afford him.

The second installment of Delarue-Mardrus's story presents Charles's ideas on the relationship between husbands and wives, the female "nature," and the "proper" conduct of modern women. The view of marriage that Delarue-Mardrus presents, similar to the image of the "angel in the house" common in British and American fiction since the nineteenth century, also replicates the representation of marriage in many of the novels studied here. Eminently spiritual, almost incorporeal, the wife brings order to her home and comfort to her husband, weary from the pressures of the outside world. Above all, she accomplishes these monumental tasks indirectly so as not to reveal the strength of her authority over him. For Charles, a woman's soul, completely different from a man's, is its counterpart and sounding board.

While I, the positive element, earn outside the means to maintain the domestic establishment, I want her, the negative element, to be the mysterious spirit of the home, that spirit through which the miracle of daily life is accomplished—the miracle of order and direction in the household. All my being, absorbed in work without, counts on her for repose of that interior, made miraculous by her presence. In hours of difficulty I expect from her, also, good advice, rather murmured than spoken, which, once again outside, I shall follow without realizing too much the influence on my life which my wife, that priestless-like authority, exercises (105–06).

The letter format of the story lends a sermon-like quality to Charles's pronouncements, which refer to his own experience to decry women's ambition and independence, born of "the bold laugh—the Nietzschean laugh—of the epoch" (99). Yet Delarue-Mardrus does not present his criticism of modern ideas as an example of male selfishness or egocentrism, but rather as the correct assessment of what women lose in their attempt to gain autonomy. For her, the attempt to construct one's life according to personal goals and ideas can never lead to happiness. Delarue-Mardrus is careful to point out that only traditional, wholly French, marriages can bring about the fulfillment of both partners, and she portrays Géo as a victim of the German-initiated prewar aspiration for self-realization. Described in several places as a failed mother with an empty heart, Géo finds child substitutes in eccentricities, including the makeup that transforms her into a doll (97; 104).

Thus Charles's advice on the education of girls, in insisting on the primacy of domestic skills and coquetry, seeks to redress a perceived imbalance in the relationship between women and men. It is a disparity made clear by the stark reality of the war and the resulting necessity to reinforce the social fabric of the nation. Charles can accept feminism as long as it trains women to be more pleasingly intelligent companions for men, and he condemns all efforts at self-realization as attempts to appropriate male prerogative.

Women, women, while we, the fighters at the front, are eminently men, you must be eminently women in order to re-establish the equilibrium. Don't be trivial and frivolous, as my wife was; cultivated to the point of aridity, restless, self-assertive, a sort of men in miniature, creatures in transition whom their own logic would lead to grow moustaches. I know well that there is a thing called feminism; and I have no quarrel with it. It is a necessity; that's all there is about it. And, certainly, I would permit women to be [feminists] as long as they care to be on wit and intelligence. But let them not cut their hair short! (107)

The conclusion of the story, contained in the final episode "The Red Rose," endorses this denunciation of women's efforts to achieve autonomy. Ashamed at how she had so thoroughly misunderstood Charles, Géo now hopes to win him back as her husband. Although they had agreed not to meet, the need Charles feels as a soldier in the trenches for a woman's support and her own regret cause Géo to agree to his request to see him during a leave. Terrified that her months of effort to win him back will not succeed, Géo lowers her head and remains silent as she sees him coming toward her at the train station. The red rose that identifies her as the secret correspondent drops "its petals on their four hands—softly, as if to fill their future with fragrance" as Charles grasps Géo's wrists (114). The anger and the hint of violence in Charles's gesture noted by the narrator marks his acceptance of her submission to him and announces the reappropriation of his legal authority as her husband.

As in the novels and stories by Marie Reynès-Monlaur, Mary Floran, Camille Mayran, Lya Berger, Odette Dulac, and M. Maryan, the war causes Delarue-Mardrus's woman protagonist to understand the fundamental error in insisting on the freedom to construct her own life. All of these narratives demonstrate the shallowness of such autonomy and the modern values that sustain it when compared with the historic richness of traditional family relationships. Moreover, in suggesting that the Germans sought the destruction of France through the corruption of its family structure, the authors designate the preservation of the family as an important objective in the war. While defense of the home and all it represents is generally invoked as a reason for men to engage in armed conflict, these authors concentrate on the capacity of women to endanger, as well as preserve, the social order.

Chapter Five

Sex, Slackers, and Civilians

The vast majority of French women's war narratives concentrate on the sad realities of war and the resulting changes in people's lives. The female protagonists, although civilians, participate as much as possible in the war effort, and consequently, these characters are faced with unfamiliar situations, problems, and obstacles. The emotional losses and physical deprivation they endure disclose or cause to develop their nobility of spirit, and the women emerge from their experience of war with a heightened sense of virtues traditionally ascribed to the feminine, such as self-abnegation and sacrifice. The seriousness and elevated moral tone of this didactic idealism, however, are absent from the multiple war-era works of two high profile and prolific authors, Gyp and Jeanne Landre. Both of these authors concentrate on the weaknesses and failings of women civilians especially, using satire and irony to scrutinize and deride behavior they consider selfish, ridiculous, and even traitorous.

Gyp (1849–1932), the pseudonym of Sibylle-Gabrielle Marie-Antoinette de Riquetti de Mirabeau, Comtesse de Martel de Janville, was the infamous and indefatigable author of a vast *œuvre* that included more than 100 novels, numerous plays, articles, and volumes of memoirs. Known especially for her anti-Semitic novels and her acerbic caricatures of bourgeois society, Gyp published four dialogue-novels between 1916 and 1918 that indict in particular women's attitudes and activities.[1] All four, *Ceux de la "Nuque,"* (Those of the "Rear")[2], 1916, *Les Flanchards* (The Quitters), 1917, *Les Profitards* (The Profiteers), 1918, and *Ceux qui s'en f. . . ..* (Those Who Don't Give a D. . . .), 1918, share the similar setting of Parisian upper middle-class society during the war, and several of the characters reappear. Although Gyp debunks in these novels the schemes of men who evade military service as well as the projects of others seeking financial gain from the war, she castigates men only for obvious and undisputed transgressions. Women, however, are the

targets of Gyp's corrosive assault, whether they are society matrons who ignore the war or patriotic women who volunteer as nurses. The only female
characters to earn Gyp's esteem in the four novels are conservative young
women planning to wed disabled soldiers.

Ceux de la "Nuque" was the first of these dialogue-novels, and it introduces several themes and characters that will follow in the other volumes.
Here Gyp articulates unequivocally the public criticism of volunteer
nurses that continued to trouble women throughout the war. Whereas
novelists such as Geneviève Duhamelet and J. Delorme Jules-Simon recount their own experiences in a determined defense of nurses, Gyp's novels thoroughly endorse the rumors and suppositions that vanity, sexual
appetite, and husband-hunting, not patriotism or devotion, motivated the
volunteers. In *Ceux de la "Nuque,"* a male doctor vents his frustration with
the volunteers, complaining of their failure to respect hospital hierarchy in
order to inflate their visibility and importance. He portrays them as thrill-
seeking braggarts, refusing to execute tasks they judge inferior in favor of
more aggrandizing activities, such as performing operations, for which
they are obviously not qualified. As in similar comments by other characters, he emphasizes the attraction that physical sensation, especially odor,
has for the women (55–56; *Ceux qui s'en f. . .* , 178–84). "They're very
charming, my nurses, very stylish . . . but they'd always want to splash
about in the blood and breathe in the gangrene. . . . It seems like that's
their aspiration!" (*"Nuque,"* 25).[3]

Moreover, Gyp goes beyond these hackneyed allegations in her novels
to postulate the danger that such women pose to the survival of the French
family. The freedom and corporeality of the hospital render women "unfit"
as wives and mothers, either because they refuse to resume their prewar
lives, or because men will reject them as despoiled and impure. In *Les Flanchards,* a poet laments her forced return to the mundane life of caring for
her husband and children after enjoying the freedom of the hospital environment, and then bids farewell to her home: "It's wanting too much from
an Emancipated Soul / Who has savored a multi-faceted vista" (231).[4] In
Ceux de la "Nuque," a character bemoans the fate of his sister's niece, a 22-
year-old volunteer nurse, who intends to eschew her family responsibilities in order to remain in public life at the hospital when the war is over
(56). Another character thinks that only single women without children
should be allowed to volunteer, in order to stop the married women from
walking out on their husbands and children and running to the wounded
like "lunatics" (174). A third character recites a poem in praise of the soldiers at Verdun, in which she describes the erotic energy released by their
death and dying. The jocularity of such a contention that women might
be so aroused that they would abandon their husbands and children does

not obscure the extent of the author's contempt. At the end of the long poem, the intensity of their stimulation leads the women to yearn for a means to show their total devotion to the soldiers, even to the point of their own debasement.

> . . . Man of Verdun, do you wish the French woman
> To leave for your side, singing the *Marseillaise?*
> Or to lie down flat on the ground, so that all of your steps
> Might become embedded in her flesh, from top to bottom? (57)[5]

Gyp further impugns women's morality and motivations for war work in a section of *Ceux qui s'en f. . . .,* where a wounded soldier on leave engages in a long dispute with his two sisters. The young women's ineptitude occasioned their release from nursing duties, as well as the accusation of insincerity. While other characters in the story admit that the work of the Red Cross is important, they reiterate the view that it is an improper undertaking for women, except for the very pious and those older women who are unmarried or widowed. Accordingly, the brother considers his sisters frivolous and conniving, who delight in their appearance in the alluring nurse's uniform and anticipate the possibility of a flirtation.[6] His particularly harsh criticism of Vava (meaning "go, go"), "[a]s for your devotion, you'll trample your family and your country for a tango or an outfit" (179),[7] extends to her friends at the hospital, all of whom he considers to have learned too much of the world (184). Gyp here extends her denunciation of nurses to attack the modern tendency of women's increased autonomy by suggesting that such women are unchaste and therefore unmarriageable. The brother considers that only modern women like his sister could engage in work that so obviously deprives a woman of her "downy softness and maidenly freshness" (187). He feels that in a moral sense Vava has lost her virginity by caring for wounded soldiers and seeing their naked bodies. This is a view shared by a friend who affirms that he would never marry a former war nurse since her knowledge of male anatomy would make him uneasy (187–90). While these ideas are certainly humorous, Gyp characterizes their proponents with an earnestness that sanctions the underlying beliefs of these views. Chastity, whether literal or figurative, denotes the acceptance of a code that denies or controls women's sexuality, forming and maintaining the basis of the traditional family unit. With knowledge and the experience of self-direction, a woman might be able to exercise control over her own body, therefore compromising her husband's authority and power in the family. Thus the hospital becomes, in Gyp's novels, not only a school for vanity and licentiousness, but the nursery for ideas that will eventually destroy the traditional structure of the French family.

Gyp portrays in the four novels the insensitivity of society women whose constant whining about the inconvenience of the war is sharply funny. While some complain that the war is ruining their dinner parties and the quality of their pastries, others discourage discussing the war by assessing a fine each time someone mentions it. Although an occasional disabled soldier or grieving father enters the scene to proclaim patriotic and noble sentiments, the women remain unmoved. One woman counters an impassioned speech about the necessity of securing the future of France through total victory and the soldiers' enthusiasm for fighting and dying well, with the assertion that living well is more difficult (*Les Flanchards,* 62).

In *Les Flanchards,* Gyp also mocks two parents whose attempts to keep their son Edgar from going to the front are ludicrously extreme.[8] The selfishness and hypocrisy behind the entire family's spectacular efforts to help Edgar avoid military service bring into focus Gyp's view of sacrifice and devotion. While the parents of Liette know that Edgar is a shirker and an idiot, they nonetheless find him a suitable husband for their daughter because of his family's wealth. Liette, however, has already demonstrated the extent of her loyalty and passion for the genuine defenders of France. In a conversation with her grandmother, she vows to marry only a former soldier, preferring someone with "some missing part" so as to be certain of his tenure "under fire." In keeping with Gyp's rejection of the increasing autonomy for women in modern life, the grandmother notes sadly the rarity of young women like Liette, an old-fashioned girl who is neither bluestocking, nor student, nor surgeon (97–98). Liette's subsequent actions, while predictably traditional, nonetheless suggest the influence of her time. She rejects Edgar and decides on her own that she will marry Jacques, who, despite an amputated leg, has returned to the front as a fighter pilot. Although it is clear that Jacques is not opposed to the idea, it is nonetheless Liette who takes the initiative and announces their engagement publicly, seemingly without consulting him. A quip that she is too bold engenders a retort from a male character that in fact Liette epitomizes the young French woman of 1916. Gyp here joins other authors such as Démians d'Archimbaud and Broussan-Gaubert in accepting autonomy for women, but only when it serves the continued stability of family and country.

Gyp spends considerable time lampooning civilians who profit from the war. In *Les Profitards,* an alliance of business executives and politicians connive to cheat the government and each other out of enormous sums of money. Their rapacity is so absolute that they ignore the possible negative impact of their intrigue on the French soldiers' state of health. Their scheme involves the circulation of false rumors of peace to manipulate the price of their stock of "compressed lamb tablets," food that the conspirators gleefully hint is of dubious origin and quality (195).

Gyp also mocks other types of profiteering, where fame and respect are the goals, instead of money. In *Ceux qui s'en f. . . .*, a socialite and hack writer sets out to win a prestigious literary prize. However, since the award committee has ruled that the honor will go to a writer killed, wounded, or adversely affected by the war, the woman attempts to convince the jury that her stint as an ambulance nurse damaged her mental health.[9] Moreover, Gyp's sarcasm pinpoints another problem, evoked more compassionately by diverse writers in this study. Tuberculosis and other infectious diseases were a grave threat to the soldiers' lives, yet these men were sadly aware that death from these causes would not elicit for them the same level of heroic praise that they might have earned had they died in battle. Risette in *Ceux de la "Nuque"* ignores her husband's death from sunstroke, because she does not consider it heroic. Refusing to wear mourning clothes, she immediately sets out to remarry and encourages the attention of a man who is an obvious *embusqué* (war slacker) and may even be a German spy. Although the man has been "recovering" for nearly two years from what turns out to be a mere scratch, Risette admits that it was the appearance of his wound that attracted her (144). Thus Risette accepts a fake wound as heroic, because its physical manifestation can achieve for her the reflected glory that death from disease could not. As evidenced many times throughout this study, women evaluate their own worth according to the accomplishments of the men in their lives. This attitude is so extensive that even an active nurse such as Janine in Delorme Jules-Simon's *Âmes de guerre, âmes d'amour* is blind to the value of her own deeds because she has no soldier in her life. It is a significant indicator of these authors' estimation of the personal importance of their women characters that such appropriation of another's identity is never recognized as a profound denial of the self.

In three novels published between 1916 and 1918, Jeanne Landre also mocks civilians who seek personal recognition and pleasure. Like Gyp, Landre (1874–1936) gained notoriety for her prolific as well as acerbic pen, especially in the years before the war. She published dozens of novels, biographies, short stories, and literary and art criticism in newspapers and periodicals, all of which demonstrated her sharp wit and astute ability to dissect the intricate hypocrisies of French bourgeois society. She also earned the sobriquet "romancière (novelist) de Montmartre" for her short stories and biographies of that artistic district and its performers, including Jehan Rictus and Aristide Bruant. Official and established honors affirm her prominent place and acceptance in formal French literary circles. Named an Officier de l'Instruction Publique and a Chevalier in the Légion d'Honneur, Landre was also the principal founder of the Ligue des Femmes des Professions Libérales, vice-president of the Société des Gens

de Lettres, and member of the Comité de la Presse Artistique and the So-
ciété de la Critique Littéraire. Novels like *Les Pierres du Chemin* (The
Stones of the Road), 1900, *Madame Poche ou la Parfaite Éducatrice* (Madame
Poche or the Perfect Teacher), 1919, and *Le Débardeur lettré* (The Learned
Stevedore), 1921 earned for her a steady and faithful readership.[10]

Among Landre's other writing of the war period, three novels, . . . *puis il
mourut* (. . .then he died), 1916, *L'École des marraines* (The School for Godmothers), 1917, and *Loin des balles, mémoires d'un philanthrope* (Far from the
Bullets, Memoirs of a Philanthropist), 1918, disclose the egotism and self-
delusion that characterize for the author a variety of wartime activities and
attitudes. As in Gyp's dialogue-novels, Landre's narratives make use of sarcasm
and buffoonery to lay bare the pretense of virtue that she felt concealed
more selfish motives among both women and men, soldiers as well as civilians. In Landre's novels, sincere altruism, the purported goal of the civilian
war effort, is rare indeed, and good works are undertaken in the hope that
they might generate some gain for the benefactor. Further, despite the differences in their story lines and characters, the three books meditate on the
capacity of correspondence between strangers to provide a fictional space to
satisfy a wartime need for illusion. Creation of an imaginary and ideal self
through letter writing in Landre's novels alleviates the loneliness, deprivation, and boredom encountered by soldier and civilian alike.

The main character of *Loin des balles* is an independently wealthy middle-
aged man, Cyprien Piramy, whose last name, a homonym for "worst friend,"
predicts the personal disappointment he will experience as a consequence of
his activities in the novel. Cyprien decides to sponsor several charitable organizations in the hope of winning a commendation from the Légion
d'Honneur after the war, and records his memoirs in anticipation of such an
official recognition. He recounts in minute detail his early life, his moral
views, and his physical, emotional, and financial states, all of which communicate to the (eventual) reader the profound degree of self-satisfaction Cyprien derives from his life. He is particularly proud of his guileless integrity
and unimpeachable morals, a smugness that makes him equally blind to the
egotism of his own and others' motives (7–29).

Searching for a means to gain notoriety through a charitable activity,
Cyprien discovers a previously overlooked group certain to welcome his
aid, women writers.[11] In founding "Le Bifteck des Muses" (The Muses'
Steak) Cyprien hopes that, rescued from starvation, one of the writers will
one day win a prestigious literary prize that will also bring him the ribbon
of the Légion d'Honneur. However, he soon learns that some of these
writers have a problem different from that which he imagined. Since men
worship them, but also regard them as unattainable, the women writers are
both the beneficiaries and victims of their superior intelligence. Being un-

married, they could not contribute to the national effort to increase the birthrate, and accordingly, they responded eagerly when the government asked women to write to soldiers. However, they became victims of their own eloquence as their genius, combined with loneliness and free postage, led to "intellectual" flirtations and eventually, love affairs and pregnancies when the soldiers returned on leave. Cyprien agrees to establish "Aide aux Marraines-Filles-Mères" (Assistance for Unwed Godmothers), not out of compassion for the writers, but because he is certain that the French government would eventually reward his participation in such a pronatalist project. Landre's description of the group and its members skillfully lampoons the literary establishment, the fanatical disciples of repopulation, and war novelists like herself. In describing the women's increasing intoxication with writing letters to an ever-greater number of *filleuls,* Landre notes the inherent freedom in such a correspondence to create a persona.

> There is not a corner of our emotions that we did not use to benefit the combatants. A husband could live with us for years without getting to know us as deeply as did our unknown friends (42).[12]

Like Delorme Jules-Simon, Landre records the excessive emotions and sexual license engendered by the environment of war and also excuses the behavior of the soldiers. Pushed by abstinence and loneliness to accept the women's advances, the soldiers become increasingly bold, and the women, worried that they might lose the *filleul*'s interest, heighten further the level of familiarity by adding pieces of clothing and locks of hair (136–38). Landre stigmatizes the women's actions as a calculated attempt to overturn the men's common sense and ultimately control them. She explores this escalating intimacy and resulting obsession more closely in . . . *puis il mourut,* where the woman's stockings and other apparel become erotic amulets for the soldier. Nonetheless, Landre softens her overall negative judgment by intimating that a feeling of inutility and the desire to be more directly involved in the war motivates these women. In both *L'École des marraines* and . . . *puis il mourut,* several characters decry the laws that prohibit women from serving in the army, and they express the intense desire to be afraid for someone, indicating their need to close the gap that separates them from the war. In *Loin des balles,* however, such women go beyond taking a place next to the soldiers to assume their identity and devour their essence. Their identification as "malicious fairies" and mythical beasts accentuates the fictive and imaginary qualities of their relationships with the men.

> That's him, from then on the prisoner of his illusion, clutched by the claws of the monster. He is no longer Him, he is Her. It is she who wages war, it

is with her, for her, by her that he obeys, that he throws his grenade, that he charges with his bayonet. If she quits, he is lost (137).[13]

Landre judges less harshly the young working-class women who become pregnant, reserving for them the opportunity to voice the seriousness of the problem of single mothers. These women recognize, yet seem powerless to end, their many-sided exploitation by sex-starved soldiers, a pronatalist government, and civilians like Cyprien himself, who receive recognition for their charitable acts. The women proclaim the hypocrisy in citing the men's heroism as an excuse for their behavior, mindful that defense of women and the homeland is a loudly touted goal of the war (76–78; 234). In vain these women demand recognition for their contribution to the nation of France, especially since they will probably bear and rear their children alone, while other women end their economic victimization by another form of war profiteering. Landre's humorous yet sympathetic depiction of the women who take advantage of loopholes to obtain government subsidies illegally and extra rations of controlled goods redeems them from the total disapprobation accorded to middle-class women (191–200). Further, Landre satirizes Cyprien's class snobbery when he is forced to abandon his luxury apartment to seek refuge with the book's main female character, a poor woman whose manipulation of the system insures a regular supply of heat and electricity (192–93).

Cyprien's complacency dissipates even further when Lydie, his housekeeper of thirty years, leaves to take a job in a munitions factory. Tired of her servant's status, Lydie suddenly realizes her autonomy and seizes the opportunity to exercise it.

> Let Monsieur study me closely: I am, since this morning, a woman of the new social stratum, enlightened, emancipated, aware. . . . I will have the right to vote tomorrow, for I have just made an extraordinary decision: I am leaving Monsieur (164–65).[14]

However, Landre undermines Lydie's endorsement for women's civil rights by mocking feminists who support legal measures to guarantee women's autonomy. Cyprien easily bribes Lydie to return by granting her total control of the household resources, and additionally, by agreeing to hire a personal servant for her. Thus she will enjoy all of the material advantages of managing a rich man's household, yet, like a wife, she will still be indebted to him and dependent on his good will. This insinuation that self-regard, and not political consciousness, forms the basis of Lydie's motivations is seconded by Landre's comments near the end of the novel about women's suffrage and the political power of the vote. The writers in

"Le Bifteck des Muses" reveal to Cyprien their lack of happiness as independent intellectuals, and their desire to trade their future "glory" for the simple joys of marriage. Astonished by such a display of passion from these "viragos," Cyprien declares, "They no longer aspire to emancipation, but to slavery. After having brandished the flag of revolt, they dream of using it to clean the shoes of a master" (231–32).[15]

Landre also ridicules women's slavish behavior in . . . *puis il mourut,* where Raymonde fantasizes about her lover strangling her if he withdrew his affections. In *Loin des balles,* Landre insists as well on women's inability to recognize that group solidarity would bring about far-reaching advances for all of womankind. A discussion of the imminent implementation of suffrage at first elicits a politically sophisticated response from a young woman. She angrily declares that men would never relinquish any of their power to women, since women would refuse to send their children to war. Landre then immediately destroys the seriousness of the woman's comments and reveals her blind submission to traditional gender roles. When asked what she would do when suffrage became a reality, she replies, "Me, I will stay at home, because I hope to have a husband who will think, who will work, and who will vote for me" (235).[16] Whereas Landre shows the political acumen of working-class women who understand the structure and means of their exploitation, her middle-class characters cannot see beyond their own individual self-interest.

As its Molieresque title suggests, *L'École des marraines* (The School for Godmothers) is a satire on the abuses of the *marraines de guerre* program. Nonetheless, the foolishness and dishonesty Landre portrays is not confined to the women, who are for the most part misguided rather than malicious, but includes a resounding criticism of the soldiers. The novel reiterates important themes for Landre, especially the different ways civilians and combatants profit from the war and the fictional space in which war correspondence resides.

The main characters are two women, Claude, an artist, and Lucienne, a homemaker. The war has caused these two women to meditate on the direction of their lives. Claude wonders why women cannot have a more active role in the war, noting the irony in the government's rejection of their bodies but its demand for their devotion and gifts for the soldiers. Her observation that this official sequestration of women would stimulate them to try to prove their worth accurately foretells the actions of many of the numerous women in the story, including her own (8–10).

Lucienne is depressed, but only because her soldier husband has not seen any action. For her, he is practically an *embusqué,* and her decision to adopt a *filleul* is as much to annoy her husband, who has forbidden it, as it is to satisfy her need for involvement in the war. Writing from the front, the husband condemns the *marraine* program as an obsessive fad and merely an opportunity for sexual license. Nearly every character in the book outwardly denies this assessment, but their actions prove otherwise. The earnestness with which they pursue multiple correspondents, the degree of emotional investment, and the candid sexual talk in their letters demonstrate motivations that are more self-serving than patriotic. It is a theme that Landre examines in minute detail in . . . *puis il mourut,* where both a woman and man imagine and create a love relationship through correspondence. Here she illustrates this particular kind of war profiteering with an eye for slapstick and an ear for the timbre of self-righteous hypocrisy. One of the book's more humorous scenes involves a hotel in which there are so many married women having affairs with their *filleuls* that a mix-up places a middle-aged matron and her own married daughter in the same room, waiting for two men who never arrive (250).

Lucienne defends her decision to adopt a soldier by saying that she needs to be afraid for someone (47); her mother, excited by the sight of soldiers and their wounds, registers for hospital work (123). Other women satisfy this same longing to overcome their isolation from the war experience by founding charitable activities. Like Cyprien's comical "Le Bifteck des Muses," the groups in this novel also indicate the amiable stupidity underlying actions that serve nothing except their members' egotism. A group of women, congratulating themselves on how important their letters are to their *filleuls,* decides to found "L'Œuvre de la Serviette Éponge sur le Front" (Charity of the Sponge Towel on the Front/Forehead) (14). Their belief that men in the trenches would have the opportunity for bathing illustrates Landre's judgment of the women's ignorance about the war. Despite the variety of these women's activities, they share the common desire for sexual excitement or adultery.

Vignettes throughout the novel recount hilarious mishaps when *marraines* and *filleuls* attempt to realize in person the passion of their letters. Often the women are married, middle-aged, and in love with several soldiers at the same time, multiplying the comic possibilities when they finally learn the most basic facts about the men's lives. There is the story of a woman who has "ideas" about her *filleul,* but when he comes to visit her, he brings his wife and children and expects to move into her house (136). A stout matron is distressed that her *filleul* turns out to be a priest, but her friend offers to "give" her an older captain to cheer her up (78). Landre also recounts the many misadventures of Lucienne's mother and her four *filleuls.* One had been a petty criminal in civilian life, and another arrives a week before their arranged tryst, spends his leave with another woman, and returns to the front. When the mother finally reaches the hotel, all she finds is a huge bill (305). Significantly, Landre, unlike most other fiction writers, indicts specifically the exploitative behavior of the soldiers. While some men pursue the sexual possibilities of their correspondences, others are greedy for the packages the women send. When the men tire of the women, or if the number of parcels dwindles, the men simply trade *marraines* by claiming that the first soldier died in battle. Grief-stricken, the *marraine* quickly adopts the new *filleul,* and the cycle of passionate letters and boxes of gifts starts anew (218).

A rare note of sincerity in this vast panorama of self-aggrandizement and cupidity comes unexpectedly from Trik, Claude's artist friend. Trik's assignment as a camouflage artist keeps him safe and in Paris, and although he performs tasks vital to the war, he considers himself an *embusqué* (53, 106). His honesty about his personal situation lends considerable weight to his scathing indictment of industrialists, merchants, and suppliers as simple war profiteers. As in Gyp's *Les Profitards,* Landre's caustic satire pinpoints the businessmen's complete lack of patriotism or even the least concern for the soldiers. Trik's playful manual on teaching the *nouveaux riches* to talk properly has a chapter on what to say at a banquet celebrating the Allies' victory:

> Say: A businessman who risked his capital during the war had to have supreme intelligence in order to earn modest sums, thanks to which he was able to support the government with loans. . . . [Do not say:] By God! It was a great time, the war! If only it had lasted another six months, I would have rounded out at five million with my rough friends (118).[17]

Like her friend Trik, Claude is a sincere person who honestly searches for self-knowledge and improved connections with other people. Although an artist, she spends most of her time in visits and idle conversation, as required by her bourgeois lifestyle. With great reluctance, she begins a correspondence with a soldier named René, and their letters come to exemplify the solace, friendship, guidance, and mutual esteem that characterize the ideal *marraine-filleul* relationship. Both letter writers develop a better understanding of themselves and others in their lives, and René especially finds a deep level of comfort that alleviates his anxieties. Although the two gradually fall in love, their letters retain a level of purity that does not negate the paradigmatic status of their union, and René dies before the two actually meet. Similar to the outcome of the relationship between Raymonde and Jacques in . . . *puis il mourut,* the death of René exempts his friendship with Claude from the possibility of disappointment due to reality, the contamination of sex, or the deterioration of time (87–93; 310–15).

Claude and René notwithstanding, Landre's analysis of the psychology of war correspondence, important also in her other two novels, relies more often on the comedic in *L'École des marraines.* It is evident that in general the exchange of letters offers an opportunity to project a persona or a reality according to one's needs or desires. Moreover, letters written during a time of physical danger and emotional stress can provide a refuge from an increasingly difficult existence. The numerous relationships based solely on correspondence between strangers in this novel illustrate the comic result of the clash of opposing and urgent emotional needs of civilians and soldiers. For in fact, it is the received letter that fulfills the reader's desires, and the better each correspondent can discern those needs, the more successful and satisfying the exchange of letters will be. In the days before television, the personal witness of soldiers enabled civilians to feel vicariously the excitement of battle in a way that official newspaper accounts and communiqués could not. Similarly, soldiers, overextended by a daily reality that rendered the horrific banal, could find in the letters a vision of normal life in all of its different manifestations. "Their ambition," Cyprien writes in *Loin des balles* of the soldiers who try to bilk luxury goods from their *marraines,* "is to be able to give themselves, at the front, the illusion of society life" (173).[18]

Most of the correspondents are indifferent to the fact that the content of their letters erodes the distinction between what is, what may be, or what might never occur. Lucienne's need to experience the war is so strong that she insists on a *filleul* who personifies the essence of her imagined ideal, a dirty and tattered warrior, a bearded and crude *poilu,* in short, a real soldier (55). Her correspondent, worried that his fiancée might one day read the fiery sentiments in Lucienne's letters, arranges for a friend to continue the correspondence for him, while retaining his name. This Cyrano-type compromise works well for a time, and the two letter writers quickly develop an eloquently poetic and explicitly sexual attachment (224). At first Lucienne finds in these doubly fictional, ghost-written letters the relief from the boredom, embarrassment, and isolation that her husband's inactivity at the front cannot alleviate. Through battlefield letters from a "real soldier," Lucienne can finally savor the intense feelings and heightened emotions denied her by what Claude had earlier termed the "official sequestration of women." Yet Landre also demonstrates that the author of the letters projects the kind of heroic sentiments and impassioned prose that he senses Lucienne desires, not because the words communicate his thoughts or actions, but for his own amusement. Thus for Landre, the fantasy created in war correspondence is double-sided and self-referential, like an endless series of self-reflecting mirrors. She alludes to this phenomenon in a previously cited section from *Loin des balles,* and she examines it in depth in . . . *puis il mourut,* discussed below.

As the correspondence continues, Lucienne penetrates more deeply into the fictive world created by the letters. She takes seriously her role as a writer of fiction, carefully editing and writing her letters. Moreover, she saves the rough drafts in the hope of an eventual publication that could bring the couple a substantial fortune (177–78). The broad humor of their eventual meeting, more like the confusion of a fun house maze of rooms than the fulfillment of erotic longing, does not obscure Lucienne's disappointment with Paul, whom she still believes to be the author of the letters. She decides to adopt another soldier and goes to an agency where she and other women of various ages and economic status read letters from prospective *filleuls*. With the cold eye of a seasoned shopper, Lucienne searches for a man who resembles the protagonists in the nineteenth-century novels she adores and whose identification with fiction would facilitate her ability to maintain her fantasy. However, Landre, perhaps mocking her fellow novelists, shows that Lucienne lacks the talent to fulfill her future ambition to become a financially successful writer because she requires another person, mirror-like, to actualize her imagination (250–77).

Landre ends *L'École des marraines* on a less cynical note, restating her view on the redemptive power of love that is also important in her other two novels. For her, love is stronger than individual will and, although people might try to resist its inexorable force, in the end they yield to its power. Moreover, the energy of love is restorative and therapeutic, expiating all crimes and curing the ill effects of thoughtlessness, madness, and egotism (*Loin des balles,* 128). Far from being unwholesome, the little intrigues and infidelities that resulted from wartime correspondences have a good effect on the soldiers, fortifying their marriages and providing the illusion of normality in an environment that was neither healthy nor rational (*L'École des marraines,* 317).

Landre's novel, . . . *puis il mourut,* treats many of the same themes contained in the other two works from a more intimate and interior point of view. Consisting of a series of letters between a *marraine* and *filleul,* the story recounts the development of their friendship and intense love for one another and the tragic end to their relationship. While the tone of the book is certainly somber and even grim, its exploration of the subjectivity and idealism of wartime letter-writing, with its escapism, sensation, and creation of an alternative reality, mirrors especially the more humorous relationship of Lucienne and Paul in *L'École des marraines.* Although the books were published one year apart, the affinity between the two couples is apparent.

The correspondence takes place over a short period, from August 15, 1915 to Jacques's death on September 25, 1915.[19] From their letters we learn that both Raymonde and Jacques are searching for some redemptive action that will give meaning and compensation to lives that they feel have been wasted (12–13; 28–31; 71–72). Jacques has had much experience in the world, but at 32, his past life of pleasure seems like "an enormous absurdity from which he'd gladly rehabilitate himself with the sacrifice of his skin" (12).[20] Raymonde also had been resigned to the emptiness of her existence, but she too, like Jacques, sees in the war the possibility of spiritual renewal. They are drawn to each other by an intense and mutual emotional need: he for a female presence in a "totally masculine world" (7), and she, for a surrogate battle experience. "Then don't I have the right to shake your hand . . ." she writes in the beginning, " . . . since, if I am not fighting, it's not at all because I lack the desire to do it, but simply because the laws are badly constructed" (3).[21] Like Landre's other female characters, Raymonde yearns to contribute more directly to the defense of France. It is significant that her rejection of the socially prescribed way for women to participate in the war is specifically gender-determined. Characterizing volunteer nursing as rife with women's petty quarrels and little jealousies, she dreams instead of direct contact with the enemy. Her image of Jacques, a total stranger, is that of an ideal warrior, " . . . I don't know you, and yet I know that you are young, heroic, and that you adore France" (3).[22] It is an identity that replicates her fantasy of herself on the battlefield, where she later dreams of fighting side by side with Jacques, following his orders (28; 64).

Jacques, however, does not want a fictional comrade-in-arms, even one who would serve and support him. In several letters he writes of the suffering Raymonde would encounter in the trenches and the distraction of her presence that would endanger his men (77–78; 121–22). In this fictional world created by two emotionally overextended people, it is not that Jacques actually believes that Raymonde will suddenly appear, gun in hand. Rather, he is guiding the development of their fantasy according to his personal motives and will. Early in their correspondence, Jacques wrote that he wanted Raymonde to be "the maternal and amorous friend that every man hopes for . . ."[23] and Raymonde accepted the double role of "little mother" and "great friend" as agreeable to her protective nature (13, 15). Raymonde understands without romanticizing the character that each of them is to assume in the dramatization of a story that parallels that of the war itself. For her, the reading of his "heroic tales" would occupy the time spent waiting for the war to end, and her affection for him would calm and assuage the complex and disquieting emotions created by the war. Raymonde sees his affection for her clearly as a desire for catharsis that would end when the need for such relief no longer existed.

The war over, he would set out "wandering" again, without even having met his correspondent, because all that he required of her was to personify at a distance his dreams and desires, to listen to the great affection that groaned inside him, to take it for her own, to respond to it according to her heart, her nature, and her self-expression (30–31). [24]

Jacques, emotionally drained by the steady tide of devastation that slowly reduces his regiment to a fraction of its original size, also understands the depth of his need to create a refuge in an alternative reality, and he readily embraces his part in "this letter-writing game" that he also terms "our dear novel" (44; 87). Central to his fantasy is the total and mutual possession and love of an ideal woman, one who manifests all the different relationships between men and women. In a world where reality is too horrible to accept as authentic, illusion becomes a means for a person to achieve some kind of emotional balance and compensation. For Jacques, Raymonde's letters are an anchor of normality in his nonhuman world, where social custom and rational understanding no longer exist. In such a place, fantasy is superior, for it manifests artifice and creativity.

> What he wanted was the illusion of love, of love coming to him, very simply, very innocently; what he hungered for most, was not the good times, well-organized like a battalion on parade during peace time, but the expression of his lover's mind, of the instant of her feeling, of the words which came to her heart or to her head at the moment when she thought of him, of him who writes to her from the place where conventions were dead, where one could dare everything, since boldness, even excessive, entailed nothing (44). [25]

In their letters, Raymonde and Jacques achieve a level of total mutual possession that they express to each other patriotically, sexually, and metaphysically. While Jacques admires the generosity of French women, he appreciates Raymonde's infinite love of France that he feels is transferred to him, and he dreams of their nights together where their limbs would be so entwined as to be indistinguishable from one another (50–51; 97–98; 188–89; 204–05). Similarly Raymonde's visions echo and continue the narrative of this ultimate union that exists independently of their previous lives (60). Her momentary hesitation to grant his wish that she send him one of her nylon stockings, "still warm from you" signals a last withholding of herself before a complete surrender (82). Once accepted, however, her commitment is total, and she endows their relationship with otherworldly attributes. She feels his invisible presence hovering continually near her, and she is certain that she will know telepathically if he is injured (65; 67–68; 104–05; 175; 216). His love even transforms her judgment of herself. Having considered herself plain and a bit dowdy, she now declares herself rejuvenated and beautiful (159).

It is significant that interspersed in the explicit evocation of their desire for one another, the two express doubts about themselves and concerns that they might not be able to fulfill each other's expectations. Raymonde fears that when they meet, he will be disappointed, or that one day he would cause her pain (68). "I want to nourish your precious affection, at least until reality arrives" (117).[26] Similarly, Jacques worries that he is not an adequate conversationalist (187–88) and that his body is not as supple as that of a younger man (202). Like Landre's characters in her other novels, Raymonde and Jacques understand the danger that the end of the war and the passage of time pose to the fiction they have created, and they respond to this fear by intensifying their vision. Raymonde anticipates the end of their relationship by happily fantasizing her death at Jacques's hands, and Jacques's final letter, sent in the event of his death, celebrates the endurance of their "perfect tenderness," a union that death will preserve against the contamination of reality (219; 244). Similar to Claude and René in *L'École des marraines*, Landre spares Raymonde and Jacques the deception and disappointment that Lucienne and Paul experience when, as *marraine* and *filleul*, they finally meet. Still, the finale of the fantasy created by Raymonde and Jacques summarizes the self-referential goals of their relationship, an affinity that replicates the desire and vanity of Lucienne and Paul, rather than the quiet sincerity of Claude and René. Indeed, the story narrated in . . . *puis il mourut* could be the published correspondence that Lucienne, in *École des marraines*, hopes will make her and Paul rich.

In . . . *puis il mourut*, both Raymonde and Jacques achieve an image of each other that would have been impossible under normal circumstances, and they both realize, through the eyes of another person, the sense of a higher purpose for lives they had considered wasted. Jacques's letters demonstrate that he understands extremely well the fictive nature of war correspondence, and he is fully aware that his death, whether real or imagined, will enshrine forever the images the couple created. His exit from the dream affords Raymonde the additional pleasure of mourning, and she becomes "la veuve mystérieuse," (the mysterious widow). However, since they were not actually married, her widowhood must be as mythical as their relationship. The arrival of his final letter transports her to an exquisite and near-divine level of suffering and sacrifice. "Overcome, prostrate with grief, she would continue her martyrdom, and her crucifixion would be slow. She felt that she had been chosen for the greatest sorrow" (246).[27] For Landre's characters in all three of her war-related novels, as for Mary Floran's protagonist in *On demande une marraine*, the exchange of letters furnishes an opportunity to create and assume a particular identity for a variety of reasons that may tangentially help others, but that ultimately serve the needs and motives of the self. Conversely, correspondence between friends and acquaintances in works such as Reynès-Monlaur's *Les Autels morts* and Colette's *Mitsou, ou comment l'esprit vient aux filles*, provides a space to grow as a person and develop ideas with more freedom than social convention normally permits.

Chapter Six

Women of the Future, Men of the Past ✹

The themes of the novels reflect the actual concerns of civilians and soldiers, including the difficulties of life at both the front and the rear and the adjustments these new situations cause people to make in their lives and attitudes. Among these, the integration of the veteran into a reconstructed France is an especially important issue. The works discussed below consider how the war affects women's and men's social roles as well as their relationships with each other. They also investigate the meaning these changes would have for the future of France and for its citizens' individual lives. The first three novels in particular explore the physical and mental conditions of severely wounded soldiers who must adapt to life as amputees, and the attempts of the women in their lives to help them make that adjustment. The women characters in these stories willingly abandon their individual pursuits and interests to undertake responsibility for the massive needs of the soldier. Their compliant acceptance of a new life totally different from that which they had expected or planned echoes the acquiescent attitude that Hortense Cloquié advised in her *La Femme après la guerre, ses droits, son rôle, son devoir* (Woman After the War, Her Rights, Her Role, Her Duty). As discussed above in chapter 1, this 1915 publication considered the privations and deaths of the war as an unforeseen benefit that would force women to abandon their prewar selfishness and laziness. The overwhelming needs of the wounded and handicapped would develop the many female talents that the war had revealed to women unaccustomed to work and responsibility.[1]

The emphasis on altruistic service to men is the antithesis of the central problem in a second group of texts, where a conflict occurs when both the veteran and his partner actively pursue their individuality. Here the war impacts the central female character in such a way that she metamorphoses from a passive being content to parrot or at least yield to her husband or fiancé's ideas to become an autonomous citizen ready to participate in the rebuilding of France. These women are reluctant to accept these new roles, which remove them from the carefully protected lives they once enjoyed. However, they come to see the loss of this lifestyle as a sacrifice and an appropriate memorial to their loved ones who perished as heroes of the war. Written before the actual end of hostilities, these five novels and a play present different images of the France of the future. The question they attempt to answer is not how each woman will adjust to the social changes brought about by war, but how each man will react to the erosion of his traditional and legal power and authority over his wife and children. Some of the authors represent the future as a dream of harmony and hope, while for others it is a nightmare of deception and disintegration.

The visions of the future in *Chantal Daunoy* by Isabelle Sandy, *Un grand blessé* (A Severely Wounded Soldier) by Jehanne d'Orliac, and *Tu aimeras dans la douleur* (You Will Love in Sorrow) by Andrée Mars are filled with hardship and uncertainty. All three of these narratives appeared in 1917, and they recount the many psychological problems gravely wounded veterans face in their attempt to adapt to their new situations. In each case, the woman character must figure out how to restore the permanently disabled soldier's will to live. The outcome of each woman's efforts remains somewhat ambiguous, however, surely a realistic assessment of the kind of lives these men and women would face. The protagonist's hesitations and doubts about the future parallel the general discouragement of French civilians and soldiers in 1917 concerning the management and direction of the war.

As in *Chantal Daunoy*, the setting in most of Isabelle Sandy's (1884–1975) more than 40 novels is her native Ariège, the southernmost region of France. Sandy was the recipient of many literary prizes throughout her career, including the generous Montyon Prize awarded by the Académie Française for *Chantal Daunoy*. She received another prize from the Académie Française for her subsequent work, *Andorra, ou les hommes d'airain* (Andorra, or the Men of Bronze), the Prix National des Lettres in 1921 for *Dans la ronde des faunes* (In the Realm of the Fauns), and the Prix de Prose Fabien-Artigue for *Histoire d'un comte de Foix* (History of a Count of Foix). While Sandy was best known for her many novels, she also wrote several volumes of poetry, as well as short stories and articles that appeared in many large-circulation publications including *Le Journal, L'Intransigeant, Minerva,* and *Comœdia.* Isabelle Sandy was named an Officer in the Légion d'Honneur in recognition of these literary accomplishments and the notable respect she enjoyed among her fellow writers.[2]

Chantal Daunoy is the story of a sculptor and a poet who live contemplative and somewhat reclusive lives, wholly dedicated to their respective arts. They meet by chance while Jean, the artist and now soldier, is recovering from fatigue and depression in the mountains near Foix. Morose and aloof, he is nonetheless drawn to Chantal by the powerful images of her patriotic poetry, and when he returns to the front he writes to thank her for restoring his inspiration. Their letters express their philosophies of life and art, and they become increasingly, although reluctantly, connected to each other. Once declared, however, their love is all consuming. Yet their letters reflect a realistic caution and even pessimism concerning the future, fears that appear substantiated when Jean is wounded, reported missing, and presumed dead. Chantal refuses to abandon hope, and continues to write her daily letter to Jean. Several different subplots evoke the courage and loyalty of some civilians, as well as the frailty and selfishness of others.

As in other war novels, especially those of Jeanne Landre and J. Delorme Jules-Simon, letters are an important part of the narrative of *Chantal Daunoy.* The correspondence between Chantal and Jean shows the development of their love for one another and also their efforts to transcend the tragedy that enters their lives. Nevertheless letters are more than a convenient way for an author to advance the plot or to allow characters separated by long distances or social circumstances to communicate. In this novel, as in others, letters contain the good news and bad, the desire and confidence, as well as the desperation and withdrawal with which readers were familiar from their own experiences.

As the months go by and the pile of unmailed letters increases, Chantal senses a power in her writing to keep Jean alive. After four months of silence, Jean suddenly appears after being incarcerated in a German prison camp. Yet, Sandy refuses the joyful homecoming of the long-missing soldier that Broussan-Gaubert portrays in *Reviendra-t-il?* and that undoubtedly mirrored the hope of any contemporary reader. Jean returns, having lost not only his right arm and most of his eyesight, but also the will and spirit to adapt to a life without sculpture. Chantal undertakes an all-powerful, life-giving, and maternal role as she attempts to revive his spirit, but Jean rejects any possibility of a normal life as unfitting for an amputee. Undaunted, Chantal leads Jean to the scene of the battle of the Marne, where the memory of his friends' deaths and of France's victory there startles him into realizing that he must help regenerate the French nation (265–73). In causing Jean to accept marriage with Chantal, Sandy underscores the primacy of the life principle.

Throughout the world runs such a flow of life, that, like an irresistible wave, it carries away all of the debris amassed by human destruction . . . (266).[3]

It is certainly significant that *Chantal Daunoy* appeared in 1917 when civilian disappointment and dissatisfaction were at a dangerously high point. Sandy's novel specifically counters pessimism and cynicism with its story of perseverance, abnegation, and eventual triumph over the hardships of war. Moreover, its characters serve as models for readers in their patriotic rededication to the larger community of France. Yet the loss of their individual interests is not a sacrifice they make easily or willingly, and it is the war itself that teaches Chantal and Jean the true nature of idealism. Forced by circumstances to renounce their lofty, but personal goals, they come to understand that the needs of their country supercede their own. The precept that Isabelle Sandy proposes, that the war was beneficial in many unforeseen ways, is one common to much of French women's war fiction. *Chantal Daunoy* and other novels discussed in this study affirm that the war, seemingly a destroyer of individual families, would in an unexplainable and mysterious manner solidify and strengthen the collective family of France. Here the blood of the dead becomes the life force of the future as Sandy evokes the regeneration of France through childbearing and hard work. Chantal explains to Jean their new and higher calling:

> Reveal to your fellow men all that the war has taught you and prescribed as eternal truths. Among our people, there are those whom the war has not sufficiently changed; their redemption has only started; if no one summons them to advance farther, they will stop, and their initial errors will be solidified. Their childish souls will remain encumbered with shallow worries, forgetful of what must be our sole thought: the regeneration of an entire race.
>
> Carried by the blood of the dead, this race has achieved an elevated level: it must be maintained there.
>
> . . . From everywhere in France, good workers will come forth. We will be among them!
>
> Like he who plants seeds, our action will extend endlessly! We must accomplish this act! We must! (268–69)[4]

Maternal images appear throughout Sandy's narrative. France is both the mythic pelican who offered its own flesh to its starving brood and the mother whose mangled arms bring her citizens together toward a more elevated form of love (34; 104). Additionally, several of the characters are part of a mother-daughter dyad united by their enduring dedication and service to France (44; 60). Chantal is the only disconnected and solitary character among these women. Before she met Jean, she had avoided love and pleasure, convinced that her poetry elevated her to a superior level of humanity. In fact, it is Jean's new condition that ennobles her love for him and reorients her focus in a direction away from her previous individual objectives. Before the injury, Jean and Chantal had been the intellectual equals, complementary artists whose talents yielded reciprocal benefits (30–31). The amputation of his arm ends his career as a sculptor and eliminates the outlet for his creativity. Moreover, it destroys the equilibrium of their relationship. Chantal, solitary and self-sufficient, must take on the maternal role of protector to lead Jean back to life. Overwhelmed by his sudden childlike, dependent state, Jean rejects Chantal because he fears her love has turned to pity (238–39; 248; 256–57).

In the end, it is the remembrance of Jean's fallen comrades and not Chantal's love that succeeds in renewing in him the will to live. The powerful images and memories of the battle of the Marne convince Jean that he must maintain what he feels to be the superiority of the French nation, a distinction that the soldiers assured with their lives (256–64). Significantly, Jean ignores Chantal at the battle site and experiences his moment of epiphany not with a civilian, but with his fellow soldiers. This is not a rejection of her love, as much as it is a recognition of its irrelevance, for Jean abjures the personal sphere of women and their individual attachments to embrace the public sphere of the community of men and of nationhood. For Sandy, Jean can only reclaim his desire to live while performing the preeminent role of a man in 1917, that of soldier. His comrades' example of abnegation and unity at the beginning of the war had succeeded in counterbalancing his own artist's egotism. Chantal, too, replicates the consummate traditional woman's role for she finds the inspiration to carry on through dedicating her life in service to her future husband. Moreover, Chantal's thoughts on her new direction elucidate Sandy's view that such private ministration to one individual is superior to more public actions, such as volunteer nurse or charity worker. In Chantal's mind, Jean is a microcosm of France, and in dedicating her life to him, she becomes the mother of all who fight:

> She reflected that her love for this man wounded on the battlefields exceeded all that her fervent youth had taken pleasure in imagining; she had been granted to love in a single being both the chosen man and suffering France; in cherishing one, she cradled the glorious agony of the other; in loving, she cleansed and healed the wounds. What a noble and magnificent destiny! (238)[5]

Just as Chantal yields her egotism as a poet to the love and care of a permanently wounded veteran, so Jean renounces first his sense of his own importance as an individual artist, and then his despair at his infirmity, to the needs of his country. Their mutual disavowal of personal interests is symbolic of the *union sacrée* and the French people's rejection of the individualism that provoked many quarrels before the war (94–95). Sandy here joins many other writers, such as Marcelle Tinayre and Geneviève Duhamelet in considering those disputes as an important factor in Germany's perception of France as vulnerable. Her story reiterates the continued need for unity and the sacrifice of self-interest, certainly an important message in 1917.

Other examples of enduring devotion to the nation in spite of tragic personal loss support this theme of the need for perseverance and determination as necessary for victory. There is the woman from Lorraine who tells Chantal the story of her husband's departure to defend France in 1870 (121–23). At first, she was jealous, as if he had left her for another woman, but when the Germans destroyed her village, she understood at last the meaning of *patrie,* her homeland. There is also the sight of the peasants wearing mourning clothes, who nonetheless continue their work in the fields (141). These are lessons, Chantal recognizes, in the eternal and obstinate nature of life confronting death.

In *Chantal Daunoy,* however, Sandy goes beyond urging persistence in the face of the disappointments and setbacks of three years of armed conflict to portray the experience of war as a great moral teacher to the French nation. Similar to other writers, such as Reynès-Monlaur and Delorme Jules-Simon, Sandy views war as a purifying agent that, through the shock of a reversal of values, jolted the French people away from self-interest toward a higher love of the nation. The necessities of the war brought them together, and in fighting, suffering, and hoping in unison, they developed a sense of belonging and commitment to one another they otherwise would not have known (95). Moreover, it was not necessary to experience the rigors of battle to undergo the transformative effects of this mysterious and magic binding. Simply being in a barracks with other French men is sufficient to recreate a chance acquaintance of Chantal's from a spoiled dandy and dilettante to a person who has a sense of purpose for the first time in his life (161).

Sandy also analyzes the difficulty of maintaining civilian morale through the evolution of the character of Chantal. Like other noncombatants, Chantal's support of the war is clear from the beginning of the story, yet she nonetheless struggles with despair as the fighting continues. The belief that the length of the war has taught the French people to adapt and develop a hitherto unknown level of patience comforts Chantal. While she comes to accept that a prompt victory would have left her fellow citizens mired in the hereditary flaw of individualism, she regrets, nevertheless, that such wisdom would come at the price of so much blood. War destroys, Sandy asserts in her novel, but it also creates.

> Today the values are reversed, the experience of a single person, if it does not relate to the one undergone by the world, has no hold on sensitivities.

The individual himself consents not to linger over the various transformations that destiny can implement in his life. Perhaps individualism, which for too long depleted the connection among the French race, will have been strongly subdued by the war. French people struggle, suffer, [and] hope together. They have grounds for understanding; they have gathered together. The invader had not predicted that (94–95).[6]

The conflict of self-interest and public good is also a theme in one of Sandy's postwar works, *Kaali,* published in 1930. This novel, however, reverses the view of war that Sandy presented in *Chantal Daunoy,* for here a pacifist response will best serve the French nation. Kaali is the Hindu goddess of love and death, a fitting symbol for the main character, a woman scientist who discovers a particularly deadly gas. Much of the novel concerns her hesitation at making the findings public, as she attempts to balance her sense of moral responsibility with her ambitions as a researcher. Although a Christian pacifist urges her to destroy her work for the sake of her young son, it is not clear if the scientist will choose to forego the honors and fame that the public announcement of her discovery would certainly bring. The denouement of Sandy's novel resolves this conflict of maternal love with personal ambition as another mother, a woman whose son died in the war, sets fire to the laboratory to destroy the deadly invention.

As in *Chantal Daunoy,* the protagonists of Jehanne d'Orliac's *Un grand blessé* (A Severely Wounded Soldier) struggle to adapt to the permanent changes in their lives. D'Orliac's soldier is also a well-known sculptor who has lost his right arm and faces a future without art. While in Sandy's novel, Chantal sacrificed her individuality and professional goals to adopt an all-encompassing maternal role of protector for Jean, the two female protagonists in d'Orliac's story struggle with the conflicts inherent in such a choice. Unlike the main characters in *Chantal Daunoy* and Andrée Mars's *Tu aimeras dans la douleur,* discussed below, Christiane and Françoise consider how love and sacrifice will impact their own lives. While it is never a question of whether or not the women in these other novels will give up their own plans to serve the handicapped veteran, the willingness of women to dedicate their lives to such men is the central subject of d'Orliac's narrative. *Un grand blessé* presents the problem of a veteran's adjustment from a woman's point of view.

D'Orliac's story has little plot. Its lyrical narrative evokes the relationship of two friends, Christiane and Françoise, and their love for the disabled Mario, through long Proustian-style descriptions of the lush landscape of southern France. D'Orliac shows Christiane, an only child raised in freedom, to be a strong-willed individualist; however, she carefully notes that the self-absorbed young woman has paid little attention to the war and is ignorant of her duty (3). A visit to her newly inherited estate in the south of France arouses Christiane's sense of guilt at not being able to participate in what d'Orliac terms "the great sacrifice" (9). Her meditation leads her to wonder what her role in life will be, and she concludes that, unlike her friends who seek only to find a rich or important husband, her mission will be one of reawakening and resurrection (13). A woman whose greatest passion is sensation, Christiane is particularly attached to Françoise, whose husband and child were killed in an automobile accident before the war. Françoise comes to stay with Christiane so that she may visit her lover Mario, a sculptor who is recuperating from his wounds in a nearby hospital.

Outside the hospital, a group of wounded soldiers arrives, and seeing their bloody clothes and dirty faces, Christiane understands for the first time the immense distress of their hardship. She feels enormous pity and love for them "in her heart and in her flesh" (32). This experience transforms the young woman who resolves to serve the wounded as a volunteer nurse. Her decision takes on the fervent tone of a nun entering a cloister, for she vows to confine her body in the nurse's white uniform and subordinate her now disciplined thoughts to the soldiers' needs.

> And Christiane knew the disappointment of great surges of enthusiasm; she experienced infinite pity and the shame of never, ever having thought about those who sacrifice themselves. . . . She would have wanted to become their servant, and under her white veil, under the white smock, to confine her limbs and her thoughts, disciplined and subservient (31–32).[7]

The exaggerated intensity of Christiane's awakening is important to the theme of *Un grand blessé,* for it abstracts her character to symbolize love based on pity and death. Her relationship with Françoise underscores this portrayal, for it is the sadness and tragedy in the young widow's life that originally caused Christiane's profound attachment to her. The issue of love and pity is prevalent in women's war fiction, and many male characters voice their aversion to any expression of pity. While other novelists include this problem among larger themes, d'Orliac devotes her entire narrative to the analysis of women's and men's attempts to overcome it.

The friendship of Christiane and Françoise developed and intensified after the deaths of Françoise's husband and child. Christiane recalls being deeply moved by the beauty of the young widow enveloped in her black veil, an image that was for her the very incarnation of grief (50–51). Françoise, too, feels a deep bond with Christiane, and confirms the confessional character of their friendship. She confides her anguish to Christiane in an attempt to purge the negative emotions associated with her past life in favor of a new life with Mario. Françoise understands that Mario requires her to reflect his image of her as the person he loves and not as a widow in mourning. Before the war she had willingly conformed to this conception.

> If Mario had not been taken away from me, doubtless we would have joined our lives together. I was his warmth and his inspiration. And because my being thus arranged pleased him, I would have explicitly retained this appearance with him (69).[8]

From the beginning of the story, then, the elements that form the relationship between the two women are sadness, pity, and death. Moreover, d'Orliac completes the bipolar imagery by associating Mario's love with enthusiasm and vigor.

The news of Mario's amputation brings the two women together in the radiant countryside of southern France. Christiane, bewildered by changes in Françoise's demeanor, senses the loss of their previous intimacy. Françoise tries to explain that people either die of sadness or are cured of it, and that one day she simply discarded her past suffering with her mourning clothes (68–69). For the first time in her life, Françoise is aware of the energy and vitality of being, and she delights in the sheer sensuality of her new existence. Continuing her relationship with a now disabled man would negate this conscious choice for life and desire and would return her to the suffering she abandoned.

The love that Mario needs to survive also requires that Françoise forsake her newly found desire to live. It is a sacrifice she is not willing to make, although she attempts to take a middle ground by visiting Mario in the hospital. At the same time, however, she begins a new relationship, and the openly physical nature of this liaison underscores the value of Françoise as a symbol of life. Conversely, d'Orliac reinforces the association of Mario and Christiane with pity and death. The grove of mournful cypress trees and uprooted pines reflects the passage of time and beauty, a fitting place for them to discover not only Françoise's new relationship, but also to recognize their feelings for each other (89–96). However, Mario understands that love must be mutual and equal, consisting of reciprocal confidence and accord. He is drawn to Christiane, whose compassion leads him to comprehend that his duty as a soldier is to conquer his fear of his new life and continue to live. Yet he refuses a relationship with her, in spite of her role in his reawakening, for he realizes that her pity for him denies any possibility of equality of affection. Nonetheless Mario also admits that it is Christiane's love that has brought him to the understanding that complete healing is possible only with a woman who loves him in spite of his amputation and not because of it (154–67). His continued love for Françoise, the image of light and desire, symbolizes his decision for life, just as her rejection of him represented the same choice. Both of them ultimately reject Christiane, the figure of pity and death.

D'Orliac's narrative presents Christiane's role as important but transitional. Although she is selfish and childish at the beginning of the story, her experiences at the hospital mature her and cause her to assume the responsibility of service to her country. While Françoise and Mario are preoccupied with their personal feelings and problems, Christiane changes in the opposite direction of generosity and altruism. Similar to other characters, such as Chantal in Isabelle Sandy's work, Christiane considers her selfless devotion to a single soldier to represent a sacrifice to all of France. D'Orliac's praise of Christiane's attitude notwithstanding, she also shows this approach to be static and mired in the grief of the past. The story closes as Mario rejects both women, citing Françoise's betrayal and Christiane's misinterpretation of pity as love. The ending, while ambiguous, affirms d'Orliac's vision of a future in which the quality of a love relationship has a singular importance.

> Too fresh is the wound in each one of us to consider touching it, we cannot determine right now what is essential. Françoise, you ask for a pardon today that would be perhaps offensive to you tomorrow. And me who does not know whether in the future I can live with or far from you . . . how to make my choice! Christiane had pity . . . does she know what love is? And is she not confused? For both of you, I, soon rid of my plain uniform, in civilian clothes, will no longer be a casualty, a severely wounded soldier but a one-armed man, let each one consider that . . . I will live, that I know. . . . Little Amber [Christiane] bless you for having given me the self-esteem for it (182–83).[9]

Unlike *Un grand blessé,* there is no discussion in *Chantal Daunoy* of the attributes of the love relationship between Chantal and Jean, for Isabelle Sandy portrays emotional fulfillment as secondary to the necessity of the couple's role in rebuilding France. However, in Andrée Mars's award-winning novel, *Tu aimeras dans la douleur,* the author reiterates d'Orliac's examination of the incompatible nature of pity and love and the friction that inevitably results from their blending. While Mario understands that Christiane's pity will prevent his mental healing, the disabled soldier in *Tu aimeras dans la douleur* comes to hate the woman whose pity he embraces. In 1919, writer and critic Rachilde praised the young author whose first novel had won the Prix des Femmes de Professions Libérales, citing in particular the subtle manner in Mars's evocation of a woman's disappointment in marriage. Often the defender of traditional feminine modesty in other

women, Rachilde commends Mars's self-restraint in portraying the protagonist's passage from disappointed wife to contented mother.[10]

Written between March and September 1917, Mars's book begins with
the detailed and gruesome depiction of the operation that removes
Xavier's leg, but much to his regret, saves his life. Embittered and humiliated at his enfeebled state, he lashes out at France, the young volunteer
who comes to see him on her regular rounds. His angry statement that
only a woman in love would ever want him provokes and inflames France,
who gradually becomes passionately attached to him (37–39; 54–56). Similar to both female protagonists in *Chantal Daunoy* and *Un grand blessé*,
France considers Xavier to be a microcosm of all handicapped French veterans. He appears to return her affection, but suddenly avoids her to pursue a beautiful, talented, and fiercely independent woman, Marguerite
Saint-Pol. However, Xavier eventually realizes that a person in his situation
needs the love and devotion of a docile woman like France, rather than the
pity of a self-reliant free spirit like Marguerite.

Their marriage is a disappointment to France, who compares it unfa-
vorably to a romance novel. Instead of an ending where the brutish ruffian
reveals himself to be a tender lover, she is living a story in which her sweet-
heart becomes savage and cruel. She counters his implacable coldness with
increasing devotion and utter meekness, but he remains distant and nearly
indifferent. She nonetheless resists his desire to have children, considering
him child enough for her. Xavier's predictably angry reaction to France's
attitude reiterates Mars's central theme of the conflict of love and pity
(216–19). The story ends with the news of France's pregnancy, and her
thoughts on motherhood and her husband (241–56). She understands that
because of his war experience and his injury, he cannot love her or anyone else adequately. However, she also recognizes that her unborn child
may bring the only possibility for his emotional recuperation.

As in the novels by Isabelle Sandy and Jehanne d'Orliac, the primary
concern in *Tu aimeras dans la douleur* is the emotional adjustment of the
physically disabled soldier. While in all three of these novels the male character must overcome diminished pride and autonomy represented by the
loss of a limb, it is in Andrée Mars's narrative that the problem emerges in
greatest detail.

When the war began, the handsome Xavier Le Prieur had enlisted in
the army despite being rejected twice for a slight heart condition. Through
brief but precise portrayals of battle scenes and of the hospital and operating room, Mars shows the evolution of Xavier's character from that of a
spoiled son of a rich industrialist to an exceptional officer (13–23). Mars's
description evokes with resolute meticulousness the physical and emotional reality of amputation.

> In the somber compartment, the makeshift operating room set up between
> the barracks, the regular noise of the saw on the bone, fine like a gnawing,
> squeaks for a moment in the midst of silence, punctuated from time to time
> by the unconscious moan of the wounded soldier (7).[11]

Xavier's attitude reveals a degree of bitterness at his condition that few
novelists in this study deemed appropriate; most prefer a more heroic description of the amputee's view of his plight. More than simply injured,
Xavier feels a profound shame that penetrates his innermost identity as a
man, and indeed Mars describes him specifically as a "humiliated male"
(34). The idea of sacrifice for his country and family that was once an inspiration now appears to him to be empty and vain.

> To never again be able to run, never even walk like another. To never again
> be "oneself." An arm, if it were an arm. . . . He will never be loved again . . .
> or he'd be pitied. Oh no!, no pity, never . . . (34).[12]

Xavier's treatment of France, sarcastic and irritating at the beginning of
the story, changes slowly over the months of his rehabilitation and their
courtship to a combination of tenderness and cruelty. France sometimes
feels frustrated by her inability to help in Xavier's emotional recovery, but
she never speaks to him about it. Meek and self-effacing at the expense of
her own interests, she waits patiently for Xavier to ask her to marry him.
To France's bewilderment, he nearly marries Marguerite Saint-Pol, a mul-
titalented, rich, and independent woman. However, Xavier's injury repels
Marguerite, and while his handsome demeanor attracts her initially, she
soon abandons him to resume a life he could never share of skiing and
mountain climbing (104–06; 138–40). Like Françoise in d'Orliac's *Un
grand blessé,* Marguerite is so attached to life that she chooses to forfeit a
love relationship with a disabled person that would require her to renounce her vital and energetic activities. Pity is not a part of the affection
that either of these two women has for her respective soldier. It is an emotion whose presence is paradoxical at best: the men reject compassion as
humiliating, but they also come to realize that in their present state, it is a
necessary component of love. As much as Xavier enjoys the fact that Marguerite does not treat him as handicapped, he also understands that he can
never participate in the activities that are central to her rich and independent lifestyle. The complications of his long recovery, the operations, the
training necessary for use of the prosthesis, all of these difficulties make
him long for the comforting and maternal touch of France. He resents the
power that France's pity has over him, but he cannot live without her help
(120–22). He has lost not only his male traditional role as head of the fam-

ily, but also the ability to choose equality with a woman. The only option left to him as an amputee is that of a child, with France filling the role of his mother. It is a part she cherishes, but one that exacerbates his humiliation and anger.

Xavier's behavior deteriorates after their marriage. Bad-tempered and given to bouts of self-pity, he becomes increasingly violent towards France, who responds to his mixture of affection and hostility with humility and renewed devotion (206–08; 218–19). Realizing finally that Xavier will probably never be able to love her in the way she had hoped, she transfers her need for love to her unborn child. Her final thoughts echo those of her mother's: that the child belongs first and always to its mother, and that women, destined to be servants to their husbands and children, sacrifice themselves simply and willingly to the great forces of nature (201; 254–55). As in so many of the novels examined in this study, *Tu aimeras dans la douleur* establishes maternity not only as the natural role of women, but also as the preeminent means to compensate dissatisfaction and even, as in the case of Camille Mayran's *L'Histoire de Gotton Conixloo,* redeem error.

> Her child? She felt suddenly, fiercely that he belonged to her alone. Yes, the child is the mother's first—and forever. She will be able to love him, him, nourish him, watch over him, console him, and serve him. He will show self-centeredness and ingratitude; all of the mothers say it, but even so, naiveté, nonchalance, and trust. He will leave one day, but he will stay a long time. As she counted the minutes a while ago, now she counts the years: eighteen, twenty years? (255)[13]

Furthermore, the satisfaction France finds in the life of her child is one of the several ways in which Andrée Mars defends the institution of marriage. The subplot of Xavier's relationship with Marguerite Saint-Pol furnishes an especially distinctive entry point to this second major theme in *Tu aimeras dans la douleur.* Marguerite is unbeatable as a rival for France. As beautiful and intelligent as she is talented in music and art, she is both rich and self-reliant. Yet Xavier is shocked to learn that she does not sew or do any kind of needlework. That Mars considers this simple fact to be a symbolic rejection of a woman's natural role is reinforced by Marguerite's refusal of marriage because a husband is the master of his wife (114–15). The other women characters pity Marguerite and blame her mother's death in childbirth as the cause of her capriciousness and liberated attitudes. As in other novels studied here, the lack of a mother figure directly results in an autonomous daughter. In this story, however, such independence is associated with selfishness, for Marguerite cannot even bear to speak of Xavier's injury. Moreover, the only other negative character in the novel is France's cantankerous aunt, who chose not to marry and has an unfavorable opinion of marriage that closely resembles that of Marguerite. Aunt Clémentine tries to convince France not to marry Xavier, explaining that men are always tormentors. Moreover, she considers the scarcity of men untouched by the war to be an advantage for women who decide to marry. Whether the remaining men are permanently injured, or war slackers shamed by their inactivity, their humility and conciliatory nature in her view will make them ideal husbands (144). Thus, both Marguerite and Clémentine claim for women the independence traditionally reserved for men, either by avoiding marriage or by choosing a man who exhibits those self-effacing characteristics generally attributed to a model wife. It is important to note that Mars shows her opposition to these ideas by associating negative attributes to both of these characters.

While Mars's book appeared in the same year as those of Sandy and d'Orliac, its presentation of the war is markedly different in the characters' reaction to personal tragedy. The idealistic and patriotic speeches in Sandy's and d'Orliac's novels, which rationalize death or grievous injury as a great and necessary sacrifice to the nation, are conspicuously absent in Mars's novel. Xavier's bitterness at his injury and his inability to adjust to his new life contrast sharply with the determined courage of both Jean and Mario to transcend their individual misery. While it is true that these two characters must learn to adapt to their situation, and that they can only achieve this goal with the help of a woman's love, their eventual success is intimated in both novels. In Mars's book, however, France's love merely exacerbates Xavier's distress and rancor. Only the birth of a child may offer some recompense, although this outcome is uncertain. Xavier's mental attitude substantiates the comments of a minor character who worries that serious social problems will result from the veterans' instability. Moreover, acrimony and guilt, rather than the dramatic evocation of duty and sacrifice so prominent in Sandy's and d'Orliac's narratives, mark the way in which France's parents react to the news of their son's death at the front. Neither does Mars represent France's pregnancy as the fulfillment of her patriotic duty to create more soldiers and thus assure her country's future security, as both Sandy and d'Orliac imply in their novels. The author's noteworthy attention throughout her novel to portray authentically the process of amputation and the soldier's rehabilitation surfaces as well in her treatment of the psychological effects of the war on civilians. Mars explores the impact of the war on both groups without the idealism found in most other war fiction. Along with Pascal's *Noune et la Guerre* and Élie Dautrin's *L'Absent,* Mars's novel is among the few works that refuses the conciliatory notion that the war served a superior purpose.

The difficulties and prejudices faced by women on their own are the focus of Jeanne Broussan-Gaubert's *Reviendra-t-il?* (Will He Return?), published in 1918. The author of ten novels, several volumes of poetry, plays, and children's stories, Broussan-Gaubert was named a Chevalier in the Légion d'Honneur in 1936. The complexity of both the main characters and the plot in *Reviendra-t-il?* demonstrates the expansion of her skills as an author, for stereotyped women and melodramatic stories were common in her prewar novels. For example, her *Josette Chardin ou l'Égoiste* (Josette Chardin or the Egoist), published in 1912, recounts the story of a woman who marries for name and fortune and then neglects the child she resents to the point that he dies. It was exactly this type of novel that critics like the Comtesse de Courson in *La Femme Française pendant la guerre* (The French Woman During the War) (5) and Maurice Donnay in his *La Parisienne et la Guerre* (The Parisian Woman and the War) (18–20), both published in 1916, denounced as a contributing factor in Germany's decision to invade France, for it disseminated an image of France as weakened by a hedonistic and self-centered bourgeoisie.

In *Reviendra-t-il?*, Broussan-Gaubert relates the stories of three different women: Renée, a 30-year-old schoolteacher; Émilienne, a young peasant girl; and Bertha, an Alsatian refugee. Renée is devoutly religious and very proper, and when the war interrupts her wedding day, she agrees to marry her fiancé by proxy despite her misgivings, and also to live in his home in the central part of France. She begins her adjustment to the life and customs there with the help of Émilienne, also a young pious woman, who is beaten and abused by her parents. Renée befriends Bertha, an Alsatian refugee, who is partially insane and is eventually tormented to suicide by the local villagers who believe she is a spy. Much of the novel concerns the efforts of these women to combat the prejudice, rumor, and persecution that at that time inevitably burdened the lives of single women or women living alone.

Renée has an especially difficult situation, for the villagers doubt she is really married and assume that, in addition to being immoral, her education and vocation have made her haughty and pedantic. Her indeterminate marital status attracts the unwanted attention of Émilienne's banker uncle, who is cheating the villagers out of their war allocations and is also selling grain illegally to the Germans. Although Renée's husband is missing and presumed dead throughout most of the novel, his return from a German prisoner of war camp occasions the introduction of a major theme of *Reviendra-t-il?*, the role of women and men in postwar France.

Broussan-Gaubert spends considerable time developing the character of Renée. A puritanical and introspective feminist, she had planned to remain a teacher, and, by exploiting the prejudice against intellectual women, to avoid without embarrassment the sexual demands of marriage. Nevertheless, while Renée agreed with her colleagues that celibacy was a superior human state, her strong desire to have children led her to accept a marriage proposal.

> In private conversations, many of her colleagues confided to her that the absence of young people in their lives was the secret of their melancholy. Some of them missed husbands, lovers, [and] companions in their celibate lives, nearly all of them longed for children. Many of those women theorists of the salon, who live in fact without children, would be amazed to hear so many of these teachers, generally sincere feminists, deplore their lives without a daughter or son to raise, to cuddle, to love, [and] to educate. Renée, in this regard, was no different from the humblest peasant woman. This longing for a child, without the idea of lovemaking, is a feeling so true and so eternal that it has been glorified in all religions through the symbol of the Virgin-mother. Certainly, Renée loved Fernand for himself, but she loved him even now through his future children (80–81).[14]

Broussan-Gaubert's depiction of the lonely life of solitary and virginal teachers, dreaming of the children they might have had, supports her conviction that women's future advancement is contingent on their assumption of the "natural" role of mother. She underscores the intrinsic and inherent qualities of the maternal impulse by linking it simultaneously with feminism and religion, that is, the secular and political with the transcendent and metaphysical. Thus, for Broussan-Gaubert, as for other French reformist feminists of the period, the superiority and universality of motherhood dissolves and neutralizes all assumed contradictions.

Further, Broussan-Gaubert demonstrates through the characters of Bertha and Émilienne her conviction that men's assistance is indispensable for women. Bertha had tried to live independently as a private teacher in Paris, but soon found herself penniless and starving. Taken in by strangers whom she trusted, she became trapped in near slavery and was eventually seduced and abandoned by a gambler. By the time the war began, she was nearly insane, overcome by a combination of depression and superstition. Tortured by voices and harassed by the local villagers, who suspected any Alsatian of being a German spy, she drowns herself despite Renée's efforts to help her. The character of Émilienne is also tragic. Broussan-Gaubert presents her as a Cinderella-type young woman surrounded by a corrupt and abusive family. She spends her life in complete servitude to her brutish parents and war-profiteering uncle (1–12). Despite her docile nature, she does rescue Renée from her uncle's clutches in a noncharacteristic show of self-assertion, only to revert quickly to her life of submission. Eventually, she receives permission from her parents to enter a convent. Both the death of Bertha and

Émilienne's withdrawal from life demonstrate Broussan-Gaubert's view that an autonomous life for women is impossible.

When Renée's husband Fernand suddenly returns, his positive and energetic view of life shocks Renée and conflicts sharply with her chaste introspection. She is dismayed by Fernand's wish that she adopt a coquettish appearance with fancy clothes and makeup, and also by his plan to take her to Paris, a place she considers to be completely depraved. In stating his reasons for exposing Renée to the modern world in all of its beauty and ugliness, Fernand envisions a future in which everyone will work for the benefit of France. He explains that his experience in the war made him understand both the errors and the qualities of the French nation, as well as the measures necessary to rebuild and revitalize their country. Nonetheless, the collective effort he imagines retains the tradition of Republican Motherhood and separate "spheres," for although men and women would share the same goals, the women would serve France through creating and maintaining families (277–81).

Broussan-Gaubert incorporates in Fernand's future plan several common opinions concerning the connection among pacifism, feminism, women's education, depopulation, and the war. Fernand criticizes the intellectualism that results in Renée's refusal of life and reality, and he explains that the war has awakened them all from their dreams of universal peace and disarmament (277). Here Broussan-Gaubert joins several other novelists, like Reynès-Monlaur and Delorme Jules-Simon, in blaming pacifist and internationalist ideas for an ill-prepared France, whose perceived weakness attracted the aggression of Germany. Moreover, Broussan-Gaubert reiterates the criticism of feminist activists in Odette Dulac's *La Houille rouge* in defining the proper role for Renée and all women in the France of the future. Broussan-Gaubert's narrator assumes that all feminists are separatists who refuse contact with men as debasing, and she admonishes learned women especially for having chosen the principle of celibacy over the happiness of marriage. She blames their education for having indoctrinated them with too much idealism and conscience, thus diverting them from their true roles in life as wives and mothers (270–73). The male-female relationship Broussan-Gaubert imagines is a partnership, but not one of equals. For her, it is the husband who leads and instructs his wife, directing her to work, not just for women's rights, but for all forms of social progress, such as educating the poor or improving their living conditions.

> If feminists [were to be] sensible from now on, that is without revolt against the necessities of life that God, nature, and circumstances created, [and were to] rely on men to reach their goal, they would consider this war a sign of defeat. Alone, they can do nothing. Their role is to be wives and mothers,

without neglecting social responsibilities. Yes, the role of women is heavy. Cultivated, intelligent, they must be interested in the destiny of France, participate in the rebuilding of the material and moral ruins caused by the war, and they must also, because they [the men] insist, be pretty, decked out, and smiling (272).[15]

Broussan-Gaubert's double condemnation of women's education and the demand for civil rights has its basis in the debate concerning the role of population growth in the war. As discussed above in chapter 1, the steady decline in France's population had been linked to women's increasing participation in all levels of instruction, as well as their growing demand for autonomy in a variety of areas. The war, with its many deaths, disappointments, and reversals, merely intensified the incrimination and the demand that women discontinue these other activities to return to full-time motherhood. Broussan-Gaubert's emphasis on population growth also reflects the concern about the strength of France and its ability to resist future enemies, and as in Dulac's novel, maternal love triumphs over all obstacles, even the violence and humiliation of rape.

> Renée, who had read many articles and who had been fascinated for several months previous by this question, understood that scholars, philanthropists, and academicians had been asked their opinion. She saw it answered by this woman who nodded her head, agreed to the reasons [for giving up the child for adoption] but was holding the little being tightly, repeating these simple words that expressed her ultimate defeat and her greatest pride: "What do you want, it's my child" (185–86).[16]

Fernand returns from his tragic experiences with a renewed sense of life, and the mission to rebuild France and to improve society. His dream of progress, however, is actually reactionary, for, underlying his view is the assumption that modern ideas provoked the mistakes of the past. The lesson of the war in Broussan-Gaubert's novel is that women can accomplish nothing of value by themselves, and that their true goal in life is biologically and spiritually determined. Rather than turn their energies toward a personal or inner-directed fulfillment, women, according to Broussan-Gaubert, should devote themselves to the moral and physical reconstruction of France. The educated and principled women of France, like Renée, must adapt to this new society, regardless of how painful the transition.

The need for adaptation is also a theme in *Le Survivant* (The Man Who Survived) by the celebrated author Camille Marbo (Marguerite Borel) who lived from 1883 to 1969. Marbo enjoyed an especially long career filled with many honors and official accolades, among them being named a Chevalier and later an Officier of the Légion d'Honneur, and becoming the first woman president of the Société des Gens de Lettres. Her novels enjoyed both popular success and critical acclaim, earning for Marbo prestigious literary awards, including the Prix Fémina and the Grand Prix Louis Barthou from the Académie Française, as well as impressive financial gain. Her *Hélène Barraux, celle qui défiait l'amour* (Hélène Barraux, She Who Challenged Love) reached 100,000 copies, an extraordinary number in 1911.

In 1914, she and her father, the renowned physician Paul Appell, set up a hospital in Paris and founded a committee that raised and distributed money to thousands of French people and to groups of writers. Marbo assumed directorship of the hospital, establishing a reputation for efficiency that brought her to the attention of the French government. When in 1916, the officials of the Ministry of War complained that they could not find competent editors or typists among the women who volunteered to replace the mobilized men, they appointed Marbo to organize and preside over an organization designed to test the women and place them in the various service sectors. Marbo recounted the history of her own group, which recruited more than 20,000 women for service to the country, as well as the efforts that led to the induction of the 2 million women she called "the great French women's army" in her voluminous work of 1919, *La Mobilisation féminine en France* (The Female Mobilization in France). Marbo's contribution to the war effort earned her the Médaille de la Reconnaissance Française from the French government, which also named her as director of a newly-created postwar bureau of women workers. Yielding to the objections of her husband, famed mathematician Émile Borel, Marbo declined the appointment and resumed her literary career.[17]

In 1937, the literary critic André Delacour wrote that Marbo "has a virile mind but that she retains a feminine sensitivity. . . . The objectivity in her experimentation comes alive through the warmth of her affection" (475).[18] As noted previously, male critics often wrote similar commentaries in book reviews and essays about the works of women writers. Statements that credited the innovative aspect of women's writing to male qualities reiterated the standard opinion that women possessed inferior powers of imagination. By attributing women's individual accomplishments to masculine qualities, Delacour and other critics reinforced the notion of intrinsic male superiority in the arts, while rationalizing the obvious contradiction presented by acclaimed writers like Marbo. Moreover, in characterizing emotion, sensitivity, and other such "feminine" attributes as extrinsic to the work and important only in their capacity to add nuance or "flavoring," the critics reproduced the gender stereotype of women's larger role in society as accessory, whose purpose was to make men's lives more enjoyable.

Comments like Delacour's were especially common in reviews of women's novels whose main characters were not exclusively female, as in the case of Marbo's *Le Survivant*. Published in 1918, it was one of the few French women's war novels translated into English (along with Reynès-Monlaur's *Sister Claire* and Tinayre's *To Arms!*), and it enjoyed considerable success in the United States. Written in journal form and narrated in the first person, it tells the melodramatic story of Jacques and Marcel, wounded together on November 23, 1914. When Jacques wakes up in the hospital, he realizes that, although his mind and personality are intact as Jacques, in fact he has the body of Marcel. He finds out that Jacques is dead, and that the same bullet that struck Marcel in the head had passed through Jacques's brain, thus explaining what he calls "the Miracle." He decides not to tell his wife Lucette, since she would think him mad, but sets out instead to win her as Marcel. He is at first happy to see how devotedly she grieves for him; however he soon becomes aware of the degree to which she had changed since he left home. Alone and forced to take responsibility for herself and their child, Lucette had quickly adapted to her new situation and even seemed to enjoy pondering an issue and then making a decision. She is now so different from the submissive child, as he calls her, who simply mirrored all of Jacques's ideas and opinions, that he suspects her former obedience was merely an act. He begins to hate her as he realizes that his death has allowed her to realize this true self. At the same time, he notices that she has become more sensual, more passionate, and that she seems genuinely interested in Marcel. He is very jealous, yet at the same time conflicted, since he wants to marry her, although he does not want her to be in love with Marcel.

Marcel had been a heavy drinker and a seducer of women, and gradually Jacques finds himself incapable of resisting the same impulses and of overcoming Marcel's will. His marriage to Lucette in the second half of the book cannot make him happy, for as Jacques, he is jealous of the love that Lucette has for Marcel. He despairs because he wants her to continue to grieve for Jacques and to return to her submissive, former self.

Jacques and Marcel had both been engineers of war weapons, and when one of Jacques's inventions is slated to be used at the battle of the Somme, he realizes how to end his Miracle situation turned nightmare. His wounds healed, he reenlists, certain that he will fall with his men. He is finally happy, he states in his last diary entry of September 17, 1916, even though he doesn't know whether he is Jacques or Marcel, because he is serving a cause greater than individuals (185–91).[19]

Marbo's science fiction style plot is an effective vehicle for her to meditate on the nature of a human being's existence in relationship with others. Through the dual character of Jacques and Marcel, she considers questions on what constitutes the self and the role of impulses and reasoning in determining behavior. The war, with the reality of long separations and sudden death, provides both a realistic and appropriate context within which to examine the way people see themselves and relate to others. Jacques experiences anxiety because, although he knows he is still alive, he cannot find any trace of the person he once was in the eyes of family or friends. He is disappointed, shocked, and ultimately angry at how quickly they transfer their affection for him to Marcel, a man who is his complete opposite (34–38). The changes in Lucette, and his own unwilling transformation into the intemperate and unrestrained Marcel, reveal to him the interdependence of the sense of who he is and how people see him. Throughout the book he struggles to retain what he terms his real self, the real individual who was Jacques, but eventually realizes this is impossible, for he comes to understand that human beings exist only in relation to others. As he begins to comprehend the role that others play in shaping who he is, he loses his ability to resist Marcel's will, and like him becomes an absinthe addict and sexually exploitative. Unable to live as either man, he chooses to end his existential torment by sacrificing his life to the cause of France, a deed he considers to be an act of solidarity with a suffering and imperfect human race (185).

The changes in Lucette provoke Jacques to begin to ponder the relationship of external appearance and individual essence. For him, she has "remained a child while becoming a woman," (22) and although he does not intend to tell her about his miraculous survival, he feels certain that somehow she will recognize his true inner self. At their first meeting, he notes with pride that he is mourned "as a god" and also that she didn't look at the handsome Marcel's face. But at their second visit he learns that she intends to move to Paris, and he resents not only her decision to leave the house that still bears his presence, but also the tone of pride in her voice as she relates her new plans. While he understands she has more freedom as a widow, he does not expect her to exercise it, and he vows to prove to her that she still needs a man's advice and support.

> Everything that she said annoyed me. Why has she taken the habit of stating opinions in such a positive way—she who was silent with everybody but me? Why does she behave like a little girl who has suddenly gained a new dignity and makes a display of it? Does she think that as a wife she had no right to her private opinions, while as a young widow she ought to develop herself and exhibit an independent personality? Does she not see how ridiculous are all those phrases, "I consider" and "It seems to me?" (61).

As the visits continue, he begins to notice other changes, especially her sensual walk and her proud and passionate nature. He feels disoriented and bewildered because these changes took place without his knowledge, so that he cannot know if they were the honest result of her widowhood or the simple abandonment of what he believes to be her long-standing practice of deception. With horror he realizes that her opinions and ideas were only mirrors of his own (40–41). The metaphor of the mirror here is an important symbol, for without the person of Lucette to reflect Jacques's personality, the mirror would be blank, and he would lose the last vestiges of his own image. He tries to limit her social contacts, especially with other women, whose influence he feels is supplanting his own. He contrives plans to dominate her, finally realizing that Lucette's unqualified dependence on him was the basis of his happiness with her. He cannot let her former personality disappear, for he understands that that is all that remains of him.

> What I want is for my spirit to fill her as of old, master her, dictate to her her thoughts, her feelings. I laugh at my former folly—in the days when I flattered myself that I was a husband who respected his wife's individuality— as if the brightest part of my happiness had not always been this hold of my consciousness over another consciousness. Lucette, a tender and delicate parasitic flower, lived off me. It was I who transformed everything into thoughts, emotions, sentiments. The little parasitic flower withered, and now, adapting itself to solitude, it is beginning to plant its roots directly in the soil and aspires to build its own substance.
>
> I writhe in rebellion. I am determined that we shall once more be only one, that our life together shall be again what it was (64–65).

Thus, the figurative rebirth of Lucette begins with the literal loss of Jacques, and through this process, Camille Marbo presents both a critique of the past and a vision of the future. From a child whose face would change to reflect Jacques's words, Lucette has developed into a woman who understands that she has choices and enjoys making decisions about her own and her son's future. Not only has she become more confident about her mind, but more comfortable with her body. It is appropriate that eventually she fall in love with the overtly sexual Marcel, for he represents acceptance of a complete and adult woman. Her expression of desire for Marcel and the sexual independence it symbolizes repel and disgust Jacques, who mourns the loss of the purity of her love and endures the impulse to kill Lucette. He considers the passion Lucette shows him as Marcel to be an act of infidelity, and he longs for the pleasure he once derived from what he terms her "submissive tenderness" (113).

Jacques's death in the war causes the transformation of Lucette from her former childlike self into a mature woman. No longer simply a reflection of someone else's essence, she has evolved enough to be able to establish a new relationship and to keep her own individuality intact. Unlike Jacques, however, she is not aware of any change in her personality, and simply tries to cope with the tragic loss of her husband. She realizes that the war has destroyed her former life, a life of happiness and satisfaction for her, and she resolves to find a way to be happy again, albeit in a different way.

Jacques, however, chooses to die rather than to adapt to his new situation. His despair at the loss of power over his family is multiplied by his inability to resist the will of Marcel, and thus, to control himself. The conflict of Jacques, the authority figure, and Marcel, the hedonist, however, is not just the simple representation of the mind/body dichotomy. Moreover, Marbo's allegory goes beyond revealing how changing social conditions brought by war affect social roles to suggest the necessity of conscious adaptation for the future of France. Marbo presents Lucette as a model of the endurance and energy needed to persevere in the face of tragedy, whereas the alienated Jacques refuses to complete the symbolic transformation begun by the "Miracle." The war has altered the ordered patriarchal society in which Jacques was so comfortable to such an extent that he can longer find his place in it. His attempts to reverse these changes are futile and the happiness he desires eludes him because he cannot accommodate the loss of his power that the new Lucette represents. Marbo's parable for the future, much like Broussan-Gaubert's novel, confirms the necessity for all survivors of the Great War to reinvent themselves, not only to find a place in the postwar world, but also to participate in the rebuilding of France.

While Broussan-Gaubert and Marbo present their characters with choices, growth and improvement are not possible in Élie Dautrin's *L'Absent* (The Absentee), published in 1919. Dautrin was well-known in literary circles because of her many novels, plays, and articles published in the major Parisian newspapers. As in the case of other established women writers, her work received praise for its "manly qualities," proof that she was a "total" writer.[20]

L'Absent is the story of an officer who becomes so alienated from the civilian world of family, friends, and former colleagues that he becomes despondent and eventually commits suicide in battle. Dautrin examines and analyzes in this novel, as Marbo did in hers, the complex set of problems that beset soldiers and especially their wives, who ultimately become strangers to one another because of long separations.

In civilian life, Marville had been a lawyer with strong socialist and feminist ideas. Yet his commitment to all forms of individual freedom did not transfer to his personal life, and he had never noticed throughout 12 years of marriage how completely his wife's will had adjusted to reflect his own. Thus, when he returns on his first leave from the front, he is shocked not only by the deterioration of his own physical condition, but also by the transformation of his wife. At first his departure had disoriented her, but she quickly adapted to her new role as head of the family. She handled their difficult financial affairs expertly and made decisions about their son's education. She shrugs off her husband's amazement at her new abilities, saying that these tasks were not as arduous as men had made them seem to enhance their own importance. The war had taught women everywhere, she admits, a lesson of self-sufficiency and self-esteem (25–26). Marville notices that the joy of personal freedom had made his wife more intelligent and beautiful, and concludes with some bitterness that the war benefited those at the home front at the soldiers' expense.

> Marville observed to what extent his wife spoke with more coherence in her ideas, more logic in her deduction and more care in her language and resolution in its expression. He noticed the broadening of her thoughts, the scope of her concerns and to what point her judgments were more generous, more intelligent, her opinions nobler.
>
> He thought, "There was all of that in her. And for me to realize it, it took the war." An agonizing thought plagued him: "While I am decaying in combat, she is growing in liberty" (29).[21]

Each time Marville returns home, he feels more and more like a stranger to his wife, feeling certain that he has become "superfluous, awkward, and annoying to her" (109). Back at the front, his friends recount similar stories of estrangement and resentment for wives and other civilians. Having lost all hope in the future, they realize with a sense of doom the irony of their dread of an end to the hostilities. The postwar France they envision is bleak indeed: a society of immigrants in which everyone is equal in poverty, middle-class income devoured by taxes, and former soldiers hampered and limited by women reluctant to give up the freedoms they enjoyed during the war. Some of the men, like Marville and his writer friend, concede that they have become the enemies of their wives' newly found importance. Nonetheless, they conclude that as long as the women wait for and love them, they will not oppose their activities. What is hard for them to accept, however, is the increasing neglect and indifference they encounter with each visit home (117–35; 234–36; 249–52).

While Marville is away, his wife meets and gradually falls in love with a young American entrepreneur. His philosophy of practicality encourages Madame Marville to recognize new opportunities for her personal growth. Overcoming her feelings of guilt, she begins an affair with him as an expression of her emotional freedom. After some time, Marville becomes aware of their relationship, and without confronting them, decides to commit suicide. His marriage over, his son a complete stranger, and his law practice plundered by his former colleagues, he volunteers for a hopeless mission. The story ends with Marville's comrades surrounding his dead body.

While the majority of women's war novels detail the benefits of war in granting people the opportunity to express their heroism and serve their country, Dautrin's novel presents a more balanced view of the war's positive and negative effects on soldiers and civilians. Her narrative recognizes the value of personal growth, while regretting the consequences of that development. While some scholars of British Great War literature find a source of resentment toward women in the war's sudden reversal of male and female roles, Dautrin's Marville is proud, if somewhat amazed, at his wife's quick and successful adjustment to taking responsibility. Rather than take offense at her accomplishments, he despairs at the discrepancy between his egalitarian ideas and the way he treated her before the war. He understands that the intellectual development brought about by the war is his own, not hers, and he feels at fault that it took the war experience to reveal to him the extent of her intelligence. Similar to Jacques in *Le Survivant,* Marville concludes that it is impossible to know another person, but unlike Jacques, he is willing to accept his wife as an autonomous individual, for he understands the effects of freedom.

Marville also recognizes that the same event can have opposite and contradictory results, and he contrasts his wife's growth with his own physical deterioration. Rather than censure her new sense of self, he directs his anger instead at male civilians, whom he feels are taking advantage of the interrupted careers of their absent colleagues. With his successful practice gone, his family unfamiliar to him, it is understandable that Marville should cling to his fellow soldiers, who share similar experiences. In recounting their stories of divorce, children's estrangement, and the advancement of other men's careers, Dautrin develops sympathy for the soldiers. Moreover, she shifts the source of their misfortune away from women's increased autonomy to the loss of affection inevitable in war. The incidents the soldiers recount show clearly that it is the soldiers' absence that causes the women to withdraw their love and not their new, enhanced economic position. Certainly, the men are not happy about the decrease in their own importance in the family, but they are nonetheless willing to accept the change in status, as long as their wives will love and wait for them.

The conclusion that Dautrin posits is that absence does not make the heart grow stronger, but in fact, forces people apart. Although Dautrin does not develop extensively the character of Madame Marville, we do know that she married her husband in spite of the potential clash of his cold reason with her lively personality. They had little in common, but she thought that he would learn to share some of her tastes, especially for music and art. As the years went by, she stopped trying to assert herself and instead yielded completely to Marville's preferences in everything (19–20).

By the time Madame Marville meets the American Edward Hartford, she has been on her own long enough to rediscover the sense of herself that she suppressed throughout her 12-year marriage. While Edward loves France, his philosophy and outlook on life are totally American, and his practical views on politics and economics are often opposed to those of Madame Marville. His role in the novel is to provide an example of self-determination and freedom of choice, but his overly materialistic character and contingent view on the nature of good and evil reveal instead the intemperate and egotistical side of independence. When Madame Marville protests that she is not free to love him, his reply supports his moral relativism, a position identified as wholly American.

> "If only I were free."
> "Free! You become free. It is not life that must lead you, but you who must lead life," Edward expressed concisely in the American style (96).[22]

After this point, the resolution of the conflict between the American's forceful realism and Madame Marville's hesitant French idealism is no longer in doubt. While she does feel guilty for the pain she knows she will cause her husband, she begins the affair as an act of self-will. Thus, Madame Marville accepts Edward's challenge to assert her individual freedom and end her relationship with her husband. It is a step that she could not have made before the war, since the responsibilities she assumes awaken in her what Marville perceptively terms "the joy of liberty" (14). Nevertheless Dautrin is not suggesting that a woman's acceptance of personal freedom leads inevitably to a loss of affection, but rather that an individual who understands that she is autonomous will exercise that independence.[23]

While Marville is unselfish when considering the effect of freedom on his wife, other soldiers react to their spouses' transformations with dread. Their fear is economically based, however, and not concerned with a re-ordering of authority in their personal relationships. What alarms them is the application of women's autonomy in the workplace, for the men already faced competition from machines and more modern means of production, and they know that women are excellent workers. Their anxiety concerning women's efficiency is voiced at the same time as their dismay at the influx of foreign workers, rising prices, and the increased mechanization of industry that may have already eliminated their jobs. Their uneasiness about the next battle is certainly far less than their fear of an unpredictable future should they survive. Their wish that the war continue in order to delay the advent of postwar society is less absurd than it seems. The lessons of the battlefield taught them the timeless values of duty to country and friendship for comrades. When the war ends, so too will the idealism that rendered their sacrifice noble. Peace will thrust them into a now foreign world, a materialistic society dominated by the contingent morality of men like Edward Hartford. It is not surprising that they should fail to visualize themselves in such a future nation. In the true sense of the double meaning of the title of Dautrin's novel, the soldiers are both absentees and missing persons. Having left their homes voluntarily during the war, these soldiers were absent when their world changed. Failing to recognize themselves as possible participants in such a social milieu, soldiers like Marville will be lost and out of place in the future. While Jeanne Broussan-Gaubert and Camille Marbo's novels counsel change and adaptation to the new realities brought by war, Dautrin's vision of veterans and their families in postwar society is irremediable and dystopic.

Élie Dautrin is not the only author whose characters express concern about changing economic conditions, although her novel is one of the few to display those fears openly. Other authors evoke symbol-laden scenes of social unity whose didactic purpose is strikingly clear. For example, in both Broussan-Gaubert's *Reviendra-t-il?* and Isabelle Sandy's *Chantal Daunoy,* the main characters imagine a future France in which all classes of citizens work together harmoniously to rebuild the country. Moreover, these and other authors, such as Delorme Jules-Simon and Maryan, emphasize the leadership role that middle-class professionals, the educated, and the talented perform now and in the future. It is the task of such enlightened women and men as Broussan-Gaubert's Renée and her husband, Delorme Jules-Simon's Madeleine and Janine, and Maryan's Anet and Fabien, among others, to direct and instruct workers and peasants both during the war and in the reconstruction of France. The members of the "lower" and "laboring" classes, as they are called, are always ready to accept and follow the uplifting words and examples provided to them. Pointedly class-conscious and openly paternalistic, such depictions sought to counter contemporary fears of social revolution by presenting an image of community harmony. As discussed above in chapter 1, the war's duration and extensive casualties exacerbated traditional fears of the possibility of political revolution in France, even before the Russian example in 1917. As early as 1915, essayists such as Eugène Martin, Maurice Donnay, and the Comtesse de Courson began to promote the conciliatory role that they felt women should continue to play after the war. They heralded a type of *union sacrée* of the future, consisting of war-weary and potentially dangerous veterans pacified by middle- and upper-class former nurses, who had begun their social entente in the environment of the war hospital.[24]

Writing in 1916, Lucie Delarue-Mardrus also notes the future social value produced by the unintentional collaboration of "society" and "the people" in her novel *Un roman civil en 1914* (A Civilian Novel in 1914). She depicts the positive influence that women exert on all men in their surroundings, regardless of social condition.

> The nurses were bustling about, smiling. The good-natured respect of the soldiers on one hand, the compassionate attention of the women who cared for them on the other, this is how "society" and "the people," intimately brought together, perceived one another, perhaps for the first time.
> In spite of a few mistakes and some abuses, what a fine socialism the war will have created throughout France, in the pearly wards of the hospitals! (177–78).[25]

Set at the very beginning of the war, *Un roman civil en 1914* explores the difficult psychological maturation a young doctor, Francis Malavent, accomplishes by virtue of his changing relationship with Élisabeth Clèves, his grandmother's young companion. Malavent's transformation, like that of other characters such as Anet in Maryan's *Un marriage en 1915* and Claude in Reynès-Monlaur's *Les Autels morts,* results from events set into motion by the war. As in these other novels, the war furnishes a vantage point from which the character attains an angle of vision that would have otherwise remained obscure. It is a developing perspective that the reader shares with Francis, for although Delarue-Mardrus first presents Élisabeth as cold and unpleasant, gradually her greater qualities of intelligence, sincerity, fortitude, and self-reliance become evident. The character of Élisabeth grows in our estimation simultaneously as she evolves in Francis's opinion, leading to a comparison between the two that underscores his insecurity and childish behavior and accentuates the female character's determination and moral strength.

As in the novels of Camille Marbo and Élie Dautrin discussed above, *Un roman civil en 1914* concerns the evolution of a flawed person forced by the war to assess his life in ways he would not have done under normal circumstances. Francis Malavent, arrogant and self-centered, is especially disdainful of women. The birth defect that eliminates him from active duty emasculates him in his own eyes, forcing his psychological identification with women, who, like him, cannot enlist because they are "unfit since birth." Although he will be able to serve his country as a civilian doctor, he considers himself degraded because his status resembles that of "that heap of ignoramuses" he has been asked to train as nurses (72–73). Later he recognizes the courage that some of the women will demonstrate, acknowledging their receipt of the "baptism of blood" from those who had undergone the "baptism of fire" (149).

Francis's changing view of nurses parallels their portrayal in the novel as a whole. As Geneviève Duhamelet does in her account of nurses, *Ces Dames de l'hôpital 336* (Those Ladies of Hospital 336), Delarue-Mardrus displays the full range of the volunteers' attitudes and behaviors. Some show a deep level of commitment and bravery, while others simply want the prestige of a title or the selfish pleasure of a pretty uniform. Moreover, humor in both books softens the severity of any negative depiction, and even the most conceited nurses eventually contribute invaluable service to the war effort. Delarue-Mardrus, like Duhamelet, notes the gradual dwindling of the number of volunteers, until only the most sincere and courageous remain, and she praises the skill of the nuns and professional nurses who patiently endure the inexperience of the assistants. Francis finally concedes that the squabbles between the nuns and the volunteers are a microcosm of the human experience, and that working toward a common goal ameliorates all behavior, even that of the male doctors (74–85; 103–06; 127–30; 149; 200–06).

The particular target of Francis's misogyny has long been Élisabeth Clèves, whose strong will and introspective nature particularly annoy him. Delarue-Mardrus underscores the differences between the two characters, for although they are similar in age, Élisabeth is clearly superior to the childish Francis. The intellectual and educated Élisabeth spends no time trying to please or flirt with men and demonstrates a courage and strength of will as a volunteer nurse that erodes Francis's categorical animosity towards her. Already humiliated by his exclusion from "the great adventure," Francis resents Élisabeth's perspicacious assessment of his immaturity, and he vacillates between admiration and the desire to beat her (167). His determination to dominate her through either violence or marriage reaches a climatic point when Élisabeth rejects his declaration of love because of her affection for Francis's father. In revealing the details of this relationship, Élisabeth also elucidates the principles that structure and guarantee the integrity of her sense of self. Unwilling to accept a compromise of her freedom, damage to the father's family, or the degradation of concealment, she had refused marriage and decided on the celibate life of a teacher (190–92; 215–21).[26]

But me, I did not want to marry him. That was offensive to my freedom. There is in marriage an understanding, an authorization, something that exists only for others. Everything which yields, everything that makes provision for *others* is weakness, therefore humiliation. Since he had chosen me and I had chosen him, we did not need anyone's approval. . . .

We did not need anyone's approval. But it was impossible for me to injure anyone. I could not belong to him while his family surrounded him. It would have been necessary for us to hide from all of you. That was a humiliation greater than marriage (215–16).[27]

Francis, subject only to his raw desire to possess this woman, ignores her declaration of integrity and independence. Instead, he hears in her words only the indication that a sexual relationship did not exist between the couple, information that attests to her purity in his eyes and increases his determination to "steal" her from his father. Delarue-Mardrus makes it clear that Francis's lust for Élisabeth stems from a combination of divergent feelings of inadequacy and revenge against both his father and the woman, and moreover, that the young doctor is unaware of his psychological problems (250). He suffers in the comparison not only between himself and Élisabeth ("He felt physically and morally humiliated next to this upstanding and superior girl" (240)[28]), but also between himself as a noncombatant and his father, a soldier. For Francis, his father is simply, "the other, he who was not Francis" (217), and Élisabeth provides the means for him to compensate for his shame by outdoing a man who is physically superior. Delarue-Mardrus, like Andrée Mars and Élie Dautrin, emphasizes the role of the war in her character's loss of the traditional meaning of his own masculinity. Here Francis's resolve to make Élisabeth love him without regard to her own feelings, his desire to caress her but also to "crush" her, and his projected triumph over another man are part of his attempt to restore the sense of power and manhood forfeited by his civilian status (236–44). While he overcomes his attack of conscience by reasserting the importance of his own volition, he nonetheless regards himself as weak, incompetent, and impaired.

> Thus, while, lost in the horror of carnage, a man happily carries out his exalted duty, he, Francis the lame, Francis, unfit for service, Francis, the inept, accomplishes slowly, like a coward, the act of robbing from this man what was most precious and sacred to him.
> . . . But me, I love her! (243–44; 245).[29]

Delarue-Mardrus, similar to other authors, notes the lack of psychological and material preparation for war as a foil to demonstrate the eventual ennobling effects of such a tragic experience. She suggests at the beginning of her novel, as do Colette Yver, Odette Dulac, and others, that the contemporary faith in scientific progress, the hope for permanent peace, the current movement for increased political participation among all social classes, and the modern obsession with pleasure obscured the very real possibility of war. For those who anticipated the social and technological advances afforded by twentieth-century culture, war seemed like an anachronism, a remnant of the uncivilized past, no longer possible in a modern age of science (38). Delarue-Mardrus's narrator captures the shock and aversion of a society that thought itself too advanced for war and its dismay at being required to reanimate, like some vestigial organ or primitive instinct, an archaic heroic impulse.

> Are we made, we the modern, we the evolved peoples, for this episode from another time? What has war come to accomplish among our bitter European struggles for justice and equality, among our tangos and our Persian festivals? What does war have to do with us? We are no longer heroes. We will not know how to fight. We no longer have what we need for such an adventure (35).[30]

Despite some initial confusion, Delarue-Mardrus's characters, like those in other novels, quickly recognize and respond to the danger that threatens their country. "A great collective soul," exemplified by Élisabeth's purity, supercedes individual personalities and differences (44), and even the embittered Francis, despite his habitual misanthropy, feels the desire to embrace all of France (48). Moreover, the change in Francis's attitude symbolizes that of his entire generation, born during a time of peace. Proud of the rationality and tranquility they believed inherent in modern civilization, they had considered war to be a kind of ancient and irrelevant fable, an attitude they now sincerely regret (65; 70). The war so ennobles Francis that he recognizes good qualities in other people, instead of merely concentrating on their shortcomings. While the process is long, Francis eventually comes to appreciate the efforts of the volunteers, and his ultimate success with Élisabeth implies that his advancement was sufficient to appeal to this obviously superior person (284). Even the idea of disloyalty and competition with his father acquires justification as a natural outgrowth of war. The father's death, allowing the young couple to unite, is simply a heroic soldier's last opportunity to perform a type of altruism common to the defenders of France (208). Moreover, Delarue-Mardrus enlarges the symbolism of the father's death to exemplify the sacrifice of the present generation to insure the safety of tomorrow's adults, an image that has a great impact on Francis and Élisabeth. (296–97). Finally, the suggestion of the defeat of Élisabeth's plans for a celibate, and therefore childless life, parallels the symbolic restoration of the antisocial Francis to the greater family of France, ensuring that both young people will participate in the pronatalist effort to rebuild the country. Delarue-Mardrus's novel resembles others in its disapproval of individualism in favor of dedication to the nation. *Un roman civil en 1914* reveals how two young people, ennobled by the example of soldiers like the father, are able to discard their propensity for social isolation and accept their responsibilities to a totality greater than themselves.

Marie Lenéru (1875–1918) was the most important woman playwright of the prewar period. The intensity of her celebrity, as well as the unusual subject of her play of 1917, *La Paix* (Peace), warrants her inclusion in a study of French women's Great War fiction. For her, social responsibility is a moral obligation not to the people of one country, but to the entire human race. Lenéru had achieved startling success before the war, especially for her play *Les Affranchis* (The Emancipated Ones), first performed in 1910, and *La Triomphatrice* (The Triumphant Woman), which debuted in February 1914. Although Lenéru died at age 43 at the beginning of the influenza epidemic, she had already earned a reputation as a dramatist of genius. She attained the honor of the Prix Fémina in 1908 for the manuscript version of *Les Affranchis,* as well as the distinction of being the first woman since George Sand to have a play produced by the official theater of France, the Comédie Française.[31] Throughout the decade after her death, her literary friends and admirers wrote many articles and tributes, maintaining an interest in Lenéru's work that succeeded in the staging of several of her plays, including eight performances of *La Paix* in 1921.[32]

Lenéru did not live to see a production of the play, begun in 1914 and finished in 1917, or an end to the war she hoped would be humanity's last. Administrators at the Comédie Française had judged its frankly didactic content too inflammatory for a public at war, and had refused to honor Lenéru's request to present the new play in January 1918 instead of the previously scheduled *La Triomphatrice.*[33] Yet the play, despite its core of orthodox pacifism, resembles Lenéru's other dramas in its portrayal of the attempt of an intelligent and self-directed woman to resolve the conflict between expansion of her individual goals and the conventional demands of a love relationship. Unlike the degraded representation of women as victims, dupes, or imbeciles in the plays of her well-known male contemporaries, such as Henri Bataille, Paul Hervieu, and Georges de Porto-Riche, the main characters in all of Lenéru's dramas are strong women who think and then transform these reflections into action (Lavaud, 236–73).

La Paix begins in 1918 with the imagined end of the war and the beginning of the peace treaty negotiations. Lady Mabel Stanley, a pacifist of international reputation, has come to France with Graham Moore and other activists to persuade the delegates of the Congress of Paris to adopt the principle tenets of the Wilsonian and Wellsian models for world peace.[34] The beginning of the play finds Mabel at the home of her friend Marguerite de Gestel, who has lost her husband and two eldest sons in the war. Mabel's continued presence at the château solicits the anxiety of several characters. Moore, a former government minister and plenipotentiary member of the peace congress, wants Mabel to return to her lobbying efforts in Paris. Marguerite's brother, a famous war poet, fears the influence of Mabel's pacifist ideas on his nephew Jean, but more importantly, on General Peltier, a high-ranking member of the general staff in the French army. Peltier fell in love with Mabel while recovering from wounds at the hospital where she was a nurse, and he traveled to the château to ask her to marry him. The principle focus of the play concerns whether the pacifist Mabel and the professional soldier Peltier can overcome the personal and political ramifications of a marriage between such well-known and ideologically opposed public figures. Their efforts to explain their beliefs, and the attempts of other characters to influence their ultimate decision, provide a backdrop for Lenéru to explore the psychology of war and to assert her views on the creation of world peace. She portrays both peace and war as a matter of simple will, for war could not endure in her opinion without the assumption of its inevitability. Rather than dismiss world peace as a utopian dream, she believes that public opinion could bring it into existence through demand and further, that a vigilant and powerful international congress would ensure its permanence. Her position in *La Paix* differs from the call for a simple cessation of hostilities by those labeled during the war as defeatists, for it anticipated a strong treaty to control aggressive nations in the future. For Lenéru, the soldiers had died to create a lasting peace, and to subvert or fail to support that goal was to debase their memory.[35]

La Paix investigates in particular Lenéru's conviction that the most important role in the creation of world peace belongs to women. As witnesses to the agonizing deaths of their men, women become for Lenéru the sacred guardians and sole repositories of their *souvenir* or memory. The multiple connotations of *souvenir* as remembrance, keepsake, and memorial lend depth to Lenéru's insistence on the concrete action necessary to fulfill the process of memory. She thus extends the stereotypical identification of the passivity of emotion with the feminine by infusing it with an active quality for change. Recollecting the soldiers' sacrifice without continuing their effort to secure world peace is to disregard the power to end war that the memory of their deaths bestows on women.

> But I also ask the women, because I reserve for them a mission, the mission that is specifically theirs, which is mine, that of memory. . . . I have come to this belief, only one thing is essential, one single thing would suffice, but of which humanity is perhaps incapable: not to forget. . . . Ah! if only each person had seen . . . if only a single one of these horrors, which played across our cowardly imaginations by the thousands, were truly a part of the actual life of each one of us, if only we considered ourselves in fact to be charged with exacting revenge. . . . They assassinate your brothers in your houses, and you listen behind your latched door . . . (30–31).[36]

Mabel's arguments for the possibility of peace have at their core an attempt to convince the other female characters of the essential importance of women's support to continue any policy of war, something already known to generals and politicians alike. The women in the play represent an array of different attitudes and responses to the consequences of war, from Marguerite, the *mère douloureuse,* to the sanguinary and vengeful Simone. Their individual struggles to understand or even merely to endure their situations provide the means for Lenéru to elucidate carefully her pro-peace position, and counter any arguments that could dispute her doctrine of women's responsibility.

Lenéru creates debates between characters who hold opposing views, but who came to those conclusions from similar life situations. These arguments delineate all of the rational and emotional arguments for and against the idea of a permanent peace and the role of women in its realization. For example, both Marguerite and Mabel served as volunteer nurses, where they experienced firsthand the physical reality of war. Marguerite even lost the use of her arm to an infection transmitted from a patient, and Mabel was a witness to her beloved brother's slow and agonizing death. Words like honor and glory do not grant solace to Marguerite for the loss of her husband and two sons, for she is haunted by the image of her son Gérald. He did not experience the kind of heroic battlefield death that people had been led to imagine by writers like Marguerite's brother, the famous war poet. A machine gun sheared off the top of his head, and Gérald died in a hospital, screaming continuously for 29 hours. Despite the similarities in what they experienced, the women responded differently. Marguerite reacts to her tragedy by retreating to her memories of the past and refusing to continue her life, while Mabel rejects this mute resignation and embraces an active concept of remembrance. She recognizes the inherent transformative power in the grief of mothers to preserve the peace that the soldiers died to obtain. She urges Marguerite to translate her acquiescence into resistance, her sorrow into action, so that the war just ended would truly be the last (21–27).

Lenéru also contrasts the ideas on war, men, and marriage held by two young women characters, Perrine and Simone. Perrine, a childhood friend of Marguerite's sons, has lost three brothers and a brother-in-law in the conflict. Introduced early in the play, Perrine gives voice to the traditional argument for women's pacifism, a long-standing rationale mentioned and generally discredited in the works of other authors studied here, such as Marcelle Tinayre. Perrine decides to reject any personal participation in the cycle of violence by remaining celibate. Her denial of motherhood is a direct repudiation of her prescribed role in the creation of French soldiers for the future. Unlike Marguerite, who chastises her for rejecting her patriotic duty, Perrine understands her power, however small it may be, to affect events in the society to come.

> I sacrificed my happiness in this world. And so that God might never permit, as long as I am alive, that children of others be killed again. . . . I made a vow to never have any of my own (18).[37]

Simone, however, sees beauty and grandeur in sacrifice and unlike Mabel, believes that war, rather than peace, honors the memory of the dead soldiers. She identifies heroism so completely with war, that she vows to marry only a soldier, someone who has experienced the "sacred fire" (90–91). Moreover, Simone and her father Delisle, the famous war poet, espouse the proposition directly opposed to that of Mabel. Simone considers peace an impossible dream, and both of them accept war as inevitable because they believe that it is part of a divine plan to punish sin and purify the earth. Thus to defeat war, as Lady Mabel proposes, is to blaspheme by opposing the will of God and further, to rob the world of virtues like nobility and self-abnegation that can only arise through war (89–95).

Lenéru skillfully emphasizes the viability of Mabel's views on the potential role of women in creating peace by unmasking Delisle's attempts to obscure the force of women's power. Like Mabel, he acknowledges the considerable influence that women possess. As women remain largely unaware of their power, he correctly perceives the danger in Mabel's attempts to stimulate women to exert their energy for peace. He concedes that in order to continue to exist, a politics of war must have the undiluted support of women, whether as mothers of future soldiers or as the conscience of those presently in arms. His concerted efforts to prevent the marriage of Peltier and Mabel stem from his fear that the high-ranking general will lose the inspiration needed to wage the next war. Delisle's religious tone elucidates Lenéru's view that war and peace depend on belief systems, and that war becomes inevitable only when people act according to those doctrines, "[t]he only reality in the world is in our convictions" (113).[38]

> But you are at the highest level of the national defense. . . . The man charged with anticipating, with ordering future sacrifices, future slaughters, if you like, cannot live in the unbelieving atmosphere of pacifism. He will not take from the eyes of a woman in mourning, from the arms of a defiant woman, the self-confidence, the composure, the certainty to accomplish the essential task, the indispensable responsibility, the supreme mission of salvation! (120–21)[39]

Further, Lenéru compares the sentiments and actions of Peltier and Jean, the only remaining son of Marguerite, to explore the illusions that ensnare people in a politics of war. Peltier, the 50-year-old professional sol-dier, freely admits the absurdity and uselessness of war. His judgment on war and peace, however, is interwoven with a static and gendered view on the respective responsibilities of men and women. Peltier's approval of Mabel's pacifism results from his certainty that such a position is normal for a woman, just as waging war is normal for a man. So firm is he in this conviction that he condemns women who are warlike or even resigned to war, and declares that he could only love a pacifist (44). Although Peltier concedes that a man might be a pacifist, he cannot envision himself in any other role than that of soldier. His chosen profession transmits a sense of honor so integral to his definition of himself as a man that he cannot aban-don it, even knowing that war is futile.

Like Peltier, Jean had decided to become a professional soldier and likened himself to a monk, called to holy orders (141). However, he soon accepts Mabel's argument that peace would exist if people desired it more than they wished for war, and he resigns his commission in the army to join the pacifists. His decision frees him from the static definition of honor and masculinity that constrains Peltier and aligns him instead with the vig-orous activism of Mabel. Choosing pacifism over war, that is, female qual-ities of caring over masculine violence, he accepts a "call to the heart" that grants him a higher image of himself as a man than if he had yielded to the temptation of following in his brothers' footsteps to avenge their deaths (142). His fiancée, like Peltier, is not able to relinquish her belief either in the inevitability of war or of a man's natural desire for glory in battle, and she breaks her engagement with Jean, just as Mabel ends her relationship with Peltier (150–51). Thus, both Jean and Mabel reject individual happi-ness through marriage for the possibility of universal welfare. In uniting love and action, emotion and intellect, Mabel and Jean transcend station-ary gender-determined categories to personify the aggregate qualities es-sential to enact Lenéru's vision of the future. The play, however, ends on a pessimistic note that proved to be prophetic. The pacifists, determined to end the cycle of brief truces that merely interrupt continual war, vow to continue their campaign, despite the failure of the congress to adopt any of Wilson's or Wells's doctrines (158). Writing in 1917, Lenéru would not live to see the accuracy of her prediction of a failed peace, or her premo-nition that visualized, as did that of Wells, explosions that would reduce the cities of Europe to volcanic rubble (148).

The central role of women as repositories of the memory of those who died for France is also an important theme in J. Delorme Jules-Simon's sec-ond war novel, *L'Impérieux amour* (The Essential Love), published in 1918. The diary format of the novel accommodates the confessional tone that also characterized Delorme Jules-Simon's earlier *Âmes de guerre, âmes d'amour,* and the structure of both novels permits the main characters to examine their consciences without fear of impropriety. As in the earlier book, *L'Impérieux amour* explores the difficulties faced by French women in war as they strive to meet their traditional obligations, while also struggling to understand and fulfill society's new expectations for them as women. The protagonist in this novel is Suzanne, a 30-year-old woman whose parents died when she and her brother were young. Nine years his senior, Suzanne is more like a mother than a sister to Michel, and he often calls her "Little Mother" and acknowledges the values of patriotism and valor with which she has raised him. Suzanne is strong and independent, and like other orphaned women in the novels studied here, the tragic death of her parents authorizes the development of a sense of autonomy and self-reliance that would not have otherwise been permissible.

The central interest in the novel is the growing conflict between Suzanne and her fiancé, Roger, concerning Suzanne's participation in the war effort. It is a discord that forces Suzanne to reevaluate the priorities in her life, bringing about a new understanding of her responsibilities as a French woman. Nevertheless, the emotional maturity she acquires develops not from her own activities, but primarily as a reaction to the opinions of the three men in her life, Roger, her brother Michel, and Philippe, a former suitor of Suzanne and surrogate father for Michel. The disagreement among the men concerning the meaning of sacrifice and love of country launches a process of self-reflection in Suzanne that will expand to a meditation on duty and the glory of heroic resignation applicable to both men and women.

With the beginning of the war, Suzanne finds herself forced to consider issues and make decisions that are completely new to her. While she supports the war effort, she resists her brother's enthusiasm for glory in battle and thinks only of the tragedies and loss of life to come. Her patriotic words at his departure mask her "selfishness" and "lack of enthusiasm" (8). It is this reticence, although presented as natural and maternal, that will evolve into an understanding of the preeminence of the love of country, the "essential love" of the title, over any affection between people. Although Suzanne has released Michel physically from her care as a parent, the events of the story will teach her that women must also relinquish their emotional attachments so that their soldiers can offer themselves without reservation to the service of France.

With both Michel and Philippe at the front, Suzanne searches for a way to contribute to the war effort. Stressing her maternal responsibility, she organizes a daycare center for the children of soldiers, which puts her in contact for the first time with the working class. Similar to the idea presented in the novels by Duhamelet and Sandy among others, it is the resignation of the poor that exemplifies the error of individualism to middle- and upper-class women. Moreover, Suzanne, much like these other characters, accepts the moral responsibility of her class to lead and inspire those of lower status (16–20). Her zeal for volunteer activities leads to the conflict with Roger, who has been assigned to essential services in Paris. While Roger is grateful that he is out of danger and that he can still see Suzanne every day, he also mocks her feeling of guilt for his safety and disparages her desire to serve her country as a childish whim. The comparison of Roger's attitude with the patriotic ardor expressed in the letters from Michel and Philippe causes Suzanne to question her fiancé's motives and judgment (34–51). Although she defends Roger's work in Paris as vital to the war out of her duty as his future wife, her brother's suggestion that Roger is a war slacker (*embusqué*) raises doubts in her mind. Still, her hesitancy remains covert, confined to the secrecy of her diary. Even when Roger refuses to allow her to become a volunteer nurse, since this would put her in daily proximity with officers, she remains silent, allowing Michel to argue with Roger on her behalf (61–77). The dispute over nursing, however, is only a symptom of a greater conflict that Suzanne senses between the traditional obedience she wishes to accord to her future husband and the obligation to devote her energy to her country. She reproaches herself for being afraid to displease Roger, yet she knows that he should facilitate, rather than hinder, her desire to serve. With sadness, she realizes that although she might truly aspire to fulfill the conventional expectations for her as a wife, the experience of war has rendered that impossible.

> Never do our thoughts coincide, never do our two hearts beat in unison outside of those rare instants when, succeeding in setting aside the war, we speak only of love. And even during these fleeting moments, a shadow lingers; I would like to be able to say to him: "I am your creation, my voice is only the echo of your own, my soul is the reflection of your soul, your strength fortifies my weakness," and I cannot pronounce these words! (86–87)[40]

As the novel progresses, Roger becomes increasingly sensitive to allusions to his safety, even accusing the frontline soldiers of seeking praise for their bravery. He also impugns the integrity of women volunteers and the young recruits, predicting a breakdown in traditional French social and family order after the war. For Roger, the authority and responsibility women exercised during the fighting and the extreme hardships that characterized the young men's trench experience would encourage arrogance and self-assertion in both groups, thus usurping the traditional authority of older men (80–85).

While Suzanne does not entirely accept Roger's ideas, she does fear that they may prove correct. Suzanne's visit to a friend whose husband is at the front allows Delorme Jules-Simon to address directly the issues of civilian conduct and relationships with soldiers. Arriving a few days after the end of the husband's first leave, Suzanne finds her friend both depressed and angry. Charlotte had taken care of the three children, managed the household finances completely by herself for many months, and had expected praise from her husband. Instead he felt alienated from his family and embittered that his traditional role had evaporated. The pitiful situation stimulates Suzanne's reflections on the psychological needs of soldiers and the problems that sometimes result in depression, drunkenness, and other negative behaviors. She concludes that the solution resides in the compassion of women who would preserve paternal authority and importance by creating the illusion that all decisions came from the father. Such stratagems would not only safeguard the family structure, but would also invigorate the soldier by proving to him that his wife and children understood the value of his courage (90–105). Moreover, by appropriating the husband's thoughts and opinions and totally subsuming her identity to his, the wife would insure that his will and character would survive his death.

It is significant that the lesson of heroism that Suzanne seeks to impart to her friend is in fact the one she is in the process of learning herself: the insufficiency of human love without love of country and the impossibility of love without esteem. When Roger receives the respected *croix de guerre* medal, normally given for valor in battle, for his work at the home front, Suzanne's embarrassment deepens to shame as she compares his ordinary job with the hardships of soldiers at the front. She fears that Roger is in fact avoiding active service because he lacks the courage that motivates men like Philippe and Michel. Her guilt deepens as she struggles to maintain her affection for him despite his willingness to remain in the rear (109–60). Nevertheless, she shifts her attention from Roger to herself for, at this point in the novel, she is still searching for a middle course between her obligations as a wife and her duty to France. The stirring words in her brother's letters and his courageous example illuminate for her the means to accomplish both responsibilities without lessening her commitment to either. Reiterating the values of the Republican Mother ideology so prevalent in the novels studied here, Delorme Jules-Simon depicts a self-directed protagonist who willingly chooses to embrace a purely maternal role that requires total submission to her husband.

My duty is to prevent my uneasiness from affecting my health, because as the far-off voice of Michel whispered to me, I might need my strength for him or for others, my duty is to bring to my fiancé an affectionate, sweet,

[and] cheery soul because we have the obligation to make love many times in order to give a considerable number of little Frenchmen to a crippled France. This idea brings a smile to my lips. I am going to make myself beautiful and throw myself into Roger's arms as soon as he arrives. . . . He is really my master, my only ruler, and I love everything from him, even his domination (123–24).[41]

Yet the harmony that Suzanne constructs between her role as wife and mother assumes that both partners accept unconditionally the preeminence of the "essential love" of the nation. Despite Suzanne's doubts about Roger, she is determined to fulfill her obligation to him and to France. It is not until she realizes how the experience of war had ennobled her friend Charlotte that she understands how her own affirmation of patriotism had elevated her beyond Roger. Nonetheless, Suzanne's epiphany comes not from any personal accomplishment or idea, but from the awareness of the importance of her responsibility as a future mother of French children. Seeing the hero-worship and devotion that her friend instills in her children, Suzanne realizes that her own children will suffer unbearable humiliation if they cannot relate with pride their father's exploits in battle (192–200). When both Michel and Philippe are killed, Suzanne ends her relationship with Roger, considering her desire to honor their memory impossible if she were to marry a man who had not exhibited the same degree of love of country as they had. Conscious of the invisible presence of all of the patriotic dead, she feels their strength authorizing her to assert her new consciousness. Understanding at last the greater meaning of the war, she assumes her supreme duty as a French woman to become the storehouse of their greatest love, the love of country. Thus preserved, the sacrifice of Michel and Philippe will become a model for future generations and perhaps even for Roger himself, whom Suzanne hopes to inspire to renounce his post for one at the front that would test his love of France.

A sort of joyful premonition came over me. Michel, Philippe, will [the fact of] your death reopen the tomb of my love to enact a magnificent resurrection? Will it make Roger understand the beauty of your life, of your heroic sacrifice?

A single ideal inflamed and directed you both. You were the champions of right and liberty.

Michel, Philippe . . . dead? No, eternally living to exemplify, to glorify in us the essential love (242–43).[42]

In suggesting the eventual rehabilitation of Roger, Delorme Jules-Simon indicates far more than a happy conclusion to a love story. Similar to many of the authors studied in the preceding chapters, she subscribes to the conviction that despite its tragedies, the war brought unforeseen benefits, causing people to grow and change into more mature and better citizens. Although Suzanne breaks out of her prescribed role as a submissive fiancée and future wife, she does so only for the greater good of France and not for any individual goal. Moreover, her revolt is of course temporary, because without Roger she would not be able to fulfill her primary intent to repopulate her weakened country.

For Delorme Jules-Simon, as for Broussan-Gaubert, Delarue-Mardrus, and others, the war forced the French people to confront formidable tasks for which they were not prepared. Nonetheless, their great moral strength, love of country, and historical traditions and faith enabled most of them to develop the new abilities required in such unexpected circumstances. These authors portray the process of that evolution in women protagonists who adapted more easily than their husbands to the demands of modern French society. It is their intelligence and awareness of their unique maternal responsibility, along with their self-discipline and abnegation, that will build the France of the future. These authors indicate that in order to find a place in the postwar world, men must relinquish part of their traditional authority and accept some new expressions of women's autonomy. To fail to do so, the writers insist, would be to harm themselves and impair the restoration of their nation.

Conclusion

"The Unchanging Core at the Heart of Change" 🏵

The image of the war that emerged from French women's fiction was that of a great teacher of moral and civic virtues. The gravity and tragic finality of the consequences of war provided life lessons impossible to achieve under normal circumstances. The experiences endured created situations in which each individual developed into a better person through service to the nation. Whether self-centered or simply naive before the war, women especially became aware that they possessed talents and emotional resources previously unknown to themselves and their families. Humility, self-sacrifice, and duty replaced egotism and complacency, stemming the erosion of eternal "French" values that had been invigorated by modern society with its freedoms and optimism for peace. The fiction writers presented war simultaneously as a destroyer of individuals and as a creator of a strong French national family. For them, the war was a purifying agent that expunged individualism and created, as one of the novelists declared, a "great collective soul." This patriotic spirit subdued and superceded all disputes, differences, and personalities to restore the people's connection with a national identity historically associated with the development of Christianity and Western civilization. In this definition of civic responsibility, the nation appropriated and subsumed religion so that *la patrie* preceded and was superior to all things. Uniting the historical with the sacred in the novels and short stories, textual references to national and religious figures such as Joan of Arc and Saint Genevieve elevated the primacy of the nation to the highest level of purity and transcendence. Concurrent images of Germans as godless and innately evil, intent on destroying Latin civilization and Catholicism, provided the antithesis necessary to underscore the righteousness of the French cause.

The cultural tradition that ascribes a variety of symbolic meanings to women and their bodies is transhistorical and multinational. The history of an idealized image of maternity in France, the Republican Mother, which identified procreation with civic duty, was the focus of chapter 1. As a construction based on characteristics deemed inherent in women's nature, and which guaranteed the home and family, the Republican Mother designated the nation's past and its future, as well as the purity and sanctity of maternal love. In creating characters and plots that conveyed their reaction to the national event of war, the women fiction writers drew on this and other received values and symbols. Whether literal or figurative mothers, the women in these stories eventually exemplified the ideal of sacrifice and duty to the nation through the maternal function. It was an ideal of service that granted priority to the family of the nation over that of the individual, and therefore the "sacrifice" of offering soldiers to the nation was more laudatory than the "selfishness" of preserving a son's life. The acceptance of such a proposition was central to the successful functioning of the ideology of Republican Motherhood during the Great War, for it erased the contradiction between the creation of life inherent in maternity and the destruction of life innate to armed conflict. Asserting the primacy of a woman's duty to the family of the nation promoted and assured their continuing support for the war, not only in the encouragement of soldiers and in the performance of essential services, but also in facilitating women's return to the home when the war was over. It is noteworthy that although the contemporary manifestation of maternal ideology transmitted a distinct moral authority to women that resulted in an increase in women's agency, it was nonetheless a limited power bound to the aims of the government of France in waging, and eventually winning, the Great War.

The novels and short stories explored in chapter 2 detailed the challenges faced by middle- and upper-class women whose previous lives of isolation from the outside world left them unprepared to confront the exceptional problems brought by war. As dedicated wives and mothers, these women sought to fulfill their prescribed duties of service and charity; yet, ironically, it was the willing acceptance of this ideal that placed the characters in dangerous situations. Nursing the wounded and caring for refugees required a level of interaction with the outside world that exposed the women to disparate people, issues, and ideas. The characters did not welcome the freedom of movement and thought that accompanied their new activities, but rather feared the loss of the tranquility and safety of their former lives. Their stories demonstrated, however, that their faith in God and devotion to France provided the moral strength and guidance necessary to allow them to serve their country without losing their respected and traditional roles as Republican Mothers. These characters became more self-directed and autonomous, but they exercised that freedom of thought in an attempt to reconstruct the security of their prewar lives.

The protagonists examined in chapter 3 also found themselves in abnormal and perilous situations, but they faced risks to their persons as well as to their moral reputations. Caught in circumstances where their actions would directly affect the outcome of the war, several of these protagonists metamorphosed into warriors who engaged the enemy and were victorious. Yet these sheroes carried out this traditionally male activity without rejecting those qualities considered essential to femininity. While their authors created stories that made prominent their characters' active courage, there was no direct challenge to the authority of men in matters of armed conflict, nor any attempt to usurp the male role in war. Writers in a second group of novels also placed their characters in situations that forced them to act heroically.

In chapter 4, the experience of war led the main characters to realize the harm that had been inflicted on the larger community by the ideas and projects undertaken before the war for their personal satisfaction. The authors confirmed the view that the war provided an unforeseen benefit by revealing to the protagonists the authenticity of their obligation to family, nation, and God. Whether they attempted to express their freedom intellectually, professionally, or socially, these main characters eventually renounced their autonomy as inappropriate and injurious to the greater interests of the nation. Perhaps the most destructive aspect of the women's independence had been the choice against motherhood, presented by the authors as having contributed to the weakness of France and rendering the nation vulnerable to attack. Abstention from maternity for any reason, be it to attend parties or to attend medical school, brought the same severe condemnation and charge of egotism. Despite the importance of the doctrine of Republican Motherhood, the patriotic reason for childbearing was secondary to the belief that the instinct of mother love was universal, undeniable, and unaffected by any personal choice on the part of the individual woman. In these stories, it was the simple presence or idea of a child that annulled even the most elaborate of personal goals.

The authors of the fiction explored in chapter 5 chose satire to express many of the same themes contained in the majority of French women's war novels and stories. However, while other writers occasionally mentioned the selfishness and other failings of civilians, it was in the works of Gyp and Jeanne Landre that the wartime behavior of noncombatants was closely scrutinized and judged not only egotistical and foolish, but even disloyal and seditious. Both authors used sarcasm and facetiousness to expose the pretense of virtue that they felt concealed the rapaciousness of many private citizens, both men and women. However, women of the upper class were targeted in particular, presented as petty, vain, insensitive, social climbing, and sexually aroused by wounded soldiers. Such reproach closely paralleled the censure in the press of "society" women, the group of civilians whose daily lives underwent the greatest amount of social change during the war.

Perhaps the most complex of French women's war fiction are among those works examined in chapter 6. While the authors of these works concurred with many of the prevalent themes and ideas explored in other war novels, they analyzed in much greater depth the psychological dimension of the impact of war on their characters. Centered on the relationships of soldiers with their wives and children, these works concentrated on the problems of the veteran's reintegration into the civilian world. Some of the women responded to the men's new situations by renouncing their individual goals to devote themselves entirely to their husband's or fiancé's rehabilitation. Other women, however, experienced emotional changes that brought them into conflict with their soldiers. The choices made by these protagonists reflected their own understanding of the impact of the war, rather than that of the men. Nonetheless, regardless of the ex-soldier's viewpoint, the decisions and actions of these women generally acknowledged the overriding importance of the psychological and material rebuilding of France. These authors indicated that the restoration of France required the cooperation of all sectors of society, and that to facilitate this unity, some sharing of authority and power with women was now necessary.

It is important, however, to view the partial empowerment of women displayed in these novels within the context of the theme of patriotism manifested in the majority of the fiction. Independent decision making and autonomy were authorized only when in service to the collective needs of France, and individualism, regardless of its source, was specifically condemned, only to be transformed by the experience of war. The strength of this new knowledge, although acquired through pain and tragedy, was powerful enough to overcome the greatest of transgressions, as well as the tiniest of peccadilloes.

The cumulative record of women's activities in the Great War became in the novels a testament of the benefit of their contribution to the survival of their nation, characterizing their effort for victory as similar to that of any uniformed soldier. Moreover, the motive and capacity to serve the nation originated from those qualities of self-sacrifice and forbearance that the authors established as integral to maternal love, and not from any desire to usurp male privilege or assume male social roles. Thus, for these authors, women's participation in the world outside the home did not challenge or subvert the traditional values of French society, nor did it degrade the "womanly" virtues of devotion, service, and sacrifice. Instead, the experience of war intensified and concretized those innate qualities essential to the realization of the responsibilities of the Republican Mother. This notion of the complementarity of women's biological and social roles and the fusion of the private and public "spheres" mirrored the dual philosophy of reformist feminists of the period. In this view, the maternal function transcended and synthesized any separation between such seeming opposites, and empowered self-reliant and autonomous women to work with men for the greater good of their nation.

By assimilating an expanded role for women within an historically validated definition of the responsibilities of French citizens to their nation, the Great War authors included women in the ongoing discussion of the meaning of national identity and the relationship of their people to *la patrie*. They certainly concurred with the accepted definition of "Frenchness" as the embodiment of the eternal values of service, piety, honor, and other qualities identified with the long history of Catholic France. In their works of war fiction, these writers claimed for women the same obligation to safeguard and perpetuate those essential virtues that had long been the responsibility of male citizens.

The French women writers acknowledged the destruction and upheaval of war, changes that caused devastation of lives and property as well as emotional and social instability. While modifications in borders and frontiers, like the loss of Alsace and Lorraine in 1870, were part of the reality of history, the endeavor to preserve a national identity and to defend its basic values constructed a space outside of time where that essence was protected from the power of events. In general, such efforts seek to insure permanence and continuity even within an atmosphere of anxiety and uncertainty, establishing "an unchanging core at the heart of change." The values that express these essential qualities connote spirituality and morality, characteristics that confirm the continuance of the nation regardless of any temporal circumstances.[1]

In their novels and short stories, the women writers of the Great War recognized the duality of permanence in the midst of transformation. They confirmed the constancy of the core values of the French Nation and its People, virtues that would subsist unblemished, despite enormous loss of life, partial occupation by enemy troops, and countless hardships endured by both soldiers and civilians. For them, the essence of France was invariable, even if war devastated its surface appearance, just as the essential qualities of French womanhood were eternal and immutable. These writers validated the continuity of women's devotion to their families and country, despite outward changes in their everyday lives brought about by war. Even while advocating and supporting women's agency in the modern France of the future, the writers reasserted the identification of women's biological role with the preservation of the Nation, as symbols of home and family and of the past and future. Their fiction demonstrated that the freedom of movement and independent decision making required of these women in the service of their imperiled country did not diminish, but in fact, strengthened the core values of maternal love, abnegation, and service of Republican Motherhood. Derived from these "innate" female qualities, the feminine force amplified by the war experience would continue to manifest itself in all places women might wish to go, whether they remained at home or were active in the public arena. For these writers, the changes in women's daily lives, even including the possibility of increased civil rights, were external only, much as the differences in the postwar French landscape were merely superficial. In French women's Great War fiction, the essential qualities of its female citizens, just like the core values of the Nation, were constant and changeless, durable and enduring, eternal and outside of time.

Notes

PREFACE

1. Judith Lowder Newton, *Women, Power, and Subversion: Social Strategies in British Fiction, 1778–1860* (Athens: University of Georgia Press, 1981); "History as Usual? Feminism and the 'New Historicism,'" in *The New Historicism,* ed. H. Aram Veeser (New York: Routledge, 1989): 152–67; and Deborah Rosenfelt, "Introduction: toward a materialist-feminist criticism," in *Feminist Criticism and Social Change: Sex, Class, and Race in Literature and Culture,* ed. Judith Newton and Deborah Rosenfelt (New York: Methuen, 1985).
2. Sharon Ouditt, *Fighting Forces, Writing Women: Identity and Ideology in the First World War* (New York: Routledge, 1994), 2.
3. Two recent critical works are a notable exception: *Feminist Novels of the Belle Epoque* by Jennifer Waelti-Walters (Bloomington: Indiana University Press, 1990), and *The Forgotten Generation: French Women Writers of the Interwar Period* by Jennifer Milligan (New York: Berg Publishers, 1996).
4. Roger Chartier and Henri-Jean Martin, *Le Livre concurrencé 1900–1950* (The Book Contested), vol. 4 of *Histoire de l'édition française* (History of French Publishing), ed. Roger Chartier and Henri-Jean Martin (Paris: Fayard, 1986), 270–75.
5. As cited in Milligan, 2–3.
6. Jean Vic, *La Littérature de guerre: manuel méthodique et critique des publications de langue française* (War Literature: Systematic and Critical Guidebook of French Language Publications), 5 vols. (Paris: Payot, 1918–1923); J. Norton Cru, *Témoins: essai d'analyse et de critique des souvenirs de combattants édités en français de 1915 à 1928* (Witnesses: analytical and critical essay of soldiers' recollections published in French from 1915 to 1928) (Paris: Les Étincelles, 1929).
7. Margaret R. Higonnet, "Another Record: A Different War," *Women's Studies Quarterly* 3,4 (1995): 87.
8. A fraction of French women's war fiction centers on the male experience, with few or no women characters. These include a play by Rachilde, *La Délivrance* (Deliverance), 1915, the novel *Vers la Gloire* (Toward Glory),

1918 by Jean Bertheroy (Berthe Le Barillier), and *Baptême du courage* (Baptism of Courage), 1916, the sixteenth novel by popular writer Maria Star (Ernesta de Hierschel Stern). There were also a small number of children's stories, such as Hortense Barrau's *Les Gaufrettes de Guerre* (War Waffles), 1916, and Marie de La Hire's *Deux Boy-Scouts à Paris pendant la guerre* (Two Boy-Scouts in Paris During the War), 1916.

9. Margaret R. Higonnet, "Not So Quiet in No-Woman's-Land," in *Gendering War Talk,* ed. Miriam Cooke and Angela Woollacott (Princeton: Princeton University Press, 1993): 206–07.

10. Jean Bethke Elshtain, "Thinking about Women and International Violence," in *Women, Gender, and World Politics: Perspectives, Policies, and Prospects,* ed. Peter Beckman and Francine D'Amico (Westport, Conn.: Bergin and Garvey, 1994): 109–118, and *Women and War* (New York: Basic Books, 1987); Sara Ruddick, "Maternal Thinking" and "Preservation Love and Military Destruction: Some Reflections on Mothering and Peace," both in *Mothering: Essays in Feminist Theory,* ed. Joyce Treblicot (Totowa, New Jersey: Rowman and Allanheld, 1983), 213–30; 231–62, "Notes towards a Feminist Peace Politics," in *Gendering War Talk,* ed. Miriam Cooke and Angela Woollacott (Princeton: Princeton University Press, 1993):109–27; "Pacifying the Forces: Drafting Women in the Interests of Peace," *Signs* 8 (1983): 471–89; and "'Woman of Peace': A Feminist Construction," in *The Women and War Reader,* ed. Lois Ann Lorentzen and Jennifer Turpin (New York: New York University Press, 1998): 213–26. Many other writers have explored the various aspects of the complex relationship of women, militarism, and nonviolence. In addition to the studies cited here and below in chapter 1, see also Helen Cooper, Adrienne Munich, and Susan Squier, *Arms and the Woman: War, Gender, and Literary Representation* (Chapel Hill: University of North Carolina Press, 1989); Micaela Di Leonardo, "Morals, Mothers, and Militarism: Antimilitarism and Feminist Theory," *Feminist Studies* 3 (1985): 599–617; Cynthia Enloe, *Does Khaki Become You? The Militarization of Women's Lives* (Boston: South End Press, 1983); Sandra Gilbert, "Soldier's Heart: Literary Men, Literary Women, and the Great War," *Signs* 8 (1983): 422–50; and Erika A. Kuhlman, *Petticoats and White Feathers: Gender Conformity, Race, the Progressive Peace Movement, and the Debate Over War, 1895–1919,* Contributions in Women's Studies, no. 160 (Westport, Conn.: Greenwood Press, 1997).

11. Lorraine Bayard de Volo, "Drafting Motherhood: Maternal Imagery and Organizations in the United States and Nicaragua," in *The Women and War Reader,* ed. Lois Ann Lorentzen and Jennifer Turpin (New York: New York University Press, 1998), 240–53.

12. Joyce Berkman, "Feminism, War, and Peace Politics: The Case of World War I," in *Women, Militarism, and War: Essays in History, Politics, and Social Theory,* ed. Jean Bethke Elshtain and Sheila Tobias (Lanham, MD.: Rowman and Littlefield, 1990), 140–61; Leila J. Rupp, *Mobilizing Women for War: German and American Propaganda, 1939–1945* (Princeton: Princeton University Press, 1978), 62–64.

13. Nancy Scheper-Hughes, "Maternal Thinking and the Politics of War," in *The Women and War Reader,* ed. Lois Ann Lorentzen and Jennifer Turpin (New York: New York University Press, 1998), 231.

14. Joan W. Scott, "Rewriting History," in *Behind the Lines: Gender and the Two World Wars,* ed. Margaret R. Higonnet et al. (New Haven: Yale University Press, 1987), 27; Jennifer Turpin, "Many Faces: Women Confronting War," in *The Women and War Reader,* ed. Lois Ann Lorentzen and Jennifer Turpin (New York: New York University Press, 1998), 15.

15. Margaret R. Higonnet and Patrice L.-R. Higonnet, "The Double Helix," in *Behind the Lines: Gender and the Two World Wars,* ed. Margaret R. Higonnet et al. (New Haven: Yale University Press, 1987).

CHAPTER 1

1. Recent examples include Catherine O'Brien, *Women's Fictional Responses to the First World War: a Comparative Study of Selected Texts by French and German Writers* (New York: Peter Lang, 1996); Susan R. Grayzel, "Mothers, Marraines, and Prostitutes: Morale and Morality in First World War France," *The International History Review* xix (1997): 66–82; and Agnès Cardinal, "Women and the Language of War in France," in *Women and World War I: The Written Response,* ed. Dorothy Goldman (New York: St. Martin's Press, 1993). Incredibly, Cardinal characterized French women artists and intellectuals as silent on the war (152).

2. Roddy Reid, *Families in Jeopardy: Regulating the Social Body in France 1750–1910* (Stanford: Stanford University Press, 1993); Barbara Corrado Pope, "Revolution and Retreat: Upper-Class French Women After 1789," in *Women, War, and Revolution* (New York: Holmes and Meier Publishers, 1980), 222–28; Linda Clark, "The Primary Education of French Girls: Pedagogical Prescriptions and Social Realities, 1880–1940," *History of Education Quarterly* 21 (1981): 411–28; Carol R. Berkin and Clara M. Lovett, "Introduction/Retreat to Patriotic Motherhood," in *Women, War, and Revolution* (New York: Holmes and Meier Publishers, 1980), 209–13. Berkin and Lovett also noted that the Republican and Patriotic Motherhood ideology arose in several other countries, including the United States, as a postrevolutionary role for women (209). Linda K. Kerber's *Women of the Republic: Intellect and Ideology in Revolutionary America* (Chapel Hill: University of North Carolina Press, 1980) is among several works that have explored the role of this maternal ideology in American cultural history.

3. Anne Martin-Fugier, *La Bourgeoise: femme au temps de Paul Bourget* (The Bourgeois Woman: Women in the Era of Paul Bourget) (Paris: Grasset, 1983), 279–84.

4. Jonathan Cole, "'There Are Only Good Mothers': The Ideological Work of Women's Fertility in France before World War I," *French Historical Studies* 19 (1996): 640, 645, 658–59, 665–69; Karen Offen, "Depopulation, Nationalism, and Feminism," *American Historical Review* 89 (1984): 652;

664–65; passim; Françoise Thébaud, *Quand nos grand-mères donnaient la vie. La Maternité en France dans l'entre-deux-guerres* (When Our Grandmothers Gave Birth. Maternity in France in the Period between the World Wars) (Lyon: Presses universitaires de Lyon, 1986), 13–19; Judith F. Stone, "The Republican Brotherhood: Gender and Ideology," in *Gender and the Politics of Social Reform in France,* ed. Elinor Accampo, Rachel Fuchs, and Mary Lynn Stewart (Baltimore: Johns Hopkins University Press, 1995), 31–35.

5. Michelle Perrot, "The New Eve and the Old Adam: Changes in French Women's Condition at the Turn of the Century," in *Behind the Lines: Gender and the Two World Wars,* ed. Margaret R. Higonnet et al. (New Haven: Yale University Press, 1987), 51–60; Annelise Maugue, "The New Eve and the Old Adam," trans. Arthur Goldhammer in *Emerging Feminism from Revolution to World War,* ed. Geneviève Fraisse and Michelle Perrot, vol. 4 of *A History of Women in the West,* ed. Georges Duby and Michelle Perrot (Cambridge, Mass.: Harvard University Press, 1993), 519–32; and *L'Identité masculine en crise au tournant du siècle 1871–1914* (Paris: Rivages, 1987). Margaret H. Darrow, among others, considered the resurgence of nationalism after 1900 as an expression of the crisis of masculinity fueled by the defeat of France in 1870. Margaret H. Darrow "French Volunteer Nursing and the Myth of the War Experience in World War I," *American Historical Review* 101 (1996): 81. For a discussion of the German view of France after 1870, see Modris Eksteins, *The Rites of Spring: The Great War and the Birth of the Modern Age* (New York: Doubleday, 1989), passim.

6. Anne-Marie Käppeli, "Feminist Scenes," trans. Arthur Goldhammer in *Emerging Feminism from Revolution to World War,* ed. Geneviève Fraisse and Michelle Perrot, vol. 4 of *A History of Women in the West,* ed. Georges Duby and Michelle Perrot (Cambridge, Mass.: Harvard University Press, 1993), 483–84.

7. Christine Bard, *Les Filles de Marianne, histoire des féminismes,* 1914–1940 (The Daughters of Marianne, History of Feminisms, 1914–1940) (Paris: Fayard, 1995), 27.

8. For a comprehensive history of the campaign for suffrage, see Steven C. Hause with Anne R. Kenney, *Women's Suffrage and Social Politics in the French Third Republic* (Princeton: Princeton University Press, 1984).

9. Vernet (1878–1949) implemented her progressive educational policies at L'Avenir Social (Social Future), a secular orphanage she founded at Épone, France, which also functioned as a shelter for abused women and a publishing house for antimilitarist essays, poetry, and fiction by activists such as Noélie Drous (Léonie Sourd) and Vernet herself. For a discussion of Vernet's and Drous's poetry, see my *En l'honneur de la juste parole: la poésie française contre la Grande Guerre,* and note 75 below.

10. Bard, 86–87; Laurence Klejman and Florence Rochefort, *L'Égalité en marche, le féminisme sous la Troisième République* (Equality on the Move, Feminism in the Third Republic) (Paris: Des Femmes, 1989), 196–97.

11. Françoise Thébaud reported that such military language was common among contemporary feminists of all combatant nations. Françoise Thébaud, "The Great War and the Triumph of Sexual Division," trans. Arthur Goldhammer in *Toward a Cultural Identity in the Twentieth Century,* ed. Françoise Thébaud, vol. 5 of *A History of Women in the West,* ed. Georges Duby and Michelle Perrot (Cambridge, Mass.: Harvard University Press, 1994), 36–37.

12. Françoise Thébaud, *La Femme au temps de la guerre de 14* (Women During the Time of the War of 14) (Paris: Stock, 1986), 16. All translations of quoted French material are mine except where noted.

13. Marguerite Borel (Camille Marbo), *La Mobilisation féminine en France (1914–1919)* (The Female Mobilization in France) (Paris: Imprimerie Union, 1919), passim; Hortense Cloquié, *La Femme après la guerre, ses droits, son rôle, son devoir* (Woman After the War, Her Rights, Her Role, Her Duty) (Paris: Maloine, 1915), 21–22; Marie de La Hire, *La Femme française, son activité pendant la guerre* (The French Woman, Her Activity During the War) (Paris: Librairie Jules Tallandier, 1917), 57.

14. Berthem-Bontoux (Berthe Bontoux), *Les Françaises et la Grande Guerre* (The French Women and the Great War) (Paris: Bloud et Gay, 1917); Yvonne Pitrois, *Les Femmes de la Grande Guerre* (The Women of the Great War) (Geneva: Jeheber, 1916).

15. Negative images of women, from hateful invective to patronizing admonition, are characteristic of much of French men's written judgment of women. Texts that are often cited as "classic" or "definitive," such as the novels by Henri Barbusse, *Le Feu* (Fire), 1916, and Paul Géraldy, *La Guerre, Madame* (The War, Madam), 1916, or the cultural history by the veteran Gabriel Perreux, *La Vie quotidienne des civils en France pendant la Grande Guerre* (The Daily Life of Civilians in France During the Great War), 1966, are no exception. For a discussion of the portrayal of women in songs and films of the era, see Charles Rearick, *The French in Love and War: Popular Culture in the Era of the World Wars* (New Haven: Yale University Press, 1997.)

16. Mathilde Dubesset, Françoise Thébaud, and Catherine Vincent, "Les Munitionnettes de la Seine" (The Women Munitions Workers of the Seine), in *1914–1918, L'Autre Front* (1914–1918, The Other Front), ed. Patrick Fridenson (Paris: Éditions ouvrières, 1977), 216.

17. Similarly, critics today neither problematize the accusations nor analyze the motives of those who made them. Historians concerned with French women during the war tend to accept as fact subjective and undocumented statements on women's activities and attitudes toward men from former combatants, whether they come from historical accounts or novels. Unfortunately, this presentation of veterans' beliefs as historical fact, rather than as indicators of gendered ideology and social values, is lent authenticity by the inappropriate identification of the authors of the novels with their first person narrators.

18. Romain Rolland, "À l'Antigone éternelle" (To the Eternal Antigone) 1 *demain* (1916): 20–21.

19. Tony D'Ulmès, "La Mobilisation des Femmes" (The Mobilization of Women), *La Revue hebdomadaire* 8 (1915): 77.

20. Berthem-Bontoux, *Les Françaises,* 6.

21. As cited in Geneviève Colin, "Writers and the War," in *The Great War and the French People,* by Jean-Jacques Becker (Providence: Berg Publishers, 1993), 161.

22. Claude Laforêt, "La Mentalité française à l'épreuve de la guerre" (French Mentality Tested by the War), *Mercure de France* (1918): 577–600. "La femme française est courageuse, intelligente et cultivée; elle est aussi voluptueuse. C'est un reproche que nous ne saurions lui adresser sans ingratitude."

23. Robert de Flers, "La Vraie Charité" (The True Charity) *Le Figaro* (Paris), 17 August 1914, p. 1.

    Sans doute, à côté de ces fécondes initiatives, nous avons parfois remarqué dans ce zèle ambulancier quelques excès et peut-être même un soupçon de snobisme. Un esprit amer n'avait-il pas été jusqu'à estimer que certaines mondaines semblaient avoir pris pour devise: "Je panse, donc je suis." C'est là une injuste boutade.

24. See Accampo et al., Bard, Hause, and Thébaud in *Femme* for extensive examinations of the legal position of women before and during the war.

25. Louise Compain, "Souvenirs de l'ouvroir de guerre" (Memories of a War Workshop), *La Grande Revue* 4 (1915): 262–279. Bard (56) and Thébaud (*Femme* 114–18) also noted the economic hardship of working women during the war.

26. Jean-Jacques Becker, *The Great War and the French People* (Providence: Berg, 1993), 21–28; Klejman, *L'Égalité en marche,* 191; Thébaud, "The Great War," 28–30.

27. Scott, 27; Margaret Allen, "The Domestic Ideal and the Mobilization of Womanpower in World War II," *Women's Studies International Forum* 6 (1983): 403–04; Darrow, 89–92. See also the other essays in *Behind the Lines.*

28. Stéphane Audoin-Rouzeau, *Men at War 1914–1918, National Sentiment and Trench Journalism in France during the First World War,* trans. Helen McPhail (Oxford, Berg Publishers, 1995), 128–35; Mary Louise Roberts, *Civilization Without Sexes, Reconstructing Gender in Postwar France, 1917–1927* (Chicago: University of Chicago Press, 1994), 6–9; Thébaud, "The Great War," 35–39; *Femme,* 182.

29. Darrow reported that at the end of the nineteenth century the French public considered nursing as menial drudgery to be performed by the working class or nuns. It was only after an extensive publicity campaign by the Red Cross in the prewar period, which stressed the potentially patriotic and benevolent contribution of nurses in future conflicts, that the image of nurses changed (84–88).

30. Borel has a detailed description of the nurse's uniform and the different insignias worn by the members of the various volunteer organizations (54); see also Thébaud, *Femme,* 87–94.

31. Bard, 56; Marcelle Capy, *Une voix de femme dans la mêlée* (A Woman's Voice in the Melee) (Paris: Ollendorff, 1916), 79.

32. Frédéric Masson, "Les Femmes pendant et après la guerre" (Women During and After the War), *La Revue hebdomadaire* 9 (1917): 12–15.

33. Tony D'Ulmès, "Ces Dames de la Croix-Rouge" (These Ladies of the Red Cross), *La Revue de Paris* 6 (1915): 414–17. The notion of the war as a learning experience for women is also important to the narrative, *Réfugiée et Infirmière de Guerre* (Woman Refugee and War Nurse), 1915, by Jack de Bussy. While de Bussy's identity and gender remain obscure, the degree of faultfinding and reproach directed against civilian women is infrequent among women writers and far more typical of the criticism voiced by men. De Bussy's first person narrator, although female, repeats most of the same accusations directed against women in the press: frivolity, voyeurism, insufficient mourning, pleasure-seeking, and inappropriate use of the government allocation.

34. Pitrois, 86.

> Les dames de la Croix-Rouge, tout de blanc vêtues et coiffées, avec leur voile flottant et leur brassard orné du signe rédempteur, s'empressaient autour des lamentables arrivants; désormais, c'était leur propriété, leur trésor; c'étaient "leurs enfants," comme elles disaient toutes, et rien n'est plus jolie que de voir telle jeune fille de vingt ans, aux joues fraîches et roses, soutenir un territorial vieux déjà, brave papa à la moustache grise, et lui faire monter l'escalier en lui répétant, encourageante: "Allons, mon enfant!"

35. Berthem-Bontoux, 6–12; Comtesse de Courson, *La Femme Française pendant la Guerre* (The French Woman During the War) (Paris: Lethielleux, 1916), 6–7; Maurice Donnay, *La Parisienne et la Guerre* (The Parisian Woman and the War) (Paris: Crès, 1916), 18–20; 26–35; Geneviève Duhamelet, *Ces Dames de l'hôpital 336* (Those Ladies of Hospital 336) (Paris: Albin Michel, 1917), 6–7;17–18; François Le Grix, "Sur quelques livres de guerre" (On Several War Books), *La Revue hebdomadaire* 7 (1915): 362–87; Tony D'Ulmès, "Ces Dames de la Croix-Rouge," 415–17; "La Mobilisation des femmes," 75–79.

36. Courson, 40–42; Donnay, 64–65; D'Ulmès, "La Mobilisation des femmes," 79–83.

37. Dans une ambiance toute familiale, les blessés ont le temps de réfléchir et de comparer; plus d'un, en voyant de près ces "aristocrates" et ces "bourgeois," que dans les réunions publiques de jadis il entendait vilipender par les camarades, se demandera, avec son bon sens simple et droit, si ces mêmes camarades avaient jamais pratiqué ceux qu'ils dénonçaient si vigoureusement. Mis en défi-

ance, par là même, contre les doctrines révolutionnaires, les blessés d'hier, devenus les électeurs de demain, auront, après la guerre, une mentalité plus saine et plus clairvoyante; la Croix-Rouge, guérisseuse des corps, aura contribué à refaire aux générations françaises une âme nouvelle.

38. See chapter 4, note 3.

39. J. Delorme Jules-Simon, *Visions d'Héroïsme* (Images of Heroism) (Paris: Librairie Payot, 1915), 8–9.

Servir! Pour pouvoir dire que nous ne sommes pas des inutiles. Servir, pour essayer de nous élever à nos propres yeux et devant les yeux de ceux que suit notre âme, en nous efforçant de faire cette âme un peu semblable à la leur. Servir avec cet espoir que nous achèterons ainsi la vie de ceux qui nous sont chers.

40. Henriette de Vismes, *Histoire authentique et touchante des marraines et des filleuls de guerre* (Authentic and Moving History of War Godmothers and Godsons) (Paris: Perrin, 1918). See also Grayzel.

41. J. Becker, 193–322; Jane Clement Bond, "Women Workers in the Bourges Government Arsenals During World War I," (paper presented at the Conference on World War I and the Twentieth Century, Wichita, Kansas, November, 1998); Dubesset, Thébaud, and Vincent, "Les Munitionnettes de la Seine"; Leonard V. Smith, *Between mutiny and obedience: the case of the French Fifth Infantry Division during World War I* (Princeton: Princeton University Press, 1994).

42. . . . leur pitié s'étend à des inconnus, à des "filleuls" de guerre, que leurs bienfaitrices n'ont jamais vus, qu'elles ne verront jamais, mais qu'elles adoptent pour les vêtir, les nourrir, et les réconforter.

43. . . . l'adoption par les gens de l'arrière des soldats du front, isolés et malheureux, l'amitié des Marraines et des Filleuls, est digne de figurer parmi les plus beaux traits d'une histoire de France épisodique. Ne conviendrait-il pas, par exemple, de donner comme sœurs aux femmes de Bretagne filant le lin pour la rançon de Duguesclin, ces femmes de nos jours, les marraines, tricotant la laine pour vêtir les défenseurs de la patrie, séparés des leurs ou orphelins?

44. For a discussion of the internationalist pacifist movement that attracted a wide following at the turn of the century, see Sandi E. Cooper, "Pacifism in France, 1889–1914: International Peace as a Human Right," *French Historical Studies* 17 (1991): 359–385.

45. "Le désordre, l'indépendance, l'égoïsme, l'aveuglement, tout cela devient ordre, discipline, altruisme et lucidité."

46. Aurel (1882–1948), known primarily as a moralist, was a celebrated woman of letters whose political commentary, book and cinema reviews, and articles on women's psychology appeared regularly in nearly every im-

portant periodical of her era. The author of many volumes on conjugal love, she believed that only equals could achieve true happiness in marriage, and she urged women to reject their traditional subservience in order to become real companions to their husbands. Her work of 1937, *Flammes aux yeux* (Flashing Eyes), provoked much discussion with its challenge to readers to choose between being "femmes poupées" (doll women) or "femmes cerveaux" (intellectual women). During the Great War, Aurel inaugurated a literary salon as a psychological means to counter the horror that surrounded writers and artists. Continuing each week for nearly 20 years, more than 200 guests gathered to celebrate poetry. Well-known men and women writers, including Jehanne d'Orliac and Lucie Delarue-Mardrus, whose works are discussed below, read and discussed the works of generally undiscovered young artists. Both Geneviève Duhamelet and Jeanne Landre satirized the famous salon in their respective war novels, *Les Inépousées* (The Unmarried Women) and *Loin des balles, mémoires d'un philanthrope* (Far from the Bullets, Memoirs of a Philanthropist). Aurel received the Légion d'Honneur medal in 1936 in recognition of her contribution to French letters. Dossier Aurel, Bibliothèque Marguerite Durand; Henri Clouard, *Aurel, bibliographie critique. Les Célébrités d'aujourd'hui* (Aurel, critical bibliography. Celebrities of Today) (Paris: Chiberre, 1922), 4–5; *Annuaire Général,* 781.

47. Aurel, "Mœurs de guerre" (War Mores), *La Grande Revue* 9 (1915): 35.

> Quant aux femmes, n'ont-elles pas été amenées par la guerre à renoncer à leurs indolences d'oiseaux, à leur fatuité de jeunes paons, à leurs empanachements d'esclaves ruineuses? Regardez leurs visages. Ils ont été, semble-t-il, *touchés de respect.* Chacune porte en son cœur un compagnon, un ami, qui souffre pour la victoire. Et l'Ève trouble de jadis qui tirait tout à elle, est devenue la femme sûre et forte, celle qui, de nouveau, respecte, admire l'homme.
>
> Il vivait jadis pour ses aises. Comment l'eût-elle respecté, elle qui ne s'incline que devant la souffrance? Au regard de la femme, l'homme est redevenu par la guerre le grand sexe, grand par la fatigue vaincue, grand par la guerre bien portée.
>
> Je ne crois pas qu'il vive en ce moment une femme qui se moque de l'homme. C'est tout un avenir de magnifiques mœurs que nous ouvre la guerre en rendant à l'homme le respect de la femme. (Italics in original.)

48. Ontological or maternal pacifism has a long tradition, with many adherents from antiquity to the present. Contemporary feminist scholar Sara Ruddick has studied the relationship between maternal practice and pacifism. Drawing on the work of Nancy Chodorow and Carol Gilligan, Ruddick argued that the specific biological experiences of women caused them to develop a moral concept she called "preservation love." The female connectedness to

and responsibility for life that others termed "maternal thinking" became for Ruddick a preservative caring that resembled and was parallel to pacifism. Sara Ruddick, "Maternal Thinking," "Notes towards a Feminist Peace Politics," "Pacifying the Forces: Drafting Women in the Interests of Peace," and "Preservation Love and Military Destruction: Some Reflections on Mothering and Peace."

49. Opposition to the war encompassed several different ideas and ideologies, including socialist, feminist, motherist, and assorted combinations. The goals also varied from immediate cessation of hostilities (called "defeatism" by its detractors), to negotiated settlements that differed on the subject of treaties, territories, and reparations. There were those like playwright Marie Lenéru (see chapter 6), whose profession of absolute pacifism in fact resembled closely the patriotic sentiments of most French people—that the war, fought to the end, would bring about a permanent peace. The number of declared peace activists was small, estimated at 300 by the police in 1916, but more than 800 by the adherents themselves. Brion, Duchêne, Saumoneau, and Vernet are representative of other feminist pacifists, such as Marthe Bigot, Louise Bodin, Marcelle Capy, Lucie Colliard, Jeanne Halb- wachs, Andrée Jouve (first wife of famed poet Pierre Jean Jouve who also opposed the war), Jeanne Mélin, Marthe Pichorel, Madeleine Rolland (sis- ter of Romain Rolland), Nelly Roussel, Marguerite de Saint-Prix, Séver- ine, Marguerite Thévenet, and Noélie Drous (Léonie Sourd), whose poetry inaugurates this book. Brion (1882–1962) was a teacher arrested for sedi- tion in 1917. At her trial she defined her pacifism as the expression of her female morality, the opposite of male brutality. Gabrielle Duchêne (1870–1954) founded the French section of the International Committee of Women for Permanent Peace, in solidarity with the principles and work of the International Congress of Women held at The Hague in April, 1915. Members of the group, known by the address of its meeting place, the Rue Fondary, included many of the activists named above. Louise Saumoneau was one of the rare socialists to oppose the war openly, for which she spent time in prison. For Madeleine Vernet, pacifism was the natural and instinc- tive response of all women, as carriers of life, to male violence and brutal- ity. Daniel Armogathe, "Les Femmes et la Paix en France aux XIXe et XX siècles," (Women and Peace in France in the Nineteenth and Twentieth Centuries), in *Féminisme et Pacifisme: même combat,* ed. Danielle Le Bricquir and Odette Thibault (Paris: Les Lettres libres, 1985); Bard 89–124 and pas- sim; Hause 191–94, 196–97; Marie Lenéru, "Les Femmes n'entraveront pas la guerre" (Women Will Not Hinder the War) *L'Intransigeant* (Paris), 20 July 1917, n.p.; Thébaud, *Femme,* 247–58.

50. Bard 47; 79–108; Hause 169–211; Thébaud, *Femme,* 247–59.

51. Louis Madelin, "La Vertu française" (French Virtue), *La Revue hebdomadaire* 10 (1917): 208.

Trois août mil neuf cent quatorze! Plaisirs frivoles, luxe éclatant, querelles politiques, discussions religieuses, luttes sociales, tout parut en une heure oublié. Le pays, debout, face à l'ennemi, face au danger, face à la mort, se révéla plus beau qu'il ne l'avait jamais été. Tous les idéalismes se fondirent d'un élan, l'esprit de la croisade et l'esprit de 89 parce qu'avec la Patrie on allait défendre le Droit contre la Barbarie et le Dieu de nos pères contre Odin destructeur.

52. For a discussion of the situation of women working in offices and factories during the war, see Borel, 32–37; 47–52; J. Becker, 205–301; Thébaud, *Femme,* 147–89.

53. Frédéric Masson, "Les Femmes de France et la Guerre" (The Women of France and the War), *L'Écho de Paris,* 2 May 1915, 1. "Il a donné sa vie pour la France, il a bien fait. La France, c'était sa mère, je ne suis que sa femme." See also René Bazin, "Elles écrivent" (They [women] Write), *L'Écho de Paris,* 8 February 1916, 1; René Bazin, "Trois Françaises" (Three French Women), *L'Écho de Paris,* 1 August 1915, 1.

54. James F. McMillan, "Reclaiming a Martyr: French Catholics and the Cult of Joan of Arc, 1890–1920," in *Martyrs and Martyrologies,* ed. Diana Wood (Oxford: Blackwell Publishers, 1993), 359–70.

55. Eugène Martin, "Préparons l'avenir: aux épouses et aux mères en deuil" (Let Us Prepare for the Future: to Wives and Mothers in Mourning), *La Croix* (Paris), 5 November 1915, supplement, p. 1.

Épouses et mères françaises, le Seigneur, par la voix de la patrie en danger, vous a demandé vos époux et vos fils. . . . En donnant vos époux et vos fils, ô Françaises, vous avez donc contribué au rachat, au salut de notre France! . . . par vos chères et tant regrettées victimes, vous avez protégé la patrie du plus redoutable péril qui l'ait jamais menacée . . . et, avec la patrie, la civilisation que tant de générations de chrétiennes ont fait s'épanouir, bienfaisante, sur la terre de Clotilde, de saint Louis, de Jeanne d'Arc, de Vincent de Paul, de Pierre Fourier.

56. In his antifeminist and pronatalist play of 1917, *Les Mamelles de Tirésias* (Tiresias's Tits), Apollinaire satirized the ambitions of women for careers outside the home by attributing to them the desire to become men. As a result of the refusal of feminists to have children, men develop the capacity to reproduce countless children unisexually, thus eliminating the need for women's participation in the repopulation campaign. Guillaume Apollinaire, *Œuvres complètes* (Complete Works), vol. 3, ed. Michel Décaudin (Paris: Balland and Lecat, 1966), 609–50.

57. Cited in Bard, 64.

58. Also cited in Thébaud, *Femme,* 282.

59. Capy, 65. "En avant! La croisade pour les berceaux . . . Chantez les langes blancs après le crêpe des veuves."

60. Jacques Bertillon, "La Dépopulation en France" (Depopulation in France), *La Croix* (Paris), 8 October 1916, supplement, 1; "Aux jeunes filles" (To Girls), *La Croix* (Paris), 21 October 1915, supplement, 1.

61. Frédéric Masson, "De la repopulation" (On Repopulation), *L'Écho de Paris,* 20 October 1916, 1.

62. "Aux jeunes filles," 1. "Elles auront pitié de la race française, déjà si étiolée et si appauvrie avant la guerre, si décimée et si meurtrie par la guerre; et elles se permettront de la relever et de la ranimer."

63. Henry Spont, *La Femme et la Guerre* (Women and the War) (Paris: Perrin, 1916), 1. "La fonction essentielle de la femme, sa raison d'être, c'est la pro-création et la conservation de l'espèce."

64. Rolland, "À l'Antigone éternelle," 21. "Ce n'est pas en faisant la guerre à la guerre que vous la supprimerez, c'est en préservant d'abord de la guerre votre cœur, en sauvant de l'incendie *l'avenir qui est en vous.*" (Italics in original.)

65. Marthe Borély, *L'Appel aux Françaises. Le Féminisme politique* (Paris: Nouvelle Librairie nationale, 1919): "La maternité est le patriotisme des femmes"; Cloquié, "Nous aurons à repeupler la France."

66. Cited in Thébaud, *Femme,* 282. "Avant leurs bras, le pays blessé veut leurs flancs."

67. See also Grayzel, 68–70; Thébaud, *Femme,* 177–181.

68. Women teachers, whose duties were generally limited to the primary education of girls and therefore considered an extension of their "natural" maternal roles, were exempt from the prevailing domestic ideology that maintained that married women were not to work outside the home (Fugier, 283–84). While both Fugier (280) and Siegel reported that many women teachers married and continued to work, it is clear that the authors of these articles written during the war, as well as of the novels discussed below, assumed not only that the majority of women teachers were celibate, but also that these educators considered their professions and marriage incompatible. Mona Siegel, "Lasting Lessons: War, Peace, and Patriotism in French Primary Schools, 1914–1939" (Ph.D. diss., University of Wisconsin, 1996).

69. René Bazin, "Le Rôle maternel des institutrices" (The Maternal Role of Teachers), *L'Écho de Paris,* 7 December 1915, 1.

70. Louise Zeys, "Les Femmes et la Guerre" (Women and the War), *La Revue des deux mondes* 9 (1916): 184. "Nous ne serons pas trop de mères pour les orphelins."

71. For example, Eugène Tardieu, "Un mariage émouvant" (An Inspiring Marriage), *L'Écho de Paris,* 7 August 1915, 1.

72. Frédéric Masson, "De la repopulation, le Mariage" (On Repopulation, Marriage), *L'Écho de Paris,* 2 November 1916, 1.

Répandre la loi morale, et rétablir une loi religieuse, provoquer au mariage par piété, par patriotisme, par pitié, les jeunes filles qui, par esprit d'indépendance, par crainte des charges familiales, faute d'avoir rencontré le *prince charmant,* faute d'avoir compris que le premier devoir c'est la formation d'une famille, adoptent le célibat, d'abord comme régime d'attente et plus tard à perpétuité, c'est là une première victoire à préparer. (Italics in original.)

73. Although historians have long disputed the issue of German brutality against French women, Thébaud reported that women were raped during the invasion and occupation of France (*Femme,* 58). While it is not my purpose here to examine the historical accuracy of these abuses, it is worthwhile noting that skepticism concerning claims of assault and molestation during the war duplicate the common cynicism and imputation of women's morals and motives that have traditionally mitigated the behavior of rapists.

74. Judith Wishnia, "Natalisme et Nationalisme pendant la Première Guerre Mondiale" (Natalism and Nationalism during the First World War), *Vingtième Siècle* 45 (1995): 30–39.

75. Odette Dulac (Odette Roche). *Le Droit à l'enfant, Conférence faite à l'Action des Femmes* (Rights for Children, Lecture Given to Women's Action) (Paris: Figuière, 1916); "La Tache originelle" (Original Stain), *Le Journal* (Paris), 28 January 1917, 2; Lucie Delarue-Mardrus, "L'Enfant du Barbare" (Child of the Barbarian), *Le Journal* (Paris), 22 March 1915; Madeleine Vernet, "L'Enfant ennemi" (The Enemy Child), *Contes d'hier et d'aujourd'hui* (Stories of Yesterday and Today) (Épone: Editions de l'Avenir social), 1917; Thébaud, *Femme,* 58–59; Wishnia, 30–39.

76. "Nous réclamerons le droit de vote pour faire des lois pour protéger les femmes qui travaillent, les filles-mères, et les abandonnées."

77. Pauline Valmy, "La Guerre et l'Âme des femmes" (The War and the Soul of Women), *La Grande Revue* 10 (1915): 305–310. "Le salut d'une nation exige des bataillons de chérubins" (308).

78. La guerre a fait s'unir, dans un même élan de foi patriotique, des concitoyens séparés par leurs autres convictions, elle a fait naître aussi un second miracle: les hommes ont découvert en l'âme des femmes, enrichie et rénovée, de quoi fonder le couple de demain selon une formule non plus de revendications mais d'amour et d'intelligence.

79. "L'Œuvre féminine et le Féminisme," 527. "Elles auront pris conscience de leur valeur, de leur force personnelle, elles se seront essayées."

80. Among them are Dorothy Goldman, *Women Writers and the Great War* (New York: Twayne Publishers, 1995), 26–50, Margaret R. Higonnet et al., introduction to *Behind the Lines: Gender and the Two World Wars,* ed. Margaret R. Higonnet et al., (New Haven, Conn.: Yale University Press, 1987), 1–2; Higonnet, "Not so Quiet," 206; Claire Tylee, *The Great War and Women's Consciousness: Images of Militarism and Womanhood in Women's Writings, 1914–64* (Iowa City: Iowa University Press, 1990), 13–14.

81. Gilbert, passim; Goldman, *Women Writers,* 38–39.

82. Trudi Tate and Suzanne Raitt, introduction to *Women's Fiction and the Great War,* ed. Suzanne Raitt and Trudi Tate (Oxford: Oxford University Press, 1997), 3.

CHAPTER 2

1. Gérard d'Houville, "Il faut toujours compter sur l'imprévu," *La Revue des deux mondes* (1916): 259–93. Gérard d'Houville was the pseudonym of Marie de Régnier (1875–1963). She was a member of a distinguished family of poets and writers. Her numerous publications in a variety of genres, including novels, poetry, and dramatic proverbs, earned for her an outstanding literary reputation, especially in the first twenty years of this century. She won the Grand Prix de Littérature from the Académie Française in 1918. The didactic dramatic proverb, a genre that flourished in literary salons from the seventeenth century, seems particularly appropriate for the aristocratic d'Houville. Dossier Gérard d'Houville, Bibliothèque Marguerite Durand.

2. "Rapport des prix littéraires décernés, 1917," Archives de l'Académie Française, 3 Br.1.

3. While this theme is present in the majority of novels, it is of central importance in *La Houille rouge* by Odette Dulac, as discussed below in chapter 4.

4. Nous avons trop fui la souffrance. La Providence nous rappelle son rôle de rédemptrice. Voyez, les hommes qui ont été les esclaves du plaisir sont appelés comme à une expiation directe au martyre de la chair. . . . Et la femme partage leur expiation, c'est la loi.

5. Avec douleur, mais irrésistiblement, la jeune femme obéissait à l'impulsion qui lui ordonnait de s'éloigner sans retard. Pourtant, le chaos des circonstances l'isolait dans une entière liberté. Autour d'elle, pas un conseil, pas un appui. Mais en elle toute la force d'un ordre secret qui émanait d'influences profondes, invincibles: de son amour pour ses enfants, de la pensée de son mari et de leur foyer, de ses remords confus, de ses sentiments religieux, de toute l'harmonie de son existence.

6. See chapter 6.

7. This same idea appears in Lya Berger's short story, "Renoncement" (Sacrifice), published in 1919. A French nurse takes care of a soldier she knew before the war. When she learns that he is married, she realizes that she is in love with him and that he shares her feelings. The situation becomes more complicated when the wife visits and asks the nurse to protect him for her. The nurse, having promised to do so, requests a transfer to the Orient (71–76).

8. " . . . puisque c'est notre champ de bataille à nous l'hôpital!"

9. . . . il y en a, d'ailleurs, pour qui cette habitude de penser au malheur est devenue un véritable snobisme de la douleur. Une catégorie curieuse est celle de la femme compatissante à l'excès; celle-ci recherche toujours la douleur d'autrui, elle a toujours une amie à aller consoler; je crois vraiment qu'elle y trouve une volupté.

10. La guerre aura remis la femme à sa vraie place, elle lui aura procuré le moyen de donner avec intensité son dévouement, sa pitié, son admiration, sa gaieté. Je vois bien l'influence des femmes à l'avenir, que je voudrais être à la fois toutes les femmes être mère, épouse. . . .

11. Dossier Geneviève Duhamelet, Bibliothèque Marguerite Durand.

12. Je ne me marierai pas, maman. Les garçons de mon âge sont morts presque tous. Génération sacrifiée, a dit quelqu'un en parlant d'eux. Eh bien, nous autres, les jeunes filles, nous sommes la génération du sacrifice. Celui qui m'aurait aimé est tombé au champ d'honneur. Nous serons, ainsi, une légion de veuves qui n'auront jamais été des fiancées. Mais notre sacrifice compte pour la Patrie; et l'amour que nous n'avons pas eu ne peut être perdu. Monique le donne à Dieu, Marthe à ses blessés d'aujourd'hui, à ses malades de demain. . . . Moi, je veux ce petit.

13. "Justement, la guerre menaçait la France et le monde et Mme Marcelle Tinayre s'est dit: 'Tiens! Voilà un sujet de roman!' Elle écrivit ce roman sans tarder. . . . Mme Tinayre, pour célébrer l'héroïsme français de la veillée des armes, a écrit son livre le plus fade." Jean Ernest-Charles, "La Vie littéraire: *La Veillée des armes* par Marcelle Tinayre," *La Grande Revue* (1915): 119–22.

14. Waelti-Walters, 31–53; 186.

15. Marcelle Tinayre, *To Arms!*, trans. Lucy Humphrey (New York: E.P. Dutton and Company, 1918), 117; 164–66; 181–87; 237; 259–61; 264; 271–80; 283–84.

16. The union of French socialists created in 1905 the Section Française de l'Internationale Ouvrière (S.F.I.O.) under the leadership of Jules Guesde, Édouard-Marie Vaillant, and Jean Jaurès. Jaurès (1859–1914), celebrated especially for his eloquent call for justice, was assassinated on August 31, the eve of the war. The majority of socialists, trade unionists, and others on the left supported the war effort, agreeing to respect the political truce known as the *union sacrée* (sacred union). Hervé (1871–1944) edited the newspaper, *La Guerre Sociale,* in which his socialist, trade unionist, and antimilitarist views appeared. His endorsement of the war was such that he changed the name of the periodical to *La Victoire* in 1916.

CHAPTER 3

1. Dossier Jehanne d'Orliac, Bibliothèque Marguerite Durand.

2. J.-E. Weelen, review of *La Légion d'Honneur,* by Jehanne d'Orliac, *La Revue bleue* 75 (1937): 625.

3. Ainsi s'installèrent-ils à la Kautre, tous trois réunis, pour l'accomplissement de l'œuvre. Tous trois non seulement réunis mais unis en un indissoluble amour, me semblent former la trinité parfaite du monde spirituel. Hubert le père, le créateur; Jean le fils, l'exécuteur;

Marguerite, l'esprit par la douceur qu'elle dégage, la tendresse qu'elle impose.

4. Y a-t-il donc des gestes indépendants de nos vouloirs? Des vouloirs évadés des consciences? Des consciences qui ne contrôlent plus. . . .

5.   Quels idéologues, atteints de myopie, ont pensé que se battre équivalait à s'épargner; se civiliser, c'est augmenter les moyens de se détruire pour avoir ceux de se sélectionner. Il n'y a qu'une justice, celle qui donne la permission de vivre à celui qui a le pouvoir de vaincre, cela en paix comme en guerre, dans le passé comme dans le présent. Hors de cette évidence, il n'y a que ténèbres.

6. "J'ai sauvé l'*Agneau* et j'ai sauvé mon honneur aussi . . . et j'ai rassasié mon cœur. . . ."

7. *Annuaire Général des Lettres,* 797; Clarissa Burnham Cooper, *Women Poets of the Twentieth Century in France: a critical bibliography* (New York: King's Crown Press, 1943), 76.

8. A more personal kind of heroism motivates the main character in the short story, "L'Espion au Foyer" (The Spy at Home), 1917, by André Corthis (Andrée Lécuyer), who also defeats the enemy while maintaining the standards of female decorum. In occupied territory, Jacquette receives letters from her soldier husband through clandestine means, and because of her naiveté, nearly divulges the secret to the cleverly manipulative German officer who lives in her home. Aided by an old servant, Jacquette realizes that the officer's mission is to destroy the underground network of communication. She engineers a plan that both neutralizes his activities and safeguards the couriers by blackmailing the officer with letters from his wife that criticize the German emperor. Calmly facing his loaded pistol, Jacquette maintains proper courtesy while ordering the officer to leave her home, thus preserving both her reputation as a French woman and the lives of the women who carry the letters from the front lines to occupied France (115–79). Corthis's story, "Une mère" (A Mother), 1917, is discussed below in chapter 4.

9. *Rapport de M. Georges Lecomte, secrétaire perpétuel, sur les concours littéraires* (Paris: Firmin-Didot, 1952), 19.

10. Firmin Roz, "Un grand roman féminin," *La Revue bleue* (1926): 314–16.

11. "Il y a un peu de miracle dans tant de chasteté à exprimer de telles audaces. On sent là une pureté native qui dépasse l'habileté, et à laquelle l'homme de lettres le plus avisé, le plus ferré sur les tours du métier s'efforcerait en vain." Fernand Vandérem, "Les Lettres et la Vie," *La Revue de Paris* (1918): 415–420.

12. La tragique secousse qui ébranlait toutes les âmes avait résonné pour elle comme la trompette du Jugement. Il lui semblait que la fin du monde al-

lait arriver et elle se voyait avec épouvante enchaînée hors de la chrétienté dans les liens d'un amour coupable.

13. Son désir d'être mère lui avait fait comprendre ce que peut être l'amour des parents pour leurs petits. Il lui semblait inévitable que cet amour finit par être le plus fort, et par vaincre, dans le cœur paternel, l'amour de la femme.

14. Lya Berger's "La Fée aux Roses" (The Rose Fairy), published in 1919, has a similar plot and resolution. An elderly woman whose husband and son died in the Franco-Prussian War confesses to throwing a rock at German soldiers in order to avenge their deaths and to save her village from destruction. Refusing to commute her death sentence because of her age, the German officer coldly explains that there are no old women, no children, nor men—only enemies (108–13).

15. Je les aimerais, eux me détesteraient peut-être: ils auraient bien raison. J'en mourrais de honte et de chagrin. Toi, maintenant, tu dois vivre pour eux; tu dois te marier: il faut qu'ils aient une mère, et que ce ne soit pas une indigne comme moi.

16. *Noune et la Guerre* was the first novel of Pascal, who herself had aspirations for the stage. Despite the abundant body of commentary of those works of Colette dealing specifically with the music hall, as well as her well-documented personal experiences on the stage, *Mitsou, ou comment l'esprit vient aux jeunes filles* has attracted little attention.

17. Colette, *Œuvres*, vol. 2 (Paris: Gallimard, 1986), 699.

18. Et puis une fierté naît en cette petite femme de se sentir là, tout prête, si brave, attendant les Boches. Elle pense, pitoyable, aux autres femmes qui doivent dormir, ou pleurer inutilement.

. . . Oh! Bien sûr, elle ne pourra pas faire grand'chose, Noune, n'est-ce pas? Mais enfin, elle se défendra! Et puis, s'ils passent dans la rue, elle tirera dessus, c'est entendu!

19. "Se pourrait-il qu'elle, Noune, petite femme inutile, certaine de sa non-valeur, fût mise au monde uniquement pour donner de la vie à son tour?"

20. For a detailed explanation of the Zimmerwald Program and its connection to French pacifists, see my "From Whitman to Mussolini: Modernism in the Life and Works of a French Intellectual," *Journal of European Studies* xxvi (1996): 153–73.

21. . . . je leur dirais: "Écoutez, vous, les gars, vous avez des femmes, des mamans, des gosses? Nous aussi. Eh bien, pourquoi se bat-on? Pour faire plaisir à des salauds qui sont à l'abri, et pour faire pleurer vos femmes, vos mamans et vos gosses? . . . Ne vous battez plus, venez avec moi, devenez les amis de tous les peuples, et unissons-nous pour casser la figure aux tyrans, aux empereurs, aux rois, aux ministres! . . . Tous des frères; voilà ce qu'il faut être."

22. See chapter 1 for a discussion of the impact of the charities established for the financial relief of working women. Jeanne Landre caricatures such efforts in her *L'École des marraines* (The School for Godmothers) and *Loin des*

balles, mémoires d'un philanthrope (Far from the Bullets, Memoirs of a Philanthropist), discussed below in chapter 5.

23. Oui, bien sûr, dans le peuple, c'est comme ça: on a "un homme," et puis, c'est pour toujours. On est à lui, et il est à vous; alors on le garde, sans bras ni jambes, si la vie—se croyant généreuse—consent à vous le rendre un jour, du même geste qu'un gosse riche donne à un gosse pauvre le jouet qu'il vient de casser. Et l'on est ravi, et l'on joint les mains, et l'on dit merci. On vous le rend; tant pis s'il est abîmé: c'est "votre homme."

24. On sait bien que le théâtre n'est pas un métier de fainéant, pour les femmes surtout. Elles, en plus des rôles à apprendre et à travailler, elles devront aussi tenir une maison, soigner des gosses—dont le plus enfant est souvent le mari,—accomplir, chaque jour, la tâche éreintante d'une bonne ménagère et, en outre, jouer le soir.

25. "Mon pays, ma patrie, c'était lui, mon Jacques, mon grand si beau, mon homme."

26. Delarue-Mardrus's first war-related novel, *Un roman civil en 1914* (A Civilian Novel in 1914), published in 1916, is discussed below in chapter 6.

27. Pauline Newman-Gordon, "Lucie Delarue-Mardrus," in *French Women Writers: A Bio-Bibliographical Source Book,* ed. Eva Martin Sartori and Dorothy Wynne Zimmerman (New York: Greenwood Press, 1991), 108–120.

28. The controversy surrounding the fate of these children is explained above in chapter 1. See also chapter 4 for a discussion of Dulac's views.

29. "Décidément, Toutoune, tu ressembles tout à fait à la tante Dorothée."

Au moment d'aller se coucher, comme la petite venait embrasser sa mère, celle-ci se prit à examiner sa fille comme si elle ne l'avait jamais vue. Elle lui releva ses nattes, sans doute pour juger l'effet de coiffure, pencha la tête de côté, puis dit d'un ton complaisant:

"Tu as de jolis yeux, Toutoune . . ."

L'enfant sursauta, frappée au cœur. Elle comprit en cette minute que, jamais de sa vie, elle n'entendrait quelque chose de pareil. La gorge serrée, elle eut le désir d'exprimer un peu son immense plaisir, un peu de son étonnement ravi.

30. "Je le trouve très gentil. Mais c'est si ordinaire d'épouser un vendeur! J'aurais aimé un jeune homme qui eût fait quelque chose de grand, un mari dont j'aurais été fière: un aviateur par exemple."

"C'est comme moi," dit Louise. "Mais que veux-tu? A la triste époque où nous vivons, il n'y a plus d'héroïsme. Les hommes tiennent avant tout à leur guenille. Leur idéal, c'est de rapporter le dimanche un poisson plus gros que celui du voisin ou d'aller faire la manille à l'apéritif."

31. Pour moi, j'ai pensé plusieurs fois qu'Henri pourrait revenir mutilé. Ne craignez point qu'alors j'aie à me contraindre pour ne pas m'enfuir comme une sotte. Non, non, trop heureuse s'il revient, fût-ce un bras, un œil, ou une jambe en moins!

32. This is the main idea in Odette Dulac's second war-era novel, *Faut-il?* (Must We?), published in 1919. A young woman reads the diary of her disabled grandfather, whom she affectionately calls "Trois Pattes" (Three Paws), because of injuries he sustained during the Franco-Prussian War. Impressed by his bravery and understanding for the first time the nobility of a soldier's sacrifice, she agrees to marry the disabled *poilu* she had first refused. The story ends with her exclamation to her proud grandfather and parents, "Grand-père! Voici mon Trois Pattes à moi!" (303). (Grandfather! Here is my very own Three Paws!)

33. "D'ailleurs nous nous aimerions mieux ainsi, car c'est moi qui lui servirai de lumière...."

34. Aujourd'hui comme hier je retrouve chez les femmes la même noblesse, la même vaillance, la même idée de l'honneur. Chez les hommes, l'indomptable courage et l'abnégation au profit de la gloire du pays. Quelle harmonie entre les siècles! Malgré les vicissitudes, les évolutions, les transformations, la France est une et toujours semblable à soi. Telle elle était il y sept cents ans, sous le manteau blanc de la chevalerie, telle je la retrouve aujourd'hui, le visage plus grave, un peu assombrie par les méditations de la science, environnée des fumées de l'industrie, des chemins de fer et des paquebots, mais ornée de la même flamme, de la même jeunesse et du même attrait qui séduit le monde, et trouble jusqu'à ses barbares ennemis.

CHAPTER 4

1. Review of *Jérusalem*, by Marie Reynès-Monlaur, *La Civiltà Cattolica* 3 (1949): 292–93. Henri Bremond, writing earlier in *Le Correspondant*, praised the skillful blending of fiction and reality in *Les Autels morts*, as well as Reynès-Monlaur's courteous depiction of the Protestant world. Henri Bremond, review of *Les Autels morts* by Marie Reynès-Monlaur, *Le Correspondant*, 25 August 1917, 756–58.

2. In her recent article, Annette Becker explored the spiritual interpretation of the war and its suffering among certain Catholic intellectuals. Annette Becker, "Tortured and Exalted by War: French Catholic Women, 1914–1918," in *Women and War in the Twentieth Century*, ed. Nicole Ann Dombrowski (New York: Garland Publishing, 1999), 42–53.

3. The desire to earn merit, a Catholic concept certainly familiar to Reynès-Monlaur's readers, is also a motivation for characters in other works studied here, especially in Delorme Jules-Simon's *Âmes de guerre, âmes d'amour*. More than just an act of charity or a prayer, a meritorious deed is a charitable activity accomplished in total surrender of the self. The more intense the act, the greater the reward in heaven.

4. Among the several accusations of sedition denied by the French clergy as "rumeurs infâmes" (infamous rumors) was the allegation that Pope Benedict XV, while publicly neutral, in fact supported Germany and its allies

(McMillan, "French Catholics: *Rumeurs Infâmes* and the *Union Sacrée* 1914–1918," in *Authority, Identity and the Social History of the Great War*, ed. Frans Coetzee and Mailyn Shevin-Coetzee (Oxford: Berghahn Books, 1995): 113–32, and "Reclaiming a Martyr," 370).

5. The story of Joan, the martyred heroine who rallied her king and country in defense of the nation, had obvious parallels to a France at war in 1914. It is not surprising that she is the most frequently cited historical figure in women's war fiction and poetry. See chapter 1.

6. . . . je ne peux pas les regarder sous cet angle, comme des bandits ou des bourreaux. Autant je les repousse comme Française, autant je les admire au point de vue de l'esprit. Vous savez le mot d'un de nos maîtres: "L'Allemagne, la seconde patrie de tout être qui étudie et qui pense."

7. Mais mon premier maître, c'est moi-même. . . . Le Christ n'intervient que dans la mesure où je le juge bon. C'est le seul gain—ou le seul maléfice—que je conserve de l'Allemagne. Et je ne puis pas parler autrement que je ne pense.

8. C'est une sensation si nette que cette guerre est une guerre de dieux! Malgré notre gouvernement athée, la France est ici avec ses grands instincts chrétiens, la générosité, la bonté, la pitié! Devant l'adversaire brutal elle garde le caractère chevaleresque que quatorze siècles d'amitié avec le Christ lui ont donné. On sent cela, dans ce corps à corps, comme on sent la vie.

9. "Nous avons cherché nos maîtres chez nos pires ennemis, et j'en ai honte."
   "Ils sont les ennemis de nos âmes latines, autant que ceux de nos frontières."

10. Reynès-Monlaur again relates events in her novels to real incidents. On Good Friday, March 29, 1918, at exactly 3 p.m., German shells bombed the Parisian church, Notre-Dame de Saint-Gervais. Ninety-one people died in the attack, with at least that number wounded. Gilbert Guilleminault, *La France de la Madelon* (Paris: Denoël, 1965), 311.

11. Du sol se levait une poussière aveuglante, si dense que l'on crut d'abord à des gaz asphyxiants. Des débris humains s'entrechoquaient au travers. Les épargnés eux-mêmes, près du chœur, poussaient des hurlements de folie. . . . Les Allemands avaient choisi ce jour et cette heure—le Vendredi Saint à trois heures—pour étonner le monde par un des traits de leur culture. Ils rendaient inoubliable, ainsi, l'un des crimes significatifs de leur race. L'obus avait brisé un pilier, entraînant la voûte.

12. Dieu l'avait entendue, exaucée, dépassant ses espérances et comblant les désirs de son cœur. Son offrande était acceptée. Son sang servirait à la rançon de cette France qu'elle avait aimée plus qu'elle-même, au baptême de l'âme chérie qu'elle remettait aux mains de Dieu sous cette aspersion héroïque.

13. *Annuaire Général des Lettres*, 1003.

14. Elle est venue pour purifier la terre, peut-être de tels monstres, ou pour la punir de les avoir portés. Croyez-m'en, marraine, après le baptême de sang qui a lavé l'humanité, on ne verra plus de ces forfaits, on ne verra plus de ces caractères.

15. Tout leur est machine. Eux-mêmes fonctionnent comme des pièces d'une machine énorme. Le plus étonnant, c'est que, pris en particulier, souvent les soldats ne sont pas méchants. Mais ils font partie de la machine, et cela rend tout possible.

16. "Je compris que mon cœur trop cupide avait mérité son désastre."

17. Quand nous sommes seuls ensemble, et que la pensée de notre commune misère et faiblesse m'accable, je prends sa petite tête entre mes mains, et je sens alors que cette pauvre petite miette d'amour dont nous faisons notre nourriture, lui et moi qui avons tout perdu, suffit à nous tenir en vie, mêlés à l'immense communion des êtres qui s'aiment. Pour un cœur qui s'est cru retranché du milieu des vivants, c'est une résurrection.

18. Dossier Odette Dulac, Bibliothèque Maraguerite Durand; *Annuaire Général des Lettres,* 878; *Grand Annuaire des littérateurs et de notabilités,* 204.

19. See discussion above, chapter 1.

20. Berthem-Bontoux, 6, 9; Capy, 36–37. This view also appears in Henry Spont's *La Femme et la Guerre,* 183.

21. Ken Silver discusses the connection between modernism in art and German and French cultural perceptions during the war in *Esprit de corps* (Princeton, NJ: Princeton University Press, 1989).

22. Nous avons juré sur le Progrès universel, et lui seul est le but de notre œuvre; nous sommes les pionniers de la Sublime Race.

23. "Oh! blasphéma la faiseuse d'anges, pourquoi mettre des enfants au monde, puisque voilà ce qu'on en fait?" Mais la noblesse de cette mort de saint-cyrien ripostait victorieusement: "Pour sauver la France!"

24. Dulac, "La Tache originelle," 2.

25. Depuis trop longtemps, les faiseuses d'anges, l'amour du luxe, la sottise des modes et maintenant du canon, ont anémié notre Race. . . . Le Nombre seul peut sauver notre avenir. . . . J'y ai vu grouiller le Nombre hostile, je l'ai vu défiler au pas de parade, j'ai vu les innombrables cheminées d'usine qui attestent l'industrie de cette foule, et je vous supplie de sauver la France. S'il fallut une pucelle pour délivrer un Roi, il faut des mères pour sauver une République. Les hommes ont donné leur sang; donnons le nôtre. Que soient flétries désormais les tantes ridiculement vierges et les sœurs mystiquement réservées. Plus de mains croisées sur des bustes plats, plus d'égoïstes vertus grassouillettes et gourmandes. Que toutes les femmes enfantent dans la douleur, comme sont morts nos héros dans les tranchées.

26. " . . . formons les bataillons des futures épopées!"

27. "[L]a France à laquelle elle avait peu songé, qu'elle ne savait pas aimer . . . soudain prenait possession de son âme avec une violence douloureuse."

28. Les cloches des églises sonnant l'alarme, sonnant le devoir, ont fait surgir la vraie France, une France guerrière, une France religieuse qui, se reconnaissant demain, sera éperdue de fierté et de joie devant sa beauté retrouvée.

29. Vous n'êtes plus la jeune Parisienne ennuyée et futile que j'ai vue arriver il y a si peu de temps, ne cherchant dans la vie que son plaisir. Le

grand coup qui va nous frapper tous a fait surgir une femme avide de dévouement. . . .

30. Cloquié extols throughout her book the moral benefits of physical labor for women, seeing in work the beginning of wisdom (32). Borel's *La Mobilisation féminine en France (1914–1919)* (The Women's Mobilization in France) traces the remarkable increase since 1900 in the number of women in all sectors of the labor force.

31. "Car ce n'est pas seulement là la tendresse d'une femme aimante, c'est la foi d'une chrétienne et la force d'une Française."

32. Elle resterait toute sa vie veuve de cet amour mort, dont il lui faudrait même cacher le deuil, et la douleur qu'elle en éprouvait était si grande et si vive, qu'elle se comparait à une martyre de la Patrie!

    Cette pensée soutenait un peu son énergie en élevant sa résolution jusqu'à l'héroïsme. Choisir entre son amour et la France, la France, lui semblait une action d'éclat comme celle qui, bientôt peut-être, illustrerait nos soldats sur le champ de bataille, et elle s'exaltait à la consentir.

33. Protégé contre toute répulsion personnelle par cette discipline barbare dans sa conception et son exécution, Otto se prêtait sans scrupules aux plus dégradantes besognes. On le vit donner des ordres d'exécutions qui étaient de véritables assassinats. Des incendies furent allumés sur son commandement, et il toléra, sous ses yeux indulgents, des orgies que la plume se refuse à décrire.

CHAPTER 5

1. Willa Z. Silverman, *The Notorious Life of Gyp: Right-Wing Anarchist in Fin-de-Siècle France* (New York: Oxford, University Press, 1995), 4. See this meticulous biography for details on Gyp's life and a bibliography of her works. A fifth novel, *Journal d'un cochin de pessimiste* (Diary of a Pig of a Pessimist), 1918, is semiautobiographical and will not be discussed here.

2. A more literal translation of the word *nuque* (back of the neck) would indicate Gyp's satirical turn on the word *front,* which means forehead as well as the military connotation. Thus, civilians enjoy protection at the "back," whereas soldiers "face" the enemy.

3. "Elles sont très charmantes, mes infirmières, très chics . . . mais elles voudraient barboter toujours dans le sang, et humer la gangrène. . . . Il paraît que c'est leur idéal!"

4. "C'est trop vouloir de l'Âme Émancipée
   Qui a goûté d'un multiple horizon."

5. Verdunois, voulez-vous que la femme Française
   S'en aille à vos côtés, chantant *La Marseillaise?*
   Ou s'étende en tapis, afin que tous vos pas
   S'incrustent dans sa chair du haut jusques en bas?

6. Even the socialist journalist Marcelle Capy, certainly no political ally of the right-wing Gyp, agreed that the nurse's uniform was largely inappropriate

and promoted coquetry and other abuses (79–85). See also the discussion of nurses in chapter 1.

7. "Quant à ton dévouement, tu piétineras ta famille et ton pays pour un tango ou une toilette."

8. Silverman notes that Gyp was guilty of this herself, having used her connections in the War Ministry to effect her son's repatriation in 1916 (193–96).

9. This is most likely a sarcastic allusion to the writer Harlor (Jeanne Perrot, 1871–1970), whose *Liberté, liberté chérie* (Liberty, Beloved Liberty) was nominated for the prestigious Prix Goncourt in 1915. The prize committee decided that only combatants were eligible and Harlor's book was disqualified. The director for many years of the feminist library, Bibliothèque Marguerite Durand, Harlor wrote countless essays and newspaper articles on art, music, decorative arts, and writers. During the war she was Secretary General of the Ligue Républicaine de Défense Nationale, Droit et Liberté (Republican League for National Defense, Law and Liberty), for which she wrote pamphlets and engaged in fact-finding missions (Dossier Harlor, Bibliothèque Marguerite Durand).

10. Dossier Jeanne Landre, Bibliothèque Marguerite Durand; *Annuaire Général,* 968–69; *Qui Êtes-Vous?,* 435.

11. Landre also caricatures the civilian mania for founding charitable associations in *L'École des marraines.* In both novels the difficulty in finding a neglected need or group yields absurd results, such as Cyprien's Muses' Steak and the uniform repair unit, B. P. S. L.F., "Œuvre de Bouton Pression sur le Front" (Action for Button Pressure on the Front/Forehead) in *École des marraines.* Like Gyp, Landre makes full comic use of the double meaning of *front.* For a serious view of civilian charitable groups, see Marguerite Borel's (Camille Marbo) *La Mobilisation féminine en France (1914–1919).*

12. Il n'est pas un recoin de notre sentimentalité que nous n'ayons mis au service des combattants. Un époux pourrait vivre pendant des années près de nous sans nous approfondir comme l'ont fait nos amis inconnus.

13. Le voilà désormais le prisonnier de sa chimère, agrippé par les griffes du monstre. Il n'est pas Lui, il est Elle. C'est elle qui fait la guerre, c'est avec elle, pour elle, par elle qu'il obéit, qu'il lance sa grenade, qu'il va à la baïonnette. Si elle flanche, il est perdu.

14. Que Monsieur m'examine: je suis, depuis ce matin, une femme de la nouvelle couche, éclairée, émancipée, consciente. . . . J'aurai le droit de voter demain, car je viens de prendre une décision extraordinaire: je quitte Monsieur.

15. "Elles aspirent, non plus à l'émancipation, mais à l'esclavage. Après avoir brandi l'étendard de la révolte, elles rêvent de l'utiliser pour le nettoyage des chaussures d'un maître."

16. "Moi, je resterai à la maison, parce que j'espère avoir un mari qui pensera, qui travaillera, qui votera pour moi."

17. Dites: Il a fallu une haute intelligence à l'industriel ayant risqué ses capitaux pendant la guerre pour gagner les modestes sommes grâce auxquelles

il a pu soutenir l'emprunt national . . . Cristi, c'était le bon temps, la guerre! Si elle avait seulement duré six mois de plus, j'arrondissais à cinq millions là de mes garnements.

18. "Leur ambition est de pouvoir se donner, au front, l'illusion de la vie mondaine."

19. On September 25, 1915, the French launched major offensives in Champagne and Artois.

20. " . . . comme une immense sottise dont il se réhabiliterait volontiers par le sacrifice de sa peau."

21. "Alors, n'ai-je pas le droit de vous serrer la main, puisque si je ne me bats pas, ce n'est point parce que l'envie me manque, mais simplement parce que les lois sont mal faites."

22. " . . . je ne vous connais pas, et cependant je sais que vous êtes jeune, héroïque et que vous adorez la France."

23. " . . . l'amie maternelle et amoureuse que chaque homme espère."

24. La guerre finie, il serait reparti "vagabonder" sans même avoir vu l'épistolière, car tout ce qu'il exigeait d'elle c'était de personnifier à distance ses rêves, ses désirs, d'écouter la grande tendresse qui se lamentait en lui, de la prendre pour elle, d'y répondre selon son cœur, son tempérament et ses moyens d'extériorisation.

25. Ce qu'il voulait, c'était l'illusion de l'amour, de l'amour venant à lui, tout simplement, tout naïvement; ce dont il avait le plus faim, ce n'était point de belles périodes bien agencées qui défilent comme un bataillon en temps de paix, mais de l'expression de l'esprit de son amie, de l'instant de son émotion, des mots qui lui venaient au cœur ou au cerveau au moment où elle pensait à lui, à lui qui lui écrivait du lieu où les conventions sont mortes, où l'on peut tout oser, puisque les audaces, même excessives, n'entraînent rien.

26. "Je veux entretenir votre chère tendresse, au moins jusqu'aux heures des réalités."

27. "Accablée, écroulée, elle continuerait son calvaire, et sa crucifixion serait lente. Elle se sentait élue pour la plus grande douleur."

CHAPTER 6

1. Cloquié, 18–19.

2. Dossier Isabelle Sandy, Bibliothèque Marguerite Durand; *Annuaire Général,* 1079–80.

3. Il y a par le monde un tel courant de vie, que pareil à un flot irrésistible il emporte les décombres entassés par la destruction humaine. . . .

4. Tout ce que la guerre vous a appris et imposé comme des vérités personnelles, révélez-le à vos semblables. Parmi ceux de notre race, il en est que la guerre n'a pas suffisamment changés; chez eux la rédemption n'est que commencée; si nul ne les invite à cheminer plus loin, ils s'arrêteront et

s'endurciront dans les erreurs premières. Leurs âmes puériles resteront encombrées de vains soucis, oublieuses de ce qui doit être notre unique pensée: la régénération de toute une race.

Portée par le sang des morts, cette race a atteint un étiage élevé: il faut l'y maintenir.

. . . De tous les coins de la France de bons ouvriers vont se lever. Nous serons parmi eux!

Comme le geste du semeur notre geste s'élargira jusqu'à l'infini! Il faut le faire, ce geste! Il le faut!

5. Elle songeait que son amour pour cet homme blessé sur les champs de bataille dépassait tout ce que sa fervente jeunesse s'était plu à imaginer; il lui était donné d'aimer en un seul, et l'homme élu, et la France souffrante; en chérissant l'un, elle berçait la glorieuse misère de l'autre; en aimant, elle pansait et guérissait. Quel noble et magnifique destin!

6. Aujourd'hui les valeurs sont renversées, l'aventure d'un seul, si elle ne se rattache pas à celle que vit le monde n'a pas de prise sur les sensibilités. L'individu lui-même consent à ne pas s'attarder sur les divers changements que le destin peut opérer dans sa vie. Peut-être l'individualisme, qui trop longtemps désagrégea le bloc de la race française, sera-t-il fort atténué par la guerre. Les Français luttent, souffrent, espèrent ensemble. Ils ont des terrains d'entente: ils s'agglomèrent. L'envahisseur n'avait pas prévu cela.

7. Et Christiane connut la décevance des grands élans; elle connut la pitié infinie et la honte de n'avoir jamais, jamais pensé à ceux-là qui se sacrifient. . . . Elle eût voulu devenir leur servante, et sous le voile blanc, sous la blouse blanche emprisonner ses membres et ses pensées, disciplinés et asservis.

8. Si Mario ne m'avait pas été arraché, sans doute nous aurions lié nos vies. J'étais sa chaleur et son inspiratrice. Et parce que mon être ainsi composé lui plaisait, j'aurais gardé mon expression définitive près de lui.

9. Trop vive est la plaie de chacun pour songer à la toucher, nous ne saurions déterminer en cette minute le seul nécessaire. Françoise, vous demandez aujourd'hui un pardon qui vous serait demain peut-être une offense. Et moi qui ne sais pas si je pourrai désormais vivre avec vous ou loin de vous . . . comment faire mon choix! . . . Christiane a eu pitié . . . sait-elle ce que c'est l'amour? Et ne confond-elle pas? Pour vous deux . . . bientôt dépouillé de ma vareuse stricte, en habits civils je serai non plus un blessé, un grand blessé mais un manchot, que chacun y songe . . . Je vivrai, cela, je le sais . . . Petit Ambre, soyez bénie, pour m'en avoir donné l'orgueil.

10. "Sa déception est indiquée avec un grand tact d'écriture qui ne peut choquer personne et que seule une plume, féminine dans le bons sens, pouvait indiquer." Rachilde, "Revue de la Quinzaine," *Mercure de France* (1919): 303.

11. Un moment, dans la pièce triste, salle d'opérations de fortune érigée parmi les baraquements, le bruit régulier, menu comme un grignotement, de la scie sur l'os crissa au milieu du silence, ponctué de minute en minute par le gémissement inconscient du blessé.

12. Ne plus jamais pouvoir courir, ne plus jamais seulement marcher comme un autre. Ne plus jamais être "soi." Un bras, si c'était un bras. . . . Il ne sera plus aimé . . . ou il fera pitié. Ah! non, pas de pitié, jamais.

13. Son enfant? Elle sent tout à coup, farouchement qu'il lui appartient à elle seule. Oui, l'enfant est à la mère d'abord—et toujours. Elle pourra l'aimer, lui, le nourrir, le veiller, le consoler et le servir. Il aura l'égoïsme et l'ingratitude; toutes les mères le disent, mais, quand même, la candeur, l'abandon et la confiance. Il s'en ira un jour, mais il restera longtemps. Comme elle comptait tout à l'heure les minutes, elle compte maintenant les années: dix-huit années, vingt années?

14. Par les confidences que lui firent beaucoup de ses collègues, cette absence de jeunes êtres dans leur vie était le secret de leur mélancolie. Quelques-unes regrettaient dans le célibat le mari, l'amant, le compagnon, presque toutes regrettaient l'enfant. Beaucoup de ces théoriciennes de salon qui vivent, en effet, sans enfant seraient surprises d'entendre bien des professeurs, généralement féministes sincères, déplorer leur existence sans une fille ou un fils à élever, à câliner, à aimer, à former. Renée, sous ce rapport, ne se différenciait pas de la plus humble paysanne. Ce désir de l'enfant, sans l'idée de l'amour, est un sentiment si vrai, si éternel, qu'il a été magnifié dans toutes les religions par le symbole de la Vierge-mère. Certes, Renée aimait Fernand pour lui-même, mais elle l'aimait déjà dans ses futurs enfants.

15. Cette guerre est pour les féministes, le signal d'une défaite si, dès maintenant sages, c'est-à-dire sans révolte contre les nécessités de l'existence telle que Dieu, la nature et les circonstances l'ont créée, elles s'appuient sur l'homme pour parvenir à leur but. Seules, elles ne peuvent rien. Leur rôle est d'être des épouses et des mères, sans négliger l'œuvre sociale. Oui, le rôle des femmes est lourd. Cultivées, intelligentes, elles doivent s'intéresser au sort de la France, participer au relèvement des ruines matérielles et morales causées par la guerre et doivent également, puisqu'ils y tiennent, être jolies, parées et souriantes.

16. Renée, qui avait lu beaucoup d'articles et que cette question passionna plusieurs mois auparavant, comprenait qu'on avait demandé leurs opinions à des savants, à des philanthropes, à des académiciens. Elle la voyait résolue par cette femme qui hochait la tête, approuvait les raisonnements, mais serrait le petit être en répétant ces simples mots qui pour elle exprimaient sa défaite suprême et son suprême orgueil: "Que voulez-vous, c'est mon enfant."

17. "Une Président," *Le Journal* (Paris), 23 March 1937; Camille Marbo, *A Travers Deux Siècles: Souvenirs et Rencontres 1883–1967* (Across Two Centuries: Memories and Encounters 1883–1967) (Paris: Grasset, 1967), 162–63; 168–69.

18. "Elle a un esprit viril, mais elle garde une sensibilité féminine. L'objectivité de l'expérimentation s'anime chez elle de la chaleur de la sympathie." André Delacour, "Un romancier," *La Revue bleue* 75 (1937): 474–478.

19. Camille Marbo, *The Man Who Survived,* trans. Frank Hunter Potter (New York: Harper and Brothers, 1918).

20. *Paris-Soir,* 23 October 1924. Untitled clipping. Dossier Élie Dautrin, Bibliothèque Marguerite Durand.

21. Marville observa combien sa femme parlait avec plus de suite dans ses idées, plus de logique dans la déduction et plus de soin dans la phrase et de fermeté dans l'expression. Il constata l'élargissement de sa pensée, l'ampleur de ses préoccupations et combien ses jugements étaient plus généreux, plus intelligents, ses vues plus hautes.

    Il songeait: "Il y avait tout ça en elle. Et pour que je le sache, il a fallu la guerre." Une pensée douloureuse le harcelait: "Pendant que je me déforme dans le militarisme, elle se forme dans la liberté."

22. "Si j'étais libre."

    "Libre! On le devient! Ce n'est pas la vie qui doit vous mener, mais vous qui devez mener la vie," formula Edward, à l'Américaine.

23. Such independence is the plot mover in Dautrin's earlier war novel *L'Envolée* (The Flight), published in 1917, in which a famous woman writer becomes the mentor of a young man. Perceiving his great poetic talent, she nurtures his career to success and cares for him when he is wounded during the war. Although she recognizes his great love for her, the eighteen year difference in their ages causes her to decide to set him free (the flight in the title referring equally to a poetic flight of oratory and that of a bird) to fulfill unfettered his great potential as a writer.

24. Eugène Martin, "Préparons l'avenir: consignes de guerre aux épouses et mères," *La Croix* (Paris) 22 October 1915:1; Donnay, 62–65; Courson, 42.

25. Les infirmières s'activaient, souriantes. La bonne humeur respectueuse des soldats, d'une part, l'attention émue de celles qui les soignaient de l'autre, et voici que "le monde" et "le peuple," étroitement rapprochés, se comprenaient, peut-être pour la première fois.

    En dépit de quelques erreurs et de quelques abus, quel beau socialisme la guerre aura fait vivre tout au long de la France, dans les salles nacrées des hôpitaux!

26. The conflicts posed by Élisabeth's idealization of love, her introspective nature, and her willing separation from the world suggest an affinity with another character of the same name, Madame de La Fayette's Princesse de Clèves.

27. Mais moi, je ne voulais pas l'épouser. Cela déplaisait à ma liberté. Il y a dans le mariage une convention, une officialité, quelque chose qui n'existe que pour les autres. Tout ce qui concède, tout ce qui prévoit *les autres* est faiblesse, donc humiliation. Puisqu'il m'avait choisie et que je l'avais choisi. Nous n'avions besoin de l'approbation de personne. . . .

    Nous n'avions besoin de l'approbation de personne. Mais il m'était impossible de léser quelqu'un. Je ne pouvais pas lui appartenir tandis que sa famille l'entourait. Il aurait fallu nous cacher de vous tous. C'était une humiliation plus grande que le mariage. (Italics in original.)

28. "Il se sentait physiquement et moralement humilié près de cette fille droite et supérieure."

29. Ainsi, tandis que, perdu dans l'horreur des tueries, un homme fait avec bonheur son grand devoir, lui, Francis le boiteux, Francis le réformé, Francis l'incapable accomplit lentement, lâchement l'œuvre de voler cet homme dans ce qu'il a de plus cher et de plus sacré.
   . . . Mais je l'aime, moi!

30. Sommes-nous faits, nous, modernes, nous races évoluées, pour cet événement d'un autre temps? Que vient-elle faire, la guerre, parmi nos âpres luttes européennes pour la justice et l'égalité, parmi nos tangos et nos fêtes persanes? En quoi nous regarde-t-elle, la guerre? Nous ne sommes plus des héros. Nous ne saurons pas nous battre. Nous n'avons plus rien de ce qu'il faut pour une telle aventure.

31. Dossier Marie Lenéru, Bibliothèque Marguerite Durand.

32. See for example Aurel (Aurélie Mortier), *La Conscience embrasée* (The Ardent Conscience) (Paris: Radot, 1927), Jean Balde (Jeanne Alleman), "L'Héroïque destinée de Marie Lenéru" (The Heroic Destiny of Marie Lenéru), *Revue hebdomadaire* (1925): 405–16, as well as articles in *La Grande Revue* (1918), *Études* (1922), *Les Nouvelles Littéraires* (1924), *Les Lettres* (1926), and the special issue of *La Revue française* devoted to Lenéru in 1927. Lenéru was the subject of two doctoral dissertations in the 1930s: one in German by Maria Dissen (Rheinischen Friedrich-Wilhems-Universität), and a second in French by Suzanne Lavaud (Université de Paris), cited below.

33. Rachilde, "Mort de Marie Lenéru" (Death of Marie Lenéru), *Mercure de France* (1918): 755–56; Suzanne Lavaud, *Marie Lenéru, sa vie, son journal, son théâtre* (Marie Lenéru, Her Life, Her Diary, Her Theater) (Paris: Société française d'éditions littéraires et techniques, 1932), 145–70; 258–64.

34. The cornerstone of these models, was, of course, the establishment of a League of Nations. Lenéru also advocated many other specific objectives of the program of British novelist H.G. Wells (1866–1946), including prohibition of the private sale of armaments and the abolition of customs regulations to allow free exchange between countries. In a letter to Léon Blum in 1917, she proclaims, "Je suis d'un bout à l'autre dans la ligne officielle, et je n'éprouve aucun besoin d'en sortir" (I am from one end to the other, completely in the official line [with Wells's program] and I feel no need to get out of it). From the letter, it is obvious that the original version of *La Paix* included explicit references to the plan at the beginning of act 4, scene 3, citations that are absent from the published edition of 1922 (Lavaud, 166–67). For more on Wells's involvement with the League of Free Nations Association and the League of Nations Union, see Henry R. Winkler, *The League of Nations Movement in Great Britain, 1914–1919* (New Brunswick, NJ: Rutgers University Press, 1952); and W. Warren Wagar, *H.G. Wells and the World State* (New Haven, Conn.: Yale University Press, 1961).

35. Lenéru also expresses these ideas in articles she published in *L'Intransigeant* (July, 1917–April, 1918) and other Parisian newspapers, as well as in her diary, especially the entries for 1916. See Marie Lenéru, *Journal de Marie Lenéru* (Paris: Crès, 1922) and Lucien Roth, "Marie Lenéru et la Guerre" (Marie Lenéru and the War), *Évolution* (1930): 22–31.

36. Mais je demande aussi les femmes, parce que je leur garde une mission, la mission qui est proprement la leur, qui est la mienne, celle du souvenir. . . . J'en suis arrivée à cette conviction, une seule chose est nécessaire, une seule chose suffirait, mais celles dont l'humanité est peut-être incapable: ne pas oublier. . . . Ah! si chacun avait vu . . . si une seule de ces horreurs, qui ont passé par milliers devant notre lâche imagination, appartenait vraiment à la vie réelle de chacun de nous, si nous nous en sentions vraiment les vengeurs responsables. . . . On assassine vos frères dans votre maison, et vous écoutez derrière votre porte loquetée. . . .

37. J'ai fait le sacrifice de mon bonheur en ce monde. Et pour que Dieu ne permette pas, tant que je serai en vie, qu'on tue encore une fois les enfants des autres. . . . j'ai fait l'aveu de n'en avoir jamais à moi.

38. "Il n'y a de réalité au monde que dans nos convictions."

39. Mais vous êtes au tout premier rang de la défense nationale . . . L'homme chargé de prévoir, d'ordonner les futurs sacrifices, les futures hécatombes, si vous voulez, ne peut vivre dans l'atmosphère incrédule du pacifisme. Il ne puisera pas dans les yeux d'une femme en deuil, dans les bras d'une femme révoltée, l'assurance, le calme, la certitude d'accomplir l'œuvre nécessaire, l'œuvre indispensable, la mission suprême du salut!

40. Jamais nos pensées ne se rencontrent, jamais nos deux cœurs se battent à l'unisson, en dehors des rares instants où, parvenant à nous écarter de la guerre, nous ne parlons que d'amour. Et même dans ces instants fugitifs, une ombre subsiste; je voudrais lui dire: "Je suis ton œuvre, ma voix n'est que l'écho de la tienne, mon âme est le reflet de ton âme, ta force arme ma faiblesse," et ces mots je ne peux pas les prononcer!

41. Mon devoir, c'est d'empêcher ma nervosité d'altérer ma santé, car ainsi que la voix lointaine de Michel me l'a murmuré, je peux avoir besoin de mes forces pour lui ou pour les autres, mon devoir est d'apporter à mon fiancé une âme aimante, douce, gaie parce que nous avons l'obligation de nous aimer beaucoup afin de donner un nombre considérable de petits Français à la France mutilée. Cette idée amène un sourire sur mes lèvres. Je vais me faire belle et me jeter dans les bras de Roger dès son arrivée. . . . Il est bien mon maître, mon seul maître et j'aime tout de lui, même sa domination.

42. Une sorte de pressentiment heureux m'envahit. Michel, Philippe, votre mort va-t-elle rouvrir la tombe de mon amour pour une résurrection splendide? Aura-t-elle fait comprendre à Roger la beauté de votre vie, de votre héroïque sacrifice?

Un même idéal vous a enflammés et vous a entraînés. Vous étiez les champions du droit et de la liberté.

Michel, Philippe . . . morts? Non, éternellement vivants pour l'exemple, pour exalter en nous l'impérieux amour.

CONCLUSION

1. Prasenjit Duara, "The Regime of Authenticity: Timelessness, Gender, and National History in Modern China," *History and Theory* (1998): 290–95.

Bibliography

PRIMARY SOURCES:

Apollinaire, Guillaume. *Les Mamelles de Tirésias* (Tiresias's Tits). In *Œuvres complètes* (Complete Works). Vol. 3. Edited by Michel Décaudin. Paris: Balland and Lecat, 1966.

Aurel (Aurélie Mortier). *Les Françaises devant l'opinion masculine* (Male Opinion of French Women). Paris: Chiberre, 1922.

————. *Les Saisons de la mort* (Seasons of Death). Paris: Figuière, 1916.

"Aux jeunes filles" (To Girls). *La Croix* (Paris). 21 October 1915, supplement, 1.

Barrau, Hortense. *Les Gaufrettes de guerre* (War Waffles). Paris: Librairie Haton, 1916.

Bazin, René. "Elles écrivent" (They [women] Write). *L'Écho de Paris,* 8 February 1916, 1.

————. "Le Rôle maternel des institutrices" (The Maternal Role of Teachers). *L'Écho de Paris,* 7 December 1915, 1.

————. "Trois Françaises" (Three French Women). *L'Écho de Paris,* 1 August 1915, 1.

Berger, Lya. *Les Revanches, contes de guerre* (Revenge, War Stories). Paris: Jouve, 1919.

Berthem-Bontoux (Berthe Bontoux). *Les Françaises et la Grande Guerre* (The French Women and the Great War). Paris: Bloud et Gay, 1917.

Bertheroy, Jean (Berthe Le Barillier). *Vers la Gloire* (Toward Glory). Paris: Éditions Pierre Lafitte, 1918.

Bertillon, Jacques. "La Dépopulation en France" (Depopulation in France). *La Croix* (Paris), 8 October 1916, supplement, 1.

Borély, Marthe. *L'Appel aux Françaises. Le Féminisme politique* (Call to French Women. Political Feminism). Paris: Nouvelle Librairie nationale, 1919.

Broussan-Gaubert, Jeanne. *Reviendra-t-il?* (Will He Return?). Paris: Crès, 1918.

Bussy, Jack de. *Réfugiée et Infirmière de Guerre* (Woman Refugee and War Nurse). Paris: Figuière, 1915.

Capy, Marcelle. *Une voix de femme dans la mêlée* (A Woman's Voice in the Melee). Paris: Ollendorff, 1916.

Cloquié, Hortense. *La Femme après la guerre, ses droits, son rôle, son devoir* (Woman After the War, Her Rights, Her Role, Her Duty). Paris: Maloine, 1915.

————. *Les Soldats de France de 1914–1915* (Soldiers of France from 1914–1915). Paris: Maloine, 1915.

Colette. *Mitsou ou comment l'esprit vient aux filles* (Mitsou or How Intelligence Comes to Girls). In *Œuvres*. Vol. 2. Paris: Gallimard, 1986.

Combarieu, Jules. *Les Jeunes Filles françaises et la Guerre* (Young French Girls and the War). Paris: Armand Colin, 1916.

Compain, Louise. "Souvenirs de l'ouvroir de guerre" (Memories of a War Workshop). *La Grande Revue* 4 (1915): 262–279.

Corthis, Andrée Husson Lécuyer. *Petites Vies dans la Tourmente* (Minor Life Stories of the Turmoil). Paris: Pierre Lafitte, 1917.

Courson, Comtesse de. *La Femme Française pendant la Guerre* (The French Woman During the War). Paris: Lethielleux, 1916.

Dautrin, Élie (Marie Aglaé de la Layère, Comtesse de Duranti). *L'Absent* (The Absentee). Paris: Flammarion, 1919.

———. *L'Envolée* (The Flight). Paris: Plon-Nourrit, 1917.

———. *Nos Petits pendant la Guerre et Nos Grands.* (Our Young and Full-Grown During the War). Paris: Plon, 1916.

Delarue-Mardrus, Lucie. "L'Enfant du Barbare" (Child of the Barbarian). *Le Journal* (Paris), 22 March 1915.

———. "The Godmother." In *Tales of Wartime France.* Translated by William L. McPherson. New York: Dodd, Mead and Company, 1918.

———. "The Godmother II." In *Tales of Wartime France.* Translated by William L. McPherson. New York: Dodd, Mead and Company, 1918.

———. "The Red Rose." In *Tales of Wartime France.* Translated by William L. McPherson. New York: Dodd, Mead and Company, 1918.

———. *Toutoune et Son Amour* (Toutoune and Her Love). Paris: Albin Michel, 1919.

———. *Un roman civil en 1914* (A Civilian Novel in 1914). Paris: Bibliothèque Charpentier, 1916.

Delorme-Jules Simon, J. *A l'ombre du drapeau* (In the Shadow of the Flag). Paris: Fayard, 1914.

———. *Âmes de guerre, âmes d'amour* (Souls of War, Souls of Love). Paris: Perrin, 1917.

———. *L'Impérieux amour* (The Essential Love). Paris: Perrin, 1918.

———. *Visions d'Héroïsme* (Images of Heroism). Paris: Librairie Payot, 1915.

Démians d'Archimbaud, Mathilde. *A travers le tourment: une vie intime* (Through the Torment: A Private Life). Paris: Plon-Nourrit, 1917.

Donnay, Maurice. *La Parisienne et la Guerre* (The Parisian Woman and the War). Paris: Crès, 1916.

Drous, Noélie. *Sous la tempête* (In the Storm). Épone: Société d'Edition et de librairie de l'Avenir social, 1920.

Duhamelet, Geneviève. *Ces Dames de l'hôpital 336* (Those Ladies of Hospital 336). Paris: Albin Michel, 1917.

———. *Les Inépousées* (The Unmarried Women). Paris: Albin Michel, 1918.

Dulac, Odette (Odette Roche). *Le Droit à l'enfant, Conférence faite à l'Action des Femmes* (Rights for Children, Lecture Given to Women's Action). Paris: Figuière, 1916.

———. *Faut-il?* (Must We?). Paris: Calmann-Lévy, 1919.

———. *La Houille rouge; les enfants de la violence* (Blood Power; the Children of Violence). Paris: Figuière, 1916.

———. "La Tache originelle" (Original Stain). *Le Journal* (Paris), 28 January 1917: 2.

Flers, Robert de. "La Vraie Charité" (The True Charity). *Le Figaro* (Paris), 17 August 1914, 1.

Floran, Mary (Marie Leclercq). *L'Ennemi* (The Enemy). Paris: Calmann-Lévy, 1916.

———. *On demande une marraine* (Seeking a Godmother). Paris: Calmann-Lévy, 1919.

Gayraud, Louise-Amélie. "Le Féminisme et la Guerre" (Feminism and the War). *La Revue hebdomadaire* 53 (1916): 610–27.

———. "L'Œuvre féminine et le Féminisme" (Feminine Work and Feminism). *La Revue hebdomadaire* 30 (1916): 525–40.

Gyp (Sibylle-Gabrielle Marie-Antoinette de Riquetti de Mirabeau, Comtesse de Martel de Janville). *Ceux de "la Nuque"* (Those of "the Rear"). Paris: Fayard, 1916.

———. *Ceux qui s'en f. . . . .* (Those Who Don't Give a D . . .). Paris: Flammarion, 1918.

———. *Les Flanchards* (The Quitters). Paris: Fayard, 1917.

———. *Les Profitards* (The Profiteers). Paris: Fayard, 1918.

Harlor (Jeanne Perrot). *Liberté, liberté chérie* (Liberty, Beloved Liberty). Paris: Crès, 1916.

Houville, Gérard d' (Marie de Régnier). "Il faut toujours compter sur l'imprévu" (Always Count on the Unexpected). *La Revue des deux mondes* (1916): 259–93.

Laforêt, Claude. "La Mentalité française à l'épreuve de la guerre" (French Mentality Tested by the War). *Mercure de France* (1918): 577–600.

La Hire, Marie de. *Deux Boy-Scouts à Paris pendant la Guerre* (Two Boy Scouts in Paris During the War). Paris: Larousse, 1916.

———. *La Femme française, son activité pendant la guerre* (The French Woman, Her Activity During the War). Paris: Librairie Jules Tallandier, 1917.

Landre, Jeanne. *L'École des marraines* (The School for Godmothers). Paris: Albin Michel, 1917.

———. *Loin des balles, mémoires d'un philanthrope* (Far from the Bullets, Memoirs of a Philanthropist). Paris: Albin Michel, 1918.

———. *. . . puis il mourut.* (. . . then he died). Paris: La Renaissance du livre, 1916.

Laparcerie, Marie. *Comment trouver un mari après la guerre* (How to Find a Husband After the War). Paris: A. Méricant, 1915.

Lenéru, Marie. "Les Femmes n'entraveront pas la guerre" (Women Will Not Hinder the War). *L'Intransigeant* (Paris), 20 July 1917, n.p.

———. *La Paix* (Peace). Paris: Grasset, 1922.

———. *Journal de Marie Lenéru* (Diary of Marie Lenéru). Paris: Crès, 1922.

Madelin, Louis. "La Vertu française" (French Virtue). *La Revue hebdomadaire* 10 (1917): 174–209.

Marbo, Camille (Marguerite Borel). *A Travers Deux Siècles: Souvenirs et Rencontres 1883–1967* (Across Two Centuries: Memories and Encounters 1883–1967). Paris: Grasset, 1967.

———. *La Mobilisation féminine en France (1914–1919)* (The Female Mobilization in France [1914–1919]). Paris: Imprimerie Union, 1919.

———. *Le Survivant* (The Man Who Survived). Paris: Fayard, 1918.

Mars, Andrée. *Tu aimeras dans la douleur* (You Will Love in Sorrow). Paris: Albin Michel, 1917.

Martin, Eugène. "Préparons l'avenir: consignes de guerre aux épouses et mères" (Let Us Prepare the Future: War Directives for Wives and Mothers). *La Croix* (Paris) 22 October 1915:1.

———. "Préparons l'avenir: aux épouses et aux mères en deuil" (Let Us Prepare the Future: to Wives and Mothers in Mourning). *La Croix* (Paris) 5 November 1915, supplement, 1.

Maryan, M. (Marie Cadiou Deschard). *Un mariage en 1915* (A Marriage in 1915). Paris: H. Gautier, 1916.

Masson, Frédéric. "De la repopulation" (On Repopulation). *L'Écho de Paris,* 20 October 1916, 1.

———. "De la repopulation, le Mariage" (On Repopulation, Marriage). *L'Écho de Paris,* 2 November 1916: 1.

———. "Les Femmes de France et la Guerre" (The Women of France and the War). *L'Écho de Paris,* 2 May 1915, 1.

———. "Les Femmes pendant et après la guerre" (Women During and After the War). *La Revue hebdomadaire* 9 (1917): 5–31.

Mayran, Camille. *Histoire de Gotton Connixloo* (The Story of Gotton Connixloo). Paris: Plon-Nourrit, 1918.

———. *L'Oubliée* (The Forgotten Woman). Paris: Plon-Nourrit, 1918.

Orliac, Jehanne d'. *La Captive de Gand* (The Captive Woman of Ghent). Paris: Flammarion, 1917.

———. *Un grand blessé* (A Severely Wounded Soldier). Paris: Flammarion, 1917.

Pascal, Mme Yves. *Noune et la Guerre* (Noune and the War). Paris: Edition Française illustrée, 1918.

Pitrois, Yvonne. *Les Femmes de la Grande Guerre* (The Women of the Great War). Geneva: Jeheber, 1916.

Rachilde. "La Délivrance" (The Liberation). *Mercure de France* (1915): 447–55.

Reynès-Monlaur, Marie. *Pages de deuil et d'héroïsme: Les Autels morts* (Pages of Mourning and Heroism: Dead Altars). Paris: Plon-Nourrit, 1917.

———. *Pages de deuil et d'héroïsme: La Fin de Claude* (Pages of Mourning and Heroism: The End of Claude). Paris: Plon-Nourrit, 1918.

———. *Pages de deuil et d'héroïsme: Les Paroles secrètes* (Pages of Mourning and Heroism: Secret Words). Paris: Plon-Nourrit, 1915.

Rolland, Romain. "À l'Antigone éternelle" (To the Eternal Antigone). *demain* (1916): 20–21.

Sandy, Isabelle (Isabelle Fourcade Xardel). *Chantal Daunoy.* Paris: Plon-Nourrit, 1917.

Spont, Henri. *La Femme et la Guerre* (Women and the War). Paris: Perrin, 1916.

Star, Maria (Ernesta de Hierschel Stern). *Le Baptême du courage* (Baptism of Courage). Paris: Editions de la Nouvelle Revue, 1916.

Tardieu, Eugène. "Un mariage émouvant" (An Inspiring Marriage). *L'Écho de Paris,* 7 August 1915: 1.

Tinayre, Marcelle. *La Veillée des armes: Le Départ: août, 1914* (To Arms!). Paris: Calmann-Lévy, 1915; *To Arms*. Translated by Lucy Humphrey, New York: E.P. Dutton and Company, 1918.

Ulmès, Tony d'(Renée and Berthe Rey). "Ces Dames de la Croix-Rouge" (These Ladies of the Red Cross). *La Revue de Paris* 6 (1915): 414–28.

———. "La Mobilisation des Femmes" (The Mobilization of Women). *La Revue hebdomadaire* 8 (1915): 73–84.

Valmy, Pauline. "La Guerre et l'Âme des femmes" (The War and the Soul of Women). *La Grande Revue* 10 (1915): 305–310.

Vernet, Madeleine. "L'Enfant ennemi" (The Enemy Child)." *Contes d'hier et d'aujourd'hui* (Stories of Yesterday and Today). Épone: Editions de l'Avenir social, 1917.

Vismes, Henriette de. *Histoire authentique et touchante des marraines et des filleuls de guerre* (Authentic and Moving History of War Godmothers and Godsons). Paris: Perrin, 1918.

Yver, Colette. *Mirabelle de Pampelune* (Mirabelle of Pamploma). Paris: Calmann-Lévy, 1917.

Zeys, Louise. "Les Femmes et la Guerre" (Women and the War). *La Revue des deux mondes* 9 (1916): 175–204.

SECONDARY SOURCES:

Allen, Margaret. "The Domestic Ideal and the Mobilization of Womanpower in World War II." *Women's Studies International Forum* 6 (1983): 401–12.

Annuaire Général des Lettres (General Directory of the Literary World). Paris: n.p., 1931.

Annuaire des poètes (General Directory of Poets). Paris: R. Debresse, 1933.

Armogathe, Daniel. "Les Femmes et la Paix en France aux XIXe et XX siècles" (Women and Peace in France in the Nineteenth and Twentieth Centuries). In *Féminisme et Pacifisme: même combat* (Feminism and Pacifism: Same Fight). Edited by Danielle Le Bricquir and Odette Thibault. Paris: Les Lettres libres, 1985.

Audoin-Rouzeau, Stéphane. *Men at War 1914–1918, National Sentiment and Trench Journalism in France during the First World War.* Translated by Helen McPhail. Oxford: Berg Publishers, 1995.

Bard, Christine. *Les Filles de Marianne, histoire des féminismes, 1914–1940* (The Daughters of Marianne, History of Feminisms, 1914–1940). Paris: Fayard, 1995.

Becker, Annette. *Oubliés de la Grande Guerre* (Forgotten People of the Great War). Paris: Éditions Noêsis, 1998.

———. "Tortured and Exalted by War: French Catholic Women, 1914–1918." In *Women and War in the Twentieth Century.* Edited by Nicole Ann Dombrowski. New York: Garland Publishing, 1999.

Becker, Jean-Jacques. *The Great War and the French People.* Providence: Berg Publishers, 1993.

Berkin, Carol R. and Clara M. Lovett. "Introduction/Retreat to Patriotic Motherhood." In *Women, War, and Revolution.* Edited by Carol R. Berkin and Clara M. Lovett. New York: Holmes and Meier Publishers, 1980.

Berkman, Joyce. "Feminism, War, and Peace Politics: The Case of World War I." In *Women, Militarism, and War: Essays in History, Politics, and Social Theory.* Edited by Jean Bethke Elshtain and Sheila Tobias. Lanham, MD: Rowman and Littlefield, 1990.

Bond, Jane Clement. "Women Workers in the Bourges Government Arsenals During World War I." Paper presented at the Conference on World War I and the Twentieth Century, Wichita, Kansas, November, 1998.

Bremond, Henri. Review of *Les Autels morts* by Marie Reynès-Monlaur. *Le Correspondant,* 25 August 1917: 756–58.

Cardinal, Agnès. "Women and the Language of War in France." In *Women and World War I, The Written Response.* Edited by Dorothy Goldman. New York: St. Martin's Press, 1993.

Chaigne, Louis. *Vies et Œuvres d'écrivains* (Lives and Works of Writers). Vol. 2. Paris: Lanore, 1938.

Chartier, Roger and Henri-Jean Martin. *Le Livre concurrencé 1900–1950* (The Book Contested). Vol. 4 of *Histoire de l'édition française* (History of French Publishing). Edited by Roger Chartier and Henri-Jean Martin. Paris: Fayard, 1986.

Clark, Linda. "The Primary Education of French Girls: Pedagogical Prescriptions and Social Realities, 1880–1940." *History of Education Quarterly* 21 (1981): 411–28.

Clouard, Henri. *Aurel, bibliographie critique. Les Célébrités d'aujourd'hui* (Aurel, critical bibliography. Celebrities of Today). Paris: Chiberre, 1922.

Cole, Jonathan. "'There Are Only Good Mothers': The Ideological Work of Women's Fertility in France before World War I." *French Historical Studies* 19 (1996): 639–72.

Colin, Geneviève. "Writers and the War." In *The Great War and the French People.* By Jean-Jacques Becker. Providence: Berg Publishers, 1993.

Cooper, Clarissa Burnham. *Women Poets of the Twentieth Century in France: A critical bibliography.* New York: King's Crown Press, 1943.

Cooper, Helen, Adrienne Munich, and Susan Squier. *Arms and the Woman: War, Gender, and Literary Representation.* Chapel Hill: University of North Carolina Press, 1989.

Cooper, Sandi E. "Pacifism in France, 1889–1914: International Peace as a Human Right." *French Historical Studies* 17 (1991): 359–385.

Cru, J. Norton. *Témoins: essai d'analyse et de critique des souvenirs de combattants édités en français de 1915 à 1928* (Witnesses: analytical and critical essay of soldiers' recollections published in French from 1915 to 1928). Paris: Les Étincelles, 1929.

Darrow, Margaret H. "French Volunteer Nursing and the Myth of the War Experience in World War I." *American Historical Review* 101 (1996): 80–106.

Delacour, André. "Un romancier," *La Revue bleue* (A Novelist) 75 (1937): 474–78.

Di Leonardo, Micaela. "Morals, Mothers, and Militarism: Antimilitarism and Feminist Theory." *Feminist Studies* 3 (1985): 599–617.

Duara, Prasenjit. "The Regime of Authenticity: Timelessness, Gender, and National History in Modern China." *History and Theory* (1998): 287–308.

Dubesset, Mathilde, Françoise Thébaud, and Catherine Vincent. "Les Munitionnettes de la Seine" (The Women Munitions Workers of the Seine). In

1914–1918, L'Autre Front (1914–1918, The Other Front). Edited by Patrick Fridenson. Paris: Éditions ouvrières, 1977.

Eksteins, Modris. *The Rites of Spring: The Great War and the Birth of the Modern Age.* New York: Doubleday, 1989.

Elshtain, Jean Bethke. "Thinking about Women and International Violence." In *Women, Gender, and World Politics: Perspectives, Policies, and Prospects.* Edited by Peter Beckman and Francine D'Amico. Westport, Conn.: Bergin and Garvey, 1994.

———. *Women and War.* New York: Basic Books, 1987.

Enloe, Cynthia. *Does Khaki Become You? The Militarization of Women's Lives.* Boston: South End Press, 1983.

Ernest-Charles, Jean. "La Vie littéraire: *La Veillée des armes* par Marcelle Tinayre" (Literary Life: The Call to Arms by Marcelle Tinayre). *La Grande Revue* (1915): 119–22.

Gilbert, Sandra. "Soldier's Heart: Literary Men, Literary Women, and the Great War." *Signs* 8 (1983): 422–50.

Goldberg, Nancy Sloan. *En l'honneur de la juste parole: la Poésie française contre la Grande Guerre* (For the Honor of the Righteous Word: French Poetry Against the Great War). New York: Peter Lang, 1993.

———. "From Whitman to Mussolini: Modernism in the Life and Works of a French Intellectual." *Journal of European Studies* xxvi (1996): 153–73.

Goldman, Dorothy, ed. *Women and World War I: The Written Response.* New York: St. Martin's Press, 1993.

———. *Women Writers and the Great War.* New York: Twayne Publishers, 1995.

Grand Annuaire des littérateurs et de notabilités (Great Directory of Writers and Prominent People). Paris: n. p., 1922.

Grayzel, Susan R. "Mothers, Marraines, and Prostitutes: Morale and Morality in First World War France." *The International History Review* xix (1997): 66–82.

Guilleminault, Gilbert. *La France de la Madelon* (France of the Madelon). Paris: Denoël, 1965.

Hanna, Martha. *The Mobilization of Intellect, French Scholars and Writers During the Great War.* Cambridge, Mass.: Harvard University Press, 1996.

Hause, Steven C. with Anne R. Kenney. *Women's Suffrage and Social Politics in the French Third Republic.* Princeton: Princeton University Press, 1984.

Higonnet, Margaret R. "Another Record: A Different War." *Women's Studies Quarterly* 3,4 (1995): 85–96.

———. "Not So Quiet in No-Woman's-Land." In *Gendering War Talk.* Edited by Miriam Cooke and Angela Woollacott. Princeton: Princeton University Press, 1993.

———and Patrice L.-R. Higonnet. "The Double Helix." In *Behind the Lines: Gender and the Two World Wars.* Edited by Margaret R. Higonnet et al. New Haven: Yale University Press, 1987.

Käppeli, Anne-Marie. "Feminist Scenes." Translated by Arthur Goldhammer. In *Emerging Feminism from Revolution to World War.* Edited by Geneviève Fraisse and Michelle Perrot. Vol. 4 of *A History of Women in the West.* Edited by Georges Duby and Michelle Perrot. Cambridge, Mass.: Harvard University Press, 1993.

Klejman, Laurence and Florence Rochefort. *L'Égalité en marche, le féminisme sous la Troisième République* (Equality on the Move, Feminism in the Third Republic). Paris: Des Femmes, 1989.

Kuhlman, Erika A. *Petticoats and White Feathers: Gender Conformity, Race, the Progressive Peace Movement, and the Debate Over War, 1895–1919.* Contributions in Women's Studies, no. 160. Westport, Conn.: Greenwood Press, 1997.

Lavaud, Suzanne. *Marie Lenéru, sa vie, son journal, son théâtre* (Marie Lenéru, Her Life, Her Diary, Her Theater). Paris: Société française d'éditions littéraires et techniques, 1932.

Le Grix, François. "Sur quelques livres de guerre" (On Several War Books). *La Revue hebdomadaire* 7 (1915): 362–87.

Martin-Fugier, Anne. *La Bourgeoise: femme au temps de Paul Bourget* (The Bourgeois Woman: Women in the Era of Paul Bourget). Paris: Grasset, 1983.

Maugue, Annelise. *L'Identité masculine en crise au tournant du siècle 1871–1914* (The Crisis of Masculine Identity at the Turn of the Century 1871–1914). Paris: Rivages, 1987.

―――. "The New Eve and the Old Adam." Translated by Arthur Goldhammer. In *Emerging Feminism from Revolution to World War.* Edited by Geneviève Fraisse and Michelle Perrot. Vol. 4 of *A History of Women in the West.* Edited by Georges Duby and Michelle Perrot. Cambridge, Mass.: Harvard University Press, 1993.

McMillan, James F. "French Catholics: *Rumeurs Infâmes* and the *Union Sacrée* 1914–1918." In *Authority, Identity and the Social History of the Great War.* Edited by Frans Coetzee and Marilyn Shevin-Coetzee. Oxford: Berghahn Books, 1995.

―――. "Reclaiming a Martyr: French Catholics and the Cult of Joan of Arc, 1890–1920." In *Martyrs and Martyrologies.* Edited by Diana Wood. Oxford: Blackwell Publishers, 1993.

Milligan, Jennifer. *The Forgotten Generation: French Women Writers of the Inter-war Period.* New York: Berg Publishers, 1996.

Newman-Gordon, Pauline. "Lucie Delarue-Mardrus." *French Women Writers: A Bio-Bibliographical Source Book.* Edited by Eva Martin Sartori and Dorothy Wynne Zimmerman. New York: Greenwood Press, 1991.

Newton, Judith Lowder. "History as Usual? Feminism and the 'New Historicism.'" In *The New Historicism.* Edited by H. Aram Veeser. New York: Routledge, 1989.

――― and Deborah Rosenfelt. "Introduction: toward a materialist-feminist criticism." In *Feminist Criticism and Social Change: Sex, Class, and Race in Literature and Culture.* Edited by Judith Newton and Deborah Rosenfelt. New York: Methuen, 1985.

―――. *Women, Power, and Subversion: Social Strategies in British Fiction, 1778–1860.* Athens: University of Georgia Press, 1981.

O'Brien, Catherine. *Women's Fictional Responses to the First World War: a Comparative Study of Selected Texts by French and German Writers.* New York: Peter Lang, 1996.

Offen, Karen. "Depopulation, Nationalism, and Feminism." *American Historical Review* 89 (1984): 648–76.

Ouditt, Sharon. *Fighting Forces, Writing Women: Identity and Ideology in the First World War.* New York: Routledge, 1994.

Perrot, Michelle. "The New Eve and the Old Adam: Changes in French Women's Condition at the Turn of the Century." In *Behind the Lines: Gender and the Two World Wars.* Edited by Margaret R. Higonnet et al. New Haven: Yale University Press, 1987.

Pope, Barbara Corrado. "Revolution and Retreat: Upper-Class French Women After 1789." In *Women, War, and Revolution.* Edited by Carol R. Berkin and Clara M. Lovett. New York: Holmes and Meier Publishers, 1980.

Pourcher, Yves. *Les Jours de guerre: La vie des Français au jour le jour entre 1914 et 1918* (Days of War: Daily Life of the French between 1914 and 1918). Paris: Plon, 1994.

Qui Êtes-Vous? (Who's Who). Paris: Maison Ehret, 1924.

Rachilde. "Mort de Marie Lenéru" (Death of Marie Lenéru). *Mercure de France* (1918): 755–56.

———. Review of *Tu aimeras dans la douleur,* by Andrée Mars, "Revue de la Quinzaine," *Mercure de France* (1919): 303.

Rapport de M. Georges Lecomte, secrétaire perpétuel, sur les concours littéraires (Report of M. Georges Lecomte, permanent secretary, on literary competitions). Paris: Firmin-Didot, 1952.

Rapports des Prix Littéraires discernés. (Reports on Literary Prizes Awarded). Paris: Archives de l'Académie Française, 1909, 1910, 1917, 1918, 1946, 1952.

Rearick, Charles. *The French in Love and War: Popular Culture in the Era of the World Wars.* New Haven: Yale University Press, 1997.

Reid, Roddy. *Families in Jeopardy, Regulating the Social Body in France 1750–1910.* Stanford: Stanford University Press, 1993.

Review of *Jérusalem,* by Marie Reynès-Monlaur, *La Civiltà Cattolica* 3 (1949): 292–93.

Roberts, Mary Louise. *Civilization Without Sexes, Reconstructing Gender in Postwar France, 1917–1927.* Chicago: University of Chicago Press, 1994.

Roth, Lucien, "Marie Lenéru et la Guerre" (Marie Lenéru and the War). *Évolution* (1930): 22–31.

Roz, Firmin. "Un grand roman féminin" (A Great Female Novel). Review of *Hiver* (Winter) by Camille Mayran. *La Revue bleue* (1926): 314–16.

Ruddick, Sara. "Maternal Thinking." In *Mothering: Essays in Feminist Theory.* Edited by Joyce Treblicot. Totowa, New Jersey: Rowman and Allanheld, 1983.

———. "Notes towards a Feminist Peace Politics." In *Gendering War Talk.* Edited by Miriam Cooke and Angela Woollacott. Princeton: Princeton University Press, 1993.

———. "Pacifying the Forces: Drafting Women in the Interests of Peace." *Signs* 8 (1983): 471–89.

———. "Preservation Love and Military Destruction: Some Reflections on Mothering and Peace." In *Mothering: Essays in Feminist Theory.* Edited by Joyce Treblicot. Totowa, New Jersey: Rowman and Allanheld, 1983.

———. "'Woman of Peace': A Feminist Construction." In *The Women and War Reader.* Edited by Lois Ann Lorentzen and Jennifer Turpin. New York: New York University Press, 1998.

Rupp, Leila J. *Mobilizing Women for War: German and American Propaganda, 1939–1945*. Princeton: Princeton University Press, 1978.

Scheper-Hughes, Nancy. "Maternal Thinking and the Politics of War." In *The Women and War Reader*. Edited by Lois Ann Lorentzen and Jennifer Turpin. New York: New York University Press, 1998.

Scott, Joan W. "Rewriting History." In *Behind the Lines: Gender and the Two World Wars*. Edited by Margaret R. Higonnet et al. New Haven: Yale University Press, 1987.

Siegel, Mona. "Lasting Lessons: War, Peace, and Patriotism in French Primary Schools, 1914–1939." Ph.D. diss., University of Wisconsin, 1996.

Silver, Kenneth E. *Esprit de corps*. Princeton. New Jersey: Princeton University Press, 1989.

Silverman, Willa Z. *The Notorious Life of Gyp: Right-Wing Anarchist in Fin-de-Siècle France*. New York: Oxford University Press, 1995.

Smith, Leonard V. *Between Mutiny and Obedience: the case of the French Fifth Infantry Division during World War I*. Princeton: Princeton University Press, 1994.

Stone, Judith F. "The Republican Brotherhood: Gender and Ideology." In *Gender and the Politics of Social Reform in France*. Edited by Elinor Accampo, Rachel Fuchs, and Mary Lynn Stewart. Baltimore: Johns Hopkins University Press, 1995.

Tate, Trudi and Suzanne Raitt. Introduction to *Women's Fiction and the Great War*. Edited by Suzanne Raitt and Trudi Tate. Oxford: Oxford University Press, 1997.

Thébaud, Françoise. *La Femme au temps de la guerre de 14* (Women During the Time of the War of 14). Paris: Stock, 1986.

———. "The Great War and the Triumph of Sexual Division." Translated by Arthur Goldhammer. In *Toward a Cultural Identity in the Twentieth Century*. Edited by Françoise Thébaud. Vol. 5 of *A History of Women in the West*. Edited by Georges Duby and Michelle Perrot. Cambridge, Mass.: Harvard University Press, 1994.

———. *Quand nos grand-mères donnaient la vie. La Maternité en France dans l'entre-deux-guerres* (When Our Grandmothers Gave Birth. Maternity in France in the Period between the World Wars). Lyon: Presses universitaires de Lyon, 1986.

Turpin, Jennifer. "Many Faces: Women Confronting War." In *The Women and War Reader*. Edited by Lois Ann Lorentzen and Jennifer Turpin. New York: New York University Press, 1998.

Tylee, Claire. *The Great War and Women's Consciousness: Images of Militarism and Womanhood in Women's Writings, 1914–64*. Iowa City: Iowa University Press, 1990.

"Une Président" (A President). *Le Journal* (Paris), 23 March 1937.

Vandérem, Fernand, "Les Lettres et la Vie" (Literature and Life). *La Revue de Paris* (1918): 415–420.

Vic, Jean. *La Littérature de guerre: manuel méthodique et critique des publications de langue française* (War Literature: Systematic and Critical Guidebook of French Language Publications). 5 vols. Paris: Payot, 1918–1923.

Volo, Lorraine Bayard de. "Drafting Motherhood: Maternal Imagery and Organizations in the United States and Nicaragua." In *The Women and War Reader*.

Edited by Lois Ann Lorentzen and Jennifer Turpin. New York: New York University Press, 1998.

Waelti-Walters, Jennifer. *Feminist Novels of the Belle Epoque.* Bloomington: Indiana University Press, 1990.

Weelen, J.-E. Review of *La Légion d'Honneur* by Jehanne d'Orliac. *La Revue bleue* 75 (1937): 625.

Wishnia, Judith. "Natalisme et Nationalisme pendant la Première Guerre Mondiale" (Natalism and Nationalism during the First World War). *Vingtième Siècle* 45 (1995): 30–39.

Index

DATE DUE